Angel Of Death

"Will you look at that sucker!"

A gigantic bird was descending on outspread wings toward the corpse. Lightly, the great raven settled, cocked its head, and gave a discordant cry.

Vaughn raised his weapon.

He disintegrated. His sleek skin tightened and burst, blood boiled, muscles ripped into expanding shreds. The weapon clattered to the deck. The gory cloud seemed to spin like an obscene waterspout, moving out over the cove, leaving only pink patches of foam.

The black bird vanished, and Felice stood in the stern near the inflated dinghy. She was a pallid wraith, except for her huge brown eyes.

"It was wrong of you to kill my porpoises," Felice said. *"They're much nicer than humans or exotics. Always kind."*

"May keeps broadening her canvas into
a vast panorama, with more and more
elements and more and more characters
...and hair-raising excitement."
Isaac Asimov's Science Fiction Magazine

By Julian May
Published by Ballantine Books:

THE SAGA OF PLIOCENE EXILE
  Vol. I: The Many-Colored Land
  Vol. II: The Golden Torc
  Vol. III: The Nonborn King

The Nonborn King

Volume III of The Saga of Pliocene Exile

Julian May

A Del Rey Book

BALLANTINE BOOKS • NEW YORK

For Dave and Sam,
disaster-tech and beer baron,
still another trip on Mom

Whatever we may do, excess will always keep its place in the heart of man, in the place where solitude is found. We all carry within us our places of exile, our crimes and our ravages. But our task is not to unleash them on the world; it is to fight them in ourselves and others. Rebellion, the secular will not to surrender . . . is still today at the basis of the struggle. Origin of form, source of real life, it keeps us always erect in the savage, formless movement of history.

The Rebel, Albert Camus

CONTENTS

SYNOPSIS

*The Galactic Milieu
and the Pliocene Exile*

THE GREAT INTERVENTION OF 2013 OPENED HUMANITY'S WAY to the stars. By the year 2110, when the action of the first volume in this saga began, Earthlings were fully accepted members of a benevolent confederation of planet colonizers, the Coadunate Galactic Milieu, who shared high technology and the capability of performing advanced mental operations known as metafunctions. The latter—which include telepathy, psychokinesis, and many other powers—had lurked in the human gene pool from time immemorial, but only rarely were manifest.

The five founding races of the Milieu had observed humanity's development for tens of thousands of years. After some debate, they decided to admit Earthlings to the Milieu "in advance of their psychosocial maturation" because of the vast metapsychic potential of humanity, which might eventually exceed that of any other race. With the help of nonhumans, people from Earth colonized more than 700 new planets that had already been surveyed and found suitable.

Earthlings also learned how to speed the development of their metapsychic powers through special training and genetic engineering. However, even though the number of humans with operant metafunctions increased with each generation, in 2110 the majority of the population was still "normal"—that is, possessing metafunctions that were either meager to the point of nullity or else latent, unusable because of psychological barriers or other factors. Most of the day-to-day socioeconomic activities of the Human Polity of the Milieu were carried on by "normals"; but human metapsychics did occupy privileged positions in government, in the sciences, and in other areas where high mental powers were valuable to the Milieu as a whole.

At only one period between the Great Intervention and 2110

did it seem that the admission of humanity to the Milieu had been a mistake: This was in 2083, during the brief Metapsychic Rebellion. Instigated by a small group of Earth-based humans, this attempted coup narrowly missed destroying the entire Milieu organization. The Rebellion was suppressed by loyalist metapsychic humans and steps were taken to insure that such a disaster never would occur again. A certain number of battered rebel survivors did manage to evade retribution by passing through a unique kind of escape hatch, a one-way time-gate leading into Earth's Pliocene Epoch, six million years in the past.

The time-gate was discovered in 2034, during the heady years of the scientific knowledge-explosion subsequent to the Great Intervention. But since the time-warp opened only backward (anything attempting to return became six million years old and usually crumbled to dust), and since it had a fixed focus (a point in France's Rhône River Valley), its discoverer sadly concluded that it was a useless oddity without practical application.

After the time-gate discoverer's death in 2041, his widow, Angélique Guderian, learned that her husband had been mistaken.

The Intervention had seemed to open a Golden Age for humanity, giving it unlimited lebensraum, energy sufficiency, and membership in a splendid galaxy-wide civilization. But even Golden Ages have their misfits: in this case, humans who were temperamentally unsuited to the rather structured social environment of the Milieu. As Madame Guderian was to discover, there were fair numbers of these, and they were willing to pay handsomely to be transported to a simpler world without rules. Geologists and paleontologists knew that the Pliocene was an idyllic period, just before the dawn of rational life on our planet. Romantics and rugged individualists from almost all of Earth's ethnic groups eventually discovered Madame's "underground railroad" to the Pliocene, which operated out of a quaint French inn located outside the metropolitan center of Lyon.

From 2041 until 2106, the rejuvenated Madame Guderian transported clients from Old Earth to "Exile," a presumed natural paradise six million years younger. After suffering belated qualms of conscience about the fate of the time-travelers, Madame herself passed into the Pliocene and operation of her inn was taken over by the Milieu, which had found the time-warp to be a convenient glory hole for dissidents. By 2110, nearly 100,000 time-farers had vanished into an unknown destiny.

On 25 August 2110, eight persons, making up that week's "Group Green," were transported to Exile: Richard Voorhees, a grounded starship captain; Felice Landry, a disturbed eighteen-year-old athlete whose violent temperament and latent mind-powers had made her an outcast; Claude Majewski, a recently widowed elderly paleontologist; Sister Amerie Roccaro, a physician and burnt-out priest; Bryan Grenfell, an anthropologist following his lover, Mercy Lamballe, who had preceded him through the gate; Elizabeth Orme, a Grand Master metapsychic who had lost her stupendous mental powers after a brain trauma; Stein Oleson, a misfit planet-crust driller who dreamt of life in a simpler world; and Aiken Drum, an engaging young crook who, like Felice, possessed considerable latent metapsychic power.

Group Green discovered, as other time-travelers had before them, that idyllic Pliocene Europe was under the control of a group of maverick humanoids from another galaxy. The exotics were also exiled, having been driven from their home because of their barbarous battle-religion.

The dominant exotic faction, the Tanu, were tall and handsome. In spite of a thousand-year sojourn on Earth, there were still less than 20,000 of them because their reproduction was inhibited by solar radiation. Since their plasm was compatible with that of humanity, they had for nearly seventy years utilized the time-travelers in breeding, holding Pliocene humanity in benevolent serfdom.

Antagonistic to the Tanu and outnumbering them by at least four to one were their ancient foes, the Firvulag. Often called the Little People, these exotics were mostly of short stature, although there were plenty of human-sized and even gigantic individuals among them. They reproduced quite well on Pliocene Earth.

Tanu and Firvulag actually constituted a dimorphic race—the former metapsychically latent, and the latter possessed of operant metafunctions, mostly limited in power. The Tanu, with their higher technology, had long ago developed mind-amplifiers, collars called golden torcs, which raised their latent mind-powers up to operancy. Firvulag did not require torcs to exercise their metafunctions. Certain of their great heroes were the mental equals of the Tanu in aggressive action, but most Firvulag were weaker.

For most of the thousand years that Tanu and Firvulag resided on Earth (which they called the Many-Colored Land), they were fairly evenly matched in the ritual wars fought as part of their battle-religion. The greater finesse and technology of the Tanu tended to counterbalance the superior numbers of the cruder Firvulag. But the advent of time-traveling humanity tipped the scales in favor of the taller exotics. Not only did Tanu-human hybrids turn out to have unusual physical and mental strength, but humans also enhanced the rather decadent science establishment of the Tanu by injecting the expertise of the greatly advanced Galactic Milieu. It had been strictly forbidden for time-travelers to carry sophisticated weaponry back to the Pliocene, and the Tanu were very conservative in the types of military hardware that they permitted their human slaves to build. Nevertheless, it was human ingenuity that eventually gave the Tanu almost complete ascendency over their Firvulag foes (who never mated with humans and generally despised them).

Most of the enslaved time-travelers actually lived a pretty good life under their Tanu overlords. All rough work was done by ramapithecines, small apes who wore simple torcs compelling obedience and who were, ironically, part of the direct hominid line that would climax in Homo sapiens six million years in the future. Humans who occupied positions of trust or engaged in vital pursuits under the Tanu wore *gray* torcs. These did not amplify the mind, but did allow telepathic communication with the Tanu, who were also able to administer punishment or reward through the device. If psychological testing showed that an arriving time-traveler possessed significant latent metafunctions, the lucky person was given a *silver* torc. This was a genuine amplifier similar to the golden collars worn by the exotic race, but having control circuits. Silver-torc humans were accepted as conditional citizens of the Many-Colored Land. Rarely, and only if they proved themselves, the silvers might be granted golden torcs and full freedom.

The expanded torc technology, developed from the original golden devices worn by the Tanu, was the fruit of a single misfit genius—Eusebio Gomez-Nolan, a human psychobiologist who was eventually granted gold and who rose to become the President of the Coercer Guild, one of the five metapsychic quasi clans that formed the basis for Tanu society. Under the sobriquet of Lord Gomnol, Gomez-Nolan played a manipulative role in the power politics of the Many-Colored Land until he fatally overreached himself.

The overall destiny of both the Tanu and the Firvulag was subtly guided by a mysterious woman who belonged to neither race but served as guardian to both. This was Brede the Shipspouse. With her mate, the Ship, a gigantic rational organism of intergalactic travel, she had originally brought the exotics to Pliocene Earth. Brede could foresee the future—although not perfectly—and she came to know that the destinies of Tanu, Firvulag, and time-traveling humanity were inextricably united. A pivotal point in this joint destiny was reached with the arrival of the eight members of Group Green at the Tanu reception center, Castle Gateway.

It was Tanu custom to test all arriving time-travelers immediately for metapsychic latency. Latents, and those with unusual talents of other kinds, were sent south to the Tanu capital of Muriah, located on the Aven (Balearic) Peninsula in the nearly empty saline basin of the Mediterranean. Normal humans were shared out among the Tanu cities, taking their places in the working or (in the case of presentable women) breeding pools. Presorted caravans, escorted by gray-torc human troops, normally left Castle Gateway each week.

Group Green proved to be anything but typical when examined by the Tanu overseers in residence, Lord Creyn and Lady Epone.

Most notable was Elizabeth Orme. The trip through the time-gate had restored her to metapsychic operancy, a fact which Creyn was instantly aware of. Elizabeth's awesome power of farsensing and redaction (mind-alteration) were convalescent; but when she recovered, it was evident that she would be far superior to any Tanu having those particular powers. Creyn predicted that a "wonderful life" lay ahead for Elizabeth in the Many-Colored Land. She herself was not so sure. The Milieu had expressly forbidden the time-travel of any operant meta-psychics, since such persons would be in a position to exercise unfair mental domination over normal humans in a primitive environment that lacked the mental restraints of the Milieu's "Unity." Elizabeth was a totally nonaggressive personality as well as a self-centered one, and the only way she found to defend herself from what she regarded as a temptation to hubris was flight—either physical or mental.

A second member of Group Green, the recidivist youth Aiken Drum, was found to possess powerful latencies. He was collared with a silver torc and promised that if he behaved himself (a dubious prospect) he would enjoy special privileges after being trained in Muriah. Aiken's friend, the huge ex-driller Stein Oleson, tried to escape from imprisonment in the castle, killing several guards with his Viking axe. Stein was subdued with a controlling gray torc and was earmarked, because of his heroic physique, to become a kind of gladiator in Muriah.

Richard Voorhees, the disgraced starship captain, also tried to escape. He stumbled into the chamber of the Tanu coercer Lady Epone, who brain-burned him and consigned him to a prison dormitory where other "normals" awaited the departure of the weekly caravan to Epone's city of Finiah, situated far northeast of the castle, on the River Rhine.

The anthropologist Bryan Grenfell had no metapsychic latencies, but Creyn was nevertheless impressed by his professional credentials. It seemed the Tanu had a certain urgent need for a cultural anthropologist! Bryan was also destined for Muriah and accepted the prospect with equanimity, since he expected to find his beloved Mercy Lamballe in the capital.

Claude Majewski, the old paleontologist, and the female priest Sister Amerie were tested and showed no latencies. But when Lady Epone attempted to test the girl Felice Landry, the little athlete seemed to go into hysterics. Her agitation made an accurate mental calibration impossible. Felice perpetrated this charade because she knew very well that she possessed very strong latent mind-powers; but she had no intention of being subjugated by a torc, especially after she discovered that both she and Sister Amerie were to be used as brood stock by the Tanu. In a private moment with the nun, Felice grimly resolved to "take" the entire Tanu race. Ludicrous though this vow of revenge seemed at the time, Sister Amerie felt no inclination to doubt Felice's ability to carry out her threat.

When caravans left Castle Gateway that evening, Group Green had been split in half. Bound northward for Finiah with a sizable group of normals were Felice, Sister Amerie, Claude, and the still groggy Richard. Six gray-torc soldiers and Lady Epone conducted the train, which rode horselike Pliocene beasts called chalikos. Also in this group were Basil, a mountain-climbing former don; Yoshimitsu and Tatsuji, who wore samurai garb reflecting their heritage; and one Dougal, who had been driven half-mad by the unwelcome attentions of Lady Epone.

The southbound caravan was much smaller. Led by Creyn with a minimum two-guard escort, it consisted of the untorced Elizabeth and Bryan, Aiken Drum in his silver collar, unconscious Stein wearing a gray torc, and two other latent humans who had been gifted with silver: Sukey Davies, a former juvenile officer from a colonial satellite, and Raimo Hakkinen, a glum Finno-Canadian forester.

The caravan heading for Muriah took ship at the River Rhône and made a fairly uneventful trip south. Creyn proved to be a tolerant overlord, deeply sympathetic to Elizabeth. Aiken Drum and Raimo became buddies and co-conspirators, and Aiken discovered that the latencies inside his brain were unfolding at a wondrous pace that boded all kinds of fun and games. Stein recovered from wounds inflicted during the fracas at the castle, and he and Sukey pledged themselves to each other after she entered his mind and helped to heal a severe psychic trauma. In the riverside city of Darask, Elizabeth helped a human gold-torc woman, Estella-Sirone, give birth to twins—one Tanu and one Firvulag. And when the party eventually arrived in Muriah, they were greeted by a triumphal procession of magnificent Tanu chivalry, all clad in glowing, multicolored glass armor. The welcome was primarily for Elizabeth, who was soon to discover herself a pawn between several scheming factions at the Tanu court.

Meanwhile, on the trail north of Castle Gateway, the other four members of Group Green were plotting a prisoner revolt. Felice, a professional athlete, was abnormally strong, and her latent metapsychic powers enabled her to mind-control animals. She also had a small steel dagger, little more than a toy, which had been overlooked by searchers.

When the caravan reached a remote shore of the Lac de Bresse, Felice's plan for escape was put into action. Richard, disguised in Amerie's religious garb, surprised the head guard and stabbed him to death. Then Felice compelled the caravan's escorting pack of huge bear-dogs to attack Lady Epone and the other soldiers. In the ensuing fray, the samurai Tatsuji was killed, as well as the entire escort of gray troops. Richard approached Epone, thinking that she, too, was dead. But the exotic woman seized him with her powerful mind, in spite of the fact that she was nearly torn to pieces. Richard would have perished had he not stabbed her with Felice's little dagger.

(Much later, the nun, who was a physician, deduced that the nearly invulnerable Tanu were fatally poisoned by iron weapons. For this reason, they had proscribed the use of iron in Pliocene Europe, making do with copper alloys and a kind of supertough glass, vitredur, in its place.)

Felice coveted Epone's golden torc, knowing that the mental amplifer was capable of releasing the great metafaculties now locked within her brain. But before she could take the torc from the Tanu woman's body, mad Dougal grabbed it and threw it into the lake. Amerie had to drug Felice with a sedative to prevent her from killing Dougal.

Bewildered and frightened, the ex-prisoners realized that news of the fight must have been telepathically flashed by the dying Epone to the nearest fort. They would have to disperse quickly. One group elected to follow Basil, the ex-don. They would sail in small boats down the Lac de Bresse to the Jura Mountains.

Claude, the 133-year-old paleontologist, was more wilderness-wise after years of roughing it on wild planets in the Milieu. He advised his friends of Group Green to avoid the open lake and instead head into the heavily forested Vosges Mountains, which were much closer than the Jura. The surviving samurai warrior, Yosh, decided to go his way alone, heading north in hopes of reaching the sea.

The large group of escapees out on the lake was eventually almost entirely recaptured and taken in chains to the city of Finiah. But Claude, Richard, Amerie, and Felice went deep into the Vosges, where they finally made contact with a group of free outlaw humans, fugitives from Tanu settlements, who called themselves Lowlives.

The Lowlife leader was an old woman, Angélique Guderian, former keeper of the time-gate and the ultimate author of Pliocene humanity's degradation. Around her neck was a golden torc, the gift of the Firvulag, those deadly enemies of the Tanu, who had formed a very tentative alliance with the Lowlives. Madame had modest metapsychic powers.

The killing of Epone by the escapees were unprecedented. Never before had a mere human been able to bring about the demise of one of the tough exotics, who normally enjoyed life spans of hundreds of years. Tanu searchers, under Lord Velteyn of Finiah, now swarmed the Vosges region, looking for the ones who had done the deed. The remnant of Group Green, together with Madame Guderian and some 200 Lowlives, hid in a great hollow tree until things should cool off. Inside the refuge, Madame explained to the newcomers her great plan to free Pliocene humanity from the Tanu yoke, a task she had undertaken in order to expiate her own guilt.

Madame's deputy, a Native American named Peopeo Moxmox Burke, who had once been a judge, was keenly interested in Amerie's theory about the deadliness of iron to the exotic race. This might be an invaluable secret weapon in the liberation of humanity.

A friendly Firvulag named Fitharn Pegleg joined the Lowlives inside their sanctuary and told Group Green the legend of the Ship's Grave. The great space-going organism that was Brede's mate had died in making the leap from its home galaxy to our own. Tanu and Firvulag, passengers in the Ship led by Brede, escaped from the hulk in small flying machines just before it impacted upon the Earth, making a great crater known as the Ship's Grave.

For some time, Lowlives, working with Firvulag, had searched for this ancient site. Even though a thousand years had passed, it was possible that some of the sophisticated flying machines left at the Grave might still be operational. And inside one of them, entombed after a ritual duel, was the body of Lugonn, Shining Hero of the Tanu, together with his sacred weapon, the Spear. The latter was not a blade, but rather a photonic projector that delivered laserlike blasts of energy. This Spear, in the hands of Lowlife humanity, could turn the balance of power.

Madame's people had looked in vain for the Ship's Grave. But Claude, knowledgeable in future geology, told them that the crater could only be the astrobleme known as the Ries, located some 300 kilometers to the east, beyond the Black Forest, on the northern shore of the Danube River.

It was decided to mount a new expedition at once. With luck, the searchers might return before the end of September. The Firvulag would then join humanity in a joint attack against the city of Finiah—provided that the fighting took place before the start of the Grand Combat Truce, which began at dawn on October 1. Unknown to Fitharn, who agreed to accompany the party, the Lowlives who remained behind intended to go to another site designated by Claude, where they hoped iron ore might be found. They would smelt whatever iron they could and then forge weapons to be used in the Finiah attack. The iron was to be kept a secret from the Firvulag, since Madame was dubious of their loyalty.

After receiving permission from Yeochee IV, King of the Firvulag, the expedition set out. It comprised Madame Guderian, Richard, Felice, Chief Burke, a former aircraft technician named Stefanko, a dynamic-field engineer named Martha, Claude, and Fitharn. Felice was especially anxious to go. She was certain that the body of the ancient hero, Lugonn, would have a golden torc about its neck that she could appropriate.

Disaster struck the party even before it reached the Black Forest. In a Rhineside swamp, a giant pig killed Stefanko and badly wounded Chief Burke. Frail Martha, who had borne four children in quick succession as a Tanu slave, began to hemorrhage from the shock. It seemed that the expedition would have to be abandoned. But Martha insisted that she would recover, and Felice agreed to carry the sick woman if need be. Martha was a vital member of the group, now the only one with the technical skill to put the photon Spear and/or a flyer into operation once the expedition found them. The Firvulag Fitharn agreed to take Chief Burke back to the Lowlife village of Hidden Springs, where Amerie was recuperating from a broken arm.

After many vicissitudes, the reduced expedition crossed the

Black Forest range and came into the territory of a certain Sugoll. Only nominally under the authority of the Firvulag King, Sugoll ruled a large band of grotesque mutant Firvulag called Howlers. His own hideously deformed body was hidden beneath a handsome illusion. Sugoll at first scorned to assist the expedition and threatened to kill the humans. But when Claude pointed out the source of Howler deformity—radioactive rocks among which they had lived for many generations—the ruler relented. Claude hinted that the Howlers might relieve their plight by seeking help from human geneticists—if such persons were released from Tanu slavery. The liberation of humanity (and helping out the expedition) was thus to the Howler advantage. Sugoll finally agreed to assist the party in finding the River Danube, on which the humans could easily voyage to the Ship's Grave. Once again the four travelers set off.

On 22 September they arrived at last at the crater. Richard and Martha, who had become lovers, set about repairing one of the flying machines and the great Spear. Felice, after a fit of rage brought on by her discovery that Lugonn's skeleton had no golden torc, calmed herself and was a model of cooperation. Even so, time was getting desperately short if they were to meet the deadline before the Grand Combat Truce. Martha's old affliction returned and she grew dangerously weak from loss of blood; but she would not let them return to Hidden Springs until the testing of the photon weapon was complete.

Meanwhile, a great Firvulag army had gathered on the bank of the Rhine opposite the Tanu city of Finiah. Additionally, several hundred Lowlives had been recruited from scattered wilderness hamlets and surreptitiously armed with iron. At dusk on the twenty-ninth the flyer finally landed at Hidden Springs with the Spear ready for use. But Martha was in shock from hemorrhaging, and Amerie could only rush her away for transfusions and pray for a miracle. The distraught Richard could not even remain with his beloved; he had to pilot the flyer in its bombardment of Finiah.

Screened by Madame Guderian's limited metapsychic power, the flyer hovered over the city while Claude blasted holes in both city walls. Then he turned the Spear on Finiah's barium mine, the only source in the Many-Colored Land of the element that was vital in making all kinds of torcs. The mine was destroyed, and waves of Firvulag, wearing the illusory shapes of hideous monsters, invaded the city alongside Chief Burke and his Lowlife forces. After a desperate fight, Finiah fell. Its surviving Tanu populace, including the ruler, Lord Velteyn, fled in the direction of Castle Gateway. The erstwhile human slaves (some of whom had been quite content in their bondage) were given the choice of freedom or death. Those wearing gray or silver torcs had to submit to their removal with an iron chisel, a painful process that left many of them in a state of profound nervous collapse.

Both Claude and Madame were wounded by bolts of Velteyn's psychoenergy during the air attack. Richard lost the sight of one eye, but managed to return the flyer safely to Hidden Springs. There he discovered that Martha had died. Mad with grief, he took her body and soared away in the gravomagnetically powered aircraft, to wait for his own death in an orbit thousands of kilometers above Pliocene Earth.

Below, Felice was walking toward the ruins of Finiah. She bitterly regretted missing the war; but she knew that she would find her long-sought golden torc somewhere in the devastated city, and then she would attain the powers needed to fulfill her vow to destroy the Tanu race. Felice finally did find a torc; it raised to operancy her latent powers of farsensing, psychokinesis, coercion, and creativity. Some time would have to elapse before she learned to use these powers correctly, and so she returned to Hidden Springs in order to assist Madame Guderian in the next phases of the liberation of humanity.

Meanwhile, far to the south in the Tanu capital of Muriah, the other four members of Group Green encountered an utterly different face of the Many-Colored Land.

Upon their arrival, the Green quartet and their fellow humans, Raimo and Sukey, were presented to the Tanu aristocracy at a lavish feast. Elizabeth learned from Thagdal the High King that she was to be taken to Brede Shipspouse in order to be initiated into Tanu ways—an unprecedented honor. After the initation, which might take a month, she would be impregnated by the King and found a new dynasty of fully operant (i.e., torcless) Tanu-human hybrids. Queen Nontusvel seemed en-

tirely agreeable to this arrangement and Elizabeth herself showed
no emotion as Thagdal unfolded his plans.

The other honored prisoners learned their own fates. Bryan
the anthropologist was commanded to make a careful study of
the impact of humanity's advent upon the Tanu socioeconomy.
A certain faction, headed by Nodonn Battlemaster, the most
powerful son of Thagdal and Nontusvel and heir presumptive,
maintained that the coming of humanity had been detrimental
to Tanu culture rather than beneficial, as Thagdal and most of
the Tanu aristocracy believed. Bryan, using the advanced analytical methods of the Milieu, was to settle the matter. It went
without saying that Thagdal felt confident that Bryan would
confirm the royal policy.

The gigantic Viking Stein, Raimo Hakkinen, and Sukey
Davies were forced to display their talent before the company.
Sukey's silver torc had activated a powerful latent faculty of
redaction. She would be apprenticed to the Redactor Guild,
headed by the compassionate and civilized Dionket, and learn
the art of mental healing. Poor Raimo, who possessed only a
weak psychokinetic power, found out that he was destined to
become the sexual plaything of Tanu women, who found it
difficult to conceive by their own males. Stein was presented
to the festal throng as a gladiatorial candidate for the Grand
Combat, the annual ritual war between the Tanu and Firvulag
in which certain humans also participated. Stein was about to
be auctioned off to the highest Tanu bidder when an incredible
event threw the entire mass of Tanu aristocracy into a turmoil.

Aiken Drum put in *his* bid for Stein.

This charming young rogue's awesome latent mind-powers
had been released in a psychic torrent by the donning of the
silver torc. So great was the power of Aiken's liberated mind
that he had actually burned out the control circuits of the silver
torc. He was now in the process of going fully operant—
metafunctional without artificial augmentation. Only Elizabeth,
who had been a masterclass teacher of young metapsychics
back in the Milieu, knew what was happening. The Tanu realized that Aiken Drum was far above the usual type of human
latent; but they were not yet aware just how menacing his
potential would be.

As the Tanu nobles began to bid for his friend Stein, Aiken

was aware that the big Viking was in mortal danger. Not only had Stein taken Sukey as his life-mate (an action that the Tanu deemed treason for a silver-torc woman), but he was also one of those individuals fundamentally incompatible to the torc's operation. If Stein wore his gray collar for very long, he would go mad and sink into death. Most humans who wore gray were tested for compatibility before being torced. Stein had received his collar as a means of subjection after his bloody battle in Castle Gateway. The Tanu did not really care how long he lived. Aiken, however, did; and so he entered the bidding against the Tanu, pledging to the King that as payment he would dispose of a Firvulag monster, a certain Delbaeth, who had been terrorizing the adjacent Spanish mainland.

The King was stunned, not only by Aiken's audacity but also by the glimpse of power he had perceived upon brief examination of the young trickster's mind. It hardly seemed possible . . . and yet this little human mountebank, who wore a gold-fabric suit all covered with pockets, just might be a threat to Thagdal himself.

The King's sense of hovering doom was reinforced when a member of the Tanu High Table, Mayvar Kingmaker, the head of the Farsensor Guild, declared that she was in favor of Aiken's bid and would see that he was trained for the task as her protégé. Thagdal viewed Mayvar as a mischievous old crone who might simply be making a gesture. On the other hand, she was not called "kingmaker" for nothing . . .

Shaken, Thagdal accepted Aiken's bid for Stein. Delbaeth was a menace that the King should have dealt with long ago, and now the monarch was backed into a corner by the wily human's maneuver. Both Aiken and Stein would be introduced to Tanu chivalric practice by the Lord of Swords, and then they and a large troop of knights would go on a Quest against the formidable Delbaeth.

Following the portentous banquet, there was desperate re-active scheming among the so-called Host of Nontusvel—children of Thagdal and the reigning Queen. Thagdal had had other wives during his two-millennium lifetime, and he had had thousands of other children by both Tanu and human women, since his germ plasm was considered peerless. (This was the basis for his sovereignty.) But the Host considered themselves to be the elite, and had long entertained dynastic aspirations contrary to ancient Tanu custom.

The Host leader was Nodonn, greatest battle hero of the Tanu, head of the Psychokinetic Guild, and ruler of Goriah, a rich city situated on the coast of Armorica (Brittany). Unlike his totipotent father, however, Nodonn suffered from a reproductive handicap. His offspring, who were not numerous, did not display important metapsychic powers. Nodonn was a member of the Tanu hierarchy, the High Table, as were other Host notables such as the twins Fian and Kuhal, who shared the post of Second Lord Psychokinetic; Culluket the Interrogator, Second Redactor to Dionket; Imidol the Second Coercer, who was the reluctant subordinate to the human Coercer Guild President Gomnol; and Riganone, a female warrior who intended to challenge old Mayvar for leadership of the Farsensors. There were some 200 other members of the Host, but not all of them were first-class mental powers, nor did the Host have a majority of High Table seats. But their dynasty might attain supreme power if Nodonn succeeded Thagdal.

Now, however, this succession seemed to be endangered: not by Aiken Drum, whom the Host dismissed as a mere metapsychic nova who would burn out almost as soon as he flared up—but by Elizabeth.

If King Thagdal had fully operant children by her, these would undoubtedly form the nucleus of a hybrid elite, more powerful physically and mentally than the pureblooded Tanu. The scheme to use Elizabeth in breeding had been proposed to the King by Gomnol. The Host rightly suspected that this devious human Coercer Lord intended to make a place for himself in any new order that included human operants. After anxious consultation, the leaders of the Host decided that Elizabeth would have to die. This would not be easy to accomplish, since she was an operant Grand Master whom no single Tanu could overcome by means of mental attack. If the Host acted together, however, using the multimind thrust called metapsychic concert, they might be able to destroy her. (Unfortunately for this plan, the individualistic Tanu found such cooperation to be very difficult. Only under the most firm coordination could they achieve metapsychic concert. Culluket the redactor and

Imidol the coercer would finally succeed in organizing the effort.)

Several weeks passed. Elizabeth was subjected to rather inept attacks by the Host. Knowing that the attacks would increase in effectiveness, she escaped by accompanying Brede Shipspouse into the latter's room without doors, a chamber proof against mind-penetration. Brede had plans of her own for Elizabeth that had nothing to do with the schemes of Thagdal, Gomnol, or the Host. The Shipspouse, guardian of both the Tanu and Firvulag races, perceived Elizabeth as one who might lead them (as Brede apparently could not) out of their barbarous and feckless battle-culture into a truly civilized society of the mind.

Elizabeth was in no mood for Brede's large-hearted hopes. She was sunk in despair, feeling that she was the only metapsychic adult in a population of malignant children, who had no response to a superior being other than trying to kill it out of fear. Elizabeth rejected any thought of spiritual motherhood or sharing Brede's guardian role. All she wanted, she told the Shipspouse, was to sail away in the great red balloon she had brought with her to the Pliocene: to sail away and be left alone, at peace.

Aiken Drum, under the tutelage of Mayvar Kingmaker, became more and more adept in the use of his metafunctions. Mayvar gave him his initiate's golden torc; but he was quick to show the elderly Tanu woman that he had no need of any artificial amplifier. He would wear the torc to deceive the other Tanu, however. Mayvar also gave Aiken a certain simple device that she guaranteed would give him victory over the monster Delbaeth—provided he could use the weapon without any Tanu member of the Quest finding out about it.

Stein, too, received training as a Tanu man-at-arms. He worried about Sukey, separated from him as she prepared to begin her redactor apprenticeship. Stein's fears were confirmed when he perceived a telepathic cry of fear emanate from his wife. He rushed to the headquarters of the Redactor Guild and found her recovering from an operation. A traitorous human physician, Tasha-Bybar, had reversed the sterilization procedure obligatory to all time-traveling women, making Sukey ready for King Thagdal's droit du seigneur. (Tasha, a great heroine to the Tanu, had perfected this restoration of fertility, making possible the Tanu breeding scheme that utilized human women. Her students did their work in each Tanu city as female newcomers arrived. Because of the female sterilization requirement originally promulgated by Madame Guderian, only one-fourth as many women as men elected to time-travel to the Pliocene.)

Stein was reunited with Sukey—only to discover that the infamous Tasha was spying upon them. Realizing by Sukey's telepathic confession what Tasha had done—not only to his own wife but to thousands of other human women—Stein killed the doctor on the spot.

His deed was discovered by the redactor Creyn, who seemed oddly sympathetic. Creyn promised to conceal their part in Tasha's death, giving Stein and Sukey the first hint of the existence of a Peace Faction among the normally bellicose Tanu. This group cherished the heretical notion that one day Tanu and Firvulag would be brothers in sun as well as in shadow.

At the September Sport Meeting in Muriah, both Aiken and Stein were required to display their fighting prowess in the arena, before the grand and petty nobility of the Many-Colored Land. If the pair passed muster, they would be accepted as members of the Tanu battle-company and the Delbaeth Quest would proceed.

Stein fought first and dispatched a monstrous hyenalike animal with his battleaxe. Then it was Aiken's turn. His antagonist was a species of crocodile seventeen meters long. It had been brought to the Muriah arena just for him by Nodonn Battlemaster, who had recognized Aiken as a force to be reckoned with.

The anthropologist Bryan Grenfell had been spending his days studying Tanu culture in company with a genial hybrid, Ogmol. On the night of Aiken's testing, Bryan was in the royal box together with the King and Queen; Aluteyn Craftsmaster, the President of the Creator Guild; the fey human Genetics Master Greg-Donnet (né Gregory Prentice Brown); and other notables. Bryan was introduced to Nodonn upon the Battlemaster's arrival; but he had eyes only for Nodonn's new wife,

Lady Rosmar—who was none other than the bewitching Mercy
Lamballe, Bryan's own love-at-first-sight, whom he had helplessly followed to the Pliocene. Mercy now wore a golden torc
and had developed tremendous psychocreative powers.

In the arena, Aiken met the giant crocodile. Astride a chaliko, wearing golden glass armor and armed only with a glass
lance, the trickster was terrified. He lost control of his mount
and was thrown to the sand. The rules permitted no use of
overt mental power against the beast, but Aiken eventually
conquered it, using only his native cunning. The Tanu spectators went wild at his bold performance. King Thagdal and
Nodonn had a more chilly response.

Having proved themselves, Aiken and Stein now undertook
the Delbaeth Quest. The expedition consisted of several hundred
knights and was led by the King himself. Nodonn was there
to keep an eye on Aiken. Two High Table members, Tanu-
human hybrids of great mental power, became partisans of the
trickster. They were Alberonn Mindeater and Bleyn the Champion.

The colorful troop began the Quest at the large city of
Afaliah, at the base of the Aven Peninsula. Its crusty old lord,
Celadeyr, no particular friend of the Host, was nevertheless
scornful of the notion that a human such as Aiken might get
the better of the awful Delbaeth. For three weeks the Quest
chased the monster, who bombarded the knights with lethal
fireballs and effectively kept them at a distance. Finally the
Firvulag disappeared into a vast network of caverns out on the
Gibraltar Isthmus, and King Thagdal and Nodonn demanded
that Aiken admit he was beaten.

Aiken refused. He and Stein stripped themselves of their
glass armor and prepared to follow Delbaeth underground. By
law, the Quest had to end in three days, when the Grand Combat
Truce would begin and Tanu and Firvulag would forswear
fighting until the start of the ritual war. Aiken demanded that
he be allowed those three days; and supported by his partisans,
he was given his chance. Using his psychocreative power,
Aiken turned himself and Stein into bats and they flew into the
depths.

They encountered Delbaeth two days later and killed him
by means of the secret device Mayvar had given Aiken. Just

before they left the Firvulag's cave, Stein pointed out to Aiken that the waters of the Atlantic were pounding against the western wall. The narrow Gibraltar Isthmus, forming a sill between Spain and Africa, was all that separated the ocean from the deep empty basin of the Mediterranean.

With the start of the month-long Truce, both Tanu and Firvulag from all parts of the Many-Colored Land began to converge on Muriah's White Silver Plain, a large salt flat where tent cities, grandstands, lists, and the battlefield for the Combat proper were located. Because they had adopted war-mounts and other human innovations, the Tanu had won the Grand Combat for forty years running, and the Firvulag had become more and more bitter. However, the recent fall of Finiah cheered the Little People—and inspired them to adopt a few Lowlife fighting customs themselves in hopes of changing their luck. The new tactics were opposed by the old Firvulag Battlemaster, Pallol One-Eye; but he was forced to bow to the will of the younger generals Sharn and Ayfa, a husband-and-wife team.

In the Lowlife village of Hidden Springs, Madame Guderian discussed her plan for liberating humanity from the Tanu yoke. Phase One had been successful. Finiah with its barium mine was a deserted ruin.

Phase Two would be more audacious. Under cover of the Truce, a small group of Lowlives would infiltrate the torc factory down in Muriah and sabotage the irreplaceable machinery. The undertaking would be hazardous in the extreme, since the factory was situated inside the fortresslike Coercer Guild complex, presided over by the renegade human, Lord Gomnol.

Phase Three involved the permanent closing of the timegate. Madame had a plan for doing this herself, and Claude insisted upon helping her.

An implied fourth phase of the liberation involved the making of iron weapons by humanity. It was arranged that the freed human population of Finiah, as well as some of the Lowlives who had come from other parts of Europe to join in the Finiah fight, would found several Iron Villages. They would mine, smelt, and forge the "blood metal" in preparation for the ultimate bid for human freedom.

Eleven people, including Madame and the Group Green

survivors, left Hidden Springs to implement Phases Two and Three. They were disguised as loyalist human refugees from Finiah. At the city of Roniah, Madame and Claude separated from the others and went off to hide near Castle Gateway, while the others proceeded south to the capital. The two groups would try to synchronize strikes against the time-gate and torc factory.

The Muriah-bound group included Felice, Sister Amerie, Chief Burke, the alpinist don Basil Wimborne (liberated from a Finiah prison), and five other dedicated Lowlives. Felice's metapsychic powers were developing nicely and the longer she wore her golden torc, the stronger her mental faculties became. She also carried the photonic Spear. It had been totally discharged in the Finiah fight, but the saboteurs hoped that their former Group Green companion, Aiken Drum, would find some way of putting it back into action. As the group approached the Tanu capital, a telepathic call was sent to Aiken, telling him of the Lowlife conspiracy. The saboteurs took for granted that Aiken would be loyal to humanity and eager to assist them. But they were wrong.

Down in Muriah, Aiken and Stein and Elizabeth learned at the same time of the impending assaults on the torc works and the time-gate. Elizabeth had reluctantly helped Brede attain metapsychic operancy; but she was still determined to escape from Muriah in her red balloon and live alone. Stein eagerly welcomed the prospect of a strike against the Tanu; but Aiken feared that the exotics would read Stein's simple mind and discover the plot, and so he and his new ally Gomnol (who professed to be sympathetic to humanity) put a mind-block into the big Viking. Neither Gomnol nor Aiken anticipated that Stein would leak the sabotage plot to his redactor wife, Sukey.

The alliance between Aiken and Gomnol Lord Coercer was a devious one. Neither man really trusted the other, but they had been forced into a coalition of necessity. Aiken aspired to be King of the Many-Colored Land and would need plenty of help to fulfill his ambition. Gomnol, cordially hated by the present heir to the throne, Nodonn, knew that his previous position of strength as a supporter of King Thagdal was crumbling. The Tanu monarch was on a downhill slide and might very well take Gomnol with him.

The King had believed that the Tanu race benefited by the admixture of human genes and the utilization of human technology. But now Bryan Grenfell's cultural survey, recently completed but still secret, showed that humans would eventually dominate the Many-Colored Land if Thagdal's policy continued. The King suspected (correctly) that his eldest son Nodonn planned to use the survey to discredit him publicly during the Grand Combat. Additionally, the King had suffered another blow to his prestige when Brede forbade the implementation of Gomnol's mating scheme between Thagdal and Elizabeth. Elizabeth was now taboo, and the King would not become the father of an operant superrace as he had hoped. On the contrary, that honor might very likely fall to Aiken Drum!

Sunk in despair, Thagdal confided his fears to Queen Nontusvel, who knew just what kind of diversion would cheer her spouse. By royal command, she demanded that Sukey be given to the King. Dionket was forced to yield the young woman up. As Thagdal took his pleasure, Sukey let slip a vengeful thought about the northern saboteurs soon to invade Muriah. The Queen overheard this thought and notified Nodonn's brother Culluket the Interrogator, a sinister and powerful member of the Host faction. Culluket wrung from Sukey all that Stein had inadvertently told her of the plot, with the result that Stein and Sukey were both condemned and thrown into prison to await death at the Combat's finale.

Aiken, even though he was known to be Stein's close friend, managed to convince Culluket that he knew nothing of the plot. But the Host continued to believe that both Aiken and Gomnol were in league with the Lowlife conspirators.

Meanwhile, the party of saboteurs had reached Muriah and were ready to strike. They called Aiken to their hiding place and rather reluctantly turned the inoperative Spear over to him. He promised to attempt to recharge it, but really had no intention of giving it back to the saboteurs. It was to be a key element in his own schemes later. When Aiken failed to return at the appointed hour with the Spear, the Lowlife party began its penetration without him, trusting that Felice's growing metapsychic powers would be strong enough to destroy the torc factory.

The Lowlives entered the Coercer Guild complex in disguise. Felice melted the factory door with a bolt of mental energy—only to find that some sixty knights of the Host, led by Imidol the Second Coercer and Culluket the Interrogator, were waiting in ambush. The humans managed to kill fifteen Tanu, either with iron weapons or with Felice's mindbolts. But the girl herself was eventually stunned, and the rest of the saboteurs, saving only Sister Amerie, Chief Burke, and Basil, were killed. The torc factory was undamaged.

Gomnol arrived when the fighting was over and coolly told the Host that he had everything in hand. But they refused to believe his protestations of innocence. Having improved their teamwork in metapsychic concert during the futile attacks on Elizabeth, they now combined to mind-blast Gomnol to death, knowing that the terrible Felice would be blamed. The girl was then divested of her golden torc and taken off by Culluket for interrogation. The other three saboteurs, badly wounded, were cast into the same prison as Stein and Sukey to await the end.

Far to the north of Muriah, in the vicinity of the time-gate at Castle Gateway, Madame Guderian and Claude prepared to act. They had made message holders from amber, a material known to pass successfully through the reversed time-warp, and enclosed notes warning the twenty-second-century operators to halt all time travel because of the enslaving of humans by the Tanu. As the sun rose, the two old people, rendered invisible by Madame's metapsychic power, rushed toward the gate area.

High in the sky, Aiken was searching for them. He did not want the time-gate closed, since this would deprive him of potential subjects once he became King. Before Aiken could spot his quarry he was seized by a miniature tornado and flung far away. He had been anticipated by Nodonn—who had plans of his own for the old couple.

As Claude and Madame approached the gate, the image of Nodonn filled their minds. He was not there to stop them, but to explain why he was permitting them to succeed. Because of Tanu popular sentiment, Nodonn had not dared to close the time-gate himself; yet he knew that it posed a mortal threat to his race's survival. He now told Claude and Madame that they must do their work visibly, so that there would be no doubt where the responsibility for the gate's closure lay. Then he let them go.

Hand in hand, the two old people stepped into the recycling time-warp and returned to the twenty-second century. Their bodies crumbled to dust, but the amber message holders survived. The time-gate was shut down forthwith.

Now the time of the Grand Combat had almost arrived. The petty nobility of the Tanu showed a strange liking for Aiken Drum, and his kingly aspirations had become a very serious matter. Also, he now had the photonic Spear in working order. This sacred weapon had last been used officially in a duel of two great heroes back at the Ship's Grave, when Tanu and Firvulag first arrived on Earth a thousand years earlier. The Tanu hero Bright Lugonn had wielded the Spear; the Firvulag hero Sharn the Atrocious had used a similar laserlike weapon called the Sword. In later years, the Sword had been used as the Grand Combat trophy and currently it was in the care of Nodonn Battlemaster. Aiken's possession of the Spear gave a further air of legitimacy to his aspiration. According to Tanu chivalric usage, Aiken would be permitted to fight Nodonn, Spear to Sword, if he managed to attract a suitable number of adherents during the Grand Combat.

A threat to Aiken now materialized from a strange source: his friend Stein. Suffering in prison with Sukey, who had miscarried of their son, Stein's mind was failing under the malignant influence of his gray torc. At the same time, the mental block installed by Gomnol began to weaken. It seemed that Stein would unwittingly betray Aiken's link with the saboteurs and his conspiracy with the late human Lord Coercer.

Resisting the temptation to kill Stein and Sukey, Aiken begged Mayvar to get the pair out of Muriah, beyond the range of the Host's mental snooping. Mayvar agreed to this, then went to a meeting of the clandestine Tanu Peace Faction, which hoped that Aiken would succeed in his bid for the kingship and bring a new era of peace and civilization to the Many-Colored Land.

Besides Mayvar, the Peace Faction included the hybrid High Table members Bleyn, Alberonn, and Katlinel the Darkeyed (who announced that she was betrothed to none other than Sugoll, ruler of the Howlers), Dionket the Lord Healer, Creyn,

and two banished Tanu stalwarts who might play special roles
in the upcoming Grand Combat. One of these was Leyr, father
of the hybrid Katlinel, who had been Lord Coercer before being
deposed by Gomnol. Now that the latter was dead and his post
vacant, the Host would put Imidol forward as a presidential
candidate. The Peace Faction urged Leyr to challenge young
Imidol in order to keep the Coercer Guild from Host control.
Leyr was much older, but it was known that Imidol was weaker
than Gomnol, so there seemed a slim chance that Leyr might
win. The other banished Tanu present at the secret meeting
was Minanonn the Heretic. Five hundred years before, he had
been Battlemaster. But his pacifistic temperament was anti-
thetical to the barbaric Tanu battle-religion, and he had been
forced into exile deep in the Pyrénées. The Peace Faction hoped
that, in the event Aiken defeated Nodonn, Minanonn would
fight against Kuhal Earthshaker for the presidency of the Psychokinetic Guild. However, Minanonn refused to compromise
his principles. Leyr did agree to go up against Imidol.

Later that same night, on a mountain above Muriah, Elizabeth and her great hot-air balloon awaited the arrival of Creyn.
He was to bring Stein and Sukey to her and the balloon would
carry all three to safety. But when the Tanu redactor arrived,
he brought not two people but three. Curled up unconscious
in the carriage was Felice. Creyn had found her in a cell next
to the others, near death after torture by Culluket. Felice, like
Stein, now wore a gray torc. But Sukey had been given a pair
of iron shears to remove the devices once they were safely off
the ground.

There was only one problem: The balloon gondola carried
only three.

Elizabeth was despairing and furious. Both Brede and Dionket had pleaded with her to remain with them, doing important
work that only a Grand Master metapsychic such as herself
was capable of. But Elizabeth did not want the responsibility—
especially if it meant that the Host would never relent in trying
to kill her. Faced with the wretched Felice, Stein, and Sukey,
she felt caught in the Shipspouse's web.

Finally, Elizabeth sent the three freed prisoners away in her
balloon. Then she returned to Brede's room without doors and

withdrew into a fiery mental cocoon that isolated her from all
other minds.

The First Day of the Combat began.

It was a day of bloodless sporting events and ceremony.
Mercy came to watch the thrilling contests with Bryan, who
was literally dying for love of her. Then she left him in order
to challenge old Aluteyn Craftsmaster for the presidency of the
Creator Guild.

At the same time, the balloon carrying Felice, Stein, and
Sukey drifted westward and landed alongside the Long Fjord
east of Mt. Alborán. Felice recovered her senses—and more.
In his tortures, Culluket had unwittingly duplicated a drastic
mind-altering technique that Elizabeth had used on Brede to
raise her to operancy; now Felice had gone operant, too. She
no longer needed a torc in order to exercise her metapsychic
powers; and these powers, at least the destructive aspects of
psychokinesis and creativity, were greater than those of any
other person in the world.

Felice was finally in a position to take revenge on the Tanu.
Her plan was to blast open the Gibraltar Isthmus with psychoenergy, letting the Atlantic flood the empty Mediterranean
Basin. The battleground of the White Silver Plain below Muriah
was well below sea level. It did not bother Felice that thousands
of Firvulag and humans would also drown in the cataclysm.
She did not trust the Firvulag protestations of friendship (neither
had Madame Guderian), and most of the humans in Muriah
were creatures of the Tanu. In order to implement her plan,
Felice required Stein's help. As an ex-driller of the Earth's
crust, he had the technical knowledge to instruct her where to
blast. At first, Stein refused to consider Felice's terrible scheme.
He had no grudge against the Tanu—none, that is, worth such
a hideous retribution.

At that point, Felice triumphantly told Stein that King Thagdal was responsible for Sukey's miscarriage, the guilt for which
Stein had mistakenly borne himself. In his rage, Stein gave
Felice all the help she needed. He showed her how to steal the
fjord so that a head of water would build up in the Alborán
Basin. Then he had her begin to blast open the Gibraltar Isthmus.

Powerful as she was, Felice faltered before the job was complete. In her extremity of hatred, Felice prayed help from whatever powers of darkness might exist—and the help came from *somewhere*, and she was able to open the Gibraltar Gate at last. A monstrous cascade of seawater began to fill the Alborán Basin, backing up behind a loose rubble dam near the Long Fjord.

On the Second Day of the Grand Combat, the culminating event was the selection of the Combat leaders by means of a manifestation of powers. The nine Firvulag leaders of long standing were unchallenged and accepted by acclamation. Wicked old Pallol One-Eye, the Firvulag Battlemaster, gave a demonstration of his formidable metapsychic power.

The selection of Tanu leaders was not so orderly. Things began tamely enough when Bleyn, Alberonn, Lady Bunone Warteacher, and Tagan Lord of Swords stood forth unchallenged. And then Dionket appointed Culluket his deputy, as was expected; and Nodonn similarly deputized his brother Kuhal Earthshaker since he himself would serve as Battlemaster. But a furor broke out when Gomnol's empty place was claimed by both Imidol and the exiled Leyr. The two agreed to duel for the coercer leadership on the field of battle rather than to manifest powers at that time.

Then it was the turn of Aluteyn Craftsmaster, Lord of the Creators. He was challenged by Mercy, and in the subsequent manifestation she was victorious. Rather than banishment, proud Aluteyn chose death. He went off to a huge glass vessel called the Great Retort, in which those condemned to die at the Combat's end awaited their fate. Mercy, the new Lady Creator, declined to fight in the Combat. She deputized Velteyn, erstwhile Lord of devastated Finiah, as her champion.

The final Tanu leader to stand forth was Mayvar, President of the Farsensors. She chose Aiken as her deputy rather than the Host's nominee, Riganone. After King Thagdal designated Nodonn as Battlemaster, all of the company retired to feasting and entertainment. Tomorrow the actual Combat would begin, lasting for two and a half days with only a few recesses. During that time, the sump behind the rubble dam across the Mediterranean Basin would fill with ever-deepening water . . .

The last, fateful psychocreative blast that had let in the sea also caused Felice to fall from the balloon. Stein and Sukey could find no trace of the girl. After cutting off his wife's silver torc so she could not transmit a telepathic warning to Muriah, Stein guided the balloon into a northerly current of air and soared far away, heading for freedom in a remote part of France.

The only person at the Grand Combat with an intimation of approaching disaster was the deposed Creator, Aluteyn Craftsmaster. As the Grand Combat proper began, he perceived subtle geophysical hints of the encroaching sea and tried to give warning while imprisoned inside the Great Retort. He was ignored. Tanu and Firvulag met in their ritual war with no thought except for their ancient rivalry. The human Raimo Hakkinen, forced to take part in the battle, was rescued from slaughter by Aiken Drum. Then Raimo attempted to desert, but he was found out and condemned to the Retort for cowardice.

Unlike the previous forty Grand Combats, which the Tanu had won easily, this contest showed signs of being a squeaker. The Firvulag used new tactics, learned at Finiah, against the battle-mounts of Tanu and torced humanity. The Little People pulled ahead in the body-count scoring, even though the Tanu retained a lead in the more significant banner-capture tally. Velteyn of Finiah, too anxious for vengeance after the loss of his city, was responsible for a Tanu fiasco. Aiken Drum, on the other hand, engineered a number of triumphs by means of tricky maneuvers, which delighted the more progressive Tanu but enraged the reactionaries of the Host, most notably Nodonn Battlemaster.

The rivalry between Aiken and Nodonn for the battlemastership became more heated during the second day of fighting. At a war feast, Nodonn tried to discredit Aiken by dramatically producing Bryan Grenfell and his adverse study of humanity's impact upon the Many-Colored Land. Some of the Tanu abandoned Aiken because of this; but large numbers still were pragmatic enough to stick with him. In the duel between coercers, Imidol of the Host defeated the elderly Leyr. Tough old Celadeyr of Afaliah took the place of the defunct Velteyn as Second Creator under Mercy.

Shortly before the Combat's start, Brede Shipspouse had secretly taken healing Skin to the prison cell in Muriah where

Chief Burke, Basil, and Amerie lay dying. The three were fully
recovered by the last day of the Combat and Brede led them,
mystified, to a room high on the Mount of Heroes inside the
Redactor Headquarters, which overlooked the White Silver
Plain. Inside this room were lockers full of twenty-second-
century equipment that the Tanu had confiscated from time-
travelers. More important, Elizabeth was there, apparently in
a deep coma. Brede instructed the three to take charge of the
equipment and Elizabeth, and wait until the following morning,
when they would know what to do. On no account were they
to leave the room until then.

The Grand Combat approaches its finale, in which the champions of the Tanu and Firvulag armies would meet hand to
hand. The generalized phase of fighting had given the Tanu a
narrow lead over the Little People, but this could be upset
during the Heroic Encounters. The Firvulag were especially
hopeful because neither Nodonn nor Aiken could participate in
the first round of Encounters. Each battlemaster-candidate now
had four heroes (leaders) pledged to him, and the candidate
whose people won the most duels against the Firvulag heroes
would stand forth in the culminating Encounter of Battlemasters
against Pallol One-Eye.

In the Encounters, Aiken's partisans won two and lost two.
Nodonn's won one, lost two, and tied one. This meant that
Aiken would meet Pallol. If he lost, the Firvulag would win
the entire Grand Combat. Aiken maintained that he could beat
the Firvulag ogre if the Tanu High Table allowed him to do it
in a human way, using the same trick he had used to overcome
Delbaeth. Reluctantly, Nodonn and his people had to agree.
Aiken went out and downed the Firvulag Battlemaster just as
he had promised, and the Tanu were declared winners of the
Grand Combat.

Heartbroken by their narrow loss, most of the Firvulag decided to leave the battlefield before the award ceremonies. Not
even the prospect of seeing Aiken and Nodonn battle it out
with Spear and Sword seemed worth waiting for. Only the
Firvulag royalty and their attendants remained for the finale.

The Tanu victory was ceremoniously proclaimed and Aiken
awarded the trophy Sword of Sharn (a photon weapon like the
Spear). Instead of offering it in fealty to King Thagdal, thus

acknowledging the Tanu's overlordship, Aiken drove the Sword into the ground. Thagdal signed to Nodonn to take it up as King's Champion. Meanwhile, Aiken's allies girded him in the harness of the Spear. The two squared off and began their duel just as the cataclysmic flood from the encroaching Atlantic swept over the White Silver Plain.

The mind-cries of the thousands of drowning people roused Elizabeth from her self-imposed coma. She and her three human companions looked out from the mountain refuge upon devastated Muriah and a submerged White Silver Plain. Redactor House contained a number of survivors and Chief Burke prepared for their evacuation.

Not all of those combatants and spectators caught on the White Silver Plain perished—although a majority of the Tanu, who were especially vulnerable to immersion, did lose their lives. Some few Tanu were cast ashore by the flood wave or managed to use their metapsychic powers to save themselves. Humans and hybrids in fair numbers swam to safety. Aiken Drum climbed aboard the ceremonial Kral cauldron and later rescued Mercy. The Great Retort, with its load of condemned, floated on the surge and, ironically, brought salvation to Aluteyn Craftsmaster, Raimo Hakkinen, and numbers of others, mostly human.

At the end of Volume 2, it was evident that an entirely new balance of power would now prevail in the Many-Colored Land. The Firvulag were strong under their new co-monarchs, King Sharn-Mes and Queen Ayfa. The Tanu cities, stripped of their most powerful metapsychic talents, were now vulnerable to attacks by Lowlife humans or the Little People. Most of the Tanu leadership, including Brede Shipspouse, had perished. Those Tanu remaining alive would have to decide whether or not to pledge allegiance to a human usurper who promised that he could save them from annihilation.

Now begin Volume 3, which, after a brief review of times gone by, picks up the chronicle in the period following the Great Flood.

PROLOGUE

THE DEAD AND THE WOUNDED AND THE BRAIN-BURNED HAD all been evacuated, and the highland forest lay innocent in Pliocene moonlight. Spicebush and orchids mingled their fragrance in the undergrowth. Flying squirrels came out of their hiding places and began to soar among the rowans and birches.

Up against the slope of the Mont-Dore volcano, where the trees thinned, the deadly hemisphere was motionless, faintly glimmering. It had a diameter of about fifteen meters. Its mirror surface gave it the aspect of a colossal witch ball partially buried in the mountainside, punctured by a tall, slender snag.

A single heroic squirrel came sailing out of the woods, zoomed, stalled out, and made an expert landing on the snag not far above the mirrored curve.

"Nervy little bugger," muttered Leyr Lord Coercer.

"No, just curious," the human Sebi-Gomnol said mildly.

The little animal darted down the barkless trunk, extended a paw, and touched the hemisphere. Nothing happened. Head down, the squirrel sniffed, then appeared to come to a conclusion. It dropped onto the mirror, immediately lost its purchase, and went sliding to the ground, landing in an aggrieved heap.

Bitter laughter broke from the observers as the creature scuttled off.

"Now he knows as much as we do," Bormol of Roniah observed. "If only we had learned our lesson as cheaply!"

There were six shining personages standing at a respectable distance from the hemisphere. One was a human being with an extraordinarily large nose and the others were members of the handsome Tanu race, more than two heads taller than the man. All of them wore fantastic glass armor studded with faceted spikes and gemstones, the open helmets crested with

1

horns or heraldic beasts. The figures glowed with a soft internal radiance. The human was smoking a cigar.

"Sixteen warriors of the Roniah battle-company slain," said Condateyr, Bormol's chief deputy. "To say nothing of the twenty or thirty grays and silvers killed back at Castle Gateway before we could even bring up the Hunt. Operant humans! Great Tana, they've never let operants come through the time-gate before! That's why we called on you at once, Battlmaster."

Nodonn inclined his head in acknowledgment. The rosy-gold light suffusing his magnificent form dimmed the blue-and green-glowing armor of the others. His mind, as usual, wore an enigmatic smiling overlay, and his spoken words were very soft. "The time-gate. The damned time-gate."

Bormol said, "The mental thrusts that overwhelmed the castle guardians were easily screened off by stalwarts of my Hunt, Battlemaster. But the Lowlife invaders had some kind of high-technology weapon as well, one that projected a co-herent energy beam. When we finally cornered them, they used the thing on us. Our metapsychic shields were impotent against it until Condateyr and I thought to coordinate a massed mind-defense according to the ancient discipline. Barely in time, at that."

Sebi-Gomnol grinned at the Lord of Roniah around his cigar. "And you made a strategic withdrawal behind the barrier. Very prudent, Coercive Brother."

"I have learned to be prudent where you humans are con-cerned . . . Coercive Brother."

Gomnol ignored the insulting little pause and addressed himself to Nodonn. "Battlemaster, the weapon used by these human metapsychic operants is undoubtedly some type of port-able photon cannon. Its operation is similar to that of your sacred Sword of Sharn, the trophy of the Grand Combat."

Nodonn indicated the mirrored hemisphere. "And that thing they're hiding behind?"

"What the science of my future world would call a sigma forcefield. I presume that it took a while for the invaders to get the generator working."

Bormol said, "None of our weaponry or psychocreative energies can penetrate that bloody silver bubble. You can far-sense dimly through it if you really work at it, but these aliens use a thought-mode that's all but incomprehensible. Most of them have been asleep for several hours now ... much good it does us."

Aluteyn, President of the Guild of Creators, asked Gomnol: "Just how strong is this sigma-field, son?"

"It would be completely impervious to any attack *we* could mount against it, Craftsmaster." The human's smile had a touch of chauvinism.

Leyr Lord Coercer glared down at his human Second. "I thought the rules of your human time-gate establishment forbade taking such equipment out of your world?"

"That's true, Coercive Lord. No modern weaponry is allowed to be exported to the Pliocene. Strictly forbidden by the Concilium of the Galactic Milieu." Gomnol shrugged his sapphire épaulières. "Of course, the Concilium also proscribed the translation of operant metapsychics."

Stout old Aluteyn exploded in a picturesque blasphemy. "But somehow, more than a hundred of the bastards have sneaked through! And beat the ballocks off our brother Bormol, here! Now what? I say, *now what*?" He brandished a radiant emerald fist at the rounded forcefield, which reflected a miniature moon and an anamorphically distorted forest skyline.

"I summoned you here hoping for useful advice, Creative Brother," Bormol responded with dignity, "not rhetorical questions. The alien invaders sleep now, but they'll wake up. And when they do ... I presume they have a way of shooting their weapon from inside that sigma-field."

"It depends on the type of generator," Gomnol said. "But we can assume they do."

The six of them united in a crude metapsychic concert to scan the hemisphere with their farsense; but the interior was an inchoate blur. Straining with the mind's ear yielded only the cycling mind-waves of the sleepers and a single steely thread of awareness—a watcher—whose mental emanations were almost completely outside the normal Tanu limit of perception.

Finally, Gomnol said to the Lord of Roniah, "Recapitulate the day's melancholy events once again, Coercive Brother. Leave out no details."

Bormol's mind, with Condateyr assisting, showed the four others a full-sensory reprise of the disaster. The arrival of the crowd of alien operants was first discovered by a gray-torc soldier on the battlements of Castle Gateway. (Luckily, he

survived the enusing massacre.) The invaders passed through
the time-portal at the unprecedented time of eleven-hundred
hours, rather than at dawn, as had been the unvarying custom
for the more than forty years of temporal translation. There
was no one outside the castle waiting to intercept them during
the brief period of disorientation following exit from the time-
warp; and when gray soldiers from the castle finally did emerge
to investigate, they were felled by a powerful metacoercive
blast. This alerted the silver-torc castellan, who in turn notified
the two Tanu overlords in residence at the time.

The operant newcomers had then turned their mental weapons, as well as some type of low-power photonic sidearms,
against the castle staff. A farspoken alarm went out to Roniah,
which lay a little over 30 kilometers away. But by the time
Bormol and Condateyr arrived with a Grand Hunt two hours
later, the invaders were gone, the Tanu overlords and about
half the Castle Gateway personnel were dead, and the ordinary
time-travelers in their prison compound were catatonic from
some kind of redactive brain-drain that the operants had inflicted.

Bormol's pursuing force was hampered by metapsychic barriers and mirages thrown up by the operants; but eventually
these weakened, and the trail of the invaders' small all-terrain
vehicles could be readily followed. The aliens headed west,
across the steppe of the Plateau du Lyonnais and down into the
forest that lay between the tableland and the enormous Mont-
Dore stratovolcano. The chaliko mounts of the Hunt were more
efficient than the alien ATVs in cross-country travel, once the
chase took to the lowland. Nearly a dozen of the fat-wheeled
contrivances were abandoned by their drivers in a hellishly
dense bamboo swamp; and two more were found later on a
game trail, stomped into bloody junk amid the spoor of hoe-
tusker elephants.

It was shortly after sunset that the fleeing operants made
the mistake of following a westward-trending valley that narrowed to a box canyon as it ascended a steep slope. Fatigued,
frightened, and trapped, the operants had let their metapsychic
screen waver for a brief moment, allowing Bormol's keenest
farsensors to discern the nature of the enemy—one hundred
and one human beings, all operant, some in very poor physical
condition and all suffering from profound mental trauma. They

were equipped with eighty-nine miniature trailered vehicles that were jammed to the rollbars with twenty-second-century matériel.

A cautious offensive probe by Bormol and his top coercers brought forth only feeble metapsychic retaliation. The skirmish at the castle and the long pursuit had seemingly worn the invaders out. And now they were cornered.

Disdaining to fight mentally, the Roniah Hunt had charged, mind-yelling its exuberant battle-cry ... only to be met by the photon cannon.

After the shambles of retreat, rescue of the wounded, and regrouping, it was learned that the operants had zapped one canyon wall, built a ramp with the debris, and escaped the cul-de-sac. At nightfall, scouts reported to Bormol the new phenomenon of the giant mirrored hemisphere; and at that point, the Lord of Roniah decided to pack it in and call for help from the Battlemaster and his senior advisors ...

Nodonn said, "There is one point I find curiously disturbing. The human prisoners at Castle Gateway. The ordinary time-travelers detained in the holding area. You say they were *drained*?"

Bormol was emphatic. "Minds wiped cleaner than the White Silver Plain, Battlemaster. Tabulae rasae. Damnedest thing I ever saw. It's a good thing it was early in the week and we only had two days' worth of prisoners. Those sixteen Lowlives are nothing but vegetables now. Whoever did that job had to be the devil's own redactor."

"And he found out everything that the prisoners knew about *us*," growled Leyr.

"And wiped them clean," Gomnol added, "which implies that the recently arrived time-travelers might have been able to tell us something useful about these émigré operants. Interesting."

"We know that some of the aliens—if not all of them—are what the humans term 'masterclass'," said Condateyr. "Otherwise they would not have been able to kill the Tanu overlords. Lord Moranet and Lady Senevar were highly skilled in both coercion and redaction."

Nodonn Battlemaster opened his mind and shared his stately train of thought with the others:

Certain of these aliens have awesome metapsychic powers

greater than our own. However, they did not use them to the fullest potential against Bormol's Hunt, but relied instead upon a physical weapon. Additionally, they chose to flee our forces, rather than taking a stand. Some of the aliens show evidence of being weakened. *Hurt.* These human metapsychics, the elite of their race, have been driven to the extreme of Exile, a course officially forbidden to them. Ergo, they can only be outlaws from the Galactic Milieu. But that is a contradiction in terms! All metapsychics of the future world partake of a mental fellowship called Unity. There can be no outcasts. No rebels.

"None that we know about, Battlemaster," said Gomnol aloud. "But Tanu knowledge of the Elder Earth comes perforce from human time-travelers. And what did normal humans— even latents like myself—really know what the metapsychic faction and the inner workings of the Galactic Concilium?" His smile had a wry twist as he touched the golden torc behind the blue-glass gorget of his armor. "We had to come here, to the Pliocene, to find the true kinship of shared thought, the exercise of godlike powers. Thanks to you Tanu."

The sun-flood that was Nodonn's mind illumined dark cysts of malice deep within the human coercer's heart; but Apollo's face was serene, as always.

"Your gratitude to us is noted, Adopted Brother. Now demonstrate it tangibly! *You* are capable, as we are not, of asking these alien invaders who they are and what they want. You will use the human mode of farspeech that we Tanu cannot perceive."

Gomnol's guilty spurt of fear brought insouciant reassurance from the Battlemaster. "Oh, yes, Eusebio Gomez-Nolan. We know about it. A harmless bit of schoolboy secrecy to bolster the pride of you human gold-torcs. But now it can be useful. Mindspeak to these invading Lowlives, Second Coercer. And be sure that you tell me truthfully what response they make."

Gomnol's glowing blue form seemed to totter, his face went ashen within the fantastic helmet, and the cigar fell from his mouth. The metapsychic grip of the Battlemaster, compounded of all five mental faculties focused in precise neural assault, closed upon him for the briefest instant. It was the most frightful pain that Gomnol had ever experienced. It was replaced at once by lingering pleasure.

Nodonn waited patiently until the human recovered his equilibrium. Then he repeated, "Mindspeak, Second Coercer."

Gomnol slowly exhaled. His own mental screens were up now to mask his discomfiture, his hatred. "You . . . and the Craftsmaster must stand by. In case the invaders react aggressively. That photon cannon could—"

Old Aluteyn said, "Nodonn and I can act in concert and put up a tough little shield. As long as we know what to expect, we can shelter the lot of us. Get on with your job, son."

Gomnol's confidence rapidly restored itself. He nodded gravely, struck a pose, and reached out with all of his coercive power. His thought-pattern was now indecipherable to the Tanu; but they were fully aware of its superlative technique—the gentle insinuating flow through the force-field, the abrupt concentration into a tidal thrust, and the irresistible impact of the Second Coercer's mind upon that weary-alert pattern of cold consciousness lurking inside the mirrored sphere. Gomnol spoke and the hidden watcher was constrained to answer.

Leyr's bitter commentary on the performance of his subordinate crackled on the Tanu intimate mode:

Just look at that pushy little runt's operation, Brothers! Only ten years since we gave him gold, and already his powers of coercion nearly rival my own! How long will he be content to be Second, eh?

The others kept their minds shuttered. It was an uncomfortable question.

After a time, Gomnol withdrew his mind from the hemisphere and spoke to the others with great effort. "He says . . . his people only want to be let alone. They'll leave Europe, because of the Tanu hegemony. They'll go to North America. Never return."

"Tana be thanked!" Bormol growled. "And speed the day."

But Gomnol made urgent protest. "You don't understand. This whole group . . . all of them are masterclass operants! There's been some kind of failed metapsychic coup d'état in my world, six million years in the future. This group is what's left of the losers. But they nearly won! This small group of human rebels almost overcame the metapsychic magnates of all six races of the Galactic Milieu! . . . They're in terrible shape now, but they'll recover. And when they do, if we could ally them to us—"

"The aliens must be destroyed." Nodonn's thought and voice were storm-loud.

"But think of the advantage of an alliance! The Firvu-lag—"

"Any advantages would accrue to humanity, Second Coercer! These operant humans do not wear the golden torc. They can never be part of our fellowship."

"Of course you're right, Battlemaster!" Leyr exclaimed. He threw Gomnol a monitory thought. "You get a grip on yourself, Number Two."

Aluteyn Craftsmaster's mind-tone was withering. "Dammit, son—why should these operant humans join with us when they're probably capable of taking over the whole Many-Colored Land, given a little rest and recuperation?"

"And another photon cannon or two put into operation," muttered Bormol.

"If we all act in metapsychic concert, our will can prevail," Gomnol insisted. "There are thousands of us gold-torcs and only a handful of operant invaders. Some of them are dying. The others are devastated by failure and world-loss. They'd jump at an offer of friendship, I tell you!"

The Battlemaster said repressively, "I have farspoken the King. He concurs with my decision."

In a last effort, Gomnol sent a plea arrowing to Nodonn on the intimate mode:

Think Battlemaster think! Unique opportunity! Leaderinvaders is magnateConcilium MarcRemillard. Whole familyRemillard operated highestlevel HumanPolityMilieu! Marc/recovered + others potential KEY HostNontusvel ambitions vs. Firvulag...

No.

I saw Marc traumatizedvulnerable. Others muchweaker. Acting metaconcertcoercion Host + Me easily...

No.

Marc is JonRemillardbrother! And Jon = *Jack the Bodiless*!! Marc nearly match for brother I remember Milieupolicking...

No.

Moonlight glistened on the sweat droplets trickling down Gomnol's face. From the dark forest came a faint whickering sound and the thud of clawed feet. The armored chaliko mounts of the party came trotting forward at Leyr's telepathic command. Nodonn vaulted into his saddle, kindling his own faerie aura of rose and gold about the beast's jeweled caparisons.

"I have also farspoken my Host-brothers," Nodonn said, looking down on Gomnol. "Hual Greatheart and Mitheyn, Lord of Sasaran, will coordinate a Grand Quest. Hual will bring the Sword of Sharn down from Goriah, and I will wield it against this Lowlife crew. Mitheyn will come north from Sasaran with a land force strong in psychokinesis, creativity, and coercion. We will allow the invaders to move westward into the Valley of Donaar. Somewhere in the Grotto Wilderness, at a place of our choosing, we will annihilate them."

"As Tana wills," said Gomnol in resignation. After wiping his face with a white handkerchief, he reached for a fresh cigar, mounted his own chaliko, and rode away with the others.

Three days later, near a river that would one day be called the Dordogne, a massed body of Tanu chivalry swept down upon the crawling train of twenty-second-century vehicles; but since the operant humans, even in their weakened state, far surpassed the exotics in the faculty of farsensing, the Tanu attempt at ambush was unsuccessful. Sophisticated equipment, initially unfamiliar to the fleeing metapsychic rebels and clumsily stowed to boot, was now arrayed competently. Solar powerpacks were fully charged, small arms and personal force-screens were at the ready, and the photon cannon was emplaced for tactical advantage.

Four hundred and nineteen Tanu knights, including the Lord of Sasaran and Hual Greatheart, were slain in the ensuing conflict. Twice that number of exotics, virtually the entire roster of survivors, fell wounded.

Nodonn Battlemaster saw his Flying Hunt decimated and his favorite chaliko blasted out from under him in midair. He narrowly missed dropping the precious Sword of Sharn into the Donaar River, and lost not only his Apollonian dignity but his temper as well.

Leyr Lord Coercer forfeited an arm, half a leg, and the left lobe of his liver. He had to spend eight months recuperating in Skin, during which time his subaltern, the human Sebi-Gomnol, consolidated his own position and resolved to challenge his fading superior in the next year's Manifestation of Powers.

The invading operants made their way to the Atlantic Coast.

There they linked their modular ATVs to form boats, whistled up a fair psychokinetic wind, and vanished into the sunset.

After a two-month hiatus, the time-gate resumed normal operations.

Heeding the Battlemaster's counsel, Thagdal, High King of the Many-Colored Land, decreed that the entire alien invasion débâcle had never happened.

And for the next twenty-seven years, the Tanu kingdom in exile prospered . . . until the Gibraltar Gate was opened and the Empty Sea filled.

PART I

THE POST-DILUVIUM

1

THE GREAT RAVEN OVERFLEW THE DESOLATION OF MURIAH.

She had to travel far from her mountain these days in her searches, since the near coasts of Spain and shrinking Aven were nearly picked clean of booty, the bodies buried ever more deeply in silt beneath the rising Mediterranean. She had scavenged the easily accessible golden torcs months ago, and found the great treasure. The pickings were now all the more precious for their rarity.

Muriah, below her, had its ruin softened by a spreading verdurous shroud. After nearly four months of the rainy season, the former Tanu capital of the Many-Colored Land seemed to have surrendered to rampant Pliocene vegetation. Tendrils and runners and shoots from ornamental shrubs—unrestrained now that most of the little rama gardeners had perished—smothered the courtyards, the grand stairways, and the filigreed walls of white marble. Fresh growth even probed open doors and windows and clambered onto the roofs, thrusting the red and blue tiles awry. Trees sent out erratic withes from their splintered trunks. Spores and seeds, washed or blown into the crevices of pavement and masonry, sprouted in ghoulish abandon.

The sweeping esplanades, the sporting arena, the Square of Commerce, the mansions, and all the proud structures built by the Tanu and their clever human slaves were being inexorably pushed and pried apart. Fungi, mosses, and vulgar flowering

13

weeds loosened the once gleaming courses of alabaster and the dulled mosaics. The colonnade of King Thagdal's palace had its heavy pillars unseated by the irresistible growth of little brown mushrooms. Unlit silver torchères along the deserted boulevards were tarnished black by sea mist. The façades of the five metapsychic guild-halls had their heraldic colors defaced by dark splotches of mildew. Even the lofty glass spires, their faerie lights dark forever, were encrusted with dried salt and scabby lichen.

Circling, the raven concentrated her search along the northern perimeter of the ruined city. The entire docks area was now submerged. Sullen waves lapped halfway up the escarpment below the Coercer Guild Headquarters. Skylights in one section of the huge structure had been smashed and the torc factory inside held no treasure now. The raven had seen to it.

Her farsensing eye bored deep, seeing through water and rock into the submarine caves that once had been high and dry above saline flats rimming the Catalan Gulf. Months ago when Muriah city was alive, she had hidden in one of those caves with her doomed friends. There the trickster had come, robbing her! (But she had seen to *that* matter as well.)

And sooner or later she would see to the other unfinished business, for she was a creature methodical in her unsanity, this bird that glided in a gray March sky over a gray new sea, endlessly searching.

She scanned cavern after cavern where flotsam lay piled, cast up by the Flood's first cataclysmic surge and later entombed as the waters rose. Some of the caves still had air in their upper chambers. It was in one of these that she at last perceived the telltale density-signature of precious metal.

Gold.

Her harsh joy-cry echoed from the Aven cliffs. She plummeted, coming out of the dive just above the leaden water, and poised motionless with great ebony wings outspread. Then a small woman with a cloud of fair hair appeared in place of the raven: a woman dressed in a cuirass, greaves, and gauntlets of gleaming black. Felice laughed out loud and was abruptly naked, pale as salt-rime except for her wide dark eyes.

She pierced the water as cleanly as an arrow of flesh. A single torpedolike movement took her through the sea-tunnel and into the cave. Shining like a wan bluish corposant, she walked over the water to a narrow ledge where the body lay. She laughed again at the sight of the dead enemy—until she realized that the dingy glass armor was not amethyst, as her deceiving blue light made it seem, but ruby-red. Redactor Guild red.

"No!" she shrieked, dropping to her knees beside the corpse of the Tanu knight. His jaw hung slack and his wrinkled eyelids were closed. He wore no helmet. Lank fair hair still clung to his half-exposed skull. His golden torc was befouled in adipocere from the decomposing head and neck.

"Oh, no," she wept. "Not *yet.*"

She scratched away the moldy matter hiding the breastplate's heraldic motif, gasping and whimpering until the design was fully visible. It was a stylized tree laden with jeweled fruits, not the transfixed caput mortuum of Culluket the Interrogator.

Peal after peal of laughter rang in the dank cave. What a fool she was. Of course it wasn't him.

Felice jumped to her feet, grasped the hinged gorget plates of the ruby armor, and ripped them from place. They fell to the rock floor with a loud chiming sound. And then the severed head fell, for she pulled away the torc so violently that the vertebrae were disarticulated.

She held the torc high. It blazed incandescent and was clean. She plunged back into the water and in a moment the raven was rocketing skyward, gripping a golden circlet in powerful talons. Her mind's voice shouted triumph and profound relief. She called out to her Beloved as she had done so often, using the declamatory mode of mental speech that could span continents and oceans and reverberate around the world like the sonorities of dying thunder.

Culluket!

She called. High in the featureless gray above drowned Aven she called.

The devils answered.

Felice's exaltation changed to terror. She shrank within an opaque thought-screen and sent the bird body hurtling in the direction of the Spanish mainland, protected from friction-burn by a subconical psychocreative shield. Only when she reached the vicinity of Mount Mulhacén did she slacken the furious dash and venture a cautious peep to see whether or not the devils had tracked her.

They had not. Once again, she had eluded them.

She dropped all the screens and voiced a raucous, defiant croak. Then she flew home, the newest bit of treasure secure in her claws.

2

MORE THAN EIGHT THOUSAND KILOMETERS WEST OF EUROPE, the great bulldog tarpon of the Pliocene Epoch had once again begun their spring migration to the spawning grounds around Ocala Island and the Still-Vexed Bermoothes. It was time for the saint's elder brother to suspend his weary star-search in favor of his sole form of relaxation—hunting the silvery monsters.

The man in the skiff watched the fish come with his farsense. He was motionless and made no sound, hidden behind a mass of mangroves and flowering epiphytes in the Suwanee estuary on the west side of the island. He deliberately limited his mind's stupendous vision to the river channel within a few hundred meters of his hiding place, for he had his rules in the stalking of the big tarpon and he would not violate them. Not consciously.

In the manner of their kind, the fish surfaced and rolled in the sparkling blue water, taking gulps of air. Scales larger than a handspan reflected the tropical sun like mirrors. With their undershot jaws, glaring black eyes, and bristling gills of lurid scarlet, the tarpon resembled cruising dragons rather than ordinary fish. Numbers of them exceeded three meters in length and they were capable of attaining an even greater size as the fisherman knew only too well. When hooked, a bulldog tarpon would fight with maniacal ferocity, sometimes for twenty hours.

17

He watched them parade by while the sun soared higher, bringing a sheen of sweat to his deeply tanned skin. He wore only a pair of stagged dungarees, bleached by age and salt water. His self-rejuvenating body was as powerful and firmly muscled as ever; but his face showed, as on a chart of flesh and bone, the pain-etched odyssey of the failed idealist. Only when one particularly large specimen of tarpon glided past, its jaw-plates scarred from an encounter several seasons past, did the fisherman's mouth curve in a reminiscent, one-sided smile of peculiar sweetness.

Not you, he told the huge fish. You've had your turn on the hook. Another. A greater.

Engrossed as he was in the study of the tarpon, he was instantly aware of the featherlight scrutiny: the farsense of the children, spying on him again, even though all of the inhabitants of Ocala knew that it was strictly forbidden to disturb him when the tarpon were running. None of the surviving senior rebels would dream of it, remembering only too well the capabilities of the one who had led them in their challenge of the galaxy. But the second generation, now grown to restless young adulthood, was less inclined to reverence. Even his own children, Hagen and Cloud (never having been told of his aborted plans for them had the Rebellion succeeded), believed that his mental powers were diminished by time—and by his thus-far futile scrutiny of some 36,000 Pliocene solar systems in an attempt to locate other coadunate minds.

The disdain of the youngsters had been shaken only once: last fall, when Felice Landry in her extremity besought help from what she believed were dark forces. So powerful had been the girl's projection of need that the operant metapsychics of Ocala, there on the other side of the world, had clearly farsensed what she was trying to accomplish at Gibraltar. *He* had smiled at her temerarious rage in that whimsical manner of his, and said: "Why shouldn't the Angel of the Abyss take care of his own?" And forthwith he had combined and focused the psychoenergies of the forty-three surviving conspirators of the Metapsychic Rebellion, plus the uncoadunate but immense creativity of their thirty-two mature children, and vouchsafed the totality to the madwoman. And the Empty Sea filled.

This had been a mere hint, a shadow of his potential. But it was enough to make the more imaginative of the youngsters reassess their derogation of the lonely star-searcher.

Sitting there in the skiff, he felt them sweep him again, ever so discreetly. He knew what they were up to. They were bored with their exile on Ocala, bored with the murderous intrigues and harsh restrictions of their elders, and above all bored by their own lack of coadunate mental Unity (for none of the fleeing rebels had possessed the specialized training required of metapsychic preceptors). Now that Europe, the mysterious and alluring Many-Colored Land, was known to be in a state of chaos, the more ambitious members of the second generation were hatching callow schemes of conquest. Not for them the patient search of planet after planet for kindred minds, the dream of a rescue from exile. The children had hopes of achieving power and Unity right here on Pliocene Earth. And the bolder ones entertained an even greater ambition. An unthinkable one.

Out in the channel, the enormous fish cavorted in the sun.

He lifted his rod from its case, opened the tackle box, inspected the reel mechanism with his deep-vision, mounted it, and began to thread the line. The fly rod was laminated bamboo, crafted by himself more than twenty years ago. He had made the reel as well. But that fishing line was the product of a world six million years removed from the Pliocene Suwanee estuary. Tapered, balanced, and irreplaceable, subtly armored in the trace against the tarpon's steely jaws, it merged to a vulnerable 6.75-kilo test tippet that gave the fish an almost overwhelming sporting advantage over the angler. To catch even the least of those splendid brutes on a flyrod with such a gossamer thread (and without using any metapsychic force— that went without saying!) was a supreme achievement. But this season, he intended to aim beyond supremacy toward the ultimate. He was going to take one of the Old Ones, the glittering leviathans of the tarpon clan that approached four meters in length and nearly three hundred kilos in weight. He was going to bring in one of those fish on the frail line, with his homemade fly rod.

I can do it, he told himself, smiling the attractive one-sided smile. One old monster against another.

The farsense of the children slid over him again.

Closing his mind to every other input, Marc Remillard settled down in the skiff in the sunshine, waiting for his prey.

3

IN GORIAH, AFTER MIDNIGHT WHEN THE MOON WAS DOWN, the cloud cover broke along the Brittany shore and the meteors of March appeared in all their splendor. In a fit of playfulness, Aiken Drum ordered the lights in the city to be extinguished and had Mercy roused from sleep and brought to where he waited on a narrow parapet surmounting the highest spire of the Castle of Glass.

She stepped out into the amazing night and cried, "Ah!"

Spraying among the western constellations were countless arching white sparks, and larger meteors with lucent silver tails, and occasional orange fireballs slashing the sky with bold strokes of afterglow. All of them rushed outward from a tight central focus like spokes in a starry wheel, or petals unfurling endlessly from some astral chrysanthemum. The meteors flew over the heads of Aiken and Mercy and dived behind the mass of Breton Island across the strait. Some of them quenched themselves in the black sea. The night was filled with a faint rustling sound, like ethereal whispering.

"For you!" Aiken exclaimed magniloquently, compassing the spectacle with a possessive sweep of his hand. "One of my more modest productions, but still worthy of a Tanu queen!"

Laughing, she came to him. "Not yet a queen, my shining braggart, in spite of all your saucy promises. But the star-

21

shower is lovely—not that I believe for a moment that you caused it."

"Doubting me again, woman?" The small man in the gleaming suit all covered with pockets lifted both arms. A dozen of the meteors seemed to plummet straight down at him, emitting a scorching hiss, and shrink to form a coronet of white lights that scintillated insanely. He held it out to her with a triumphant grin. "I crown you Queen of the Many-Colored Land!"

"Illusions!" she cried. "*That* for your shifty love-gift, Lord Lugonn Aiken Drum!" She snapped her fingers at the starry diadem and it died to embers, sifting through Aiken's hands like dwindling coals through a grate. But as his face fell she suddenly smiled at him there in the blazing darkness, making his heart heel half-seas over.

"But I do love the real meteors, and you're a dear trickster to have called me out to see them."

She kissed him full and long, with her wild eyes wide open, and while he was disarmed and his mind-shields awry, she caught him unprepared with a redactive probe.

"You do love me!" she exclaimed.

"The hell I do!" He mustered his defenses, reasserting self-control, trying to escape her mental scrutiny without hurting her. The great metapsychic faculties that had continued to grow throughout the winter months—those powers that had evoked admiring subservience or sullen awe from the surviving Tanu Great Ones—failed before Mercy-Rosmar. "I don't love you!" his mind and voice protested. "It isn't necessary."

Her merriment bubbled up. "*Necessary?* But you'd take my pleasure-gifts, wouldn't you—love or not, you archdeceiver! And you want them now. Admit it! Well, then..."

The fading redactive lancet softened to a sweet searing burst that coursed along his nerves and sent him falling, aflame like the meteors in helpless sexual transport. "Enchantress," he groaned, flat on the glass floor of the turret with his feet tangled in the skirts of her flowing peignoir. Then, as he recovered, he began to laugh to cover the other emotion.

Mercy knelt beside him, cradling his head and kissing his

eyelids. "Don't be afraid," she said. "It will all work as you planned."

"I'm not afraid of anything!" he protested. "Together, we'll lick 'em all, Lady Wildfire."

"I don't mean that, you schemer." She looked down at him, relaxed in her lap with his head against her swollen belly. "But you do almost make me believe you can bring the glory back."

"I can! Trust me. I've got everything worked out. How to handle the Firvulag, the way to win the loyalty of the Tanu diehards, the restoration of the economy—all of it. I'll be king and you'll be queen, and our winter dreams will all come true."

His face with its golliwog grin was bright with jacky-lanthorn radiance. He felt Mercy's mind start with an abrupt sense of déjà vu that was so intense that it made even the sleeping fetus stir.

"I've seen your face before," she said wonderingly. "Back in the Old World. I'm sure of it. It was in Italy . . . in Firenze."

"Not bloody likely. The only time I came to Old Earth was on my trip to the auberge, and I went right to France with no detours. That was after you'd already gone through the time-gate."

"I saw you," she insisted. "Or was it a picture of you? Perhaps in the Palazzo Vecchio? But whose portrait?"

"Not an Italian gene in my bod," he murmured, reaching up to stroke her hair. Meteors sketched a surreal halo behind her head. "Dalriada, where I grew up, was a Scottish world. And all of us test-tube brats had certified tartan chromosomes."

He levitated until their lips met. She melted into him again, as he knew she would, triggering the neural conflagration that he could not help craving in spite of his fear. When he regained his senses, still lying in her lap, the baby was kicking him in the ear and the damn meteors exploding in pyrotechnic mockery.

"Shame on you for disturbing my darling Agraynel," Mercy said.

Aiken felt her maternal thought-song soothe the unborn girl. Suddenly, for no apparent reason, his eyes filled with tears. Mortified, he whirled his most impregnable mental barrier into place so that Mercy would not know how much he envied the baby. He said, "Only one more month until it's born. And then I'm going to have you, my Lady Wildfire! Find out how you knock me out of orbit—and give you some of your own back with interest!"

"Not until May," she chided him. "At the Grand Loving, as we agreed."

"Oh, no! That's just the official wedding. You aren't going to hold me off that long! . . . And come to think of it—why shouldn't I take you metapsychically right now, just the way you've been mind-screwing me?" His arms closed around her shoulders, pulling her strongly down. His coercive power began to bore into her softness. "Show me how you do your magic sex! Show me—or I'll just find out by experimenting!"

"You may not!" she cried, countering him with a psycho-creative riposte that all but blinded him. "It would make a fearful womb-quake in addition to the neural surge. That's the way we women are made. It would be bad for the baby."

He released her. The damned fear came again, and so did the tears. "To hell with the baby."

Her face came close to his. Her expression of indignation changed into tenderness. "Ah, poor little one. I see. I see."

Her lips descended to drink his tears.

He thrashed wildly to escape her physical embrace, sprawling onto the floor. His mouth tightened to a thin slot and his eyes were wide and black. "I don't want that from you! Ever."

"Ah, well." She shrugged. "But you needn't fear it, really. It's quite natural for the two womanly functions to combine in the loving."

"You don't love me, and I don't love you. So why pretend? And I don't need your pity, dammit!" He cast about desperately, to put her in the wrong. "Why haven't you ever let me pleasure you? Not once! Always ready to blast me into a coma— but never letting me touch you. Am I so disgusting?"

"Don't be silly. It's the baby, I tell you."

"When Nodonn was with you, the two of you fucked up a bloody hurricane—and no worry about the baby, then. And that poor bastard of an anthropologist had all the sweet houghmagandy he wanted from you. The whole damn capital knew what you two were up to!"

Her smile was easy. "Agraynel didn't mind then, in the second trimester. But now she's all close-crowded and impatient to be born."

"Don't give me that." He got to his feet, his face no longer alight and his voice metallic. "You won't let me get into you because you're still mourning for Nodonn."

"How could I not?" she admitted coolly. She levitated and stood before him. The pale chiffon of her gown seemed to ripple in the sidereal concussions.

He shouted in fury. "Mayvar told me all about your precious Sun-Face! A fine king he would've made! The Tanu ruler is supposed to pass on his superior genes to the people—but do you know that your wonderful Nodonn was damn near sterile? The great Battlemaster! He lived eight hundred years and had only a handful of children. And not a first-class power in the lot! Mayvar Kingmaker rejected him. He was only declared crown prince because the Host of Nontusvel forced him on the Thagdal. Why do you think Mayvar was so glad to see *me* come along? Why do you think she named me Lugonn, after the real crown prince?"

Mercy clasped his waving hands. They stood face to face in bare feet and she was several centimeters the taller.

Softly, she said, "It's true that you are the chosen of the Kingmaker. And perhaps you would have won your duel with the Battlemaster on the White Silver Plain . . . and perhaps not. Nodonn is dead. Drowned. But you're alive, Lord Aiken-Lugonn, and master of Goriah in Nodonn's place. Who would have thought that would happen, when we met all drenched and puking like puppies, adrift in a golden cauldron in the midst of the Great Flood! Less than five months we've been together—and yet I feel I've known you an age, you Lord of Misrule. You'll be king! Don't doubt it. I see—I know! There isn't a Tanu or a human gold in the Many-Colored Land with mental prowess to equal your own. No other could have picked up the pieces of this shattered world as you did and begun the rebuilding. That's why I'll stay with you, work with you. And after I bear the Thagdal's daughter I'll marry you and be your queen. In May, at the Grand Loving, as we agreed. As for your own children, we'll see what the good Goddess sends."

The rage rushed out of him, leaving only a wayward thought: But if only you loved me, I'd be safe.

Her mind smiled back, changeable as the western sea. All during their time together they had played this game; and until now, he had believed himself the winner, immune to the enchantment that had bound the others to her.

She said, "You fear me, and you hope to gain control through love. But are you willing to love me in return, giving and sharing? Or would you only rule?"

The deep barriers that hid the truth crumbled within him. "You know I already love you."

"Enough to demand nothing of me in return? Unselfishly?"

"I don't know."

Her voice and mind-tone became fey and heedless. "And what if I won't return your love, you Hermes Chrysorapis? What will you do with me then?"

He folded her in his arms, burying his face in the fragrant hair cascading over her shoulder, sensing the ironic triumph behind her question. She knew. She knew.

He broke away and stood alone. The sky was graying with false dawn. The meteors diminished. He said, "I didn't really cause the star-shower. The meteors come every spring at this time. They mark the end of the rainy season. But I wanted to surprise you with them."

"What will you do with me if I won't love you?" she repeated.

"I think you know."

He gave her his hand and they entered the lightless tower, leaving the last of the meteors exploding in cool darkness.

4

JUST ONE MORE DAY, AND TONY WAYLAND WOULD HAVE MADE his escape. Just one more day, and he could have gone out normally with the caravan to Fort Rusty—then made his getaway with nobody the wiser.

But the Howlers had attacked the Iron Maiden Mine before the caravan left. And now Tony knew he was going to die...

As that Pliocene rara avis, a metallurgical engineer and fully sane ex-silver (his psychocreative faculty was modest at best; he owed his high status under the Tanu to an improved refining technique introduced at the Finiah barium mine), Tony was under strictest orders from his new bosses in the Lowlife Steering Committee to avoid life-threatening situations. He usually undertook troubleshooting tours among the Iron Villages only during daylight, when hostile exotics were seldom abroad. Sir Dougal, the stalwart bodyguard assigned to him by Old Man Kawai, shadowed him everywhere. Dougal's pseudomedieval eccentricities were more than counterbalanced by a fanatical devotion to duty and by expertise with the compound bow. And, truth to tell, Tony was also gratified to have at least one person left who still addressed him as "Lord." The majority of the Lowlife iron-working community were offensively egalitarian, if not downright contemptuous of a déclassé silver such as himself. He had cooperated with the Tanu—and done it willingly. Thus he was a traitor to the human race.

27

Not that anyone dared snub Tony to his face! Far from it, since his talents were invaluable. If the free humans of the Vosges wilderness—Lowlives and Finiah refugees, now united —were to avoid Tanu enslavement, the Howler menace, and possible Firvulag treachery, iron production was a strategic necessity. The "blood-metal" was poisonous to all branches of the extragalactic race that shared Pliocene Europe with embattled humankind, and the use of iron weapons had been a key factor in the destruction of Tanu Finiah by a coalition of Lowlives and Firvulag. Tony Wayland had been one of the top prizes in that human triumph. Most of the other noncombatant silvers had been flown safely to Tanu territory when Lord Velteyn evacuated his doomed city. But Tony had been unlucky.

A sneering band of Lowlife invaders had caught him flagrante delicto in the Finiah Pleasure Dome, too besotted after an interlude with a Tanu charmer to distinguish the skyrockets going off in his head from the noise of the city's Götterdämmerung. So they frogmarched him off, hauled him before a Lowlife tribunal, and gave him the choice faced by every other torced human following the fall of Finiah: *Live free or die.* Tony, a total pragmatist, had submitted to the abscission of his silver torc and the ensuing weeks of agonizing psychic adjustment. But he hadn't forgotten—or forgiven. He would have run away to the Tanu in a trice, except for the still greater disaster that had destroyed the exotics' capital of Muriah and snuffed out most of the ruling nobility. The Great Flood had bred such havoc that he was at a loss to sort out the main chance. Fort Onion River and the other gray-torc guard stations along the track to Castle Gateway were long abandoned. The stronghold itself, useless now that the time-gate had closed, was reputed to have been taken over by the Firvulag. The Little People had also seized the small citadel of Burask on the dangerous western trail leading to Armorica and Goriah.

By and large, Tony had little choice but to remain in the Vosges with free humanity. He pretended to cooperate wholeheartedly with the Lowlife insurgents, even though life in the newly established Iron Villages along the Moselle was a brutish comedown from the fine-honed delights of Finiah.

There were six of the settlements, with a total population of about 400—mostly male. Five villages were clustered in the vicinity of the future French city of Nancy. Their names were Iron Maiden, Hematite, Mesabi, Haut-Fourneauville, and Vulcan. Each had an open-pit mine and a simple smeltery inside a heavy log stockade. Iron Maiden, the largest, served as a storage depot for iron produced by the others. It was situated adjacent to an area of disease-killed conifer forest, and on Tony's suggestion, had a naval-stores distillery operating on the side. Vulcan and Haut-Fourneauville had small primitive blast furnaces and rolling mills. Upstream and south of this quintet, approximately midway between them and the Lowlife headquarters at Hidden Springs, 90 kilometers distant, was the largest new settlement, Fort Rusty. Here was the principal metalworking establishment, where the pigs and bar-stock were turned into weapons. The fort also had a lime-burner and a cluster of charcoal ovens. These vital raw materials were sent down the Moselle to the mining and smelting towns via raft, as were food and other supplies. Caravans of draft chalikos and giraffid helladotheria hauled the iron into Fort Rusty.

Since the setup was so new, very little attempt had been made as yet to export iron weapons to other Lowlife bands. But the word had gone out. And all through the rainy season hardy expeditions from the Paris Basin and the High Helvetides, and even from Bordeaux and Albion, had come slinking into the Vosges, demanding their share of blood-metal. The newcomers were pressed into the labor force, crushing limestone or stoking the insatiable coke ovens for a few weeks, then paid off in cold iron and sent back to their own haunts ready for action.

All winter long, ever since late November, Tony Wayland had labored twelve and fourteen hours a day. He was a one-man training program, an analytical laboratory, a production supervisor, quality controller, and all-around soot-stained dogsbody. Everybody praised him, but no one was his friend except demented Dougal, who popped in and out of his knight-errant

persona like a Shakespearean actor who kept forgetting his
lines. Tony could only bide his time in patience, waiting for
the political situation in the Many-Colored Land to shake down.

If the rumors brought in by the last gang of iron seekers
could be credited, the times were finally ripening! An upstart
human was said to have installed himself as ruler of the late
Nodonn Battlemaster's rich domain of Goriah in Brittany. There
were hints that this usurper was accepted—even welcomed—
by the demoralized remnant of the Tanu High Table. It was
said that he would marry the Battlemaster's widow, that he
would elevate torced humanity to a parvenu aristocracy! (And
how poor Tony's bare neck had itched at that last intimation,
and how searing had been the memory of his lost torc's ecsta-
cies.)

As the rainy season neared its end, Tony planned to make
his move. Perhaps when that group of Lowlives from the Upper
Laar finished their trick and departed from Fort Rusty with a
load of axes, knives, and iron arrowheads, he could follow
them secretly, then join up at a safe distance from the Vosges,
when the inevitable posse sent after him got fed up and returned
home. Loyal, unquestioning Dougal would go along with him
if he pulled his liege-lord act; and if they reached the Laar they
could sail down it to the Atlantic and be practically on top of
Goriah. Tony never doubted that he and Dougal would receive
a fine welcome from the new human monarch—as well as a
pair of shiny golden torcs . . .

It all might have happened just as he planned, had not this
Howler attack left him well and truly fucked.

A pumpkin-sized boulder came rolling down the gully,
through the broken palisade, and smashed against the log wall
of the barracks like a cannonball.

"Dammit, boys, they're still out o' crossbow range!" The
mine foreman, a lantern-jawed crypto-hillbilly named Orion
Blue, coughed and hawked and spat. The chinking between
the half-meter-wide oak boles exploded inward with each impact. The beleaguered men inside the tiny fortress choked in
a swirling cloud of pulverized clay, moss fibers, and sawdust.

Sir Dougal ignored the bombardment. Muddy sweat dripped

from his ginger beard into the meshes of his titanium chain mail. His knightly surtout with its blazon (gules, a lion's head erased or) was spotless as always: The twenty-second-century fabric was ionized to repel soil.

"Hell-hounds! Show thyselves!" quoth he, sending bolt after bolt from his powerful compound bow through the embrasure. Another boulder slammed the wall, making the entire fort tremble. As the vibration died away, a faint screech could be heard in the distance.

"Aha! Aha!" cried Dougal. "Die, misbegotten Howler scum!"

Orion Blue squinted through the loophole next to the medievalist. "They're totin' up a big un', Doogie. Can you stop 'em from rollin' it?"

"Out of range," said the knight flatly. From upslope came a thunderous rumble.

Beniamino, his voice gone falsetto with panic, fell back from his loophole shrieking. "Back! Get back! This next mother's bigger than a VW egg! And dead on the mark!"

The defenders flung themselves to the sides, cursing. Tony Wayland alone stood at his slit, paralyzed, unable to tear his gaze from the huge chunk of granite bounding down upon them. Far up the hill, safe from the miners' iron-tipped arrows, a horde of goblins leaped and cheered. They glowed faintly in the morning mist.

"'Ware, milord!" Dougal shouted. Tony felt himself scooped up in mailed arms and flung several meters to the right. Almost simultaneously there was a cataclysmic impact. One of the great logs in the western wall buckled inward. The logs above it sagged fractionally with a hideous squeal. The structure still held firm—for the moment; but if one of those missiles hit the roof, which was of a much weaker barky-pole-and-slab construction, the place would come down around their ears.

Orion, sprawling in the dirt, didn't even bother to get up. He crawled toward the northeastern corner of the barracks, where most of the surviving miners crouched behind a wall of leather sacks filled with iron arrow blanks. "We're done for, boys. Only nine of us mother's sons left agin that whole passel

o' spooks! They'll bust up this place, then mind-fry us like
they done the other poor bastards outside."

Tony crept to join the others, useless crossbow still clamped
under one arm. Only Dougal still stood defiantly at the western
wall, where smaller rocks continued to thud against the splin-
tering oak. He smote the golden lion on his breast. "Then,
childish fear avaunt! Wilt thou stand craven before night's dark
agents, thou whoresons? Not I!" He grabbed a fresh handful
of arrows. "Now, gods, stand up for bastards!"

At his next shot, the bowstring snapped and set all the
weapon's pulleys spinning impotently. Dougal said, "Oh, shit."

He came back to the despairing huddle and dropped to one
knee in front of Tony, drawing a steel dirk and holding it point-
up before his face. "I have failed you, Exalted Lord. My life
is forfeit. But if you command it, I will use this misericord to
spare you and these minions agonizing death at the hands of
the Howler demons."

"Who you callin' a minion?" snarled Orion.

Several of the other men, mouths gaping, shrank back from
the kneeling figure. "Goddam loony!" one muttered. "Call him
off, Wayland!" said another. But at that moment three huge
rocks impacted, and the vee of the broken log jutted inward
more acutely. Little Beniamino licked his lips and rolled bloodshot eyes. "Doogie's got a point, guys. The ones that were
ambushed outside died quick. But if the friggerty Howlers
capture us, they might take their sweet time with the snuffin'
party—like when they grabbed poor Alf and Veng Hong last
month."

Dougal lowered the point of the dagger until it was level
with Tony's diaphragm. "Say but the word, milord. We will
meet again before the throne of Aslan."

"Hold it!" the metallurgist exclaimed, cringing against the
eastern wall. He held out his crossbow. After a pause, Dougal
sheathed his blade and took the weapon with a courteous bow.
Tony told him, "We still have the arbalests, Sir Dougal, even
though they don't have the range of your compound bow. And
the logs may be bending, but they're still in place. Fort Rusty
and the other villages should know by now that we're in trouble.

We missed the ten-hundred-hour sked. If we can just stand fast until they send reinforcements—"

"Keep dreaming, Wayland," a miner said bitterly. Another man curled up, head between his knees, shaking with soundless sobs. Hamid, who ran the turpentine still, consulted his wrist gyrocompass to ascertain the direction of Mecca six million years into the future, then prostrated himself and began his final prayers.

Orion Blue went to one of the eastern apertures that overlooked the Moselle and scanned the mist-hung waters through a small monocular.

"Hellfar an' white lightnin'!" he ejaculated, drawing back from the loophole as though electroshocked. "There *is* suthin' comin'! But sure's shit it ain't no troops from Rusty."

Everybody except Hamid and the weeping miner crowded for a look. A large raft was drawing up to the landing stage. It bore a towering wooden apparatus resembling a derrick on a wheeled platform. The upper part of the contraption had a pivoting arm with a scooplike container at one end and an amorphous bulky object at the other. A complex web of rope tackle linked the arm to the carriage. When the barge was made fast, three monstrous Howlers attached cables to the wooden engine, settled themselves into a troika hitch, and began hauling the thing toward the village's open gate.

"Maledizione!" wailed Beniamino. "Una bombarda!"

"What the hell is that?" Tony asked.

Sir Dougal studied the machine with professional interest. "A mangonel. Or could it be a perrier? A bricole? Funny . . . I never heard of Howlers using mechanical devices before."

"What does it *do*?" Tony yelled in exasperation.

"It just might be an onager," Dougal mused. He turned gravely to Orion Blue. "May I borrow your spyglass for half a tick?"

The mine foreman turned it over without a word. Dougal stared intently, muttering beneath his breath. "Not a classical ballista. Counterweighted. Od's bodikins—I think I've got it! It's a *trebuchet*!" Beaming, he handed the monocular back to Orion.

Tony was nearly screaming. "What—does—it—do?"

The knight shrugged. "Well, it's a medieval catapult, you see. They'll finish us by lobbing rocks at the roof."

"Hell*far*!" Orion groaned.

Tony watched the approach of the siege engine with fatalistic awe. The middle monster of the hauling team was a hideous prodigy that Dougal identified as a "fachan." It moved in awkward hops because it had only a single columnar leg. An armless hand more than a meter wide, equipped with black claws, sprang directly from its chicken-breasted trunk. Its head had a cyclopean eye and a froggy mouth from which an obscenely prehensile tongue lolled. The fachan's yokemates were somewhat more conventional horrors: a two-meter crested lizard with fiery carbuncle eyes, and a tall warthog, sky-blue, that walked on its hind legs.

As the Howler trio toiled into the village compound, they filled the air with valorous hoots. Their compeers on the high ground above the fort responded gleefully, then sent a veritable avalanche of stone cascading down on the log barracks. The sheer volume of the fresh assault now provided an ironic respite to the trapped miners. Enough rocks had piled in front of the western wall to form a salient angle, a wedge-shaped mass that tended to deflect rolling missiles to the right or left of the target. When it became clear to the exotic foe that the boulder-bowling maneuver had lost its effectiveness, the Howlers on the hill cut off their bombardment to await the arrival of the trebuchet.

Dougal raised his arms. The glittering links of mail and scarlet surcoat made him a splendid figure in the dusty gloom. "Mount, mount, my soul, thy seat is up on high! Whilst my gross flesh sinks downward, here to die." He closed his eyes with a sigh of theatrical melancholy.

"Damn *ree*-tard!" Orion grabbed up the crossbow, which the knight had discarded, and a leather bucket of iron-tipped quarrels. "Snap out of it, Doogie! Haul yer ass over yonder to the front wall. Those spooks on the machine are comin' in range of a crossbow shot!"

Dougal shed his aura of detachment. "What sayest thou, 0 lean unwashed artificer?"

"They got their infernal slingshot over next t' naval-stores shop! And they're climbin' all over it. Gettin' ready, I 'spect. But they're exposed, and you kin pot the suckers if you calc'late a good trajectory."

Dougal, Tony, and most of the miners rushed to join Orion at the northern wall. The flat area between the barracks and the industrial buildings was strewn with bodies, both human and chaliko. When the Howlers launched their surprise attack, a caravan loaded with pig iron had been on the point of leaving for Fort Rusty. The trebuchet now rested in a position about 90 meters from the barracks, partially screened by one corner of the wood-distillation shed. A large pile of conifer stumps next to the naval-stores shop provided partial cover for the enemy, but the men inside the barracks could see a dark shape moving in the upper part of the siege engine, probably adjusting its tackle.

"Enemy on the move!" Beniamino peered through one of the western loopholes. "They're coming down the hill— circling to the north. Gonna help their buddies with ammo for the bombarda, I bet."

Shapes far out of crossbow range now drifted between the far section of the village palisade and the iron pit, where the red ore made a shocking contrast to the jungle greenery, like an open wound in the land. An eerie silence had fallen, broken only by creaking noises as the Howler engineer tinkered with the trebuchet.

Dougal took aim. *Wunng* went the crossbow. On the other side of the compound, something let out a gurgling bellow. A sky-blue carcass tumbled from the trebuchet tower, seeming to shrink to a much smaller black form before disappearing from view. A chorus of angry howls went up from behind the stump pile.

"Hee-*yah*!" Orion smote his thigh joyously, still holding the monocular to his eye. "Look sharp! T'other side o' the pile! Suthin' movin' in that palmetty thicket!"

Wunng.

An apparition like a fanged furry pushball leaped into the air, vestigial limbs flailing, uttering screeches like a catamount.

As it dropped out of sight it, too, shape-shifted into a different form.

"A hit, a very palpable hit!" quoth Dougal.

"That's two," Orion chuckled.

Tony clapped the big knight on one mailed shoulder. "Well done, my man."

"Your servant, milord."

Beniamino drew in a sharp breath. "Hey—the throwing arm on the machine is moving. They must be getting ready to fire."

Dougal squinted desperately through the arbalest sight. "I can't see a fuckin' thing . . . I mean, the foe eludes mine eye, Goodman Napoli, and I—hoo boy! Here she comes!"

The counterweighted lever was drawn fully down. The entire mechanism vibrated. Abruptly, the counterweight fell, the arm whipped up, and a block of granite that must have weighed 50 kilos came whistling over the roof of the barracks. It landed on the far side with an echoing crash.

"Bismallah!" cried the Son of the Prophet, falling to his knees once more. "That's cooked us."

"Do something, Dougal!" Tony urged his heroic vassal. But the ginger-bearded head wagged in helpless chagrin. "I cannot descry the demons clearly, milord. They skulk behind the still-shed."

"Still!" Tony's face lit up. "The naval stores! Tar, pitch, turpentine—barrels of the stuff in the wood-distillation shop. If you could hit it with a flaming arrow—"

A heavy thud betokened the fall of another rock less than five meters *short* of the barracks.

"They got us bracketed," groaned Orion. "Get outa the line o' fire, ever'body!"

They scattered. Tony cursed wildly, trying to modify an arrow shaft so that it could be launched by the crossbow. Somebody found a parfleche full of flammable pitch and Beniamino used his skill as camp cook to quickly kindle a light.

The first missile to find its mark fell through the roof just as Tony solved the arrow problem. The place became a bedlam of noise and swirling debris. A falling timber struck one of the miners across the shoulders, pinning him to the floor. As men struggled to rescue the victim, shouting and coughing, Tony finished lashing the pitch-smeared wad to the shaft and touched it off. He thrust the firebrand at Dougal.

"Only one chance. Right through the open window of the still-shop. Kill, big fella!"

Dougal aimed and let fly—and then everything seemed to happen at once. Another great rock shattered the roof just above the loophole where Tony and Dougal were standing. Planks and rafters rained down while they tried to shield their heads. Tony felt himself falling, there was a tremendous *whoomp*, a prolonged clatter, a ragged chorus of distant exotic screams.

As Tony fetched up in a tangle of roof poles like a broken doll caught in a pile of giant's pick-up-sticks, he heard Orion's Johnny-Reb yell and presumed that the fire-arrow had found its target. Then oblivion claimed him.

He woke up, splinted and bandaged. The face of Denny Johnson, Lowlife Warlord Pro Tem, beamed down at him like a bitumen-painted mask. The Hidden Springs medic named Jafar was there, too, and so was the chief honcho, Old Man Kawai himself.

Tony tried to speak. His mouth would not open. "Wha' hop'n?" he inquired mushily.

The doctor lifted Tony's head, proffered a glass of water with a straw, and helped him to drink. "Your broken jaw's wired shut. Take it easy."

"Aths muths be'er." The metallurgist managed a crooked smile. "So cav'ry 'rive juths in thime, eh?"

Denny nodded. "Our barge from Fort Rusty landed a gang of fighters while the spooks were trying to douse the burning catapult and rescue their wounded. We finished them all off."

Old Man Kawai said, "You and the other defenders put up a magnificent resistance, Wayland-san. Free humanity owes you a priceless debt."

"Thum friggin' vic'ry," Tony muttered wearily. "Thpookths nailed thir'y, for'y of uths."

Kawai hastened to explain. His sallow, incredibly wrinkled

face trembled with animation. "The human losses are lamentable, Wayland-san, but even so, these comrades have not died in vain. We gained invaluable intelligence from this encounter."

Tony interrupted with an invalid's petulance. "Doogy! Where'ths Doogy?"

The doctor messed around with some kind of monitor device stuck onto Tony's forehead. "He's becoming overexcited."

Tony tried to rise up. His eyes were wide. "Don' mean ol' Doogy'ths *dead*?"

Kawai said, "Sir Dougal is alive and recovering. So are five other of your companions."

Tony gave a sigh and relaxed. "Riii'." He began to drift off—but then his eyes snapped open and he regarded the aged Japanese with piercing intensity. "Intelligenths? Wha' intelligenths?"

Denny Johnson bent over the bed. "All these months, we've blamed the spook attacks on Howlers—the deformed mutants who never accepted the alliance between humanity and the Firvulag. We knew the hostiles had to be Howlers, because the Little People have been our bosom buddies ever since the Fall of Finiah. That's what we *thought*."

"You mean those thpookths—"

Kawai's black button eyes glittered angrily. "The dead bodies of your attackers shape-shifted back to their normal form. What Denny and his troops discovered during the mopping up was not the remains of mutants, but of normal Firvulag. Our putative allies." He shook his head. "Madame Guderian never trusted the Little People. Her doubts have been confirmed. The Firvulag have mounted these treacherous strikes hoping to force us to abandon the Iron Villages. They fear the blood metal, in spite of our avowals that we would never use iron weapons against our friends."

Tony blinked. "Mebbe . . . juths Firv'lag hotheadths."

Denny said, "The corpses wore obsidian armor. They were regulars in the army of King Sharn and Queen Ayfa. And their use of the siege engine shows that they aren't wasting any time in adopting new methods of warfare now that the balance of power has shifted in their favor."

"We would never have discovered this," Kawai added, "if you had not withstood them so valiantly."

Tony moaned. He turned away.

"He's got to rest now," the doctor insisted.

The wounded metallurgist mumbled one last phrase, then subsided into sleep.

Kawai's brow wrinkled anxiously. "Doctor Jafar? What did he say?"

"I think"—the physician frowned in puzzlement—"it was: 'Take me back to Finiah!'"

5

LADY ESTELLA-SIRONE, THE WIDOWED HUMAN CHATELAINE OF Darask, had been so certain that Elizabeth would approve the chalet that she sent her major domo on ahead to make preparations, together with those who had volunteered for the domestic and security staff. The main body of refugees remained encamped at the western end of Lac Provençal. From there it was only a half-day's ride to the hunting lodge on Black Crag, in the midst of the Montagne Noire region of southern France.

By the time that Elizabeth and her four friends and their escort of loyal human and Tanu gold-torcs arrived for their inspection tour, the redoubtable Hughie B. Kennedy VII had his mistress's rustic retreat swept and garnished and ready for guests. A table in the private dining room adjoining the master suite (which was proposed as Elizabeth's apartment) had been set with the Irish major domo's idea of a light lunch: marinated mushrooms, poached froglegs in champagne aspic, stuffed green olives, smoked salmon, plovers' eggs à la Christiana, ham soufflé with asparagus tips, glazed quails cerisette, cold roast hipparion, Waldorf salad, pâté de foie gras, sourdough breadrolls, oranges rubanées, and carob-chip cookies.

It was the first festive and civilized meal that the five leaders of the Muriah evacuation had seen in months. They fell to in an atmosphere of bittersweet celebration.

It was evident that the mountain hideaway was eminently

40

suitable for Elizabeth's needs, and Creyn would stay with her. The others, however, would continue to Hidden Springs as they had planned. It was possible that the separation would be permanent, despite their being able to communicate through the golden torcs now worn by Basil and Chief Burke. Thus the conversation was desultory, with the pain of parting spoiling everyone's appetite.

Finally they left off the attempts at false cheer and reminisced about the terrible journey that was now virtually at an end. The interminable trek along the devastated Aven Peninsula, during which the triracial mob of evacuees grew to a logistic and psychosocial nightmare. The treacherous moonlight flit of the Firvulag contingent, who absconded with the bulk of the survival gear just as the worst of the rainy season came upon them. The struggles with sick and injured and defeated and exploitative refugees. The headlong flight from Celadeyr of Afaliah and his gang of ancien régime fanatics. The dreadful trip across the Catalan Wilderness, following a little-used track that degenerated into a quagmire alive with venomous snakes, giant mosquitoes, and biting leeches...

And then sanctuary. The foothills of the eastern Pyrénées, rich in mines and plantations, and the dangerously depleted cities of Tarasiah and Geroniah eager to welcome new citizens. (By then news of the Firvulag seizure of Burask in the distant north had seeped southward, and there were hints that other inadequately defended cities were next on the hit-list.) Perhaps a third of the 3700 displaced humans and Tanu decided to resettle in Spain. The rest, hoping to reach their old homes, continued to the smiling shores of Lac Provençal, where the generosity of Estella-Sirone of Darask showered them with every comfort. (They were, after all, the companions of Elizabeth, who had saved the Lady's life in childbirth.)

The decimated Languedoc cities vied with one another in sending recruiters to the refugee camp. Even more intriguing offers came from distant Goriah in Armorica, where Aiken Drum was consolidating his position, offering high status and riches to any rootless Tanu who rallied round, and a golden torc to any human fighter who pledged fealty to Lord Aiken-

Lugonn. Aiken had sent his personal farspoken invitation to Elizabeth herself, promising her complete autonomy "under his protection." She had declined with cool thanks.

Dionket Lord Healer and other surviving members of the Peace Faction went off to join Minanonn the Heretic in his remote Pyrenean enclave, where the erstwhile Tanu Battlemaster presided over a tiny population of Tanu, Firvulag, and a few free humans, all dwelling together in Spartan amity. Dionket had urged Elizabeth, for her own safety, to go with them. But she knew, even without metapsychic foresight, that pacifistic withdrawal could never be her destiny in the Many-Colored Land. Later, it had been more difficult to tell Chief Burke and Basil Wimborne and Sister Amerie Roccaro that she could not accompany them to the Lowlife center at Hidden Springs. She required an isolated retreat, where she could stay for the immediate future, recuperating and meditating upon the new rôle she had freely chosen.

"And so," Elizabeth said, rising from the luncheon table, smiling as she brushed crumbs from her black gown, "the fatal moment is almost upon us. Shall we go and explore the balcony? I think it goes all around the chalet."

Creyn was out of his seat and opening the half-glazed doors before the others could stir. The Tanu had put off his rough traveling clothes for the meal and wore again the scarlet and white formal robes of a high-ranking redactor. As he followed the others into the sunlight, his pupils shrank to pinpoints, the irises within his deep eyesockets becoming an unearthly, opaque blue. His fair hair had been cut short for the exodus, and he towered behind Elizabeth like some attenuated El Greco seraph, looking both worldly and vulnerable. He was six hundred and thirty-four years old, and he was prepared to stay at Black Crag Lodge for the rest of his life, if need be, acting as the senior servant of the human woman whom Brede Shipspouse had called "the most important person in the world."

Basil leaned on the railing, affecting to admire the eastern panorama. "I should think this place would suit you admirably, Elizabeth!" His voice was too hearty. "Isolation, security, a magnificent natural setting—and our friends at Darask on the other end of the lake near enough to keep you comfortably supplied. Lady Estella-Sirone was quite right. The lodge is a perfect hermitage. It's an Odin-seat! A perch for scanning the world!"

All of them laughed at the mental image he projected, except torcless Amerie, who growled, "Not another damn mindreaders' in-joke!"

"A funny picture." Elizabeth took the nun's arm. "Imagine a third-rate production of a Wagner opera. A plaster mountain with a lot of strobe lightning and tinny thunder. And me as a Nordic goddess, posed on top of my fake Asgard, wearing a winged helmet and a terribly portentous expression as I survey Middle Earth down below. If I spot any mortal jiggery-pokery, I have this handy basketful of thunderbolts to smite with."

"Except, you *don't*," Amerie said.

"No."

"And therein lies the bloody rub." Peopeo Moxmox Burke spoke fiercely, even resentfully, all the while trying to shore up the inexpert mental screen that decently veiled his emotions from Elizabeth. Damn the golden torc! If it weren't necessary . . .

Good old Basil caught wind of his floundering, the impending gush of anxiety and maudlin sentiment that was going to make things even worse for Elizabeth and all the rest of them. And with his donnish tact, Basil bespoke Creyn on the intimate mode:

Help him. Help us all put a lid on it.

There was no overt sign that the Tanu had heard. But immediately the two human men found that it was possible to rein in their misgivings and present a civilized front, both externally and in the outermost, "social" aspect of their mental auras. Basil was the epitome of practical common sense. Burke, the former judge, was the archetypal Red Man, all stoic and stern like a carving in cedar.

If Elizabeth was aware of the metapsychic maneuvering, she let none of them perceive it. She walked along the balcony inspecting the quaint woodwork, marveling at the breathtaking vista. In the southwest, glittering against the sky and dividing it from the dark lowlands, was the white fess of the high Pyrénées. The air was calm, faintly oppressive, with that pre-ternatural transparency that often forecasts a storm in the mountains.

"I can farsee Minanonn's country," she said. "A valley, with tall snowy peaks all around it, like Shangri-La."

"You would have been safer with him and Dionket," Amerie said. "Or even up in Hidden Springs, with us. We can't trust that bastard Celadeyr. He can fly, you know, and carry one person. What's to prevent him from coming up here and kidnapping you? You'd make a great hostage. And our tricky little pal Aiken Drum might just have similar plans."

Elizabeth faced her three human friends, projecting a great wave of comfort and reassurance. Creyn hovered in the background. She said, "I've tried to explain why I can't live with Minanonn, or even up in the Vosges with free humanity. I can't show partiality. I must remain approachable by all factions in the Many-Colored Land if my new rôle is to be successful. And that especially includes Aiken Drum and Celadeyr of Afaliah."

With one finger, Basil traced the features of a grotesque carving on the balustrade. It was a goblin face. "And what about the Firvulag? They outnumber us nearly ten to one now, and Sharn and Ayfa are quite a different breed of cat from poor old King Yeochee. Lady Estella's man Kennedy told me that Little People from the Helvetides had been farsensed gathering in the vicinity of Bardelask. That's a rather small citadel on the Rhône, about 80 or 90 kloms north of Lac Provençal. The place is exceptionally vulnerable, with Lord Daral and most of his banner-knights having been drowned in the Flood. Kennedy thinks that the Firvulag plan to pick off the weaker cities one by one in spite of our cardboard armistice agreement. Sharn and Ayfa can always blame the attacks on Howlers."

"If you came to Hidden Springs with us," Burke said, "we could protect you with iron."

Elizabeth laid a small hand on one of the Native American's massive, scarred forearms. "I have my own methods of defense now, Peo. Believe me. The Firvulag won't harm me. Neither will anyone else."

Burke scowled, touching his new golden torc with a ritualistic gesture. "If there should be the slightest threat—from any quarter—you must call on us. We can't forget what Brede said about you."

"Brede!" Elizabeth laughed, turning away from them. "The Shipspouse always was a melodramatic old soul. And she knew very well how to manipulate the lot of us!" The Grand Master metapsychic whirled around, arms opening. She seemed to embrace the three of them, enfolding their souls in great wings. "But manipulation's not my way. I'm going to be a magnet— not a force majeure."

Amerie appealed to the Tanu redactor. "If she needs us, Creyn—will *you* call?"

"I will, Sister." He hesitated, then added with regret, "If you intend to continue on to Sayzorask with the caravan today, you must leave here very shortly. I'll wait downstairs to say goodbye." He withdrew with a courteous nod.

Tears gleamed in Amerie's eyes. The symbolic separation of the three human friends from Elizabeth had been made in an instant, with none of them expecting it until the finality was upon them.

"Don't worry." Elizabeth's face and mind still smiled. "It'll be all right. We all have our jobs to do. That will help."

Basil broke the spell, stepping forward to take Elizabeth's hand. "Creyn . . . fine chap. Human as they make 'em. He and his people will take good care of you. I'm confident."

"Dear Basil." She kissed him on his weathered cheek.

He moved back, then paused at the balcony door. "You can count on me to do my utmost in the Sugoll matter. And when this is over and things have quieted down, I'm going to take you mountain climbing, just as I promised."

She projected mock skepticism. "You're going to have to prove to me that there's a Pliocene Everest over there in the Alps! I can't farsense anything of the sort, you know."

"It exists!" He waved an admonishing index finger. "Very difficult for amateurs to estimate height, you know. Especially with the mind's eye." With a last farewell gesture, he vanished inside the chalet.

It was Burke's turn. He loomed over the woman in black, his face immobile, and spoke haltingly through the unfamiliar mind-amplifying device:

I will learn farspeech technique. Talk you overkilometers. My dearest Peo . . . I am still not sure that it was wise for you and Basil to take the golden torcs.

Creyn tested us. Wecompatible he proved. You not worry aboutus. Only answer when weneed advice.

"You know I'll always be ready to advise you," she said aloud. "That *is* my way. But you and Basil and the other strong ones must lead humanity and the exotics of good will. I can't. The evacuation of Muriah was only the beginning, but it was a good start, thanks mostly to you. Even the Firvulag who ran away learned that friendship between the human and exotic races is possible. Necessary."

"Hah." The Native American let all his lawyer's cynicism show. "The exotics were docile enough right after the disaster, when they were still glassy-eyed from shock. None of those Tanu and Firvulag ever had their world pulled out from under 'em before." Unlike us poor time-traveling human schmucks! "So they were willing enough to follow my leadership on the trek out of Aven. But you saw how fast things deteriorated once we approached Afaliah on the mainland. Just one sniff of business-as-usual, one psychological anchor—and ka*pow!* Same old arrogant Tanu and bloody-minded Firvulag mindset as before. Things could have turned very nasty if the Little Folks hadn't scarpered off into the bushes about then."

They communed wordless reassurance for a moment. Then she asked, "How many human refugees do you plan to take all the way to Hidden Springs?"

"We've narrowed it to thirty stout hearts and true. Useful technicians, daredevils who won't stick at our little aircraft salvage expedition. We've scraped up twelve former gravomag specialists with flightdeck training."

"Wonderful! And if Sugoll and Katlinel will help—"

"They'd better." Burke was somber. "Felice and the others who knew the precise location of the Ship's Grave are dead."

Elizabeth and Burke had forgotten Amerie. But at the mention of Felice's name, the nun could not help uttering a low cry. Burke's thoughts were written on his face: Oh, hell. Me and my big mouth. Aloud he said, "It's time for me to go." He wrapped his great arms about Elizabeth, said, "Mazel tov!" and strode rapidly into the lodge.

"I'm sorry that I interrupted," Amerie said stiffly. "But when he reminded me that—that Felice was—" Anguish drew the nun's face taut. "And with Gibraltar on her soul—to die that way—"

Elizabeth said, "I thought it best for the others to believe that. But you loved her. You deserve to know the truth."

The priest stood stock-still before the mindreader. Sister Amerie Roccaro wore no golden torc, possessed no overt metapsychic powers; but at that moment the terrible knowledge passed from the other woman's brain to her own.

"Felice isn't dead," said Amerie.

"No."

"How long have you been sure of it?"

"Perhaps six weeks. I'd been hearing—farsensing, that is to say—these peculiar calls. They hardly seemed human at first. I paid little attention. The day-to-day problems of the journey were so overwhelming. You tend to screen out other mind-emanations to conserve your own energies, otherwise you'd go crazy from the mental static. But this calling—"

"You're certain it was Felice?"

"She farspoke me only once, when you were all on your way down the Rhône to invade the torc factory. But I remember her mind-signature." Elizabeth turned away, staring at the distant mountains. "It's a thing we Grand Masters are rather good at."

"Elizabeth, why—why—" Amerie's voice broke as she tried to regain control of herself. "Why did she do it? I knew she wanted revenge, of course. When we were first tested together in Castle Gateway, when the Tanu woman told us we'd have to bear Tanu children like the rest of the human slaves, Felice was beside herself with fury. It was . . . as if the enslavement of humanity in the Pliocene was a personal affront."

"You're a doctor as well as a priest. Do I have to spell it out to you? You love her—but you know what she is."

"Yes." The nun's tone was desolate.

Elizabeth began to move along the balcony, with Amerie following. They came to the eastern side of the chalet. Lac Provençal was an azure expanse fading to slate near the horizon. The storm would come from that direction.

"Do you remember Culluket, the King's Interrogator?" Elizabeth asked.

"I saw him only once. After our strike at the torc works failed and we were captured—he was the one who clapped gray slave-torcs on us and sent us away to die in prison. Yes, I remember the Interrogator. He wore glowing red-glass armor and he was the most beautiful Tanu male I've ever seen."

"He took Felice and tortured her."

"Oh, Jesus."

"He worked her over quite a bit more than was necessary to extract information. Dionket told me about it during the evacuation. As the head of the Redactor Guild, Dionket knew what Cull was up to—but there was no way Dionket could interfere in the private affairs of the Host. The torture—the algesis—is what forced Felice into metapsychic operancy and enabled her to take a full measure of vengeance. According to her lights." Elizabeth paused. "Cull's handiwork also seems to have forged some perverse link between the two of them. That's why she looks for him, keeps calling his name on the declamatory mode. Felice isn't sure that her dear torturer survived the Flood. Unfortunately, I am. Cull is alive, and he's gone to Goriah, where he hopes Aiken will be able to protect him from Felice. God help Cull if she ever tracks him down."

The physician warred with the lover in Amerie; momentarily, the professional won. "Yes, I see what you mean. Felice's character is profoundly sadomasochistic, of course. The Interrogator gave her not only terrible pain but also the mental power she'd been searching for all her life. No wonder she loves him . . ."

Elizabeth said nothing.

"What—what's to be done about Felice? Her powers—! My God, not even Saint Jack the Bodiless or Diamond Mask could have blasted out that Gibraltar cut! Not single-minded."

"Felice hasn't used her destructive power since the deluge. Perhaps she *can't*. Most of the time, she imagines that she's a black scavenger bird. She gathers golden torcs and hides them. I don't know where. She's very clever at screening, except when she calls to Cull."

The women stood side by side at the railing, Elizabeth in her long black gown and tall Amerie in a white coverall with a clerical rabat and dog collar at the neck. A breeze had begun to stir the dark firs that crowded close to the lodge's isolated knoll. A rock thrush, invisible, gave plaintive warning of changing weather.

"Could you help Felice with your deep-redact faculty?" Amerie asked. "Cure the psychosis?"

"Possibly. If she gave full cooperation. But it might be safer to let her stay as she is, if it means restraining her use of the psychoenergetic functions. This is . . . one of the matters I have to think deeply about."

The nun drew back, looking at the other with dawning horror. Elizabeth only smiled, resigned. Amerie said, "You'll have to decide so many things."

Elizabeth lifted a wry shoulder. She had turned so that the priest could not see her face. "It's cold and lonesome on Olympus."

Amerie said, "If only I could help. If any of us could—!"

Elizabeth's hands were clutching the wooden rail, the tendons white. "You can do one thing. Again. For the sake of my scruples."

"Yes. Of course."

From one pocket of her coverall Amerie took a narrow violet ribbon, kissed it, and hung it about her neck like a yoke. She recited the ancient formula again—as she had recited it for the sleeper wakened in the mountain sanctuary where they had watched the Flood; as she had recited it on countless nights during the long exodus while Elizabeth wept along with the winter rain pounding their improvised shelter.

"Only *believe* it, Elizabeth."

"I try." I try.

Amerie blessed the head still turned away. "Come, child of God, and lay your burden down. For he has said to his Church, 'Whose sins you shall forgive, they are forgiven them.'"

"Bless me, Sister, for I have sinned."

"Let the person who is thirsty come. Let whoever wants it accept the gift of the water of life."

"I confess pride. I confess hubris, the sin of surpassing arrogance. I confess blasphemy of the healing Spirit. I confess contempt for lesser minds. I confess refusing love to other rational beings. I confess despair. I confess the unforgivable sin and ask forgiveness. I am sorry. Help me to believe it! Help me to believe that there's a God who forgives the unforgivable."

Help me believe that I'm not alone.

Help me.

6

THE BIG WILD CHALIKO WAS TEARING UP THE SQUEEZE CHUTE
with his claws, screeching and blowing, flinging his massive
barrel against the stout wooden planks until the spikes fastening
them seemed about to give way. There were four gray-torc
wranglers trying to hold him—two on the hackamore longe-
line and two on a foot rope. They were broadcasting sheer
panic when Benjamin Barrett Travis led the three Exalted Ones
over to the corral to watch the breaking.

"You really gonna face down that clawfoot killer, Brazos?"
Aiken Drum inquired, awestricken. "Sweet houghmagandy!"

The penned chaliko reared up on its unfettered hind leg and
gave a ringing bellow. It was a blue roan standing at least
twenty hands, with black fetlock feathering and mane and a
startling black-rimmed walleye.

"Tana's left tit!" blasphemed Alberonn Mindeater. "It's as
big as a rhino!"

Brazos Ben fingered his silver torc. The chaliko settled back
into the chute with a *wooof*! "Hell, he ain't near as snorty as
some wild ones I've suppled out. He ain't even mean by nature.
Just scared."

"Travis is quite right," said the Interrogator. "The animal's
mind is awash with profound fear. The bridling device, the
equipment affixed to its feet, the saddle—these, combined with
its loss of freedom and the presence of people, have nearly

51

driven it insane. Only its natural intelligence, and the fact that it has not actually been hurt, restrain it from suicidal violence."

Brazos Ben smiled thinly at the redactor. "And don't you forget I been talkin' to him for a week, Lord Cull. You saw how he eased back when I give him a farsqueak. Chalikos are smarter'n horses at recognizin' a friendly mind."

"Then why not just mind-bend the beast to tame it?" Alberonn wanted to know. "Why go through all this ride-'em-cowboy physical tosh?"

"A chaliko's gotta be broke both ways, Lord Alby. Otherwise he's only good for gold or silver riders. No gray or bareneck could even touch him. After a chaliko's been suppled and trained to the usual body and voice commands, *then* he gets mind-broke. Course, I speak to my critters all along the way, even in the physical schoolin'. But with my method, you can train up twenty times the wild stock you could mind-bendin'—and take less time doin' it. You can use gray and bareneck trainers steada silvers right up until the final postgrad telepathic autopilot programmin'. It's a little different trainin' domesticated beasts. Easier. But the Battlemaster"—Brazos Ben broke off, eyeing Aiken—"I mean, the *late* Battlemaster wanted Goriah to be the best-mounted outfit in the Many-Colored Land come Combat time. And that meant usin' plenty o' wild stock."

Across the corral, the chaliko neighed. Brazos Ben extracted a small tin of snuff from his breast pocket and tucked a pinch behind his cheek. "Well—you Exalteds ready for some action?"

"Sic 'em, BB!" Aiken chortled.

The breaker went off to the chute while Aiken, Culluket the Interrogator, and Alberonn Mindeater approached the fence of the round enclosure and found a spot that was not too muddy. Although it was not raining, the sky was dark and louring and a cold wind blew in from the Strait of Redon beyond the stables. The three men wore traditional Tanu storm-suits of colored leather with peaked capuchons and over-knee boots. Aiken's suit was gold with black piping, the Interrogator's deep red, and Alberonn's turquoise to indicate his status as a creator-coercer. Alberonn's human heritage showed in his chocolate skin, which was a striking foil to his green Tanu eyes and the bush of fleecy blond hair that escaped from his hood. The hybrid High Table member was half a head taller than Culluket and towered over diminutive Aiken like a fairytale giant.

"My late brother Nodonn counted this man Travis as one of the most valued of all his servants," Culluket remarked. Across the corral, Brazos supervised the removal of the hind-foot hobble.

"I wish we had fifty more like him," Aiken said. "Getting large numbers of trained mounts will be critical to my strategy against the Firvulag. At least, until I track down those aircraft."

"It's a bad sign that the Little People have chucked their old prejudice against riding," Culluket said.

Aiken nodded. "One of my spies reported that they're even trying to domesticate those little hipparions for the gnomies to ride! And we know they've been stealing tame chalikos from all the outlying plantations around the eastern cities for the warrior-ogre battalions."

Alberonn said, "Bleyn farspoke me that the same thing is going on down around Rocilan. Raids, sneak attacks, ambushes. All blamed on Howlers, of course. But the situation is getting beyond makeshift countermeasures down there in Candy City. The petty lordlings and the torced humans just aren't responding to Bleyn's leadership, not even when Lady Eadnar commands it. Bleyn's an outsider, even if he is her brother-in-law, and he has no authority. Dammit, Aiken—! I've a good mind to go down and marry Eadnar now, not wait until the Grand Loving in May!"

"You cannot, Creative Brother," said the Interrogator. "It would be even more inflammatory than Bleyn's action. Old Lady Morna-Ia is mulish about respecting the mourning period for her late son. She thinks that even May is too soon for a wedding."

Alberonn was glum. "I should have let the old bat drown. But there she was on the floating wreckage with Eadnar—so what could I do?"

"Here comes trouble," Aiken observed, poking his head

through the corral bars. The wranglers were opening the chute. Brazos Ben, chewing meditatively, now held the longe-line in his left hand and another rope, attached in some complex fashion to the chaliko's front ankles, in his right. The animal skittered out into the heavy mud, its walleye rolling and its prancing claws making loud squushing sounds.

"What the hell's that rig on its feet?" Alberonn asked. "I thought Ben was going to ride the beast."

"Shut up and watch," ordered Aiken.

Brazos Ben was no longer soothing the chaliko's mind through his silver torc. In fact, he seemed to be deliberately provoking the creature to misbehavior, tugging sharply on the hackamore line. The animal's flanks began to heave. Its neck twitched and its head strained. Just as Ben maneuvered it to the center of the corral, it exploded into a frenzy of bucking. The stirrup-pieces of the big, chairlike saddle slapped against its withers. Mud flew to the four winds and Aiken hastily slammed up a PK shield.

Now Ben carefully drew in the foot line, which ran from the right side of the saddle down through a ring on the right ankle hobble, up through a pulley at the cinch, down to the left hobble, up over the high stirrup plate, and out to the breaker. "BB calls it a running W," Aiken said. "You gotta use it right, or you ruin the chaliko. But it really puts the fear o' God into uppish brutes."

With the line tightened, the huge chaliko perforce fell to its knees in the muck. Ben held him there, talking softly and making a clucking sound. He rubbed the creature on both sides of its neck but didn't try to catch its panicked eye. After a few minutes, he slacked off the W-line and let the chaliko rise. Still speaking to it, he urged it to begin walking with a gentle tug on the longe. The chaliko reared, shrieking, and gathered itself to run; but before it could step out, Ben pulled the W-line. Once again the big animal stumbled slowly to its knees, sinking deeply into black ooze.

"Now Travis is back in the beast's mind," Culluket said, admiration brightening the somber beauty of his face. "Telling it who the master is—but gently. See? The animal responds.

It's no fool. But it's going to try to break loose again, just to be sure."

The procedure was repeated, with Brazos Ben now humming tunelessly as he managed to have the chaliko move a dozen obedient steps at the end of the longe-line before it erupted into defiant bucking and claw-slashing. Ben spat tobacco juice and tipped the animal ignominiously into the slop. Hunching down, he massaged the chaliko's face, remonstrating and clucking. The skinned-back ears turned forward and the corded neck muscles relaxed. Ben let the big roan up, flicked the longe, and stood with a satisfied smile as it trotted slowly around him, responding now to the command of the hackamore. And the dry thought came:

He's all broke, Exalteds.

They gave him a heartfelt *Slonshal*! The trainer motioned to one of his assistants to take over the two ropes, stood for a few minutes probing the chaliko's mind to insure that it plotted no more deviltry, then waded out of the soupy corral back to Aiken, Culluket, and Alberonn.

"You won't ride him today, then?" the hybrid asked, disappointed.

"I could, usin' the W. But I'd rather not. Those claws can cut a rope too easy at a trot. All he really needed was to figger out who was boss. A few days now to get him halter-wise and we'll start ridin'. I don't think this baby'll need any more hobbles."

"Terrific work, BB!" said Aiken.

"I presume you handled livestock back on Elder Earth," said Alberonn.

Benjamin Barrett Travis spat politely over his shoulder. "Hell, no, Lord Alby. Wouldn't I've loved to, though! Naw— I inherited my daddy's desk as comptroller of Westex Foodex of El Paso, the biggest exporter of Hispano-American foodstuffs in the Milieu." His pale eyes twinkled. "Never want to see another refried bean long 's I live . . ." He hitched up his jeans. "I plan to mosey over'n' begin mind-breakin' a really top-notch white stallion, lords. Y'all wanta help? If you ride longside, it reinforces the programmin'."

"Sounds great!" Alberonn enthused.

"You go on with Ben, Alby," Aiken said. "Cull and I have some things to discuss." To the breaker he said, "You come on up to the Castle of Glass for supper tonight, BB. And bring Sally Mae."

"Right y'are, Battlemaster." With a casual wave, the man in the mud-caked Levis ambled off in the company of the titan warrior, reminiscing telepathically over ornery steeds he had known.

"Commander Congreve just farspoke me," Aiken told the Interrogator. "There's a whackin' big batch of recruits just arrived, and you and me better get back to check 'em out. Thirty-eight Tanu and nearly a hundred humans—including twelve golds and a gang of silver technicians. Most of 'em are from Afaliah. Old Celadeyr has instigated some kind of purge—thrown out all his human executives and managing technicians, and made things so hot for the hybrid aristocracy that they fled lock, stock, and barrel."

"I'll find out soon enough what's going on down there."

"The rest of the arrivals are from that Spanish town the Craftsmaster took over. Calamosk."

"Bleeding Goddess! They'd be cravens from the Retort—the riff-raff scheduled to be executed at the end of the Combat! You'd accept such trash?"

Aiken's beady gaze was cold. "Bull me no shit, Pretty-Face. It's all a new deal in this Many-Colored Land. You forget? And once upon a time, I was considered a bit riff-raffy myself!... Let's fly."

They pulled down the transparent face-shields of their cap-uchons and soared into the air. Little splatters of rain ticked against their moving bodies. They flew over the chaliko farm, which was north of Goriah alongside the strait, crossed or-chards, olive groves, and gardens, and approached the city itself.

Goriah was built upon a great rise and covered nearly four square kilometers. Most of the buildings, except the magnifi-cent central citadel and certain dwellings of the Great Ones, were built of cleanly whitewashed stone roofed in rose-red tile.

The mansions of the Tanu were adorned with spires and filigree buttresses of rose and gold, honoring the Psychokinetic Guild heraldry of the late Nodonn. Formerly, the glass castle had featured the same color scheme; but since the coming of the usurper, most of the rosy elements had been stripped away and replaced with accents of jet-black or midnight-purple, these unique tinctures having been adopted by the new Battlemaster. At night, every dwelling of the commonalty was picked out in a myriad of small oil lamps strung along roofs and garden walls. The Tanu structures were completely outlined in meta-activated faerie lights of many different colors, and the Castle of Glass blazed golden and amethyst— brighter than it had ever shone during Nodonn's tenure—a beacon visible all the way to the disemboguement of the River Laar, 30 kilometers away.

As the two levitants descended toward the main receiving area near the eastern city gate, Aiken observed, "Commander Congreve has discovered a really big human gold in the net today. His name is Sullivan-Tonn, originally from Finiah on the River Rhine. Ever heard of him?"

The Interrogator blasphemed luridly. "That fat funk-pisser! If he'd only used his powers as a warrior should, Finiah might have withstood Guderian's attack! Do I know him—!" And the data were spread out for Aiken to study:

Aloysius X. Sullivan, yclept Sullivan-Tonn. Ninety-six years old, rejuvenated, resident in the Pliocene nearly thirty-two years. Once Küng Professor of Moral Theology at Fordham University, and later a highly placed supervising psychokinetic under Lord Velteyn of Finiah. Tonn's primary metafunction was enormous (he was capable of levitating forty people or nearly five tons of inert matter), but his usefulness to the Tanu was limited by his pacifism, which masked an invincible timidity. He was notorious for having refused point-blank to use his PK in Grand Combats, Hunts, or any other aggressive activity, but he had performed his other duties faithfully. After the fall of Finiah, he assisted in the aerial evacuation of noncombatants and ultimately made his way to Castle Gateway, which was then being used as a relief center for refugees. When the deluge

came, Tonn was safely ensconced in the small Spanish city of
Calamosk, attendant upon his teenaged Tanu fiancée Lady
Olone, who had been forced to miss the Grand Combat because
she was recuperating in Skin, having broken her back in an ill-
considered attempt to fly on her own. Olone, a luscious honey-
blonde and a coercer of formidable raw talent, had accompanied
Tonn to Goriah.

"I'll deep-probe the pair of them for you," Culluket said,
"but it's obvious why they've come. Olone's father died in the
Flood and the Craftsmaster's too tough to give in to her winsome wiles. Tonn can be a self-righteous ass and Oly is a sly
chit, but I think we can count on their loyalty."

Aiken and Culluket descended to the receiving barracks,
where the Tanu and gold-torc human newcomers had been
segregated from the humbler arrivals. Congreve, a hulking gold
wearing full blue coercer armor, smote his breastplate in salute
and lost no time in presenting his telepathic appraisal:

   Greetings Battlemaster and Exalted Lord Interrogator! Aside
from Sullivan-Tonn and Lady Olone, the day's tot-up in the
gold includes mostly minor powers. Those from Afaliah are
respectable hybrid nobility who couldn't stomach the reaction-
ary dictates of Lord Celadeyr. Eleven pureblood Tanu from
Calamosk are former fellow prisoners with Aluteyn in the Great
Retort [classification].

   Thanks Congreve. Suffering shit. Four traitors six wife-
murderers and a tax-evader among our exotic jailbirds. But
with so few Tanu survivors every one who's willing to follow
me has to be made welcome. Cull . . . you give 'em a good
vetting. Especially the traitors!

   That goes without saying Shining One. And I will also take
pains with these twenty lesser human golds from Calamosk in
like manner Retort-fodder condemned for cowardice during the
Combat. Now please give courteous attention to Tonn and his
doxy who take their detention here with ill grace.

   "All hail to you, conquering Battlemaster Aiken-Lugonn!"
declaimed a portly individual attired in splendorous vestments
of cerise and gold. But before Sullivan-Tonn could continue,
there was a guttural shout:

"Aik! Aik—is it really you?"

From the motley group of gold-torc humans burst a scrawny man with tow-colored hair and flat, vaguely Mongoloid features. He wore a plaid flannel shirt, twill trousers, and heavy forester's boots with lug soles. Dropping to his knees before the diminutive usurper of Goriah, he mumbled, "I mean, Lord Lugonn. Sorry to bust in on this other guy's shtick, but—"

Thunderstruck, Aiken threw back the golden hood of his rain-suit. "Raimo! You ol' woodchopper, you!"

"If you want me, kid, I'm all yours. And I brought some pals, too."

"If I want you—" yelled the Shining One. The two fell into each other's arms, giggling like maniacs.

"Well!" Sullivan-Tonn drew himself up in frosty hauteur.

The tender reunion was interrupted as Culluket's mind bespoke Aiken on the intimate mode:

Congreve prelimprobe finds thisRaimoHakkinen loaded hotdata urge you permit me fulldeep ream him immediately.

?! Forget it. Indignation. "Ray, baby—you mean they were gonna *roast* you? Just for going over the hill in the Combat?"

Listen ShiningOne thisone muchinfo PeaceFaction Dionket + MinanonnHeretic countertactic CeloAfaliah also—

Sullivan-Tonn brayed, "Lord Aiken-Lugonn, please let me continue!"

The thoughts of Aiken and the Interrogator crackled on the intimate mode:

Cull question sillyfartTonn not Raimo handsoff MINE.

I know RaimoyourfriendShiningOne but he knows muchvalue even re *Felice.* Allow squeezeout—

You keep clawsoff Raimo FeliceobsessedsadistCullutortugator.

Raimo rumor Felice took SPEAR from bottomNewSea.

Christ!

Selfjustification. Thought that get yourattention. Well? You agree interrogation?

. . . Raimo know where Felice + Spear are?

Nodata. DeadpalRaimo saw Birdgirl flying Betics. Local-Firvulag bespoke pal re FelicehavingSpear. Must deepdig to get straights. You agree ream?

No!... Yes... *shit*! Later then. But when *I* say so and with *My* supervision reamout job and you fullrepair his brain after. You hear RedactiveBrother/GrandVizier/CullPrettyFace?

I hear and affirm your authority King. (But you/I must find scatophilousalgolagniacbitchgoddess before she comesafter US why did I notkill her when I had chance?)

Scorn. Don't you know?

"Now!" Aiken exclaimed brightly out loud. The mental repartee with the Interrogator had lasted approximately ten seconds. Aiken thrust the continuing mental admonitions of Culluket aside and let the full wattage of his charm flow out upon Raimo, Sullivan-Tonn, the willowy Lady Olone (who had been watching Aiken intently ever since his arrival), and all of the other Tanu and human newcomers standing about the cheerless reception chamber. Emboldened, Sullivan-Tonn exclaimed:

"We've been treated outrageously by this military flunky of yours, Lord Lugonn. His men have presumed to examine our baggage—and a clumsy oaf dropped a priceless bottle of twenty-four-year-old Jameson's Reserve! I was barely able to rescue it in time with my PK."

"Shocking," said Aiken, frowning. He tipped a subliminal wink to the commandant. "Surely you know, Congreve, that an Exalted Personage of Lord Sullivan-Tonn's rank is exempt from such procedures. You are rebuked."

Congreve gave the chest-high salute. "I abase myself, Battlemaster. Such examinations have been a standard security precaution taken with all human persons seeking permanent residence in Goriah. Because of the blood-metal peril, the ruling was enforced stringently under Lord Nodonn."

"Nodonn," Aiken noted, "is fish food. And I say that from now on, both human and Tanu arrivals will be given an equally cordial welcome. Remember that, or you'll answer to me."

Sullivan-Tonn simpered with pleasure. He drew the demure Olone forward and presented her to Aiken and the Interrogator. "Lady Olone of Calamosk, daughter of the late Lord Onedan

Trumpeter, who is to become my bride at this year's Grand Loving."

A momentary flash of fire from the girl's mind was hastily curtained. She bowed gracefully. Grinning, the Shining One planted a lingering kiss in the palm of her hand. In a low voice, she asked, "Is it true, Lord Battlemaster, that you will be king?"

The black eyes sparkled. "As Tana wills, lovie!"

"With . . . all the kingly prerogatives?" A smile stole over her coral lips. Sullivan-Tonn's face was immobile.

"The game," Aiken assured her, "goes with the name."

He strode over to the smirking Raimo, draped one arm over his old pal's shoulder, and called out: "Now, all you folks— be of good cheer! Aiken Drum is here! No more detention, no more searches, no more nasty interrogations. You're all coming along with me to my Castle of Glass, and we're going to have a party!"

7

OLD ISAK HENNING NAGGED AND NAGGED AND FINALLY HUL-
dah agreed to make the weary climb up to the promontory—
even though she knew it was going to rain—and keep watch
until midnight.

"We're the only ones left to give warning, girl!" Bony
thumbs dug into her strong upper arms. Isak's filmed eyes
rolled anxiously in the direction of the cave's inner chamber.
"It's the most dangerous time of all! Full moon after the vernal
equinox! The Hunt's bound to come. Every year it happens.
Now you listen to me, girl! When you spot 'em flying over
the lagoon from Aven, you light the signal fire. All Kersic is
depending on you!"

"Yes, Grandpa."

"He might be calling to 'em! Even in his sleep!" The old
man's voice was a malignant hiss.

"Yes, Grandpa."

Trembling, Isak scooped up glowing coals from the cooking
fire into a ceramic beaker. He heaped on ashes to slow com-
bustion. Huldah took the beaker and the thick torch of tallow-
soaked reeds he had prepared.

"Now you know what to do with these!" he barked at her.

"What?" she asked.

"The signal, you damn stupid cow!" he exploded. "If you

see the Flying Hunt, you use the hot coals to light the torch. Then use the torch to light the big pile of wood!"

Huldah smiled. "Light the torch. Light the wood. Yes, Grandpa."

The old man fairly screeched. "But only if you see the Hunt, dammit! Only if you see them coming at us from among the stars—all twisting and rising and falling like a knotted snake made of rainbow light!"

"All right." She stood staring down at him with an air of detachment. There was no physical beauty about her, only strength and health. Her lips and cheeks were shiny from the butter-fat roast dormice they had had for supper. Her doeskin shift was still fairly clean. Her breasts, swelling now for a reason Isak could well guess, stretched the leather between their outthrust nipples.

"Well?" he roared. "Get going, you overgrown bitch!"

She remained standing in the cave antechamber. Her burdened hands hung slackly at her thighs. "You will not hurt the God while I'm gone, Grandpa."

Isak's glance shifted. "You just get going on up to the promontory. Do your duty and leave him to me." He was breathing rapidly. "The Flying Hunt could be on its way to Kersic right now!"

"You will not hurt the God."

Huldah set the pot of coals and the unlit torch down on the rock floor. Isak tried to dodge away but she was too fast for him, seizing his sticklike arms and pressing them against the sides of his rib cage as she lifted him up. He kicked and howled and spat rage at her, dangling in the air, held at arm's length by the titaness. Finally he burst into tears. She put him down with great solicitude, crouched beside him as he collapsed, and wiped his face with one corner of her slit skirt.

"You will not hurt my God from the Sea," she said, satisfied.

"No." He could not stop shuddering. The musky smell of her was overpowering.

"I'll go then," she said. "And if I see the Flying Hunt, I'll light your signal fire. Even though there are no other people left on Kersic to see."

"There are, there are," wailed the old man. He covered his face with his hands.

"No," Huldah told him. "They sailed away when the salty water rose. There's only you and me and the God now." She gave Isak a tender pat on his sun-freckled bald crown and picked up the firemaking things. "And the Flying Hunt won't ever come again. The water's too deep. It's deep enough to pour into the slot where the sun goes down, so the Hunters can't come through any more to get us."

"Damn crazy cow," Isak mumbled. "Go, Go. Keep a sharp watch."

"All right. It won't do any harm."

She left him still huddled in a heap and set off into the dusk. The sky was the color of a duck's egg over the water, deepest blue lashed with violet mare's tails above the spine of Kersic. A few stars, fuzzy, were coming out. Huldah hummed tunelessly as she strode along. It was damp and chilly, but she didn't mind. And the God was well-covered with his rug of woven rabbitskin strips.

Her heart lifted with thinking of him. So beautiful, so joy-bringing even in the endless sleep! (His poor lost hand would soon be fixed when lazy Grandpa finished the last sanding and smoothing.) If she hurried back after the futile vigil there would still be time to worship him; and Grandpa would wake up and watch and groan.

"I hate you, Grandpa," she said.

Pushing through the high marquis, she came at length to the land's end where there was a cleared space among twisted umbrella pines, and a tall silver-gray pile of wood. Huldah put down the firepot and the torch and went to the sheer western tip of the promontory. She sat on the edge with her strong legs dangling and the rising wind tickling as it blew up her skirt.

Down there in that cove, in a place of sharp reefs that the waters now covered, she had found him. The wonder. The marvel. The joy. The God from the Sea. His eyes had never opened during the months she had nursed him; but she knew that they would some day, now that his terrible hurts were healed. He would awaken and love her.

"Then we will kill Grandpa," Huldah decided.

8

ON THE MAGHREB SHORE OF AFRICA, BLACK WAVES LAPPED
at the base of the Rif Range and the old volcanic hills that had
once anchored the southern end of a broken rubble dike. A
thin drizzle had started.

Kuhal Earthshaker, Second Lord Psychokinetic, had camped
in the most sheltered spot he could find, a steep-walled wadi
carrying a trickle of water that vanished into beach shingle
before ever reaching the New Sea. There were palms and
blooming acacia trees, and a poignant cluster of pink narcissus
nodding in deep shadows beside a little spring.

He had propped the Firvulag coracle up like a dome above
a fairly dry niche. Fian rested beneath it. Kuhal had managed
to light a fire with his feeble creativity, but the supper pickings
were meager: a palm heart, a couple of baked bird's eggs with
their embryos, some delicious but insubstantial acacia flowers
fried in the last of the hamster fat. A snake of mouth-watering
dimensions had got away. Kuhal knew better than to cook the
abundant but poisonous narcissus bulbs.

Fian moaned. The drizzle was turning into sharp gusts of
rain that tapped on the coracle skins.

COLD!

cold   cold

COLD   COLD

COLDCOLD   i/i know.   *COLDCOLD*
cold   *cold*

cold   cold
COLD

The sleeping-robe that Kuhal had made from small animal pelts
was now almost falling to pieces. Its sinew threads had rotted
and most of the fur had fallen from the fragile leather. He had
tried to mend it with fresh skins, but the older portions tended
to tear away from the patches. He tucked the ragged thing as
closely as he could about Fian, then went off to scout more
wood for the fire. He found dead branches on a tree up the
arroyo. Thorns ripped his hands as he broke them up and heaped
them onto the smoking fire. He crept back under the coracle's
shelter and took off his soaked and slimy poncho, draping it
over a thwart to serve as a curtain and heat-trap. The antelope
hide stank abominably.

Fian stirred, plucking at the bandages of dirty rose-gold
fabric that covered his dreadful head wounds. Kuhal restrained
his brother's hands and pressed them firmly back beneath the
fur coverlet. They were clammy, the skin stretched tight over
stark bones and tendons, pulse fluttering in the web of blood
vessels.

dying . . .
   No.
      we die together . . .
         No.
            we die cold? . . .
               No!
               socoldbloodslowsheartslows
               NO I/I WARM US!!

The conjoined mind struggled. One half was frantic to cut
loose and make an end to months of suffering. The other,
remorseless in love, commanded life.

[*psycho* A *kinetic*]
[*vaso* A *dilator*]
[*stimu* A *lation*]
A
A
H
!

The pain was coming mostly from the infected facial nerves. That and the damp cold. Having mustered up barely enough PK to boost his brother's impeded circulation, Kuhal now steeled himself to assume the pain again with his redactive faculty. His strength was almost inadequate to manage the shunt. This would be his tenth night in a row without sleep, the outer limit. They would have to lay up here tomorrow. Rest well, get warm and dry, find some substantial food. Fian's will to live had diminished almost to nullity.

Sleep, Fian.
  yes
Sleep, dearbrother.
  yes
Sleep, soulmirror.
  yes
Sleep, gentleintuitor.
  y e s
Sleep, lovedselfwounded
  y e s
Sleep, Fianmindofmymind, sleep.
  [*slow-wave theta rhythm*]
Sleep.

For most of the day, Fian had been delirious, and the mental tempests of the right hemisphere of the Brain assaulted the fatigue-drugged defenses of the left until Kuhal himself suffered a hallucination.

He had trudged along the eternal beach, towing Fian through the shallows in the derelict Firvulag coracle. Suddenly he had seemed to see a city in the mists far out on the water. It was as luminous as an earthbound sun— Muriah, reborn in splendor! Kuhal heard the Tanu women singing the Song, cheering arena crowds at the Spring Sport Meeting, glass trumpets sounding, and the clangor of jewel-bright swords beating on glass shields.

Bewitched, he dropped the coracle rope. Home! They were almost home! After months of creeping westward along the African shore, wretched castaways, half-crazed and starving, battered into metapsychic impotence, a miracle had happened.

Arms outstretched, Kuhal waded toward the vision, into deep water.

The more seriously injured brother, with greater intuitive power in his share of the Brain, recognized the phantom for the sham it was. Summoning up a pulse of coercive force, he had compelled Kuhal to return, to take the rope in hand.

"Now we will go to the Blessed Isle together," Fian had said.

But Kuhal's brainstorm had passed. Obstinately, he chose life for them. They came ashore.

"I am dying slowly," Fian had said. "Why not make an end to it?"

"You won't die. I won't let you. We're going to get back to the European mainland. Just as soon as the rains stop, the wind will shift to the south. I'll rig a sail for the coracle."

"It won't do us any good to cross to the other shore. The others are all dead in the Flood."

"We don't know that! Our farsensing power is too weakened to perceive beyond earshot—if that far."

"Kuhal! Mind of my mind. Death is all there is for us . . . if we are to remain united."

Screaming, Kuhal had denied it. Death was unthinkable. Separation was unthinkable. "Trust me! You've always trusted me, followed me. We're *one*."

And the pain flowed forth, and hopelessness, and Fian said, "If you won't follow me, I may have to go alone."

"No!" At Kuhal's lowest conscious level the truth crept out: *I am afraid . . .*

Sitting in the rain-beaten shelter, Kuhal Earthshaker who had been Second Lord Psychokinetic to the great Nodonn held his sleeping twin tightly. The fire was hissing; soon the rain would put it out. Fian's brainwaves were slow and peaceful. He felt no pain. But for the wakeful brother it was otherwise:

[*slow theta*]

[*slow theta*]   **FEAR**   [*slow theta*]

[*slow theta*]

9

It was pouring and getting pretty dark by the time that the ronin Yoshimitsu Watanabe came to the twelfth troll-gate on the Redon Track.

"Rotten Firvulag extortionists," he grumbled.

He reined in and considered the matter with weary disgust. He'd lost so much time already, swimming flooded fords and detouring around washouts and landslides. If he reached Goriah at all tonight it would be in the wee hours, when hospitality was hard to come by, even if a traveler had money. And if he was broke...

Yosh's famished chaliko took advantage of the halt to scratch up a few chufas from the muddy earth. He urged her forward again with a soft, "Hup, Kiku." She came to the edge of a precipice and looked down at the foaming torrent below, whickering uneasily. The defile was narrow but extremely steep, clogged by downed timber. It was spanned by a simple bridge of adze-flattened logs. At either end of this were the "gates," man-high cairns, each topped by a pole from which dangled a colored parchment lantern shaped like a fantastic horned skull. Large fireflies imprisoned inside were a fitful source of illumination.

If a wayfarer wanted to use the bridge, it was obligatory to drop the customary offering into holes at the base of the cairns. Gate-crashers were subject to being eaten by the troll.

Yosh unfastened his capelike straw mino and let it slide off so that the ominous magnificence of his red-laced uma-yoroi would be clearly visible to any nocturnal predator. In two swift movements he replaced his straw rain hat with the armored kabuto. When his hands came down from his head, they gripped the makeshift (but lethal) nodachi that had been sheathed behind his right shoulder.

He held the longsword before him. He and Kiku stood as motionless as an equestrian statue. The ghostly lanterns bobbed and flickered. Tepid rain rattled on the jungle greenery and a few tree frogs peeped a spring madrigal.

"Now, listen here, you!" Yosh said in ringing tones. "I'm a man of honor. I hold to the Human-Firvulag Alliance. I've paid your damn tolls all the way from the Paris Basin without a mumbling word. But now I've got only three silver bits left. If I give them to you, I'll be flat skinned when I pull into Goriah city tonight. No money for a bed, for food, fodder for my mount, anything. So I'm not paying! You'll have to take it out in trade!"

The frogs fell silent, leaving only the sound of rain and the cascade's muffled drone. Suddenly a green glow sprang into being at the near end of the log bridge. Something tall and dripping and hideous bounded onto the trail, menacing the Japanese warrior and his horselike steed. The apparition was reptilian, with webbed hands and a scaly body. The head resembled the horned skull of the lanterns, covered in pebbly hide, and there were enormous bulging eyes that shone like green searchlights.

Before the thing could pounce, Yosh opened his mouth. He summoned forth the kiai—the spirit-shout of the ancient bujutsu masters—a vocal vibration of such stupefying volume and horrific timbre that it seemed to strike the troll like a physical blow. The creature staggered and fell back on one knee, clapping its taloned flippers over the sides of its head.

Urged on by Yosh, the chaliko mare leaped. She was a huge animal, more than nineteen hands. Her forefeet, armed with semiretractile claws larger than a man's palm, landed only centimeters from the troll's paralyzed body. The point of Yosh's great nodachi hovered above the belly of the Firvulag.

"The sword is iron—not bronze or glass," Yosh said. "You speak Standard English? This is a blood-metal weapon! Nopar o beyn! One prick, and you're warm meat. I've killed twenty-two Howlers and two Tanu with this nodachi, and I'm ready to pop for my first Firvulag if you just *blink* ugly."

The troll let its breath out in a fluttering gasp. "You—say you hold to the Alliance, Lowlife?"

"I have so far. Are you going to be reasonable about the toll?"

The creature's eyes blazed. "Don't I deserve to make a living? Three times the bridge washed out this winter and I had to fix it! Two bits is cheap. I'm not even making my maintenance expenses. And besides, the royal tax gougers take a thirty percent rake-off."

The sword didn't waver. "I can't afford it. Times are hard in the North Country with the world turned upside down since the Flood. That's why I'm going to Goriah. Well? You ready to die for a lousy two bits?"

The monster's radiance dimmed. "Oh, hell. Pass and be damned to you. Look—can I shape-shift and get up? This cold mud is murder on my lumbago."

Yosh nodded and lifted his sword. The reptilian form quivered and seemed shot through with sparks of color that coalesced into the softly gleaming body of a medium-sized exotic. His face was seamed, his nose long and pointed, and his beady little eyes glowered from under extraordinarily bushy red brows. He wore a conical scarlet cap with matching breeches (now soaked with mud), a ruffled shirt laced at the throat, a leather jerkin embroidered in exquisite designs of twined stylized animals, and hobnail jackboots with turned-up tips.

"Look, we can make a deal," the troll said. "You're still more than thirty Lowlife leagues from the City of the Shining One. A long way to go on a bad night. And like you said, your wallet's short of the jinglies. You'd need even more than those three bits to find decent up-putting in Goriah. But my brother-in-law Malachee runs a nice tavern just a few kloms

from here where you can get a good meal and a flop and a bag
of roots for your brute for only two bits. Then in the morning
I'll let you across for a cut rate: one silver piece instead of the
usual two. What say?"

Yosh's eyes narrowed. "No shit?"

The Firvulag turned up his hands. "Humans and Little People are allies! King Sharn and Queen Ayfa made it official.
Nobody'll zap you in your bed at Malachee's."

"But a human staying at a Firvulag tavern—"

"Not so common in the hinterlands, but getting pretty usual
around this neck of the woods, especially since the Shining
One sent out his call for recruits. Our people can use the
business! Look, I sent two other Lowlives to Malachee's already tonight. Footsloggers. You'll have company."

Yosh grinned. He slid the longsword back into its scabbard
on his back. A touch of his heels and a slight body movement
on his part caused the chaliko to draw away from the bedraggled
exotic. "Okay. I accept the deal. How do I find this place?"

"Go back along the trail until you come to that turn leading
to the cliffs alongside the Strait of Redon. Hang a right at the
cork-oak grove, then follow the ley until you run smack into
a tumulus. That's it. Malachee's Toot. Tell 'em Kipol Greenteeth sent you."

He shambled to the edge of the gorge, then looked back
over his shoulder. "That battle-yell of yours is really a traditional Firvulag gag, you know. But the old tricks are the best.
No hard feelings." Giving a sardonic salute, Kipol Greenteeth
sank into the ground.

The tumulus, when Yosh found it, was the size of a large
circus tent and overgrown with brush. It looked utterly deserted
there in the stormy night, isolated on a wind-swept heath perhaps half a kilometer from the strait. The rain had quit for the
moment. Torn bits of wrack scudded across the sky like squad-
rons of witches. Along the southwestern horizon was a pearly
glow that silhouetted low coastal hills. That tantalizing light
behind the headland came from Goriah, Aiken Drum's new
headquarters, now the de facto capital of the Many-Colored

Land. With a human operant ruling the old Tanu kingdom, it was going to be a whole new ball game in the Pliocene Exile.

"And I can hardly wait to play!" Yosh told patient Kiku.

He'd make a more impressive entrance arriving at Goriah in daylight, anyhow. Kiku would be fresh and sporting the handsome garniture that he'd made. They'd tow a gaudy stack of hawk kites right up to the city gates to catch people's attention. Then he'd ride into Goriah dressed to the nines in his gorgeous Muromachi Period samurai armor, with his sword at present-arms. He'd offer that sword of hand-wrought iron to Lord Aiken-Lugonn. And at last Yoshimitsu Watanabe would no longer be a ronin, a masterless wave-man adrift on the sea of life. He'd be a goshozamurai—an imperial warrior!

Briefly, Yosh wondered what his twenty-second-century colleagues at Rocky Mountain Robotics back in good old Denver, Colorado, would say if they could see him in that hour of glory...

Reality brought him back to Pliocene Earth. His laminated armor was heavy and leaked like a sieve. His belly flapped empty against his spine. Poor Kiku was reduced to mouthing a scraggly broom bush.

Where could the damn tavern be? He rode around the hillock, shining his solar-battery torch into depressions and shrubbery. All he found was a little standing stone, thin and about half a meter high, with a black ideograph painted on it. As he leaned from the saddle, studying this, he heard distant coarse laughter and music.

Coming from *inside the hill*—?

"Hello!" he shouted.

The congenial sounds melted into the whistling wind.

"Is anybody in there? Is this Malachee's Toot? Uh—Kippy Greenteeth sent me!"

There was a grating rumble and the chaliko shied back. A rectangle outlined in dim yellow light, measuring nearly three meters high and somewhat less in width, appeared on the slope before him. The earth sank to reveal a sizable tunnel lit with flaming wall cressets. Passageways led off right and left. At the far end was a big wooden door with two peepholes like

crimson eyes, from behind which came muffled noises of ine-
briate laughter, singing, clinks and smashes, and other indi-
cations of rampant conviviality.

"You stand there all night, Lowlife—or come in?"

A Firvulag adolescent, hunched and slightly spotty, but
wearing a superior smile, beckoned Yosh forward. As the warrior followed the exotic youth into the righthand passage, the
entrance to the hollow hill sealed behind him. Keeping his
panic in check (as well as Kiku, who had gone skittish in this
novel environment), Yosh rode into a dry earthen chamber
where all manner of bales, sealed jars, filled sacks, and odd-
ments of domestic equipment were lying about.

The stripling slouched against a barrel, picking at an in-
flamed blackhead on his nose with one grubby fingernail. He
indicated a space along one wall where straw covered the floor.

"You put animal there. Tie to ring in wall. Roots to eat in
sacks. You do feeding, grooming. Chalikos no like me." He
giggled and a shadow of sinister felinity distorted his features.
Kiku snorted and showed the whites of her eyes.

Yosh dismounted. As he tended to the animal's needs, he
felt the gaze of the exotic seeming to bore into the backplate
of his corselet, where the great curved nodachi was still strapped.

The boy's halting English was truculent. "You leave blood-
metal sword here. In storeroom."

Yosh didn't look at him. He continued to rub down Kiku
with a handful of straw. "No. I keep my weapons and my
armor with me. And in the morning, I check to be sure that
none of the gear I stashed out here has been . . . misplaced. I'd
really be cut up if any of my things got lost—"

In a split second he whirled about, the sword chopping down
in a lightning iaijutsu motion to stop just short of the stunned
Firvulag's forehead.

"—and you might be cut up, too, kid. If you fuck around
with my chaliko. Understand?"

"Mala-*chee*!" the youth screeched.

Yosh was using the sword innocently to slice open a sack
of roots when the dwarfish exotic innkeeper came bustling in.

"Now, now! What's this commotion, Nuckalarn, my lad?

A new arrival? Welcome, human friend!" Malachee's face was plump and rosy. His pointed ears protruded from a crown of silky white hair. He had sleeves rolled to the elbow, very clean hands, and wore a bibbed leather apron. Giving the sword a brief glance, he winked at Yosh. "Of course you may keep your weapon with you, sir. But sheathed at all times, please. No demonstrations of martial art are allowed in Malachee's Toot."

The boy Nuckalarn, his face broken out in ugly white fear-patches in addition to the original spots, curled his lip with forced bravado.

"He say he cut me up with blood metal! Sonabitching Low-life!"

Malachee hoisted a reproachful eyebrow at Yosh.

"A misunderstanding." The warrior beamed suavely at Mala-chee, ignoring the epithets that the Firvulag youth mumbled in his own tongue. After his sword was cased on his back again, he took two silver slugs from his uchi-bukuro and held them out to the innkeeper. "Permit me to pay in advance as a measure of good faith. Your good brother-in-law recommended your establishment highly."

Malachee twinkled, took the money, and led the way to the public room. As the wooden door swung open, Yosh had an impression of pulsing ruddy light, tumultuous noise, a smell of roasting meat and spilled beer, and a press of exotic merrymakers who ranged in size from apple-cheeked manikins carousing un-derfoot to chandelier-grazing ogres. Not one of the Firvulag wore an illusory aspect, as was the almost invariable custom of the race when having commerce with humankind. Yosh was interested to see that in spite of the size variance, none of these Firvulag were physically deformed, like the mutant Howlers, nor were they meanly dressed. The medium-sized individuals, had they been attired in twenty-second-century garb, would have passed unnoticed in a typical barroom crowd on Elder Earth.

Malachee had to shout above the din. "Right this way to a nice table! You can sit with two compatriots of yours!"

The décor of the public room featured polished gnarled

roots, slabs of ornamental minerals, massive supporting timbers embellished with gargoyle carvings, and ingenious use of fungoid motifs. As Yosh followed his host through the throng, Firvulag patrons drew away with wary expressions. Some scowled and muttered. For all the royal decrees, detente was obviously still a fragile thing.

In the hazy glare at the other end of the room a gigantic tosspot was flailing his arms in the air like a demented windmill. He sang out a single imploring word in a surprisingly rich baritone:

"Vaaf-na!"

The rest of the company chorused: "Vafna! Vafna!"

Yosh felt himself being pushed down onto one of the mushroom-shaped wooden stools at a wall table. Malachee yelled in his ear. "Enjoy the entertainment! I'll have your supper sent out! The two bits includes all you want to eat and drink! You'll share your sleeping room with these travelers, here! Thanks for coming!"

The deep red light was brightening to orange at the far side of the room. Yosh cast an appraising glance at the two humans seated with him. One was a strapping youngster with a peach-fuzz beard, wearing shabby fringed buckskins. The shy smile with which he welcomed Yosh hinted at a childish simplicity. The other man was considerably older. His threadbare blouse and torn cape were of the type worn by gray trooper noncoms. He had a stubbled underthrust jaw, greasy hair falling over eyes slitted in hostility, and the coiled-spring demeanor of an incorrigible hard case.

"Hey, guy," the young man exclaimed to Yosh. "That's a hell of a bonzo outfit! And didn't those spooks give you *room*? Shooo!" He lowered his voice to a conspiratorial rasp. "Is that a sword on your back? Hey—is it *iron*?"

"Yes," said Yosh.

The hard case glowered above the rim of his beer mug. "You some kinda Mongolian, slaunch-eyes?"

"Japanese extraction," said Yosh equably. "North American native."

"Man, are we ever glad to meet up with you!" said the

youth. "All's we got's between us is a bronze pig-tickler and a vitredur skinning knife. I's sure we'd get massacreed in our bed tonight, y'know? Shooo! But with your iron, we'll rate *respect*! Hey—I'm Sunny Jim Quigley, and this here's Vilkas. Who you be?"

"My name is Watanabe." Yosh's reply was almost drowned out by the reiterated musical howl of the big Firvulag.

"*Vaaaaf*-na!"

"Vafna! Vafna! Vafna! Vafna!" chanted the other patrons. They thumped beakers, knife handles, and fists on the tables. Unseen drummers took up the beat. There was an abrupt hiss, a *poof*, and a flash. The tavern rocked with cheers.

A pianolike instrument struck up a strong bass figure and five little Firvulag women came prancing coltishly into the area of fiery radiance. They sang teasing challenges in the exotic language, and the male taverngoers responded in mellow harmony. The damsels wore full skirts reminiscent of bucolic Mitteleuropa. Their headpieces, bodices, and the cuffs of their scarlet boots were lavishly adorned with gemstones that gave off hypnotic glints, filling the room with whirling tiny lights as the dancers circled to accelerating tempo.

Yosh strained to see clearly in the red murk. Those women! Were they really—?

The singing grew wilder. The dancers' challenge and the response of the Firvulag men blended into a rapport of almost palpable eroticism. One short musical phrase, almost shouted by the spectators, cued the women to leap one by one into the air. As they rose, their costumes vanished like smoke and it seemed that smooth-skinned nymphs with blazing hair writhed inside an inferno of hot colors. Percussion instruments clashed and rang and the mixed voices reached a hammering crescendo. And then the incandescent bodies were consumed. The sound fell away, lost in languor, melancholy as the fall of bright ashes.

The light cooled. A different female form materialized, solitary and rarefied, her breasts and thighs scarved in flowing vapor. She sang a brief lyric of heart-stopping purity and sadness. When the last note died, so did the auroral light.

There was silence. Then every exotic in the place leaped up to utter a final deafening *"Vafna!"*

"My God," said Yosh.

Drops of sweat trickled down the youth's brow. "Shooo!"

The rough-hewn bareneck named Vilkas emptied his mug, slammed it onto the table, and blasphemed the Tanu Goddess. "Gave you a nice little buzz, didn'ey? Real turn-on—right? Well, enjoy it, suckers, and eat your hearts out. 'Cause that all you're gonna get. All any of this peg-up lot'll get." He swept his arm wide to indicate the mob of bleary-eyed, grinning habitués, slowly emerging from the dance's spell. "Damn Firvulag bitches! They only do it by remote control till their menfolk marry 'em. And us humans're on the wrong frequency, so we don't get none—and they know we can never force 'em because of the goddam teeth. So the spook cunts laugh at us! They know we got hardly any Lowlife women."

"Teeth?" said Yosh blankly. "I never got close enough to a Firvulag female to look one in the mouth. What's special about their teeth?"

Sunny Jim looked away, abashed.

Vilkas gave a bark of mirthless laughter. "Not regular teeth, slaunch-eyes." He glared meaningfully at Yosh for a moment, then whispered, "Other teeth. Down there."

"Ah." The ronin smiled coolly. "I can see how that would cramp your style. You don't look like the type to ask politely. Or get many offers of free samples."

A serving lad materialized at Yosh's elbow and began to unload a tray. There was a platter of big broiled ribs coated with pungent sauce, a bowl of something smelling like oyster stew, a loaf of purple-tinted bread, and an enormous tankard of beer. As a final touch the waiter set down a saucer filled with tiny mushrooms, the caps scarlet with white flecks.

Yosh reached out. "What's this? The appetizer?"

A hairy hand clamped his wrist. "Go easy on those hoobies, slaunch-eyes. Firvulag get high on 'em, but they'll send a human to hell faster 'n' methyl alcohol." Vilkas released his grip with insolent slowness. "Unless cheap fungo trips are *your* style." He scowled at the waiter. "More beer, dammit!"

Sunny Jim ventured a conciliatory smile. "Aw, Vilkas. Hey! Why'n'cha stash that crap?" His eyes appealed to Yosh. "Vilkas don't mean nothin'. He's just a li'l squiffed from too much spook beer. Past month's been mighty rough on him. He was in Burask when the Howlers tore the town to pieces, and before that—"

"Shut up, Jim," said Vilkas. His beer arrived and he downed a liter without pausing for breath.

Yosh regarded Vilkas without passion. "Kampai!" he toasted, taking a swallow of the brew. "Ah, Burask. I missed the festivities, worse luck. But a week or so afterward I did meet up with a party of Tanu fleeing the city." He began to spoon up the oyster stew. It was fit for the Galactic Gourmet.

Jim's eyes bugged. "Holy blue shit, guy! What happened?"

"Their offensive mind-powers were weak. I decapitated two. The others fled. Unfortunately, the golden torcs of the vanquished were damaged by my sword. But I did acquire a fine chaliko for my efforts."

"Lucky bastard," muttered Vilkas through the suds. "Lucky slaunch-eyed friggerty bastard. You wanna know what my luck's been?"

Jim interrupted what was evidently a familiar tirade. "And now you're on your way to Goriah, are you?" At Yosh's nod, he exclaimed, "Hey! So are we! When the word come that this human who wants to be king was passin' out gold collars— why, I like to busted my butt hittin' the trail outa the home swamp! And ol' Vilkas . . . well, he didn't need that much persuadin' to come along after Burask."

"And Finiah before that!" shouted the man who wore the blouse of a gray trooper. "I escaped the soddin' Lowlives after they barenecked me, but the Tanu at Burask treated me like a traitor! Never have any luck. Not here—not back 'n the Milieu. Lithuanians just *born* stone losers. Wouldn' even give us our own planet! Hell—even fuckin' *Albanians* got a planet, but not us. Y'know what the highass Concilium told us Lithuanians? 'Go colonize a Cosmop world!' Said we di'n have nuff ethnic dynamism, f'chrissake. So we could go share a planet with a lot of lousy Letts and Costa Ricans and Sikkimese!" He choked down the last of his beer and slumped forward, head on the stained tableboards. "Bloody Yanks got twelve planets. Bloody Japs got nine. But nothin' for the poor Lithuanians." He began to sob.

"Aw, Vilkas," said Sunny Jim. "Hey—come on."

Yosh considered the precious pair. They weren't much to look at, but even a couple of scruffy ashigaru would give him greater face than if he arrived at Goriah unattended. He had enough extra gear to fix them up. The boy could manage the string of hawk kites while the reprobate soldier bore the standard and the mesh bag with the Tanu heads.

"The track between here and Goriah is still somewhat hazardous," Yosh said. "You can come along with me tomorrow, Jim, if you like. Vilkas, too. All I'd ask is that you carry a few of my things."

"Hey—that's damn nice of you, guy!" Sunny Jim was jubilant. "No spook gonna mess with us if we stick close to you and that iron sword! Isn't that a great idea, Vilkas?"

The greasy head lifted. "Super." The bloodshot gaze fixed on Yosh had become horribly sober. "What did you say your name was, slaunch-eyes?"

Yosh put down the rib he had been chewing and smiled, as if at a peevish child.

"*You* can call me Yoshi-sama," he said.

10

THE RECEPTION PARTY WAITED ON THE GORIAH QUAY AS THE
ship from Rocilan was slowly warped into its slip.

All the sable banners emblazoned with Lord Aiken-Lugonn's impudent golden finger hung sodden in the thin rain.
The aristocratic riders on their elaborately caparisoned mounts
were quite drenched; but Mercy had warned Aiken against
tampering with the elements today, even in the interests of
hospitality. Screening off the rain—or indeed any extraordinary manifestation of metapsychic prowess—would be a sole-
cism in Tanu eyes, marking the kingly aspirant as deficient in
humility.

The gray-torc docking crew wrestled an ornamental gang-
way into position. In a fine show of pageantry, Aiken's new
company of gold foot soldiers took up honor-guard formation,
their gleaming brass-and-black-glass half-armor looking all the
more resplendent for the sparkling drops of water beading it.
Flunkies brought a mounting stool to the foot of the ramp.
Alberonn Mindeater himself led forward four white chalikos
for the disembarking guests.

On board the ship, a single horn note sounded. Several
Tanu ladies in Aiken's train raised their glass carnices and
responded with a fanfare. Eadnar, widow of the late Lord
Gradlonn of Rocilan, began to descend the gangplank, followed by her venerable mother-in-law Lady Morna-Ia, her

sister Tirone Heartsinger, and Tirone's husband Bleyn the Champion.

Aiken doffed his golden hat with its dripping black plume, levitated discreetly until he stood full upright on his saddle, and threw wide his arms in a gesture of welcome.

"Slonshal!" cried the mind and voice of the diminutive usurper of Goriah, and the power of his utterance made the rocky harbor walls reverberate. "Slonshal!" he said again, reaching out to join Mercy's greeting with his own as the visitors mounted the waiting chalikos. And "Slonshal!" he roared for the third time, making the ship's sails billow and the gulls rise up from all the piers and pilings like a confetti cloud of gray and pink and white. From the throats and minds of those assembled on the quay came the haunting strains of the Tanu Song, its melody so strangely familiar to the exiles of the twenty-second century:

Li gan nol po'kône niési,
'Kône o lan li pred néar,
U taynel compri la neyn,
Ni blepan algar dedône.
    Shompri pône, a gabrinel,
    Shal u car metan presi,
Nar metan u bor taynel o pogekône,
Car metan sed gône mori.

There is a land that shines through life and time,
A comely land through the length of the world's age,
And many-colored blossoms fall on it,
From the old trees where the birds are singing.
    Every color glows there, delight is commonplace,
    Music abounds on the Silver Plain,
On the Gentle-Voiced Plain of the Many-Colored Land,
On the White Silver Plain to the south.

There is no weeping, no treachery, no grief,
There is no sickness, no weakness, no death.
There are riches, treasures of many colors,

Sweet music to hear, the best of wine to drink.
  Golden chariots contend on the Plain of Sports,
    Many-colored steeds run in days of lasting weather.
Neither death nor the ebbing of the tide
Will come to those of the Many-Colored Land.

The honored guests from Rocilan joined in the singing; but at the last verse, bereaved Alberonn and Eadnar wept openly, and old Lady Morna's seamed visage hardened into a mask of grief, and Mercy's mind-voice lost its music and keened instead the Celtic lament, *Ochone, ochone!*

They all fell silent. The seabirds drifted back to their resting places. The harbor waters were dead calm, a rain-pocked leaden sheet.

Aiken said, "Welcome, Most Exalted Ones of Rocilan." His mind declaimed: The laughter and the joy will come again—and the love and the sport and the many-colored treasures of the heart. The Shining One promises it!

Lady Morna-Ia peered at him sharply. "You are shorter of stature in person than your farseen image hints, Battlemaster. And *much* younger."

"I'll be twenty-two years old on the day before the Grand Loving, Farseeing Lady," said the rogue. "On my home world, Dalriada, I'd already be four years into my majority. And old enough for elected office if my fellow-citizens hadn't banished me as a menace to the public welfare!"

Morna's subvocalization was still mentally audible: Understandable.

"As for my size," he added, smirking, "I was quite big enough for Mayvar Kingmaker, your late guild-sister." She bridled dangerously at the innuendo, but he swept on. "And if the Flood hadn't interrupted my duel with Nodonn, I'd have cut *him* down to size, too."

"So you say," the lady retorted. "Lofty talk seems to be a commodity in long supply about Goriah this time of the year. That, and the flouting of sacred tradition." Her glance fell on her widowed daughter-in-law, Eadnar, communing wordlessly with Alberonn, who still held the bridle of her chaliko. "It is your shameless example, Battlemaster, presuming to affiance yourself to Mercy-Rosmar in defiance of our mourning customs, that has led Eadnar to profane my late son's memory."

Aiken shifted elocutional gears abruptly, abolishing any hint of saucy bravado and speaking to the older woman on the intimate telepathic mode with all of the earnest charm he could conjure:

Farseeing Lady Morna-Ia, you're a First Comer—a pillar of your guild, a person of great wisdom as well as metapsychic strength. You're aware of the danger we face, with so many of the battle-company having perished in the Flood. The Foe is poised to take advantage of any show of weakness now that they outnumber us, and *they* will not scruple to go against tradition if it will hasten our downfall! Consider the so-called Howler attack that devastated Burask, in which the invaders made unprecedented use of bows and arrows. And the skirmishes in the alpine foothills around Bardelask where ogres and imps have been seen mounted on chalikos and hipparions, in contravention of their most ancient custom!

The Foe are planning to pick off, one by one, those cities that have lost their strong lords and fighting ladies. Even Rocilan, on the Atlantic coast and a protectorate of Goriah, is vulnerable to the Firvulag of the Grotto Wilderness. The lovely Eadnar is a creative genius in textiles and the confectionery arts—but she is hardly the person to undertake the defense of your city against a well-armed force of mounted monsters! This is why, at my insistence, Alberonn Mindeater has pressed his suit in spite of your mourning customs. You know he's eminently qualified. Why—it's to Rocilan's honor that it be governed by a High Tabler, and a fighting specialist, to boot! Add to this the fact that Alberonn saved Eadnar's life, and your own, in the Flood . . .

"We owe the Lord Mindeater more than we can repay," Morna said aloud, stiff-faced. "We welcome him with humility and joy. Nevertheless—"

Aha. I see what you take little trouble to hide! It's Me you really object to. My meddling in Rocilan affairs. My trampling your tradition. My taking of Goriah and aspiring to be king!

You are a human.

And a rascal! I know. But if you'll just use your great ultrasenses to look past my sawed-off body and my humanity and my youth and my bragging, naughty ways... you'd see that I'm the very one this kingdom needs now to lead it. I'm the one who can rebuild at the same time that I send the Foe packing! Who believes it? Bleyn and Alberonn do, and follow me now as they did in the last Grand Combat. Mercy-Rosmar, the President of the Creator Guild, has agreed to be my wife. And here's the Second Redactor, Lord Culluket, come to Goriah just this past month to throw in his lot with the Shining One. Four of the five eligible High Table survivors accept me at my word! Won't you?

"It's true what they say about your sly mind and forked tongue." But the old woman's face had softened into a wintry smile. "One moment you're a disingenuous mountebank, and the next—"

"Not all that impossible a candidate for High King!" He giggled, clapped his broad-brimmed golden hat back onto his head, and squinted at the wet plumes that now dripped in front of his eyes. "At home on dear, soggy Dalriada, we'd call this a fine soft morning. What say, lady dear, that we take a jaunt of inspection? Just a wee detour on our way to the Castle of Glass? I'd like you and the other Exalted Ones of Rocilan to see all the great things I've done, refurbishing the Grove of May for this year's Loving. You'll be amazed!"

"Oh, very well," said Morna.

The other guests and the members of the welcoming party, who had been mingling and chatting gravely, now fell silent and expectant. Mercy, sitting her white chaliko sidesaddle, took up Aiken's suggestion as though it were a spur-of-the-moment thing and not something the two of them had planned from the start. Psychocreative force streamed from her, and her wild opalescent glance made even the lovely sisters of Rocilan look almost wan in comparison.

"Let's fly!" Mercy exclaimed. "It's a grand day for a

Faery Rade!" She threw back the hood of her velvet Kinsale cloak, so that her fine auburn hair darkened and coiled in ringlets from the rain. "Away with all you soldiers and attending lords and ladies—we'll not be needing your company until we return to Goriah. You dear guests, follow me! Fly away! Fly away!"

She mounted aloft into the downpour, leaving Aiken momentarily open-mouthed. This detail of flying had definitely not been planned, and of the others, only Culluket was capable of self-levitation. Aiken would have to carry the four Rocilan guests and Alberonn himself, violating the humility precept. No stigma attached to the pregnant Mercy, who by Tanu custom was permitted any caprice; but she'd put a right one across him.

"What the hell," Aiken said, shrugging. "Up, up and away! I'll be breaking a whole raft more of your holy fewkin' rules to save you from the Firvulag, so we might as well wipe the slate of this piece of silliness right now."

He waggled both hands. The rain stopped falling on the Tanu aristocrats and the trickster, deflected by his psychokinetic power. "If we were on Dalriada," he said, "we could ride in nice comfy aircraft instead of on these overgrown turnip eaters. But hang tight! I'm working on *that* little problem, too!"

Effortlessly, he drew them all along with him, the chalikos seeming to canter through the moisture-laden clouds. They caught up quickly with Mercy, who only laughed, and soared eastward over a low range of heavily wooded hills. Beyond them the broad River Laar made a northerly bend before curving down to the Tainted Swamp and its outlet to the Atlantic. A well-graded roadway from Goriah paralleled the river at this point, and it was alive with traffic. Carts drawn by hellads and chaliko caravans brought loads of dressed stone, carved timbers, rolls of sod, and balled-and-burlapped ornamental plant stock into a raw clearing adjacent to the Laar. The eight flying riders swooped low, decelerated to a walking pace, and drifted just above the crowns of big magnolia and black-gum trees. Workers were everywhere down below. Humans, both bareneck and gray-torc, supervised gangs of diligent, child-sized ramapithecine apes who dug and raked, cleared and planted, fetched and carried.

"This area along the river is all new since Tirone and I were married," Bleyn remarked. "What's it going to be, Aiken?"

"A fancy campground for the Firvulag guests. Surprise!"

Bleyn's jaw dropped. He looked like a thunderstruck Siegfried. "Tana's Teeth! You can't invite *them*!"

"It goes against all precedent!" Morna said. "Firvulag would never—"

"They've already accepted," the Shining One interrupted her blithely. "Only the biggies, of course. King Sharn and Queen Ayfa and their close henchfolks. We kept the guest list modest. Two or three hundred. With luck, they'll bring presents."

Tirone Heartsinger protested, "But the Little People always have their own Grand Loving celebration. Tanu and Firvulag join in the Combat, as is proper for Foes. But never in the Loving!"

Aiken said, "The common ruck of Firvulag can do as they please, dear lass. But I have special reasons of state for getting the royals to attend our bash. It'll be very educational for 'em to see how the Tanu and torced humanity have rallied round Me!"

"If we can be sure that the city-lords will," Alberonn growled, his mind troubled and showing it clearly.

Aiken now brought the party wafting down. They rode along a broad tanbarked way that wound through the riverside grove. Mercy said, "My Lord Lugonn and I have devoted a lot of thought to this year's Maying. We've been planning all winter long to show the people of the Many-Colored Land a Loving such as they've never seen before." Her mind opened to them, showing the work she had done on Elder Earth, where she had directed historical pageants recreating the heritage of medieval Europe for sentimental colonials. The tricks of Mercy's theatrical trade would lend a fresh and erotic luster to what had been, in Tanu tradition, a charming but rather naive fertility festival. Thanks to Aiken, that polymathic jack-of-all-trades, and to her own expertise as President of the Creators, she had been able to translate her most fantastic designs into reality. No matter that it meant looting Goriah of resources and tying up the city's labor force for most of the winter and spring: A spectacle had been announced, and would be duly produced.

"We'll keep all the good old aspects of the Grand Loving," Mercy said, projecting reassurance at Lady Morna. "The pledging of hearts and the Maypole Dance and the marrying and the lovemaking on the dew-starred grass of May. But there'll be wonderful new delights as well." The visions rolled forth from her mind in a flamboyant cascade. "The old trysting grounds will be gloriously redecorated—finer than our dear people ever dreamt of! There'll be fresh entertainments as well as the familiar ones—new songs and dances and comical skits and dramas of romance, and bright masquerade costumes for everyone in our innovation of the Night of Secret Love. And the food—! You know how I adore creating good things to eat. Wait until you taste our new picnic lunches and moonlight feasts, and the grand aphrodisiac wedding banquet to climax the nuptial celebration! Even the visiting Firvulag will find our hospitality impossible to resist. You know what perfume fetishists they are . . . well, we've transplanted nearly sixty cartloads of orchids and night jasmine and scented waterlilies for the riverside lagoons. The Little People should be almost embalmed in fine fragrance!"

"And when they finish exercising their noses," Aiken said, "they can try out other parts of their anatomy. Back against the slope we've built a whole rabbit warren of new mossy grottos. Just the kind of nooky-nooks the Wee Folk fancy for their spring jollification."

"With an added feature." Culluket the Interrogator smiled coldly within the shadow of his hooded burgundy cloak. "Observe the fine line of sight through that northwestern notch between here and the high turrets of the Castle of Glass back in Goriah . . . Do you perceive it, Lady Morna?"

"Very clever," said the farsensing dame. "No rock formations to block your surveillance of the Foe. I'm glad to see some evidence of prudence amid this frantic ostentation."

Aiken grinned indomitably in the face of her disapproval. "It's *all* for prudence's sweet sake, Lady Morna, don't you see?"

"Perhaps I do," she admitted grudgingly.

"Let's see how the main amphitheatre is shaping up!" Mercy suggested. And she was off and galloping.

The company followed the tanbarked avenue inland. Ancient plane trees with mottled trunks, some more than four meters in diameter, stood sentinel on either side of the arrow-straight traditional Tanu ley that extended off into the mist. On either side of the allée ramas worked on flowerbeds, or pruned shrubs, or scraped moss off the benches of the soon-to-be-refurbished bowers. More little apes clambered over the roofs of the many vine-hung pergolas, removing wasp nests, killing bird-hunting spiders, and driving off the colonies of bats that had made free with the Grove of May since last year's Grand Loving.

They rode on more slowly, and finally the focal point of the pleasance loomed ahead. "A new maypole!" exclaimed Eadnar delightedly. "And so tall!" She went dashing off to examine it, followed after a moment's hesitation by her laughing sister, Tirone. They ignored the rain that pelted them as they left the shelter of Aiken's PK bubble. Casually, he expanded the mental force-field's radius to nearly half a kilometer.

"Tana's mercy!" cried Lady Morna in spite of herself. "You surpass the powers of Kuhal and Fian of the Host, when they used to roof over the sports arena in Muriah!"

"You don't say?" chirped Aiken. He cocked his head at distant Eadnar, who had now stopped, together with Tirone, to accept a bouquet of daffodils from one of the silver-torc landscape architects. "Nice to see the little widow acting more cheery. Perhaps she's looking forward to May."

He gave Alberonn Mindeater a playful mental jab, to which the hybrid responded with decently veiled emotions.

Morna said, "My daughter-in-law is young—scarcely seventy-three—and bears up under our tragic loss more readily than I." Morna studied a goldfinch with a bright red face that sat on a budding bush, singing sweetly. "But life must go on."

"Especially in spring," said Aiken.

Mercy, riding sedately at his side, had her thoughts enclosed in bright opacity. A secret smile turned up the corners of her mouth.

They rode into an open area that had been a mere meadow before Mercy's imagination got to work on it. Now it was transformed into a smaragdine bowl, a gently sloping amphitheatre that swept down to a flat dancing ground. Flocks of sheep cropped the lawn. Beyond was a turfed earthwork stage framed in evergreens; and in back of this, jutting from a truncated knoll, rose the towering maypole. The tip of the bare wooden spar was lost in low-hanging nimbostratus. Some 30 meters to the left of the pole waited a heavy-duty cart with a crew of grays.

"Now for my biggest surprise!" said Aiken. He winked at Mercy. "I had this up my sleeve, etiquette or no etiquette!"

Eadnar and Tirone now rejoined the party. "It's a splendid maypole," said Tirone. "I wonder you could find a slender tree of such imposing height."

"We couldn't," Aiken admitted laconically. "It's an artifact. Reinforced. But that's just for starters, Creative Sister. Here comes the real scouseroo!" He called out in farspeech: *You guys all set?*

The teamsters chorused: *Ready boss!*

The jester made a mesmeric pass in the air. Tarpaulins whipped from the cart, revealing squat wooden crates. Another pass, and lids flew off, to pile into a clattering heap. Aiken frowned, pushed back his hat, unbuttoned the cuffs of his golden suit, and shoved up his sleeves.

"Stand back!" he bellowed. Every sinew tensed as he gathered his psychokinesis. *"Shazoom!"*

From the open boxes flew hundreds of thin metallic sheets that fluttered in the misty air like golden leaves. A directorial gesture from Aiken made them rise and fall, dancing in a butterfly swarm. The gold foil formed a stream, split, twined, braided, and writhed. Like glittering fluid the sheets circled the pole; then those nearest the base spun faster, seeming to melt onto the wood. More swiftly than the eye could follow, the rest of the gold blended into place, gilding the tall spar from butt to tip in a seamless sheath of yellow brilliance. The psychocreative welding job having been accomplished, the maypole stood steaming in the rain while the workmen cheered.

"There has never been such a splendid maypole," breathed Eadnar. "You know its symbolism, do you not, Shining One?"

Aiken nodded solemnly. "Oh, yes. That's why I worked so hard. It's got to be extra glorious if it's to represent Mine."

"And how much of Goriah's treasury was expended in this quest for verisimilitude?" inquired Lady Morna archly.

Aiken was polite. "Not so much . . . that we won't replace it twenty times over with what I'm going to take away from the Firvulag. And not by plunder, either! Fair and square—almost—provided I can con Sharn and Ayfa into agreeing to my modification of the Grand Combat come next October."

"*Another* human novelty?" Morna was almost resigned.

"I'm just loaded with 'em," Aiken told her warmly. "You'll get the complete scoop at the Loving."

Mercy said, "This is why the festival this year must be the most magnificent in all the history of the Tanu exile on Earth—to lift the spirits of our people and to impress the Firvulag. To force them all to take our new regime seriously. We'll have three days of nonstop celebration."

"And at the grand finale," said Culluket the Interrogator, "all of the guests—Tanu and Firvulag and human—will witness the coronation of Lord Aiken-Lugonn and Lady Mercy-Rosmar as King and Queen of the Many-Colored Land."

The minds of the hybrids, their ladies, and the dowager of Rocilan were frozen in astonishment. Nobody noticed that the PK shelter had evaporated with Aiken's pole-gilding ploy and the rain was softly falling on them once again.

"Too soon!" cried Bleyn. "Eventually, yes. But the full-blooded Tanu aren't ready to accept a human king, Aiken! It

was more than sixty years before Alberonn and I were admitted
to the High Table—and Katlinel only last year—because of
our human genes."

"The High Table admitted Gomnol," Aiken said. "He was
human."

"He forced acceptance—and was hated for it," Morna
snapped.

"Mercy's human," Aiken said.

"Is she?" the Interrogator murmured, smiling. "My late
brother, the Battlemaster, thought not."

This was news to Aiken. On the intimate mode he bespoke
her: Say *what*?

Telepathic mirth. Nodonn had GregDonnet do my geneti-
cassay. Olddear claimed I more Tanugenes than human.
PoorGreggy mad ofcourse.

Later I winkle *this* LadyWildfire!

Aloud Mercy said, "There are only twenty-five hundred or
so pure-blooded Tanu left alive—and most of those are minor
powers. Nearly twice as many hybrids survived because of
their greater physical endurance. My Lord and I have estimated
that he will have a clear advantage in petty-nobility acclamation."

"Celadeyr of Afaliah and his traditionalists might fight rather
than acquiesce," said Lady Morna grimly. "And I can well
understand their feeling. Celo and I are both First Comers—
and you, Young Battlemaster, flout the very religious principles
that drove us to this exile in the first place!"

Tirone, who had secretly been a member of the Peace Faction, now interjected a thought that was soft but clear: That
old battle-religion must pass away now dearest Kinsmother.
Brede herself said it. And many of us see Lord Aiken-Lugonn
as the agent of this change.

Morna's consternation flared. "You'll see what battle means,
my girl, if this human youth tries tó seize the throne without
High Table consensus!"

Eadnar's objections were practical. "Even if you count a
majority of the High Table electors on your side, Shining One,
the obduracy of Celadeyr may provoke a fatal division in our

cities' chivalry. The Firvulag would take advantage of any infighting—and perhaps finish what the Flood began."

Bleyn said, "All we ask, Aiken, is that you act prudently! Don't declare yourself until you're sure that the city-lords will follow you and not Celo. If you seize the crown and the dissidents ignore your proclamations and commands, you'll look like a fool."

Morna said, "The entire Tanu power structure is based on *unanimous* loyalty to the sovereign. He's not a mere ruler, elected in the way the Little People choose their vulgar democratic monarchs. Our king is a father to us all!"

Aiken was still grinning, but contempt burned behind his black eyes. Softly he said, "There are more than eighty thousand Firvulag waiting to pounce on our asses, friends. Do you want a king and battlemaster? Or would you prefer a daddy to tuck you in while the demons howl outside the window? Someone to wipe your little twats when your bowels gush the fear of death?"

"We want you," the Interrogator stated. His probing ultrasense flicked over the others like an icy beacon. "Only you have the fullness of aggressive power and the ability to develop the metapsychic concert that we must have to defeat our enemies." He paused. "And the Firvulag are not the only Foe."

The scathing mental face of the trickster underwent a lightning transformation. Now his loyalty, his willingness to defend them if they would only accept and love him shone incontrovertible. For an instant he let them glimpse his vast metapsychic strength before veiling it with an acid drape of self-mockery. And then he conjured up memories for them to ponder, and wooed them with that lilting mental eloquence that so rarely carried over into his spoken words:

Away with your doubts and fears, my friends! Remember the Kingmaker's prophecy about me. She never lost confidence in the man of her choice. Remember how I killed Delbaeth the Shape of Fire, and the Firvulag Battlemaster Pallol One-Eye! And if you hesitate because I conquered them by trickery, then recall how I triumphed on the field of the

Grand Combat, and how the great captains and the petty lords flocked to my impudent banner. Tagan Lord of Swords hailed me! And Bunone Warteacher, greatest of the fighting tacticians! And you, Alberonn—and you, Bleyn! Remember how the commons and nobles alike loved me for my audacity and daring? Remember the mysterious way that the Spear of Lugonn came to my hands? (And even though that sacred Spear is lost for the moment, I know where it must be and I'll have it back—never fear!)

Remember how my right to challenge Nodonn was acknowledged by the whole battle-company? And by Brede! I would have won the Duel of Battlemasters if Tana hadn't had her own ideas about sweeping the chessboard clean and setting up a new game.

You still hesitate? . . . Have you no religion, then? Consider, my friends: Aiken Drum is alive and well, lord of the Castle of Glass and ruler of Goriah by manifest usurpation, suzerain over Rocilan and Sasaran and Amalizan and sundry other settlements about Bordeaux and Armorica! And where is the one who once held all that? Drowned.

(Mercy could not help the mind-cry, and Aiken heard: Nodonn! My Nodonn!)

Oh, friends. You know the Tanu must have a king—and if it's not me, then who? Do you want Celadeyr of Afaliah? He says he doesn't aspire to the throne, and I believe him. My sources have told me that the poor old boy is convinced that the Flood presages the end of the Many-Colored Land! He's training his little army for something called the Nightfall War—and as I understand it, that's a kind of Ragnarok or Armageddon that'll ring down the curtain on both the Tanu and Firvulag. And it's balderdash! Sharn and Ayfa aren't anticipating any apocalypse. They're out to win and stomp our necks!

(And they had to respond: It's true. No fatalism in the Little People. They're scuttling the traditions that held them back. The Flood was a Goddessgift to them.)

Listen to me! If we stand on our hind legs and fight them, we must have a leader. You High Tablers know that I'm stronger than you. Then who . . . ? Minanonn the Heretic? I understand he was a real ripper when he was Battlemaster. But he's a pacifist now—no more suitable to defend you from the Firvulag than Dionket the Healer! The only other High Tablers eligible are Katlinel the Darkeyed and Aluteyn Craftsmaster—if you want to forgive her treason in marrying the Lord of the Howlers, and his deposition by Mercy.

(And once again they had to say: No. None of those could lead us against the Firvulag.)

Aiken Drum sat his big black chaliko. A single drop of water clung comically to the tip of his long, well-shaped nose. The mouth that could tense in an instant to a malignant slot now smiled as he mind-embraced them all, letting his power shine forth.

Aloud, Aiken said, "You see how things stand. In the king sweepstakes, I'm the only candidate who hasn't been scratched. Those who object to a human ruler on principle may kick and scream and cuss—but in the end, they'll be forced to accept me. Hell—even old Celo might come to his senses if he thinks we have a real chance to lick the Foe."

Culluket said, "My redactive knowledge of the Lord of Afaliah affirms the last comment of the Shining One. Celadeyr is stubborn, and he has been incredibly stupid to expel his human technicians. But he is by no means insane. Nor suicidal."

But Bleyn was still inclined to cavil. "The trouble is, the reactionaries just don't *know* you as well as we do, Aiken. That's why they're balking. Why—eight cities have yet to reply to your Grand Loving invitation, and Celo's turned you down flat. If you announce a May coronation, you're laying yourself open to a fiasco."

"Somehow," Alberonn said, "we must force the hand of the fence-straddlers and win as many of the diehards as possible."

Aiken's brow screwed and his visage glowed with intense cogitation. Then his eyes began to dance and he turned to his affianced bride. "Merce, lovie, d'you remember when we were noodling all this, and you told me some of the canny things the old English monarchs did to keep their vacillating vassals in hand? Henry VIII and Good Queen Bess especially. How they traveled around the realm, stopping at one city after another, putting the arm on the wishy-washy and exerting the royal charm and even rattling a sword or two?"

Mercy saw Aiken's drift at once. "Royal progresses, they were called. A grand political tool!" And again there came to her that strange feeling of déjà vu, the tantalizing certainty that she had seen Aiken's crafty and triumphant face before. Italy! The portrait in the palace in Firenze.

"I'll do my royal progress *before* the coronation—not after," he was saying. "I'll visit each city in turn and explain just how things are in this Many-Colored Land, using my own brand of friendly persuasion and sweet reason. And a few surprises I've been cooking up!"

"And who could deny you to your face, my devious Shining One?" A current passed between Aiken and Mercy. Was the old wariness weakening against her better judgment? But he was a rare one!

"This maneuver could work," Culluket said. "It has just the right mix of humble pie and regal condescension and blatant gall. You go to the cities first, as an aspirant should, and then the city-lords may come confidently to you in recognition of your power."

Alberonn nodded to the Interrogator. "And we three to provide High Table prestige as we accompany Aiken. The Lady Creator's absence will be understandable."

"I like it," said Bleyn tersely. "We have enough Tanu and human gold recruits now in Goriah to mount a respectable show of strength."

Aiken refastened his cuffs and straightened his hat. With an offhand PK chicane, he banished the moisture from all their garments and reerected the metapsychic umbrella. "We'll sneak up the Garonne Valley very quietly, and ooze over into Spain. And the first place we hit . . . is Afaliah!"

Lady Morna was speechless. Eadnar and Tirone radiated strong anxiety.

"There's not that much danger," Aiken reassured them. "Celo's gang of mind-benders are strictly second-rate, and I can easily put the clamp on the old gaffer himself. We'll put a fine face on it. Pretend that we don't know how he's been undermining me. I mean—he's never come right out with any blatant provocation. Even his refusal of the Loving invitation was medium-polite, and I can say we never received his letter."

Culluket said, "If Celo cracks, the others should fall into your lap like ripe oranges."

"Ready for juicing," the jester agreed. "Well, how about it? What say we get back to Goriah and start polishing up the fancy armor!"

He launched them and their animals into the air, still fending off the rain, saying to Mercy, "I hope old Peliet and his sages are right about the rainy season being almost over. I'm still a little green at levitating big groups. And there aren't any computerized flight vectors to help a guy fly through soupy mountain passes in this Pliocene Exile."

Mercy laughed gaily. "You'll manage somehow, my tricksy one." *You nonborn kingling from far Dalriada six million years hence! And had some fine Italian genes migrated to stern Scotland? And had they gone on, frozen in vitro, to burgeon again in an obstetric lab on a Milieu planet, engendering this strange young man who was determined to make her his queen?*

Whose portrait had worn Aiken's face?

The train of riders sped through the sky toward Goriah, where glass turrets shone against a widening patch of blue. The obsessive question gnawed at Mercy and spilled over into an inadvertently projected thought.

Aiken's mind was elsewhere; but the Interrogator responded with flawless courtesy, on her intimate mode:

May I assist your recollection with my special talent Lady Creator?

If you would Redactive Brother. This maddening image! If you could sort out my memories and let me put a label to it.

A matter of utmost simplicity for a redactive specialist . . . Oh!

I'm glad the revelation amuses you Lady. I must agree that the resemblance is remarkable. What a dangerous-looking fellow that Florentine politician seems to be! Some day you must tell me all about him.

11

THE FARSEEING RAVEN RANGED ABOVE THE MAGHREB SHORE. The rains had brought grass and drifts of pink and yellow flowers to the slopes, and all the gullies were turned into slim oases that seemed to point in astonishment toward the new blue sea. The bird rejoiced in the many-colored landscape. Natural beauty, more than anything else, helped her to keep the terrors at bay. Aloft in spring sunlight, climbing the wind above this world she had helped to create, there was sanity and forgetfulness.

She detected sentient life—and gold.

Her mind engendered a psychokinetic gale and she sped eastward. The initial flare of life-aura fell below her farsensing threshold, but the predatory bird managed to track it into a wooded ravine with steep sides. The scent of precious metal, living and dead, excited her to the point of madness. She accelerated her metapsychic wind until black feathers ripped from her pinions and she shrieked with pain and elation. And then she arrived, calmed the air, and landed on an outcropping of rock near a trickling spring.

There in a little clearing, one Tanu castaway knelt beside another's body. The raven studied them, feeling that she knew this pair.

They were identical twins. This was clear in spite of the fearful head wounds that disfigured the corpse. The weeping survivor was still beautiful, with the classic features of the Host of Nontusvel. He had evidently just returned from hunting, for the body of a fawn gazelle and a crude spear fashioned from a glass dagger tied to a sapling lay on the ground beside him. He wore rose-gold rags, and the dead twin was similarly dressed in remnants of Psychokinetic Guild finery.

It seemed that the dead man had been unwilling to wait for his brother to return with food. A clump of deadly pink narcissus growing beside the spring had been partially grubbed up, and one half-eaten bulb lay on the ground.

The gigantic raven lifted her shoulders. Her harsh call— *pruuk pruuk*—caused the mourner to look up, trembling and wide-eyed. With great interest, the raven perceived that this twin was literally half-witted. He and his brother had evidently shared a mental symbiosis of the utmost intimacy; they must have been capable of mighty feats before the Flood had smashed them and marooned them here in North Africa. But with the death of his brother, the living twin was reduced to a state of latency even lower than that of a "normal" human being.

The enormous bird glided down to stand near the head of the corpse. The bereaved Tanu stared mutely at the bird, his green eyes dim with tears and his mouth a taut square of anguish. Only when the raven's beak poised above the dead man's throat did the other cry out:

"Fian!"

She *did* know them, these rose-gold twins! A paroxysm of anger dissolved the bird body, and a slender human woman wearing blue glass armor stood there. She wore no helmet and her hair was a buoyant platinum cloud. Her eyes flashed with the wrath of Hecate.

Kuhal Earthshaker recognized her, too. He remembered the vast dark room inside the Coercer Guild stronghold, the massed force of Nontusvel's Host awaiting the human assault on the torc factory, the Lowlife saboteurs armed with iron. They had been led by this small awful woman. Kuhal remembered psychocreative detonations, falling masonry, mental and physical strife—and the glory of the Host victorious amid the smoke and blood, in spite of this female monster's power. This was

Felice, who had slain his sister Epone and vowed to destroy the entire Tanu race—only to fall defeated in Imidol's ambush and then submit to Culluket's torture.

Felice laughed. She held his puny consciousness as if in a pair of tweezers and poked among the wreckage.

Kuhal and Fian! My Beloved's brothers. What a funny kind of mind . . . you were the left hemisphere and he was the right. A syzygy, an aion couple! Kuhal Earthshaker the Second Lord Psychokinetic and Fian Skybreaker his better half!

Her mad giggling coarsened into grating croaks. The great raven again flapped black wings and Kuhal cringed away, both hands gripping his golden torc.

Felice's mind-voice turned petulant:

But where *is* the Beloved where is he? I call and call and only the faraway devils and the nonborn Shining One answer. They try to trick me! I reject them. *He* is the only one I love and want! Where is he who willed my destruction and instead raised me to operant life?

Kuhal whimpered aloud. His broken identity teetered on the edge of dissolution.

Cull is gone! And Imidol is gone and Mayvar and the King and the Queen and the glorious Battlemaster! They are all gone. As dearFian my Self is gone and i/-am alone and powerless. You have conquered avenging DeathBird.

The raven's glittering eye seemed to wink. Once again her cruel beak approached dead Fian's throat. The knobbed catch of his golden collar rotated, impelled by Felice's PK, and the semicirclets opened. The bird jerked the gold free.

Now the living twin groveled on the ground. His arms were wrapped protectively about his own neck. Derision colored the raven's thought:

Oh . . . keep your torc for a while, Earthshaker.

She leapt into the air, carrying the gold, and set off for the Spanish mainland. Kuhal uttered a single mind-cry, so profound in its desolation that it rang from one end of the New Sea to the other. Then he collapsed unmoving.

* * *

Felice crossed the Mediterranean and flew tirelessly into the Betic Range, up the valley where the swollen Proto-Andarax raged through jungles on the flank of Mount Mulhacén. Even in the time of the Galactic Milieu, Mulhacén thrust above the rest of the Sierra Nevada and had small glaciers on its shaded slope. In the gentler Pliocene Epoch the mountain rose some 4200 meters, with snowfields only on the summit.

The bird flew higher and curved around to approach the north face. The growth of tropical hardwoods gave way to laurel thickets. In more arid places there were pines and tangled rhododendrons bearing clusters of white or carmine blossoms. A sabertooth cat sunning itself on a rock yawned. Its slitted eyes followed the giant raven, puzzled by the glint of gold against the sky.

She rode an upwelling air current that let her view the distant turquoise embayment of the Gulf of Guadalquivir to the north. Beyond that hunched the Dark Mountains where wild Firvulag lived. She sideslipped, lost altitude, and dived toward the inviting gorge of the River Genil, nearly home at last after the long day's hunt. Rock thrushes and warblers trilled a welcome. Fat brown trout leaped in the river. As usual, her friends waited outside the entrance to her lair. Otter with his gift of fish. Roe Deer and her child, who would share sweet milk. Yellow Panda holding tender bamboo shoots fetched all the way from the lowlands. Squirrel and Woodrat with nuts and mealy tubers. Dwarf Mastodon cheerfully waving a branch with gleaming purple fruits.

Felice stood before them and smiled, holding the golden torc. "See? Another one!"

The lynx, Pseudaelurus, rubbed adoringly against her bare legs. The other friends, basking in the warmth of her mind, crowded close with their offerings. She accepted them all: the food, the garlands of flowers brought by the weaverbirds, the fragrant dried grass that the mice and coneys had heaped for a fresh sleeping couch. "Thank you! All of you," she said, dismissing them after they had had their fill of communion.

The sun set and a chilly wind began to blow from the Genil Canyon. Several of the song sparrows lingered to sing to her while she kindled her fire with mental flame and got supper cooking. As often happened in the evening, the devil voices started in again, telling their lies and displaying their marvels, reminding her how they had helped when her strength failed at the sundering of the Gibraltar Isthmus.

She ignored them, and presently the devils fell silent. Mad she might be; but she wasn't foolish enough to mindspeak them on a far-carrying mode that might betray her precise whereabouts. Let them just try to triangulate her! Let any of them try—the faraway devils, Aiken Drum, or even futile Elizabeth! Felice knew how to hide from them. (And she only called for the Beloved from high in the sky where there was no danger.)

The cooking fire fell to embers. She made the verandah area of her lair neat and then stood quietly for a moment under the brightening stars. It was good that the rain was nearly over. The flowers in her hair and around her neck exhaled a richer perfume now that they had begun to die, and that was good, too.

Felice took Fian's golden torc and entered the cleft in the mountain. She could see quite well in pitch-darkness, but she wanted to enjoy the treasure at its best, and so she lifted two fingers and generated a bright flame of psychoenergy. The mica-laden rocks glistened. Her den was a talus-cave, not one carved by water, and the interior was perfectly dry. Beyond her sleeping place the way was blocked by a slab of rock weighing many tons. Felice waved the torc at it negligently and the rock slid aside.

In the smaller chamber behind, gold lay piled in heaps higher than her head: a Niebelung hoard acquired through four months of patient searching. These thousands of exquisitely fashioned mind-amplifiers had once clasped the necks of Tanu and their privileged human minions, liking their latent brainpowers into metapsychic operancy. But now those proud torc wearers were dead in her Flood, their bodies swept from the submerged White Silver Plain and flung up for the scavengers to find—and Felice. She had robbed bodies rotting in the shallows and sought out skeletons buried in silt. And when this plunder dwindled she hunted down wretched survivors and seized gold from those too weak to defend themselves from a bird with a body longer than a human arm. She fought them fairly and refrained from using her operant powers in offense. Beak and talons alone were usually sufficient to defeat the demoralized castaways who once had lorded it over the Many-Colored Land.

Felice pitched her new acquisition onto the nearest pile. There was a rich clang as the equilibrium was upset. Golden torcs went slipping and rolling in all directions—to reveal something else, half-hidden in the tangle of precious metal.

She lifted it easily in spite of its considerable weight. It was a great lance of gold-lustre glass, attached by a cable at its butt to a jeweled case, from which hung broken straps. Felice brandished the Spear and pressed one of the studs on the armrest. As usual, there was no result. Immersion in salt water had shorted out the photon weapon's power-supply module. It was as inoperative as it had been when Felice took it from the real Bright Lugonn at the Ship's Grave.

The false Shining One had duped her later and got the Spear away; but the Flood fixed *him*. Now the Spear was hers again forever.

She lay the trophy gently on its bed of gold and left the treasure-cave for her own couch of dry grass. The middle of the night brought cold air from the mountain summit, and she had the nightmare again. But toward dawn, when the lynx curled up at her feet to keep warm, Felice slept in peace.

Kuhal Earthshaker lay insensible throughout most of that day, crushed by bereavement and Felice's desecration. When he finally awoke, evening had come, and with it small things seeking his brother's body. Cursing, he drove them away, and then set about washing and preparing. There were no fresh clothes; but around Fian's neck he hung the heavy Janus-face medallion of their joint escutcheon, the only ornament that they still retainèd.

He carried Fian to the shore, then brought down the coracle. Setting his brother adrift, he knelt on the salt-crusted rocks and tried to sing the Song. But without Fian, there would never be music again, so he merely recited the words. Once again, out over the water, he seemed to see a glowing city in the haze. Fian in his skin boat followed the light-path that led to it, going home.

After a long time Kuhal summoned up his last reserve of strength. His farspeaking voice shouted: *Wait for me Brother!*

And a disembodied answer came:

. . . So there you are!

The reverie of grief vanished and Kuhal again knew terror. He stood paralyzed, staring at the luminosity out over the sea. It was no pearly mirage this time but a harsh glare, krypton-discharge green, rapidly growing in intensity. A farspoken voice emanating from the light spewed obscenities about the aether and addressed Kuhal on the intimate mode:

Why the bloodyhell you been hiding in frogfucking basalt ravine instead of staying in open where I could track you down? We heard your Fiandeathshout allway over in Afaliah!

A Tanu knight all armed in glowing aquamarine and riding an enormous chaliko materialized out of the mist and floated down to earth.

"Celo? Is it you?" Kuhal's physical voice was a cracked whisper.

"Of course it's me, you poor stupid shithead. Who else? I'm the only levitant left with the power to carry another, short of that little gold rapscallion or Tonn the Turncoat. And small chance they'd come and save your ass!"

"I thought . . . Fian and I thought that we were alone. The only ones left."

The fierce old face with its silver brows glowered. Celadeyr of Afaliah sent an inexpert redactive probe into the younger man's deranged mind. "Great Goddess, what an idea! But I don't wonder you thought so, considering the state you're in. We've managed to rescue other survivors, but all from Aven or the European shore. How in Tana's Name did you ever get yourself marooned in Africa?"

But Kuhal did not reply. He had fainted.

The old hero of Afaliah gave vent to his pity in more curses. He spotted the coracle far out on the water and used his creative power to englobe it in a pyre of astral flame. When he had sung the Song for the dead twin, he loaded the living one behind him on the chaliko's broad back and launched them into the air.

12

ELIZABETH RELAXED HER CONCENTRATION AND SMILED. "I'M glad he was finally rescued. Poor man. Imagine him thinking he and his brother were the last Tanu alive."

Creyn could not help the thought: I remember Another who also despaired at being alone.

"I learned how wrong I was." (The deep doubt persisting was far beneath Creyn's perception.)

The Tanu healer reached across the table with his long arm and poured more coffee for both of them. Thunder grumbled around the heights of the Montagne Noire. Rain started again, spraying the small leaded window panes on the eastern side of the chalet until it was impossible to see outside.

"Aside from Culluket," Creyn observed, "Kuhal Earth-shaker is the only High Table survivor of the Host of Nontusvel. The other fifteen members of the Host who escaped the Flood are minor talents."

"I presume that Celadeyr will put Kuhal into the Skin and try to cure him so that he can be enlisted into the disloyal opposition. After all, the Second Lord Psychokinetic would be quite an ally if his powers were restored. What are the odds for full recovery?"

"Not high. The Skin depends not only upon the skill of the practitioner but also upon the patient's own willpower. And Kuhal has lost half his mind. Celo's healer is Boduragol, a

109

competent enough operator—but I doubt whether even Dionket himself could restore Kuhal completely. Even under the most favorable prognosis, he'll be laid up for the better part of a year."

"His power of telepathic projection was almost nil," Elizabeth said. "I had no idea the twins were there in Africa until Kuhal gave that terrible cry last night."

There was a simultaneous flash and explosion as lightning struck Black Crag Lodge for the fourth time that stormy evening. The electrical charge drained harmlessly away.

"With all these atmospherics," Creyn remarked, "I wonder that you're able to farsense to Africa at all. I find that my own mental vision is completely blocked beyond Amalizan. But then, I am not a Grand Master."

She smiled at him, setting down her cup. "No. But it's time I began teaching you some of the specialized techniques of higher farsensing. The static filter is well within your competence, given practice." She demonstrated the program and worked with him, strengthening and correcting, while his wide-field farsight strained to penetrate the ionization of the storm.

Finally, she told him: Enough.

He sank back into his chair, his ageless seraph's face bathed in perspiration. "Yes . . . I see." The mind-tone was rueful. "I also see that I have a depressing amount to learn before I can be of much assistance to you in your surveillance."

"Have some more coffee," she suggested. "It helps. We're lucky that the bush thrives here in the Pliocene! . . . But seriously, you *can* be a real help to me, even now. I'm still not as strong as I was back in the Milieu. I must use a disproportionate amount of effort just to maintain the focus at great distances. You can be an extra set of mental eyes if you link up with me during observation—seeing details I might miss."

"I understand." For a moment his mind was silent, private. "Will my helping you increase your chance of locating Felice?"

Elizabeth's brow tensed. The image of the Raven Girl was ominously clear in both their minds. "Creyn, I don't know what we're going to do about her. She presents the most appalling danger! No metapsychic of the Galactic Milieu possessed such creative and psychokinetic powers. As far as I know, there has never been such potential for physical destruction concentrated in a single individual before."

"Not even in your patron saints? Or their adversaries in the Metapsychic Rebellion?"

"No single operant of our Milieu could have done what Felice did." Rain beat upon the black windows. "Especially that last psychocreative stroke that opened Gibraltar. I never had an opportunity to examine Felice's mind after she attained operancy. But if we could locate her, and if I could do a deep-redact, it's just barely possible that the danger from her could be . . . neutralized." Even though the operation might be fatal to both of us.

Creyn's mind cried out: You must not sacrifice yourself! That is not your destiny! You are to be our guide O Brede Revenant!

"Don't call me that!" she cried, her mind shrinking away. "I don't know my destiny and neither did Brede, damn her!" The old bitterness glared from Elizabeth's subliminal levels. "The Shipspouse was very confident in her self-righteousness . . . but perhaps her transporting you here to Earth was a great objective evil. It seems obvious to me now that you Tanu and Firvulag will survive here on Earth long enough to affect human development in some manner. But my race might have been better off if the lot of you had snuffed each other out a thousand years ago back in the Duat Galaxy!"

"Brede's prescience foresaw a greater good for both races," Creyn said.

"After how much suffering? For how many millions of years?" Elizabeth's voice broke. She had erected a featureless curtain hiding her emotions, but Creyn, as an experienced redactor, perceived the prideful truth.

He said, "If Brede's meddling with the destiny of our races was presumptuous—evil—then surely the manifest results show that her action was a fortunate sin. What your philosophy would call a felix culpa."

Elizabeth's laugh was brittle. "You're getting to know humanity quite well, aren't you? Even to playing our little casuistical games."

"I only know," he said simply, "that the motivation of Brede and her Ship was noble and unselfish. As was her guidance of us until the end."

"We all know she meant well. Even when she dragooned me. A lot of autarchs have been convinced that they knew what was best for their subjects. The human rebels in the Milieu had that sense of conviction. Very top-lofty they were! You see, they knew for a fact that human minds have the greatest metapsychic potential among the races of our galaxy. Therefore, it was logical to them that humanity must play the dominant role in the galactic civilization. Immediately. The Milieu was far too important to be left to the guidance of inferior mentalities ... But the Milieu could not be force-fed into accelerated mental evolution, any more than children could be matured to superadulthood by the insane techniques that the rebels advocated. To force maturation is not only evil but ultimately futile—whether we speak of the advancement of a single child or the perfection of a galactic Mind."

She showed the Tanu healer a brief glimpse of the havoc engendered by Marc Remillard and his cabal, and the price paid to restore mental equilibrium. "And this is why I am afraid ..."

"You see an analogy," he said, "between the Metapsychic Rebellion and Brede's manipulation of Tanu and Firvulag destiny. You fear that if you take Brede's place, you may abet her—sin."

Elizabeth sighed. "If that's what it is ... Back in the Milieu, the Concilium had billions of minds to provide a consensus. The Mind knew it was right, and the rebels were wrong. But what do I know?"

The wind rising outside the chalet made a noise like coursing beardogs on a demonic Hunt. A gust came down the chimney, scattering balsam-scented smoke from the fireplace, and it was Creyn who had to block the swirling ashes, since Elizabeth seemed helpless to deflect them and even welcomed the stinging tears that they evoked. After the distraction, when she had wiped her eyes, the two of them settled down to the serious business of the night.

It was by far the most favorable time for farsearching, when the sun—a much greater obstacle to ultrasensitivity than any storm—was blocked by the mass of the planet. At night a mind could roam more freely, delve more readily into secret places, listen to the remotest whispers, speak most persuasively to the reluctant mind's ear. Even in premetapsychic days this was common folk knowledge: Night was when the sorcerers did their work, when unseelie beings prowled and danced, and when mortal men most fitly let their consciousness rest along with their bodies, breaking free of the day's pain and tedium in dreams.

As Elizabeth's mind linked to that of Creyn, the room around them seemed to dissolve, leaving them suspended above the tempest-washed massif of the Montagne Noire. Concentrating all volitional force into her farsensing faculty, towing him along with her as easily as a kite, she ranged afar.

Observe and learn!

See below us, huddled against Black Crag, small islets of life-aura marking the mining settlements. Concentrate *this* ultrafaculty and zoom in to view individual people, one by one or in small groups. Use *this* power to hear ordinary speech or the declamatory or conversational modes of telepathy. (It is virtually impossible, even for a Grand Master, to probe the deep thought levels at distance. It is also difficult or impossible to farsense a person who has erected a superior thoughtshield. There are certain artificial screening devices—for example, Brede's "room without doors" projector—that similarly block farsight.)

Now observe how we search for a known mind. We have stored its signature, so our coarse searching faculty can range swiftly afar, ignoring all the other auras, until we home in on the sought-for personality. And there he is!

It is Chief Burke, asleep with the other members of his party in a camp just off the Great South Road, some thirty kilometers below Roniah. (Blessings on you, loved brothers and sisters. Rest safely and well.)

And now, Creyn, it is your turn to work. Join me and strengthen me as we attempt a much more difficult search, pinpointing a known mind that is certain to be half-screened and wary. We will do this so insinuatively that he will not detect us. We will make no attempt to eavesdrop upon his words or thoughts.

Range northeast—for he is most likely in residence at his capital of High Vrazel in the Vosges Mountains. See Sharn-Mes, the new young monarch of the Firvulag, who has impudently styled himself High King of the Many-Colored Land.

Behold the doughty general at home . . . His six children roast chestnuts at the fire and use a hot poker to mull another mug of cider for their hard-working daddy. The fierce general wields a sharp obsidian blade, mutters a blood-chilling oath. We are sure of this, even though we can't hear him, from the disapproving expression on the face of his wife, Queen Ayfa, leader of the Warrior Ogresses. Again Sharn's black-glass knife flashes. Chips of wood fly. The axle slips sweetly into its socket and the children cheer. Sharn sets the completed wooden chaliko onto the living-room tiles and the children crowd around the wheeled beast, each one eager to be the first to break tradition by riding the novel toy. Tradition is a frangible and sometime thing in High Vrazel these days . . .

And now let us attempt the most difficult search of all: Felice.

Consider her signature. Consider potential modes of screening. Untrained in metapsychics, her concealment mechanisms would be primitive; but the great creative potential resident in the madwoman makes refinement of technique unimportant. We will not likely succeed in our search. Nevertheless, we will try. On each and every pervigilium we will try.

Range south. South beyond Amalizan, beyond Tarasiah. Curve westerly, afar. Beyond Aluteyn Craftsmaster's new establishment on the River Iberia. Beyond the frowning turrets of Afaliah where the grim old creator-coercer lurks behind strong stone ramparts, brooding over the broken-minded one who now sleeps dreamlessly in Skin.

Soon it will be dawn. The approaching sun is heralded by a distinctive aetheric thunder. There is a program to counter solar ionization, but it is much more difficult than the storm-emendator. Observe and follow. Cling fast and look sharp.

We search! *This* is her aura that we seek, and it is known that she hides in the Betic Cordillera, the southernmost range in Spain. Sweep. Scan. Ignore the fuzzy mental blobs of the Firvulag, of the scattered Howlers, of the tiny colonies of outlaw humans, of the occasional outpost of Afaliah dependents. Focus wide, focus narrow! Use the mind's eye and ear and the special seekersense that tunes only to the aura . . .

There is nothing.

(But why? Sharn was screened, and you found him easily.)

Sharn's powers are those of an infant. But we'll wait. The black bird flies at dawn, and sometimes it calls. When that happens, her mind opens as she listens for him, for her Beloved. She would not respond to us, but she may let fall an inadvertent clue to her eyrie's location. Then we can—

(Elizabeth. *That*.)

I see. I see and hear. Above Mount Mulhacén! Of course . . . She would be holed up there! And now come forth to call.

Culluket!

The raven soars toward the stratosphere. The sky above the Sierra Nevada is cloud-free and lucent in dawn.

Culluket! I know you're alive.

She calls to him who joined with her in mutual thanatophilia, satisfying himself but unaware that her fulfillment would also come, after she had escaped from him, when she did to the helpless earth what had been done to her.

Culluket, answer!

See her wheeling in the high light, glistening. No mind-screens cover her now, no psychocreative wall guards her casting farsense as she seeks the hated love. But he is a redactor, a mind-changer, a mind-borer, a mind-masker. He is guileful and strong and the shadow of the bird passes over him unaware.

Culluket . . . you must be there. Help me to find him, YOU!
(Elizabeth! Has she perceived us?)
No. Creyn, be silent!
You helped me before. I turn again to you now! Help me find my Beloved. Tell me where he is. Talk to me! Do you see me flying here? If you speak to me, this time I'll answer you!
See her triumphal replay of the love-deed, the opening of the Gibraltar Gate. See, through her memory, exactly how the cataclysm was accomplished. O God, how. (In simultaneous relief and shock, for her power was not singular after all, but augmented.)
Help me again. I won't hide from you. We can be friends.
Listen, Creyn! No, wait—I must phase in still another emendator. Not only is this transmission faint, but it is also multiple: an inexpert metaconcerted effort, poorly aimed, coming from a vast distance. And it is not on the exotic thought-mode. Not on the bastard mode of the torced humans here in the Pliocene. It is on the unique human-operant mode . . . God almighty, my own mode! Help me, Creyn. Prop me up, dear friend. Trace this, identify its source, find out anything you can about it . . .

Devils? Is that you?
Yes, Felice.
Hello, Devils.
Hello, Felice. We've called you for such a long time.
I know. But I didn't trust you. I have so many enemies.
Poor Felice. We only want to help. We did help you.
Help me again. Show me where Cull's hiding.
Who? . . . Ah. So. How interesting.
Never mind that. Show me now!
Dear Felice. We would if we could. But we're far away from you. Far from him, too. To find him, we'd have to come to you. All the way from North America.
Ohhhh.
Not to worry. We'll be glad to do it. We've been so anxious to meet you.

*No! You could steal . . . could try to trick me! Just like
that damn little gold swindler, Aiken Drum!*

We wouldn't do that, Felice. We're not like Aiken
or your other enemies. We'll prove our friendship.
We'll do more than find your lover. We'll bring him
to you!

You could do that?

One of us is a coercer-redactor of masterclass stature.
The rest of us are strong, too. And we're young,
Felice. Like you! We believe in action.

You won't mess around with ME.

Of . . . of course not. We want you to be our leader.
You're stronger than any of us.

*Maybe. But when you act together . . . Listen. Only one
of you can come.*

That won't work, Felice. We'll need at least five to
coordinate the retrieval of your Culluket.

Five? All right. But that's all. You understand?

Perfectly. We can help you in other ways, too, you
know. And you can help us! . . . Now indicate your
precise location in Spain.

I'm here. Do you see my lair on Mount Mulhacén?

We do. We'll come to you in fifteen days. Wait for
us. Goodbye, Felice our friend.

Goodbye, Devils.

Elizabeth sat across the table from Creyn. The storm was
gone. Sunbeams from the eastern windows struck the embers
in the hearth, turning them into dusty white lumps.

"When I first arrived in the Pliocene," Elizabeth said, "I
farsearched the entire planet hoping to find other operant human
beings like myself."

"I remember. It was the evening that we rode from Castle
Gateway to Roniah. You put a strong barrier up, but I was
aware that you were ranging."

Elizabeth slumped in her chair, her face haggard. Creyn
sent a telepathic summons to Mary-Dedra, the gold-torc human

woman who had once been a confidant of Mayvar, who now served as Elizabeth's personal attendant.

The farspeaker said, "I detected only a single ambiguous trace on the human mode. It seemed to be clear over on the other side of the Earth. I knew my scan was incompetent because my ultrasenses were still convalescent, and so I dismissed that faint indication as an echo. But it was real."

"You were unable to scrutinize it closely?"

"Long-distance farsensing is a specialized business requiring great stamina. A healthy Grand Master can make brief stabs—something like the way human swimmers make deep skin-dives. But it's impossible to sustain the effort without special supportive equipment or help from a number of other minds." She passed a weary hand over her forehead. "Now, with your help, I should be able to gain some information about these so-called devils. But I know who they must be." God, I know too well.

They shared the knowledge. Creyn said, "They have been out of the Tanu mind for a long time. Twenty-seven years. When the group of operant humans came through the time-gate and contended against our battle-company, we suffered a terrible defeat. The affair was expunged from the official record when the invaders left Europe. Only a few of us—most notably the late Gomnol—actively speculated on what had become of the human operants. We can guess why he would be interested! But Gomnol's farsensing ability was only moderate. He never tracked them down."

"The rebels are in the Western Hemisphere. In a region that was called Florida on Elder Earth." Elizabeth's eyes closed and she drifted in pained abstraction. "I was only seventeen at the time of the Metapsychic Rebellion. An apprentice preceptor on an obscure little snowy planet. But I was already a part of the Unity—and I'll never forget the reaction of those three hundred billion exotic minds to the attempted coup. The Milieu had taken such a *chance* with us, Creyn—admitting humanity to their wonderful civilization while we were still psychosocially immature. And we betrayed their trust."

"I understand that the Rebellion was brief, that the active phase lasted only a few months."

"True. Nevertheless, the scars took years to heal. It was humanity's most profound humiliation . . . The Human Polity acted as ruthlessly as it had to do to put down the conspiracy. There was great suffering among the innocent. In the end, though, the Milieu was stronger than ever."

"Another felix culpa?"

She opened her eyes and regarded the exotic man quizzically. "Human history seems to abound with them."

An inner door opened. Mary-Dedra, carrying a tray with breakfast, entered with a diffident mental greeting. Creyn rose to leave.

"Will you be strong enough to range out again tonight?" he inquired.

"Oh, yes." Elizabeth was resigned. "We'll have to track Felice's devils to their home ground. Count them, identify them positively if we can, then decide how best to counter their threat. You rest up and join me at seven." She smiled mordantly. "Then we'll try our first little trip to hell and gone."

13

In a bayou of the Suwanee on the west coast of Ocala Island, it was two o'clock in the morning. The gigantic silver fish was quiet for the moment, sulking deep in the moon-dappled black water, taking a recess from its contest with Marc Remillard.

For sixteen hours the bulldog tarpon had fought to break free of the pertinacious tether linking it to the man. The tarpon was 430 centimeters long and weighed 295 kilos. Set in one corner of its jaw was a 5/0 hook with a strongly armored leader (for the tarpon of the Pliocene Epoch had sharp teeth). The tippet, that section of the line that actually held the fish, was so weak that it could be snapped by a 7-kilo weight. Nevertheless, the tarpon had been unable to free itself, so great was the skill of the angler who had played it. Now both man and fish were reaching the limits of their endurance. Before long, either the fisherman would make a mistake in judgment, betrayed by his agonized muscles, and the line would break— or the tarpon would succumb to syncope and float helpless at the end of the fatal thread while the gaff descended.

Marc eased the butt of his big flyrod in the heavy leather cup of his belt, waiting for the fish to recommence the fight. The only sounds were distant splashes of leaping mullet and the squawk of a night heron. Marc's breathing was slow and controlled as he exerted a biofeedback maneuver to flush fatigue

120

products from the cells of his burly shoulders and arms. His ultrasenses were deaf and blind. He could not perceive the lurking tarpon's movements because he *would* not. Even at this climactic juncture, he gave the fish the sporting advantage he deemed suitable: He did not track it with farsight, nor attempt to coerce its movements, nor exert any psychokinetic force upon it, nor strengthen rod, reel, or line beyond their normal specifications by means of his creativity. In one way only did Marc deviate from the angling technique of nonmetapsychics: He fished alone, and so he exerted mental power to steady the skiff so that it would not founder during the struggle.

Now Marc was aware of a subtle change in the tension of the line. One moment the water of the channel was as flat as a pool of ink—and the next, it blew open with volcanic violence. An immense writhing shape, glistening under high moonlight, cannoned more than six meters into the air, turning end over end. Its saucer-sized eyes reflected a furious orange and its gill covers rattled like a gigantic raganella.

Marc bowed to the fish, lowering the tip of the fly rod to ease the line while it was vulnerable in the air. The great silver creature crashed back into the water with a splash like a falling grand piano. A split second later it was up again, twisting and thrashing in a second leap. The skiff rocked. Streaming with water from head to toe, Marc shouted encouragement to his adversary. It was the largest tarpon he had ever hooked, and it was nearly his.

The fish ran at him. Marc took in slack. As he expected, the tarpon erupted again, this time in a soaring saltation that carried it on an impact trajectory with the skiff. Laughing uproariously, Marc sent the craft whizzing out of the way— just barely. The tarpon's reentry sent a wave over the gunwale that half filled the boat. Marc banished the water with his PK a moment before the tarpon came up on the opposite side and whirled on the surface like a runaway dynamo, trying to throw the hook.

It went down again and the reel whined as the fish raced for the flats on the left side of the channel. Marc guided the skiff after it, alert for the next leap. And it came, with the enormous plated body climbing up, up, as if in slow motion, tossing diamond drops to the moon in an expanding cloud, clashing its jaws, uttering an explosive grunt at the top of its leap, and then falling back with an impact that nearly sent Marc overboard. But the hook was still secure.

The tarpon ran again and the man followed. The next leap was half-hearted, the great body leaving the water for only a fraction of its length. Its subsequent surface struggles seemed weaker, not even raising foam. Marc could not resist calling out to the fish on the declamatory mode:

Now you gorgeous bastard! Now I've got you . . .

A powerful beam of light stabbed out of the darkness upriver. It transfixed Marc standing there in the boat, ready to make the delicate adjustment of line tension. Physically as well as mentally blind, he froze.

The tarpon leaped.

The fragile 6.75-kilo test tippet snapped.

Papa we've found her we've found Felice!

Too late, the psychoenergetic beacon died. It was Hagen's, as was the thought projection so jubilant and heedless, rapt in its own triumph. The launch carrying the young people came knifing down the bayou, then slammed to a halt as though meeting a glass wall. It fetched up wallowing and shuddering in a mass of chop some 150 meters away from the fisherman.

Off the bow of the skiff, the giant tarpon was rolling, gulping air, savoring freedom. Marc scanned it carefully, making sure it had sustained no serious injury during the long battle, and then disengaged the hook with his PK. The fish sank slowly into the black water. Marc's farsight saw it swim off in the direction of the gulf.

Papa . . .

Cloud knew, even if her brother did not, what their intrusion had cost. Her regret and apology welled out only to strike another barrier. The metapsychic wall that had restrained the launch now dissolved and the current carried the larger craft down upon the skiff.

Marc reeled in the slack line, watching the launch approach. The three other occupants were, as he had expected, the arch-conspirators among the younger generation: Elaby Gathen, Jillian Morgenthaler, and Vaughn Jarrow. These were attempting to put a bold front on their blunder. It was plain that none of them had anticipated anything other than welcome when they sped out from Lake Serene to "surprise" Marc with their news.

The two craft met. Jillian stopped the launch with her PK, dropped the anchor, and ran to the stern to take the skiff in tow. Hagen put the ladder down, mind still asmile, stubbornly determined to tough out the faux pas.

"Felice is in Spain, Papa, just as we suspected. Holed up in a cave on Mount Mulhacén in the Sierra Nevada." Picture. Bearing. "And, get this! She's freely invited us to come to her!"

The wall remained up in Marc's mind. He grasped the ladder and vaulted into the launch, disdaining levitation. The young people fell back, their minds now united clumsily in apology. Only Cloud showed an overlay of genuine sorrow at the loss of the great fish.

The children of rebellion, all in their mid-twenties, were formally dressed. There had been a party that night at Lake Serene, the culmination of which had been the successful contact with Felice. Hagen and Elaby were elegant in tropical dinner jackets; Vaughn, sporting the same outfit, managed to look disheveled and oafish as usual. Dark Jillian wore a batik pareu of soft barkcloth. Cloud's gown was as luminous as her mind, shimmering faintly in the moonlight.

The erstwhile challenger of the galaxy, naked to the waist and barefoot, dripping water onto the polished deck, confronted the five.

"You were told not to come. Never to come when the tarpon are running."

Hagen expostulated, "The hell with the fish, Papa! We've *got* her! Felice—"

He broke off, hands clamped to the sides of his head, screaming. The sharp odor of vomit rose in the warm night air, and in the aether was the stench of terror as Hagen saw for the first time the true aspect of Abaddon. But then came Cloud, rushing at their terrible father with her sweet coercion fully arrayed and her redactive faculty flung wide to curtain the worst of the reality, and dull its memory.

Hagen staggered backward and fell into the arms of Elaby and Vaughn. The fisherman, his mind veiled again, waited. Under Cloud's ministry Hagen's retching and his sobs quieted. He steadied on his feet, pulled away from the others, and stood swaying, covered in filth.

"Papa—you—must—listen," he gasped.

Marc had to smile at the persistence. The slight cleft in his chin was emphasized by oblique moonlight and the shadows made his heavy brows appear winged. The thick curly hair that lately had become frosted in defiance of his self-rejuvenating faculty was still sopping wet. False tears of salt water shone on his prominent cheekbones and the thin-bridged nose with its finely flared nostrils.

Marc refused to accept the data proffered by Hagen's mind. "Tell me," he demanded.

"She—she's agreed to let us come to Europe. To meet with her. We promised we would help her locate and destroy some Tanu redactor who put her to the torture. Papa—you've got to let us go!"

The mind-vise settled softly into place once again and exerted minimal pressure, causing the young man to catch his breath in apprehension. He was a less emphatically drawn replica of his father, without Marc's bull neck and dark-socketed eyes. Like his sister, Hagen had inherited the reddish-gold hair of the long-dead Cyndia Muldowney—and her reckless perseverance as well. "It's a priceless opportunity for us! Felice can be manipulated, I tell you. If we can trick her into accepting some of your docilization equipment, then Elaby and Jillian and Cloud and I have the watts to pin her down! It'll be dangerous, since she'll only let five of us get close to her. But if you advise us on tactics through farspeech, I know we can bag her."

The brain-screws tightened. Hagen groaned and clenched his fists until the nails bit into his palms. He felt Cloud's ameliorating redaction ready itself to assume the full painburden if need be.

"Five of you," Marc repeated.

"Only five can come, she said. I don't know whether she's telling the truth about being able to detect any extras, but we daren't chance it."

"You and Cloud, Elaby and Jillian—and Vaughn for the farspeech conferences, I presume."

"Yes."

The gentle one-sided smile grew more chilling. "And what will you do with the dragon—presuming you can subdue her?"

"Use her to dominate Europe! To force Elizabeth to raise all of us to adept status—full coadunation!" Papa we can't stay here rotting with you oldones we can't we won't we'll die here on this damnisland!

The mind-clamp eased. Marc spoke mildly. "I had planned to begin training you this summer to assist me in the star-search. Of all the second generation, you have the greatest potential competence—the stamina combined with broad-spectrum metafunction."

"Damn you!" screamed Hagen Remillard. "Won't you ever admit that there's *nobody out there*? This Pliocene galaxy's too immature for coadunation of its Mind! You're alone, Papa— you and the rest of them. And we're alone with you! This Elizabeth is some kind of a Grand Master preceptor who can at least put us on the first steps toward coadunation right here on Earth."

Marc turned to his daughter. "And you think that my way is futile, too?"

She threw open her uttermost mental depths: Yes Papa. There is no coadunate nonhuman race in this galaxy to rescue us from exile. All that there is is here.

"And you support this kidnapping foray? This buccaneer's raid?"

Cloud turned away, walls again in place, voice incisive. "There are other human beings in Europe. People of our culture, who would sympathize with our aims. Now that the Flood has undermined the Tanu society, it seems likely that the entire region will fall under Firvulag domination if we don't intervene. And the Firvulag are operants, Papa. Remember that. Their mental development has been stalled by pig-headed custom up until now, and they've never learned to act in true metaconcert because of individualist traditions. But their attitudes are changing rapidly. Even if the Tanu are led by Aiken Drum, they are too greatly outnumbered by the Firvulag to prevail. But humans and Tanu together could withstand the Firvulag easily with our help."

"And with some of the weaponry you have stored away," Hagen added.

Marc said, "There is something else in Europe."

The five young people stared at him.

"The site of the temporal singularity. The time-gate."

Opacity.

"Your real ambition is to reopen it. From *this* side. That's the ultimate goal of this entire adventure! Did you really think you could conceal the truth from me?"

Resignation, a perverse relief, flooded Hagen's mind. "Of course you're right, Papa. We'd do anything to have what you threw away!... Now kill me if you think it'll help coerce the others into believing in you. But it won't, you know."

Before Marc could react, Elaby Gathen thrust Hagen aside. His thought-projections burst forth in a compelling blaze, as irresistible as it was unexpected, staying Abaddon's wrath just long enough to provoke curiosity and a wry appreciation. In that illuminating instant, Marc knew that the plan of conquest, the search for Felice, the time-gate design—all of it—was not Hagen's conception at all, but Elaby's. Elaby Gathen the unobtrusive one, the efficient one, the synthesizing one. The clever one who now waited with mind wide-open for Marc's redactive probe (and who did not flinch at the brutality of it). Elaby Gathen who dared to love his daughter and exert puppetmastery over his son. In the young man's mind was sincere respect for the leader of the Metapsychic Rebellion, together with regret for the great dream gone agley. But there was also in Gathen a determination, as implacable as Marc's own, that he and his young contemporaries be given the chance to direct their own fate.

Marc said, "I wish I had noticed you before. Before all this had solidified."

Elaby Gathen said, "Sir, we have Guderian's entire body of data in the computer archives. We have the technological parameters and the manufacturing specs for all components of the device. If we gained control of Europe, we'd have access not only to the time-gate site, but to the raw materials Guderian used, the rare earths and the niobium and cesium that are inaccessible in Pliocene North America. Based in Europe, we could compel the assistance of whatever Milieu technicians still survive among the time-traveler population. It would take time and organization, but Guderian's device could be built."

Marc laughed. "Thus effectively setting up a *two-way gate*. And you expect me to agree to this? The agents of the Magistratum have no interest in you children. But I assure you that even after twenty-seven years, they would have a lively interest in me!"

Elaby's mind and voice evoked the most exquisite tact. "After we've passed through to the Milieu, we would naturally arrange for the destruction of both pieces of apparatus. The sites themselves could be obliterated. You know that there's a unique geological factor at work in the generation of the singularity, restricting it to that small region of the Rhône Valley. If the geology is significantly altered, the time-gate will be permanently closed."

"You'd still be safe, Papa," Cloud said, moving close to Elaby. "And we..." Her voice trailed away, but her mental speech completed the phrase: We could go home.

Elaby Gathen said, "You could supervise the demolitions on the Pliocene end of the time-warp yourself, sir."

The launch turned on its cable. The tide was rising in the estuary, countering the sluggish flow of the Suwanee. Soon the tarpon would leave their feeding in the gulf reefs and come up the river again. But Marc had lost interest in the big fish now. The frustration coming just at the brink of victory had left him tight-coiled and cheated of catharsis. He had failed to master the adversary, and now it was gone. To begin all over again was insupportable.

Gathen was outlining his scheme with cool reasonableness. "We'll need two days to gather equipment and finish stocking Jillian's ketch in Manchineel Bay. The actual voyage to Europe will take up to eleven days. Phil says the Atlantic weather systems are perfect. There'll be no adverse winds to counter our PK. Vaughn will keep you informed of our every move. Once we've contacted Felice, you can advise us precisely how you wish us to carry on."

Marc said, "All of you may go—except Hagen."

"Papa—no!" the son cried.

The eyes of Abaddon burned under winged brows. "This escapade is highly dangerous—foolhardy, even. You have badly underestimated Felice. But I know her only too well, since I was the one who forged the metaconcert linkage. Your plan of binding her with the docilization equipment is futile. None of the devices would hold her—any more than they'd hold me! . . . You'd have to use guile, act on her unsane aspects and force her to chain herself."

His mind turned to Cloud: You would have the redactive skill Daughter virtually equal to my own. I am not sure you would have the courage.

She replied: Papa I would do anything to reach this goal.

I know.

His cast of mind darkened, sorrowing. He would have to let her go, even if this venture led to her death. He dared not risk her taking Cyndia's way. The daughter was lost. But the son—

"Why must I stay here?" Hagen demanded truculently.

"In case the others fail. There must be a successor for the star-search."

The young man raged, "You old fool! Can't you ever stop living in a dream world? I'll be damned if I spend the rest of my life shackled to that fucking equipment, hunting for something that doesn't exist!"

The other four drew back, appalled. There was an intolerable flash of light and a gush of heated air. Hagen's body wavered, melting in the effulgence. His cries rose in pitch, changing to harsh, rhythmic hisses. Something huge and silvery, burning in a coat of astral fire, fell over the stern of the launch with a colossal splash.

Marc said to Elaby, "You will take Owen Blanchard with you to Europe in Hagen's place. He was the best of my coercers in the Rebellion and he'll do for a backup farsensor in the all too possible event that something happens to Vaughn, here. Owen will carry my own authority, and he'll see that I receive an accurate account of your actions."

"But, sir, he's so frail," Elaby began to say.

"Then you'll take very special care of him!" Marc thundered. "Blanchard goes."

"Yes, sir."

Cloud's mind was weeping. "Papa, poor Hagen . . ."

Marc's hand suddenly held a severed leader with a big artificial fly dangling from it. Among the grizzly streamers and scarlet hackle was a glint of pointed steel. "Don't worry about him. I've decided to begin training him tonight instead of waiting until summer."

Out on the black water, a tarpon rolled and gulped air, making a patch of glistering bubbles. The fish's scales had an eerie luminescence. Marc Remillard observed the creature with satisfaction. He began to climb over the transom back into his skiff.

"I'm sure Hagen will be ready to settle down and apply himself to his education. After he's had a little time on the hook."

THE END OF PART ONE

PART II

THE
GRAND
LOVING

1

IN THE EARLY WEEKS OF THE POSTDILUVIUM, SUGOLL OF Meadow Mountain sought and obtained full franchise for his subjects, the deformed outcast Firvulag known as Howlers. These mutants, who had split off from the main body of Little People some hundreds of years previously, now once again pledged fealty to the Firvulag throne at High Vrazel and ratified the election of the co-monarchs Sharn and Ayfa. Sugoll also agreed to abide by the Firvulag-Lowlife Entente engineered by the late Madame Guderian and King Yeochee IV, as well as the armistice between the Tanu and Firvulag that had been promulgated by the usurper, Aiken Drum.

Because of the isolated location of his domain east of the Black Forest Range, Sugoll remained unaware that Firvulag forces continually violated both peace accords all during the winter months, attacking Tanu cities and Lowlife settlements and putting the blame on renegade Howlers. King Sharn and Queen Ayfa otherwise gave little serious thought to their remote mutant subjects until early in January, when the following communication was delivered to High Vrazel:

TO THEIR APPALLING HIGHNESSES AYFA AND SHARN-MES, Sovereign Lords of the Heights and Depths, Monarchs of the Infernal Infinite, Mother and Father of All Firvulag, and Undoubted Rulers of the Known World

133

FELICITATIONS FROM SUGOLL, Lord of Meadow Mountain and Chief Among Those Called Howlers, Your Obedient Vassal.

May I humbly invite you to rejoice with me upon the occasion of my nuptial celebration, in which the Most Exalted Creative Lady Katlinel the Darkeyed, late of the Tanu High Table, condescended to become my spouse, for which grace praise be to Téah the Almighty.

Know now, Highnesses, of a matter of gravity that has claimed my attention for many months and lately approaches full resolution: In times preceding the last Grand Combat there came to my lands an expedition of Humans under mandate of your lamented predecessor, Yeochee IV, seeking the site of the legendary Ship's Grave. A certain scientist of this party vouchsafed to me information that has proved to be of vital import to my people.

Namely: That our principal settlements in and about the Water Caves of Meadow Mountain have inadvertently been located adjacent to deposits of dangerously radioactive minerals; and these have, in the course of our centuries of sojourn, affected the germ plasm of my people, occasioning deleterious mutations whose melancholy manifestations are only too well known.

The hypothesis of this scientist was subsequently confirmed by another. Lord Greg-Donnet Genetics Master aka Gregory Prentice Brown, formerly of Muriah and now an honored citizen of Meadow Mountain, who was paramount among the human genetic specialists in the Many-Colored Land and who once held a prestigious position in a noted medical school of the Galactic Milieu.

Greg-Donnet has, during the past month, undertaken an analysis of our situation with a view toward amelioration. You will rejoice with us, Highnesses, when I tell you that there is indeed hope now for our poor afflicted people. Some might be restored to an approximately normal aspect through a modification of the Tanu "Skin" healing technique if suitable practitioners among our erstwhile Foe can be persuaded to cooperate with us. Others of our mutant subjects must look to the future, which may see the normalization of generations yet unborn by the abolition of teratogenetic factors, by genetic engineering, and by other eugenic measures—some of which may be implemented even now under your benevolent auspices.

Know, Highnesses, that Greg-Donnet has declared that we must go forth from this hazardous dwelling place into lands free from radioactive contamination. We have resolved, therefore, to quit our domain here in Meadow Mountain just as soon as the rains abate, and to present ourselves to you in High Vrazel—loyal subjects prepared to occupy such demesnes as it may please you to grant us for resettlement.

Know further that Greg-Donnet advises that our pool of damaged genes must be reconstituted with an influx of normal Firvulag germ plasm, this to be an adjunct of the more difficult genetic engineering operations, which must await the training of skilled technicians. To this view, our people avow to you that they hereby renounce the old antagonism that precluded social and sexual intercourse between us and our normal brothers and sisters.

At this year's Grand Loving of Firvulag, I intend to lead forth in the mating rituals a contingent of winsome virgins from our most distinguished families, who will take husbands in the traditional manner from the ranks of your stalwart lads. The damsels will, of course, be adorned with the most alluring of illusory bodies, and they will come lavishly dowered with Meadow Mountain's considerable material substance. As a further expression of our affection, gratitude, and goodwill, and so that all Little People may share with us our joy at reunion with long-separated kinfolk, we are prepared to underwrite

the entire expense of this year's Grand Loving of Firvulag.

Expect us at High Vrazel about two weeks after the spring
equinox. At that time you will doubtless have selected
a suitable site for our habitation, as well as given thought
to the matter of interim fosterage of the brides with the
families of suitable bridegrooms-elect.

I am, ever at your service, Highnesses, SUGOLL.

"I call that nerve!" exclaimed Sharn, fetching his writing-desk
a smash with one massive fist. Sealing wax and account books
and memo-plaques and a twenty-second-century voicewriter and
the King's favorite goblet (the one made from Lord Velteyn's
skull) went dancing over the polished oak planks. "Call in that
Howler courier, dammit! I'll give him a return reply that'll zorch
that misbegotten Sugoll from his stinking deformed toenails to
his horny crested occiput! Move in on us, will he? And with a
sex-mad mob of monster brides I'm to foist off on our people at
the Loving? Ten thousand tumbling turds!"

"But he sounds rich," Afya remarked meditatively. Sitting
at her own desk adjacent to that of her husband, she nibbled
the end of a silver Parker pen with delicate pointed teeth.

The royal study deep inside Grand Ballon Mountain in the
fog-bound Vosges was cosy and bright, warmed by a big brass
brazier that glowed within a free-standing ceramic stove shaped
like a hollow turnip. A sideboard still held remains of the royal
lunch, taken today in camera. The walls were hung with a
judicious selection of captured banners and Tanu weaponry,
spoils of the last Combat. Fat candles that incorporated three
wicks in each waxy barrel illuminated the twin desks.

"That shambling bastard won't get away with taking me for
granted," Sharn snarled. "Does he think he's dealing with a
caretaker monarch like poor old Yeochee?"

"*We* are the monarch," said the handsome ogress with the
apricot-colored hair. "And I find Sugoll's letter intriguing."
She retrieved the piece of vellum with her psychokinesis from
where Sharn had flung it to the floor. "Resettlement. H'mm."

"There's no room for them here in High Vrazel. There must be seven, eight hundred monsters up on Meadow Mountain! We'll have to try to divert them down to Famorel, in the Alps. Or maybe to the Grotto Wilderness, or even Koneyn. Té on a tightrope! As if we don't have enough trouble keeping the hinterlanders in line. Now we'll get a fresh batch of headstrong types who'll want to do things their own way, and never mind how it screws up my royal strategy!"

"Nionel." Queen Ayfa smiled at the letter. "That's where they must go."

Sharn's great mouth snapped shut, aborting another tirade. His brows hoisted. His mind sent a gout of joyous appreciation splattering over his wife's psyche. She smiled indulgently. He bellowed, "Nionel! Of course! Refurbishing and staffing the place will keep those Howlers gainfully employed for years. We can have the Loving there in May, and then later on, this fall—"

"The new Games. On our own Field of Gold at last."

They embraced mentally, savoring the delicious suitability of it. Sugoll and his horde, undoubtedly wealthy, would be an asset to the Firvulag if they could be persuaded to repopulate and restore the ghost city of Nionel in the western wilderness, near the Paris Basin. Within Nionel's ambit lay the ritual battleground of the Little People, which had been virtually abandoned during the forty years that the Tanu had dominated the annual Grand Combat.

"It's the only logical place to hold this year's Games," Sharn said. "Even if that treacherous little torcless cockerel did steal victory from us at the last minute, there's no way he can prepare a suitable Tanu fighting ground this year. And the White Silver Plain is under fifty-five meters of salt water."

"If we couch the offer diplomatically, I think Aiken will agree. And there's your idea for donating a new trophy in place of the lost Sword to sweeten the deal . . . Oh, yes. This is all going to work out splendidly!"

"There's still one dead mouse in the skilligalee, Ayfe. The damned brides."

Ayfa considered. "They *might* be presentable. If their shape-shifting powers are sufficiently strong. And they'll have the doweries. Besides—how many of them can there be? Probably only twenty or thirty, given the size of the Howler gathering that the Lowlife Guderian reported to Fitharn. Surely we have that many families who'd be eager to get off our shit-list by making marriages of convenience."

"Yes," he mused. "It could be worked out. It'll *have* to be. We really can't afford to antagonize this upstart Sugoll, you know. Aside from staving off civil war, we mustn't forget that he's the one who knows the route to the Ship's Grave. One of these days, that information might be extremely useful."

FROM SHARN AND AYFA, High King and High Queen of the Many-Colored Land

TO SUGOLL, Lord of Meadow Mountain, our Beloved and Loyal Vassal: GREETINGS.

It was with pleasure as well as sympathy that we received your letter informing us of your recent marriage and your hopes for assuaging your genetic disability.

Come ahead to High Vrazel, and welcome! We do indeed have in mind an ideal new home for you and your people, which we will describe fully upon your arrival here.

You do us great honor by offering your doubtless charming daughters as brides-elect in the Grand Loving ceremonies. This matter, also, will be taken up in detail upon your arrival.

Convey our heartfelt hopes for happiness and reproductive satisfaction to the eager damsels. To your people we send our affection and assurance of continuing concern; and to you and your illustrious Spouse, the Lady Katlinel, our royal benison and the enclosed tokens of esteem, which might prove useful on your journey should you encounter any of the pestilential hyenas or amphicyons that unfortunately infest the regions west of the Rhine. Read the directions carefully before using.

We call your attention to the simplified mode of royal
address that we have adopted.

AYFA, HIGH QUEEN   Encl: 3 Solar-Powered
SHARN-MES, HIGH KING   Stun-Guns,
                                          Husqvarna
                                          Mark VI-G

With the satisfactory response from the Firvulag throne in hand,
Sugoll set in motion the monster ingathering; for Sharn and
Ayfa were mistaken in their belief that only mutants from the
Feldberg area would be coming to High Vrazel. Many other
concentrations of Howlers, who had drifted away from the
radioactive caves of the heartland over a period of centuries,
had learned about the hopeful genetic prognosis of Greg-Donnet—and they were determined to share in it.

Bundling up their portable wealth, pathetic and hideous
creatures forsook hamlets deep in Fennoscandia, trekking
southward through the Amber Lakes where the winter nights
were long and warm under perpetually cloudy skies. Other
throngs of Howlers converged on Meadow Mountain from the
haunted Swabian and Franconian Alb, and from the mineral-
rich highlands of the Erzegebirge and far Bohemia. These latter
brought with them quantities of jewels and precious metals,
which they were accustomed to mine sheerly for the sake of
their beauty, using them to decorate their twisted bodies in
ironic splendor. Mutants from the Hercynian Forest west of
the Rhine, mostly solitary and poverty-stricken, responded to
Sugoll's invitation as best they could. They made their painful
way through the Vosges and the Schwarzwald to the subter-
ranean villages of the Feldberg, where compassionate Katlinel
housed them in the dry upper caves, fattened them up, and
provided them with fine new clothes. All of the able-bodied
were put to work building boats or preparing supplies, in anticipation of the time when the meteors announced the advent
of Pliocene spring.

Finally the star-showers fell, the rains ended, and the underground rivers beneath the Feldberg dropped to navigable

levels. Everything was in readiness. The great Howler Migration commenced.

Ten days after the equinox, rank after rank of mutants, all well dressed and bearing whatever treasure they possessed, marched to the awesome borehole called Alliky's Shaft. Following a brief invocation to Téah by Sugoll, the lift machinery began to creak and the big buckets descended with parties of torch-bearing travelers: males and females, hermaphrodites and neuters, children and old folks, the diabolically misshapen and the quasi-normal—Howlers all, singing an ululating farewell that floated up out of the depths like some chorus of the damned.

Disembarking at the lowest level of Meadow Mountain's mineworkings, they tramped past heaps of garnets, yellow and pink beryls, and green tourmaline crystals that lay about in neglected profusion. The people then formed into single file and descended still deeper into the granite bowels of the Feldberg, along natural crevices in living rock where the torches smoked in the chilly damp and tinkling water-drips punctuated the eerie Howler song.

At last they came to a great underground chamber. Tubs of flaming oil blazed all along a newly constructed quay on the shore of a lake as black as a sheet of onyx. Here was massed an enormous flotilla of sturdy punts, manned by monstrous boatmen equipped with poles. Still holding their firebrands high and singing, the people climbed on board. With Sugoll's ornate craft leading the way, the boats glided off one by one until a torchlit train extended over the water as far as the eye could see, heading into impenetrable darkness.

It was a journey that few Howlers had ever made before. Beneath the Feldberg's mass were uncounted Water Caves with springs and dark cascades and streamlets and siphons in bewildering complexity. The upper levels were well explored, as were the underground tributaries to the Paradise and Ystroll Rivers; but only a few hardy adventurers had ever dared to cross the Black Lake, and these were long dead, leaving only half-remembered tales of what lay ahead.

Katlinel's farsight, limited underground, was their sole means of navigation. The boats entered a natural tunnel, wide but with a low ceiling. The torches struck wavering gleams from wet mineral formations. The singing echoed and reechoed off the walls until the people finally fell silent in confusion and dismay. Then Katlinel, to divert them, opened her mind and told stories of the Tanu world and that of the normal Firvulag, climaxing with the momentous events of the last Grand Combat and the Flood, which she had learned of from the farspeech of surviving members of her Creator Guild.

After five hours the fleet halted at a suitable place for the people to rest and eat. Then the journey resumed with a fresh crew of boatmen, and Lord Greg-Donnet took over as chief entertainer, lecturing telepathically for hour after hour on the mutagenic effects of hard radiation and on bioengineering techniques for repairing damaged chromosomes. The torches guttered out one by one, passengers in the boats fell into a doze, and presently the only sounds were the swish and thump of punt poles, the splashing of water, and muffled whimpers from the sleeping children.

More hours passed. Sugoll and Katlinel sat side by side in the bow of the leading boat while Greg-Donnet snoozed on a pile of leather cushions behind them. The Lord and Lady of the Misbegotten shared their hopes and fears on the intimate thought-mode, giving comfort to each other and even laughing over the surprise that awaited King Sham and Queen Ayfa. The monster ingathering had swelled the Howler number prodigiously, until at the end, instead of the original 700 or so denizens of Meadow Mountain, the emigrants totaled nearly 9000. Of these, 1256 were virgins of marriageable age.

About fifteen hours after leaving the Black Lake, the wakeful travelers were conscious of moving air that carried scents of humus and green growing things rather than sterile wet rock. Sleepers stirred and came alert. The children began to chatter and whisper. Interrogative howls passed from one boat to another, up the line and down. Finally, Katlinel's farsight was able to confirm that they were, indeed, approaching the river's outlet.

Ahead shone a wan glimmer. The boatmen leaned to their

poles, propelling the craft as swiftly as they could around one last lengthy curve. A thin screen of boughs hung over the cave's mouth. Katlinel stood up, fingers pressed to the golden torc at her throat, and pruned the ramage away with an invisible blade of psychoenergy. Severed branches tumbled harmlessly into the water and the boats drifted into open air. They emerged from the base of a great forested cliff into a land silvered by the moon. Steppes clothed with rippling grass stretched away on either hand. Near the river were groves of majestic flabellaria fan palms and weeping willows.

The Howler people in the crowded punts began to shape-shift spontaneously, as if eager to mask their deformities now that they had finally left the caves. The horned and crested horror who had sat beside Katlinel from the journey's beginning now metamorphosed into a tall humanoid as handsome as any Tanu, wearing a jewel-studded hunter's jerkin and a peaked cap surmounted by a small coronet.

Sugoll asked his wife, "Now that we are beyond the dense rock formations, is your farsense able to trace the course of this river to its confluence?"

She exerted her metafaculty, ranging southward for a few score kilometers. "Yes, I see it. There's a truly enormous river down there. It comes from the east, from a great lake in the Helvetides. Not far from its confluence with this stream, it makes a right-angle curve and flows northward." She showed the mental picture to Greg-Donnet.

"Oh, it's the Rhine, all right," said Crazy Greggy cheerily. "Just as we hoped. All we have to do now is float on down to the landing at the High Vrazel trailhead—and then on to Nibelheim itself!"

"How long do you think it will take us to reach the landing?" Sugoll asked Katlinel.

She concentrated. "Less than a day. The river flows swiftly with the spring runoff from the Alps. We could camp here for the rest of the night, then continue in the morning. These meadowlands should be reasonably safe from predatory animals, and I detect no sentient life whatsoever."

"If anything comes sniffing around," Greggy said fiercely,

"we can give it a blast from those presents that Sharn and Ayfa sent. Wherever do you suppose they got such contraband? Of course, it was an open secret that time-travelers did smuggle in forbidden armaments and other goodies—but we privileged humans assumed that the Tanu destroyed them. What fascinating food for speculation!" He began to giggle. "How I'd *love* to zap me a hoe-tusker! Bring ten tons of gubbertushed elephant crashing at my feet!" Wistfully, he appended, "In Muriah, I never ever got to go on Hunts. The Tanu said I was too valuable."

"And so you are, Greggy." Sugoll had been issuing telepathic commands, directing the boats to shore. Now he smiled down on the dapper little geneticist. "You are valuable to us as well. I'll see that you get to stalk some big game at a suitable time. But you must promise not to go haring off on your own. Losing you would be a catastrophe."

The elderly man was quick with reassurances. He glanced around at the grounding punts and the passengers disembarking in the moonlight. "I think you all look perfectly splendid in your illusory bodies! And you and Katy make a wonderful couple, Sugoll."

The Howler lord's brow creased slightly. "You can discern no shadow of our true monstrous shapes?"

"Not a trace! Not a—a debilissima!"

"Let us hope," Sugoll said, "that our disguises prove as impenetrable to the Firvulag royalty. And to the bridegrooms at the Grand Loving."

"Nine *thousand*?" Sharn croaked brokenly. "O Goddess."

"The riverguards counted 'em twice, Appalling One," said Fitharn. "There seem to be well over a thousand virgins, too. All shiny red boots and flower garlands with ribbons, and so stiff with opals and sapphires and rubies that they can barely stagger."

"But how do they *look*?" Ayfa inquired grimly.

Fitharn paused. He pursed his lips, screwed up his eyes, scratched one ear, and resettled his conical hat. Silence grew.

"Well?" demanded the royal ogress. "Can you tell?"

"In a dark bedroom, Majesty, if one were very horny—"

Sharn groaned. "That bad?"

"Their shiftings are ingenious and attractive, Appalling Ones, but I'm afraid they wouldn't deceive a true Firvulag for a gnat's eyeblink."

"We can't risk having an official reception for them here in the Hall," Ayfa decided. "There'd be a riot."

"At the least," the King sighed.

"If you want my advice," Fitharn said, "head 'em off before they ever get to High Vrazel. Meet 'em on the trail with a slap-up picnic feast, plenty of musicians and liquor, and a welcoming committee of trustworthy nobles and their ladies, primed to be tactful. (Don't ask any with eligible sons, of course.) Give this pack of monsters what my old friend Chief Burke would call a schmooze-job! Chat 'em up. Tell 'em you want to save an inconvenient side trip to High Vrazel—where all the palace jakes are on the blink! After all, they'll have far enough to go, marching to Nionel through the Belfort Gap."

Ayfa broke in. "We can tell them all about their fine new home. Show them mind-pictures! Promise them discounts on materials for the renovation! Send them off with plenty of pack animals and riding stock to ease their journey."

"Not my new herds of chalikos and hellads!" wailed the King.

"You can steal more," his wife said firmly. "This is an emergency. The quicker that mob of wretched little spriggans is out of the Vosges, the better."

Sharn shook his great head helplessly. "But we're only postponing the problem—not solving it. So far, our own people know very little about this migration. But what are we going to do, come May? We've agreed to let the Howlers sponsor the Loving!"

"We'll think of something by then," Ayfa said soothingly. "And besides—you and I won't be around then. Don't you recall? We're going to spend the Grand Loving this year with Aiken Drum and Mercy-Rosmar and what's left of the Tanu flower and chivalry over in Goriah."

"Well, Té be thanked for small favors. All I'll have to worry about down there is assassination!"

"Shall I put arrangements for the fancy picnic in train, then?" Fitharn asked.

"Do so," Sharn commanded, all business again. "That's a fine idea of yours, Fitharn. And you're coming, too, as master of ceremonies. Get out your best clothes and the gold pegleg studded with bloodstones. We're going to pamper and flatter that army of abominations until they're giddy. They're never going to suspect that we're all throwing up inside!... Do you think they brought their treasure?"

"The riverguards reported that the Howler horde is well supplied with strongboxes and locked pouches."

Ayfa gave a great sigh of contentment. "Then everything is going to be all right after all."

And so the festive meeting took place near the headwaters of the Onion River south of High Vrazel, in a pretty part of the forest where the bulbuls sang amid the giant ferns and blossoming trees dropped petals on a scene of rustic splendor. The King and Queen of the Firvulag, sixty of their most discreet courtiers, an honor guard of Warrior Ogres and Ogresses, and almost the entire strength of the royal culinary corps starred in a day-long fête champêtre that completely overawed the innocent Howlers.

Plied with food and drink, woozy from overindulgence in the psychoactive hooby mushrooms, the emigrants responded enthusiastically to the proposal that they repopulate Nionel. The royal donation of some 400 fully trapped chalikos, twice that number of draft hellads with carts, and a breeding herd of the recently tamed little hipparions provoked transports of maudlin gratitude among the besotted monsters. After a nice show of reluctance, Sharn and Ayfa agreed to accept their joint weight in gemstones as a partial down payment on delinquent taxes owed by the Howler nation to the throne over the past 856 years.

The matter of bride-fosterage among the noble Firvulag families was delicately skirted. This custom, Sugoll was told, had fallen into decline among the nonmutant populace; and given the large number of nubile Howler females, there would be considerable awkwardness reinstating it at the present time. Smoothly, the two monarchs declared that the brides would be far happier (and more useful) accompanying their own families to Nionel. There they could not only participate in the work force, but also prepare connubial dwellings to share with their new spouses. At the Grand Loving, the Howler damsels would celebrate the mating rituals just as other Firvulag maidens did, the girls and boys pairing off on a basis of mutual selection. Queen Ayfa pooh-poohed fears that the mutant brides would be at a disadvantage. It was true that their numbers were disproportionally great; however, she would personally extend Loving invitations to the most remote enclaves of "wild" Firvulag—those only nominally loyal to the throne—insuring an extra supply of grooms. If some of the Howler beauties went unclaimed this year, they would surely be snapped up at subsequent celebrations once word of their charm and generous endowment got round the Many-Colored Land.

Upon this gracious note, the royal party took its leave. Sugoll, feeling a mountain of anxiety lifted from his shoulders, retired to his cloth-of-gold pavilion after decreeing a two-day period of rest and recuperation. All over the littered picnic grove, happily fuddled mutants collapsed snoring, reassuming their usual forms once they drifted into slumber.

Only Katlinel and Greg-Donnet remained awake. As the moon went down and bonfires died out, the stately hybrid woman and the wispy academic in the clawhammer coat took lanterns and walked among the people to see that all were safe. Heaps of deformed and grotesque bodies, incongruous in rich clothing, lay in Dantean disarray on the trampled grass. There were empty flagons and dirty dishes everywhere.

After they had walked awhile, Greg-Donnet said, "You didn't tell Sugoll, then?"

"I couldn't bear to. Not yet. He's suffered such terrible worries all through the winter—and then the trip, and wondering about our new home. He was afraid Sharn would want to banish our people to some horrible wilderness like Albion!

Nionel will be a paradise in comparison. No . . . we must let him regain his spirits before telling him the bad news. And don't you let any hint leak out, Greggy, or I shall be very cross with you."

"No fear, no fear." The geneticist shook his marmosetlike head. "The King and Queen and their people put a very good face on it, I must say. But as I wandered about, I picked up a good many intimations of disaster. And you, my dear, with your redactive faculty, must have known the truth almost at once."

"I suppose it was only logical," Katlinel said. "Howlers can see through each other's illusions easily enough. And they and the Firvulag share the same metapsychic pattern."

Greg-Donnet gave a mournful sigh. "Only humans and nonredactive Tanu would fail to penetrate the disguises. Poor little loathly brides! Well—it was only a small part of the eugenic scheme, merging the gene pools. There's still the engineering and the possibility of using Skin."

"But the people will be humiliated at the Grand Loving! Who knows what they might do? Oh, Greggy, it's such a shame."

She paused, lifting her lantern high. Nestled together under a sheltering willow tree were three hideous little beings, pipestem limbs entwined, goblin faces relaxed and peaceful. They wore bejeweled kirtles, flower headbands, and little red boots.

2

PERCHED ON A LONE TREE IN THE MIDST OF THE BLOOMING savanna, the raven watched a pair of sabertooth cats cooperate in stalking their prey. The small herd of antidorcas gazelles, fawn-colored and lyre-horned, grazed on obliviously until the male machairodus spooked them by dashing out of a clump of high grass. They fled downwind and the female cat, lying in ambush, sprang. Almost nonchalantly she grappled with one of the gazelles and ripped its neck open with a slash of her ten-centimeter canines. Her mate bounded up, eager for his share.

While the prey still struggled, the raven flew down, on fire with the old lust. The cats withdrew before her coercive blast and crouched, snarling and hissing, as the predatory bird attacked one of the gazelle's great black eyes. The beak struck like an ebon dagger. The animal's back arched and stiffened, and then it subsided, dead. The raven drank the aqueous humor and fed on blood.

But there was no electric release. Never, as there used to be at the death.

She flew back to her perch and swayed there, logy and miserable, watching the indignant machairodus cats return to begin their meal. No pleasure! Never any more. Never the old surge of hot psychoenergy as the victim fell, confirming her power. There were small joys to be found in the gleaning of the gold, and comfort from the faithful friends on Mount Mul-hacén. But never the glorious fulfillment. Not even when she had penetrated the world.

It was his fault.

The sun above her expanded to a sanguine whirling thing. She gripped the branch and felt her mind lurch, her guts heave and disgorge clotted dark liquids. Suddenly nerveless, her claws lost their hold and she tumbled heavily to the ground, wings all awry, to land in a puddle of stinking vomitus.

And then, as before and always, she was tied to a wheel-like apparatus, prone, with hands and feet fiercely compressed by the torturer's manacles, and he focusing ever more sharply the pain that seemed to flood through every orifice of her body. The wheel turned, lowering her headfirst into the vat of filth. Even though her mouth had been wedged open, she stopped her throat with her swollen tongue, staving off drowning, while fresh agony grew in her bursting lungs. Just as the symphony of pain seemed to reach its crescendo, she was forced to a further extreme by the thrust of his impalement. The sunburst. The release. The turn of the wheel into the air. The humiliating ignominy as the combined ecstasy and anguish receded.

Stop, her mind pleaded with him. Don't...

Don't stop?

He would cleanse her tenderly, laughing, his beautiful face hovering in torn scarlet mist, sometimes kissing her unbroken body (and this was the worst of all and brought her closest to crying out hate-love and defiance, and thus to the brink of imbecility).

Scream, he told her gently. Curse me aloud and it will be consummated. But she would not utter a sound, shutting eyes and mind from the sight of him and the knowledge of what inevitably came next, the warm stream, the soft impacts on her face and eyelids.

You like it. It's what you are, where you came from, what you're made of...

Stop. Don't stop. Let me die rather than know. The agony of realization. The reaming, refining pain burning through the brain along the channels opened by fury. Stop. Don't stop...

Scream, he invited. Only scream for an end.

But she would not, and the wheel, come full circle, carried her down again into the feculent trough. Her soul shrank, her identity hid away in the tiny mental sanctuary that remained buried in contradictions of pleasure and pain, humiliation and rapture, love and hate. He was destroying her, creating her. Demolishing her, perfecting her. Driving her insane as he unwittingly set free her superhuman metapsychic potential. Killing her in the act of love.

Stop. Don't stop. Torturer Beloved.

The raven flopped weakly under the enormous blood-sun. The disk was spinning, throwing off foul-smelling drops that burned her, extruding a kind of jet—a vortex that sought her out and tried to pierce her again.

You will not, she told it. There is no pleasure in the pain anymore. None ever again until I invade and break you, O Beloved. The passive earth was not enough.

At length, the sabertooth cats finished and sat in the sun, licking their paws and washing their faces. They were magnificent things, patterned with marbled squares that merged into dark stripes and spots at the head and extremities. The male strolled over to sniff the moribund raven. But the bird was a repellent object, exuding suffering, and the cat merely gave it a contemptuous swat before turning away and leading its mate off for their afternoon nap.

The bird roused from its stupor and called: *Culluket.*

Felice.

Is that you Beloved?

No it is I. Elizabeth. My poor Felice. Let me help you.

Help? Stop?

I can help you. Stop the nightmares and the misery.

Stop? Stop painpleasure?

It's not really pleasure. That part is gone. What's left is only pain. A mind full of pain and guilt. A sick mind. Let me help.

Help? Only he can help. By dying.

Not true. I can help. Wash away all the filth forever. Make you bright and clean and new.

I can never be I am only fit to be despised shunned execrated shit upon.

Not true. You can be healed. Come to me.

Come? But *they* are coming! Coming to me! To bow down and give homage and follow. To gift me with my heart's desire. Come to YOU? Stupidstupidstupid—

They are liars Felice. They will not give you what you need. They will only use you to gain what *they* seek.

They seek my Beloved. To please me. To restore my joy!

No. They lie to you.

Theydonotcannottheyaredarkangels—

They are human beings. Operant metapsychic humans.

Not devils?

Humans. They lied. Listen to me Felice. You know that I was a powerful mindhealer in the Milieu. I will heal you if you only come freely to me. I will ask nothing in return. I will not seek to bind you. I am constrained by superego block never to harm a thinking being. I only wish to see you healthy in mind and free and at peace. The others cannot do this for you.

Perhaps they can!

Ask them.

I will! And I'll find out soon enough if they're lying about bringing me Cull.

Test them.

Yes. Yes. Elizabeth? . . . Could you really erase the nightmare? It's the wrong kind of pain you know.

I know. It's part of your sickness. To perceive pain as pleasure sometimes. Your mental circuits are dislocated. It happened when you were very young. But you can be healed if you open to me admit me freely. Will you come?

Come? Stop the pain? Don't stop! Yes? No! *CULLUKET! CULLUKET! CULLUKET!*

The raven took wing, crying harshly. Down below on the Spanish steppe, the sabertooth cats dozed and the herd of gazelles grazed unmolested.

3

HIGH ON AFALIAH'S SOUTHERN RAMPART, LOOKING DOWN UN-seeing upon the tumult of the afternoon fighting practice, the two old First Comers quarreled.

"Principles! Principles!" raved Aluteyn Craftsmaster. "Hungry people will tell you where to stick your principles! Celo, the Flood's unhinged your wits!"

"Should I have remained a hostage to Lowlife gadgetry?" Celadeyr demanded rhetorically. "The thing was a symbol of everything Nodonn warned us against. Only human operators understood it! It was a tool of soulless Milieu technocracy!"

"Well, it's nobody's tool now, you bungling idiot. Why didn't you exercise your high-minded idealism on something less vital to the local economy? There can't be two weeks' worth of flour left in the southern warehouses! Sweet tittuping Tana—every city between here and Amalizan depends on your mill. Are we all supposed to eat parched groats and mush?"

"Why not?" the Lord of Afaliah shouted. "They'd be a damn sight more healthy for you than the sissified pastries and croissants and Gil Blas pancakes you usually stuff yourself with! Just look at yourself, Al. You're toting more lard than ever. A fine excuse for a city-lord! If the Foe attacks your Calamosk, you'll look like a hippo in emerald armor leading the battle-charge! A diet of honest, old-fashioned food would do you good."

"Thank you very much for the advice." The Craftsmaster's voice was silky. He thrust his face with its silver-gold mustaches and bushy brows nose to nose with that of his old friend. "Odd, isn't it—but I had the mistaken impression you called me down here to ask my help, not to read me a health-food lecture and insult my physique! Well, live and learn. And fix your bloody flour mill yourself!" He whirled about and went stomping toward the stairway.

"Al, come back." The words were forced out. The mind-plea was desolate. "I *am* a bungler. All I intended to do was disconnect the mill's robotics. Go back to direct control by people. Modify the operation so that we weren't so dependent on the Lowlives."

The Craftsmaster paused at the head of the stairs and waited for Celadeyr to come to him. "Did you think you were tinkering with some hydro-powered grist mill back home on Duat? That was your speed, Celo! Primitive machinery for a primitive mind."

"This contraption . . . do you know it yields *forty-three* different milling products? Everything from silk-sifted cake flour to the red-dog chaff we feed the hellads. Tracing the circuits of the flour-stream blender to allow for manual operation seemed straightforward enough, but I forgot about the sample analyzer with its additive-injection unit for quality control. Bypass that and you get raw stuff with a funny color and unpredictable properties that brings the bakers screaming. Try to inject the additives manually and you end up with half-poisonous crap contaminated with benzoyl peroxide and potassium bromate and Tana knows what else."

"This could be tricky, Celo, even for me. Where's the technician who supervised the robotics before?"

"Jorgensen drowned, with most of his senior staff. They were great sports fans. The fellow that took over was an insolent bastard. Bareneck—untorcable, according to the redactors. Tried to pressure me. *Me!* I zapped him to a greasy smut."

"That's useful."

"Should I have compromised my authority?" Celadeyr bellowed. His face glowed incandescent and his hair crackled with static charges. "That wretched Mukherji thought he had me over a barrel! Said he'd do his job only if I granted him the privileges of a gold-torc! And his seditious trickery was beginning to spread among the other human technicians. Oh— they know very well that Aiken Drum has promised golden torcs to every human who's compatible—and full civil rights to those who aren't. I've had Boduragol and his redactors deep-reaming all the barenecks and the human golds in Afaliah, weeding out traitors."

"But I'm a traitor, too, Celo." The Craftsmaster's smile was sardonic. "I'm attainted! A deposed High Tabler who shirked his death-offering."

"Don't be ridiculous, Al. You chose death over exile voluntarily and then you un-chose it when circumstances changed. As far as I'm concerned, you're still Lord Creator. And to hell with Aiken Drum's redheaded Lowlife quim!"

Aluteyn laughed. "Oh, no you don't. You don't rope me into your traditionalist suicide corps. I've learned too much about Aiken Drum in the past months to go against him! I'll dance at the little gold rapscallion's wedding in May and drink Slonshal to him and Mercy-Rosmar."

"You'd accept him as *king*?" Celadeyr cried.

"Why not? Minanonn's the only other possibility—and he won't play. I'll take the kid over Sharn-Mes and Ayfa any day."

Celadeyr gripped the Craftsmaster by both upper arms. Overflowing psychoenergy enkindled a furious aura about both of them. "It's the Nightfall War that's brewing, Al! Can't you see, Creative Brother? What's coming is the final conflict between us and the Foe—the one we were about to begin when the Galactic Federation denied us our heritage and hounded us to Void's Edge! Brede forestalled the Nightfall that time when she carried us here with her Ship. But Brede's gone now, and this poor fool of an Elizabeth can never take her place. You belong with me, Al! We're of an age, coming up on three thousand orbits from our birth on poor lost Duat. Face the Nightfall with me!"

"Celo—"

The Lord of Afaliah gestured down into the courtyard of the citadel, where an armed free-for-all was under way. "We're getting ready for it! All of the Tanu who are faithful to the old traditions. The loyal members of Nontusvel's Host are here. Sixteen of them, including Kuhal Earthshaker."

Aluteyn gave his old comrade a pitying glance. "Low-power hotheads—and I know all about poor Kuhal."

"More people join us every day," Celadeyr asserted stoutly, but his hands fell away from the Craftsmaster and the glow paled.

"And the wild Firvulag in the mountains are sharpening their blades and stealing your chalikos and waiting for Sharn's reinforcements before they pounce! . . . Who's running your plantations now that you fired the human administrators? Quite a few of them stopped off in Calamosk on their way to join Aiken Drum."

Celadeyr looked away. "My son Uriet and daughter Fethneya are installing Tanu overseers. As we had in the beginning."

The Craftsmaster snorted. "And don't I know how much the younger generation's worth when it comes to hard work! When I ran Creation House, it was all we could do to find candidates for the practical disciplines. For agriculture, husbandry, game management. You'll find that your children's cronies are marvels at giving feasts and composing ballads and riding to the Hunt when the quarry's flea-bitten Lowlife refugees. But to depend on them for production of your staple commodities—? Goddess give you the brains of a nit! This broken-down flour mill will be the least of your worries if the plantations fail."

Celadeyr's face was as lusterless as the parapet stones and his mind had gone shut. He said, in tones of utmost formality, "Aluteyn Craftsmaster, I adjure thee by our sacred Creator Guild kinship to come to my aid. The Nightfall War approaches and the Adversary is nigh."

The First Comers faced each other unmoving. Then Aluteyn's ice-blue eyes misted over and the thoughts came tumbling out:

Celo Celo lads we were together fellowinitiates under old Amergan (Goddess grant him rest in light) creators makers doers workers! Never faltering even in pain caring ourpeople's welfare building sheltering affirming life. I chose Retort when death was proper but now it is right I live castingaside weariness embracing duty. As you must!

"My vision is of the Nightfall War!" Celadeyr said. "Or do you think I've gone mad?"

I think Flood loss sorrow ascendence of Foe rage at Ravensdeed have brought you to your own VoidsEdge. Perhaps beyond. We need not accept this as Nightfall! If we swallow pride unite humans we can restrain Foe renew Many-Colored-Land.

So many colors. And now all dark.

Celo our elder generation may not force end when young would choose life.

The Adversary comes! Humanity! Aiken Drum!

No Celo no. He cannot be. Not the Kingmaker's Chosen.

I had forgotten . . . that.

"Then it's time you remembered," said a loud voice from nowhere.

A dazzling point of light hovered a few meters beyond the southern edge of the parapet, where the wall of Afaliah dropped off into the precipitous gorge of the Proto-Jucar. The spark expanded into a radiance surrounding a crystalline sphere. Inside, seated upon thin air with his legs crossed, was a small human wearing a golden suit all covered with pockets.

"You," said Celadeyr of Afaliah.

The sphere drifted toward them and descended, shivering to atoms as it touched the stone pavement. Aiken Drum doffed his plumed hat.

"Hail, Creative Brother of Afaliah. I've been eavesdropping on you for the last ten minutes or so. You really ought to listen to the Craftsmaster's advice. He's a touchy old coot, but sensible in the main."

The old champion was suddenly transformed into a jovian apparition that towered hugely against the sky with one hand portentously upraised. "Die, upstart!" he bellowed in a voice of thunder, and hurled his most potent mindbolt. The resultant detonation and blast of green light caused all the knights down in the courtyard to freeze in their tracks, their mock battle forgotten.

"Battle companions! To me!" Celadeyr called . . . but the voice of the hero was now as weak as the whisper of leaves, and his mind's cry of balked wrath seemed to echo futilely within the vault of his skull. Celadeyr cast off his illusory aspect and strained to seize the usurper in his physical grip. Not a muscle would respond. He was immobile, helpless, and so were the stricken knights below.

"And we were such good friends on the Delbaeth Quest," said Aiken regretfully. "Don't you remember, Creative Brother? Chasing the old Shape of Fire up one Betic and down the next, afraid to take to the air for fear he'd fry our glass-armored scuts?" The Shining One chuckled. "If we hunted Delbaeth now, we'd have no such worry. My powers have come on nicely, as you can see. One of these days, I hope to have Dionket Lord Healer do my mind-assay right in front of the lot of you, so you can see what manner of lad aspires to be your king."

Celadeyr's incandescent face had gone chlorotic. In a raspy whisper, he said, "Free me. Fight like a true warrior."

"Fight you?" inquired the trickster lightly. "Not bloody likely. I don't take on cowards."

"Cowards—!"

Stepping close to the statuesque Tanu, Aiken floated up until the two of them were eye to eye. "You're a washed-up, worn-out, sad old death-seeking coward. *I'm* willing to take on the Firvulag. Who cares if they outnumber us ten to one? But the great High Table Lord of Afaliah would rather lie down and die. Or rather—march into the teeth of a mounted ogre battalion with a dotted line drawn on his throat and a tag that says: CUT HERE!"

The Craftsmaster said somberly, "The kid's not that far wrong about your deep motivation, Celo."

"Adversary! Fight me fairly," begged Celadeyr, his face grimacing in torment.

Aiken lowered himself to the pavement. "I fight with the weapons I have. It's the only sensible way." And he waved one hand.

In the air out over the gorge now hovered an armed and mounted host of some four hundred knights, with the brilliantly glowing forms of Culluket, Alberonn, and Bleyn poised in the van. Behind them were Tanu and hybrid warriors representing all five of the Guilds Mental, the strength of their auras confirming the power of their minds.

Respectfully, the rainbow army lifted their weapons. A resounding salute rolled over the battlement. "Slonshal, Celadeyr! Slonshal, Lord of Afaliah!"

"We're not here to fight," Aiken insisted, and the warm cajolery seeped into Celadeyr's brain willy-nilly. "We're here to demonstrate that there's hope for us all if we unite against the Foe. I had to leave most of the fighters at home in Goriah, but I did bring this bunch for you to review—and there's also my new elite guard of human golds down on the ground just outside your city's north gate, if you'd care to give 'em a fareyed once-over."

Celadeyr extended his mental vision. There seemed to be at least a thousand troops out there . . . *and the gate of Afaliah was opening to them*. The ranks of mounted men and women were led by officers with metapsychic auras. Some of the rank and file glowed and some did not—but all were collared in gold and bearing most peculiar armament.

"Go ahead," urged Aiken. "Take a really close look at their weapons. Our late great Battlemaster might have talked a good game about abolishing Lowlife technology, but he wasn't stupid enough to follow his own principles. Like you were, Creative Brother! The cellars at my Castle of Glass in Goriah were stuffed with seventy years' worth of contraband—including the things you see. Zappers. Stun-guns. Solar-powered blasters. Double-barreled Rigby .470 elephant rifles. Air guns with steel-pellet ammo. Sonic disruptors. Just about every kind of portable proscribed weapon you can imagine smuggled past the unsuspecting officials at Madame Guderian's establishment by sneaky time-travelers who wanted a small advantage over their fellow

Pliocene exiles . . . And there may be other caches besides the one I found. Do *you* have one, Celo? No? Then perhaps we'd better put the same question to your son Uriet and daughter Fethneya."

Celadeyr's eyes came back into focus. A sad smile played over his lips. "No, I didn't know about the contraband caches. But it would help explain something that puzzled me—rumors that the Foe had developed fearsome new weapons after they destroyed Burask. The late Lord Osgeyr was notoriously covetous, and it would have been just like him to have stored away the forbidden arms instead of destroying them."

Aiken said, "Thanks for the tip. I'll check into that."

The army of sky-riders was on the move, their chalikos trotting smartly on air over the city rampart, and then beginning a slow spiral down into the great courtyard. The knights of Afaliah formed into an involuntary honor guard.

"I had another reason for coming," Aiken said.

Celadeyr discovered that he was free at last. He made no move to threaten the gold-clad youth. "I think I know."

Aiken wagged a finger. "Now—don't jump to false conclusions! We're all in this together, I told you. United against the Foe! No—I came because the wedding invitation we sent you seems to have gone astray."

Celadeyr could not help an incredulous obscenity.

The golliwog was all sincerity. "We never heard a word from you. Mercy was desolated. So was I. How could I celebrate my nuptials without my old friends from Afaliah? My comrades of the Delbaeth Quest? So I'm here to reextend the invitation. Personally."

"Come on, Celo," said Aluteyn Craftsmaster gently. "I had to choose life. Now it's your turn."

Celadeyr stood there, hands at his sides, feet wide apart. His fingers clenched once and relaxed. His eyes closed, cutting off the physical image, at least, of the Adversary. The reluctant affirmation came.

Aiken fairly sparkled with pleasure. "Kaleidoscopic! You won't regret it, Creative Brother. There are lots of ways we can help each other in these tough times. For instance—" Aiken snapped his fingers.

Another astral bubble materialized and wafted down to the parapet. Inside was a samurai warrior in full Muromachi panoply, wearing a golden torc. The sphere evaporated and the warrior bowed.

"Lord Celadeyr, Craftsmaster—I want you to meet a new friend of mine named Yosh Watanabe. A technician of great ingenuity! That armor of his used to be made of hundreds of little iron plates—but he replaced them with tabs of mastodon hide and melted the iron and made himself a blood-metal sword. He's lived free almost from the first day he came through the time-gate—and yet he couldn't wait to join up with Me! Celo— you and Yosh want to get together for some serious consultation. Back in the Milieu, he was a pretty heavy robotics engineer. And he also flies a mean kite."

Yosh winked at the Lord of Afaliah, who stared back at the samurai with a wild surmise.

Aiken said, "Now, the rest of my gang and me have to be moving right along. We'll spend the night, but then we're off for Tarasiah and a few other places on an inspection tour . . . and to deliver a few more messed-up wedding invitations! But Yosh will be glad to stay on here for a few weeks to help you with your problems. You can bring him back to Goriah when you come up for the wedding. And the other fun and games."

"I see," said Celadeyr faintly.

"That okay with you, Yosh?" Aiken inquired.

"Whatever you say, Chief," said the samurai affably. He turned to the Lord of Afaliah. "What say we take a little survey of the balls-up right now?"

Celadeyr didn't move. But the Craftsmaster put an arm around his old friend's shoulder and began drawing him toward the stairway.

"That's a good idea," Aluteyn said. "And I think I know where we can find some of the special tools and components needed for the repair job. Celo—is Treonet's lab still intact?"

The Lord of Afaliah nodded.

Aluteyn explained to Yosh. "One of my late guild-brothers

was a keen fosterer of Elder Earth microprocessing and other electronic doodads. His mansion has an attached lab and one of the biggest technical libraries in the Many-Colored Land. We'll go there, set you up in style, son. You can shuck your fancy rig-out, too, and get into some more practical clothes . . . I don't suppose you'd mind if I watched while you worked?"

"My pleasure," said Yosh.

"See you all at supper," said Aiken, and vanished like a blown-out flame.

Celadeyr shook his head. "And *that* would be our king."

"The idea," Aluteyn Craftsmaster observed, "might grow on you."

4

SHE CAME OUT INTO THE EVENING CALM FOR A LAST BREATH of air before summoning the women. The moon, pregnant as she was, hung new over the Strait of Redon. It would not mature until May Day, which was an excellent portent for the Loving; but Mercy's time had come.

The balcony of her tower suite was broad, with shrubs and flowers planted in golden urns. She rarely went out there now, for the amethyst faerie lighting installed by Aiken-Lugonn seemed chilling and melancholy to her. How different it had been in Nodonn's time! Then the jewel-lamps strung along the crystal balustrade and in the angles of the opaque glass walls had gleamed warmly rose, and she had only to will it and the daemon lover himself would appear beside her to share the setting of the sun behind Breton Island, flame tones sinking at last to star-studded violet. On a night such as this one, they would make a joint wish upon the shy crescent moon.

And now the bones of the glorious Apollo rested in the New Sea's mud. "But mine will lie here," she told the babe inside her, "in this land of Brittany where I was born six million years from now. And one day, Georges Lamballe and Siobhan O'Connell will wander along the beaches and headlands of Belle Île and find a stone with a thin film of carbon and phosphor streaking it. And it will be *me*."

162

The fetus leaped, sharing the pain, and she was overcome with remorse.

Peace darling Agraynel peace Grania veinofmyheart. To-night you will be freed.

The unborn relaxed. Mercy tried again to fathom her child's mind; but under the easily perceptible surface emotions the personality was ungraspable, a fearsome bright otherness, hungering. The preconscious of the Thagdal's hybrid daughter was a humming vortex impatiently waiting to suck a new world of physical sensation, no longer comforted by the limited stimuli available to the womb-bound. The infant yearned without knowing for richer inputs than waterborne sounds of maternal heart and lungs and digestive tract, or the dim redness seen through filmed eyes, or vague tactilities dulled by her fetal coating of vernix caseosa unguent, or the omnipresent taste and smell of amniotic fluid. *More!* the inarticulate telepathic voice seemed to cry. And the mother replied: *Soon.*

Agraynel's ultrafaculties (as those of all term fetuses, whether potentially operant or latent) were totally oriented toward love-need. She beat with her weak psychokinesis against the uterine prison; plucked at Mercy's consciousness with feeble redaction; strove to create an unbreakable bond between the two of them, even as she tried to gain freedom; coerced most strongly of all. And thereby was forged that commonplace miracle, the metapsychic link between every normal mother and child.

Love! called the insatiable wee mind. *More love!*

Mother loves you. You love Mother. Sleep.

The child-mind drifted away, content.

Poor Aiken, Mercy thought, comparing.

And then: *Nodonn. My Nodonn.*

"But it is not our *way,*" protested Lady Morna-Ia. "A mother of our battle-company should travail courageously until victorious! And especially you, who may well be the founding matriarch of a new Host!"

"We will conduct the birth in the way I've decided," Mercy said. "The Lord Healer has come to assist me with the Skin, and all of the noble ladies now await us in the audience chamber."

"All of them?" Morna was as awed as she was dismayed. "For this most private, sacred moment?"

"The female knights who accompanied Lord Aiken-Lugonn will have to receive their instruction later. But the others are ready. I willingly forego my privacy. I am Lady Creator, and it's my duty to instruct all of you in this. For the future."

Morna could not mistake her intention. "Surely you don't think—"

"When the others see it—and the way it affects the baby— they won't have it any other way."

Morna bowed her head. "As you have said, you are Lady Creator. But so many things have changed."

Mercy smiled encouragement at the towering woman in the lavender robes. Her eyes were a brilliant blue tonight and her auburn hair hung free. She wore a long gauze shift, white with a golden hem, and her arms were bare, the skin very pale with a dusting of tiny freckles. The yoke of the gown, where the golden torc shone, was slashed straight between her full breasts to a point just above the swell of the child.

"Dear Farseeing Sister Morna, you're Kingmaker Aspirant now, and second ranked among the Most Exalted Ladies. But you've also been kind to a bereaved human woman—and once, eight hundred long years agone, you midwifed Queen Nontusvel when she bore her first son. The office will be only slightly different this time. And, of course, Agraynel is a girl. But as you'll see once her aura is separated from mine, she's going to be an exceptional person, worthy to be your godchild."

Mercy took one of Morna's cool dry hands and pressed it to her belly. "Feel her. Meet her! She's ready." The fetus gave a great bound and Mercy laughed. The minds of the two women embraced. "Now then. Take me to the dais of the audience chamber, where all of them are waiting."

The great room was very dim, and of course the stained-glass windows that glorified it in daylight were night-masked. There were no faerie lights, only sconces of candles casting a wavering orange glow about the stage. No couch waited, no chair, no birthing-stool. There was only a golden table with two large basins—one beaten gold, the other transparent crystal, half-filled with warm water. Beside the table waited Dionket Lord Healer, summoned from his voluntary retirement in the Pyrénées, holding a golden pouch in one hand and a glittering ruby blade in the other. Ranged behind him, looking self-important and radiating not a little apprehension, were three Tanu maidens: a redactor wearing scarlet and white, a psychokinetic dressed in rose and gold, and a blue-garbed coercer—this last none other than Olone, the bethrothed of Sullivan-Tonn.

Very slowly, Mercy came to the front of the dais and stood alone. The several hundred spectators were cloaked and hooded in white, unmoving, their minds as carefully enshrouded as their bodies.

I greet you Sisters, Mercy bespoke them.

We respond to your summoning, the minds whispered. Lady of Goriah.

I am here to demonstrate a new way of bringing forth life. You know that my powers are great, and that they are also different from those of most creative persons among the Tanu. My powers are gentle, not aggressive. They are not for battle, but for nurture. I will teach them to you. For you may all, if you desire it, follow this way that I am going to show to you now.

She stepped back to the table, to Dionket. Morna and the three girls hovered in the background. Mercy stood facing the audience of breathless women and closed her eyes. The tall Lord Healer made a gesture. From his golden pouch flowed an enveloping sheet of material thinner than the finest plass. It settled over Mercy, perfectly transparent, like a veil covering a statue. Her body began to radiate, the light concentrated most strongly in the swollen abdomen. The white gown seemed to become as clear as the Skin, and in the midst of the light was a small form.

Something almost ectoplasmic came from Mercy's body, shimmering through the abdominal wall, to float between her hands that were now outstretched. A mind-gasp, instantly sup-

pressed, arose from the crowd. Dionket's austere face softened
in a smile. The closest spectators were aware of a great web
of redactive and psychokinetic power from his mind blending
with creative forces of the mother for her almost instantaneous
healing.

Dionket gestured and the Skin whisked away into nothing-
ness. Through farseeing eyes, all of the women saw Mercy
gazing down on her newborn. The baby was still enclosed in
the fetal membranes. A gossamer bubble filled with fluid, the
amnion, hovered just above Mercy's extended hands. The um-
bilical cord, still attached to the placenta, was clearly visible.

Now Morna lifted the golden basin and held it beneath the
baby with the help of the psychokinetic lady-in-waiting. Dionket's ruby scalpel flashed briefly and the waters cascaded down.
The Healer touched the baby again, freeing the cord, and the
membranes vanished with it into the bowl.

Agraynel opened her eyes. She breathed easily after Mercy's
lung-inflating kiss, enveloped in warm air. Now the redactive
maiden stood ready with the crystal bowl, a silk sponge, and
towels. The infant continued to hover in space, wriggling gently,
as Mercy and Morna washed away the pasty vernix coating,
leaving her skin pink and fresh. Mercy kissed the child again
and she was dry. Young Olone stepped forward with clothing
and a receiving blanket, and the small form was swaddled to
the armpits.

Mercy hugged her daughter, offered a breast. The baby was
still too new to suck milk, but her mind was open and drinking,
drinking. The crowd of awestricken women hardly dared to
reach out—but with Mercy's encouragement, they came carefully, bestowing feathery mental pats of affection.

"Peace—for the naming." Morna's physical voice was soft.
Nevertheless everyone in the audience hall heard. The old woman
held high a tiny golden torc and there was a collective sigh.
The three young ladies-in-waiting went stiff with anticipation.
Who would it be?

"Olone," said Mercy, beckoning with her mind.

The maiden in the robes of the Coercer Guild took the child

into her arms, rapturous. You should be mine! How lovely you are!

"I call you Agraynel ul-Mercy-Rosmar vur-Thagdal." Morma slipped the golden ring about the baby's neck and fastened the twisting catch. "The good Goddess grant you long life, honor, and happiness in her service."

Slonshal, whispered the hundreds of female minds.

Slonshal, sighed Dionket Lord Healer.

Slonshal, Mercy told her daughter, as she took her back from the reluctant Olone. Her heart overflowed with joy for the first time since the Flood and the loss, and she reached out in playful query to Morna, who had come to lead her away.

And are you a true Kingmaker Aspirant, Farseeing Morna-Ia? Do you have the sight? And does it show you this sweet little one as a queen?...

The mind-voices in the hall were singing the Song in tones as soft as an aeolian harp.

"I see Agraynel queen of our Many-Colored Land. Yes."

Mercy uttered a delighted cry. "Do you! Oh, don't be teasing!"

There were beads of sweat on the old woman's smooth brow. Her lips were trembling. "I speak the truth. I knew as she first breathed."

Mercy stood still before the draperies at the rear of the dais. Her look was fey and wild. She had the baby drawn up tightly against one flushed cheek. The infant's eyes seemed enormous in the tiny face.

"And her king!" Mercy cried. "Who will he be?"

"He . . . is not yet born."

"But you know who he is? Whose child he will be?" Mercy persisted. "Tell me, Morna! You *must* tell me!"

Morna backed away, her face white and her mind walled up. "I cannot!" she said tremulously. "I cannot." She turned and fled through the heavy draperies, leaving Mercy staring wonderingly after. Dionket came and put a protective arm around the mother, and at the same time his redactive faculty slipped into her tired mind to fend off the inevitable question, the anxiety, and the fear.

Mercy forgot.

The baby snuggled into the front of her gown, began to nurse, and there was for Mercy nothing else to be concerned about.

5

He woke to the awful, nourishing kiss.

His food, masticated and warm, without flavor, transferred from her mouth to his. The encouraging thrust of her tongue. Moist female fingers massaging his throat until he must perforce swallow. Her rhythmic two-note humming, monotonously timed to his heartbeat.

He smelled the meaty aroma of the food and her unwashed body in its garment of half-cured skin, and smoke and enclosing rock. He heard, besides her voice, a distant tinkle of water and someone coughing and spitting far away, echoing. And birdsong. And the wind's harsh breath in mountain pines.

His farsight was blind and his body paralyzed, but he could at least open his eyes. There was pain, even though the light was dim. A low moan escaped him. The humming cut off abruptly.

"O God, is it you?"

Hanging locks of very long, very dirty fair hair. A face, doughy-pale beneath grime, the nose short and flat, the eyes small, wide-set, too gray a blue, now popping with incredulous delight. The mouth agape, lips all smeared with the food lately shared. Carious teeth.

"My God from the Sea. You're awake!"

The face approached to blurriness and again there was the kiss, not nourishing this time but alive with joyful passion.

169

When she freed his mouth her lips caressed his nostrils, his cheeks, his eyes and forehead, the lobes and shells of his ears, his beardless jaw and chin.

"You're awake! Awake and living! My beautiful God!"

He was incapable of any movement, except for his eyes: a mind immured, lacking any metapsychic faculty. When the woman leaped up and ran away, he saw stone walls, a kind of cavern arching into darkness above; but toward his feet (if they existed) was light.

A querulous, sour old-man voice, interrupted in its coughing: "He is, is he? Well, let's see this miracle."

Shuffling steps, panting exhalations all gurgly with phlegm. Her excited whispers: "Be quiet, Grandpa. Be careful. Don't touch him."

"Shut up, you stupid cow, and let me see."

The two of them bending over him. A great husky woman in a stained doeskin shift. An aged Lowlife man, bald and bearded, with reddened eyes and a cruel hawk nose, wearing tattered cloth trousers and a black mink vest, glossy and superb.

The old man squatted down. Quick as a spider, one of his hands darted out, grasping.

"Grandpa, no!" wailed the woman.

The newly awakened eyes filled with pained tears. The old man had seized him by the hair and hauled up. When the tears spilled, there was the sight of a body covered to the breast with a fur robe. The aged tormentor let loose of his hair and he fell back inert. Cackling, the old man tweaked his nose, pinched a cheek with rough fingernails, rolled his head from side to side with sharp slaps.

"Yes! Yes! Awake! But helpless, you high-and-mighty lump of Tanu shit! You heap of dead meat!"

The woman hauled the old man, squawking, to his feet. "You may not hurt the God, Grandpa!" she said in a terrible voice. There was a thudding sound, a pained gasp, whimpering. And the woman: "He's mine! I saved him from the sea and from death. I won't let you harm him." Again the thud and feeble cries.

"Goddam it, girl, I wasn't going to do anything. Owww

. . . You've put my back out, you gallumping bitch. Help me up."

"First you promise, Grandpa."

"I promise. I promise." And vicious subvocal mutterings.

"Go bring his hand. And the oil warming on the fire."

Chuntering and snuffling, the old man went off. She knelt reverently and again there was the kiss from her slightly everted lips. He clenched his teeth weakly against her probing tongue.

"No, no," she scolded gently. One hand smoothed his hair. "I love you. You mustn't be afraid. Soon I'll make you very happy. But first there's a surprise."

Grandpa was standing there with a skin bag and some kind of open container.

"Can—can I watch?" the old brute asked. His eyes had become oddly bright and he licked his cracked lips. "Please, Huldah. Let me watch."

Her chuckle was amazingly ironic. "You want to remember how it was with you."

"Didn't I make his hand for you?" the old man whined. "I won't make any noise. You won't know I'm here."

"I know you spy on us at night. Silly old Grandpa. All right. But first the hand."

A diminution of warmth. She was turning back the fur coverlet. Faintly his kinesthetic sense told of movement on his right side. Then he saw.

She raised his right arm, and halfway below the elbow it terminated in a stump.

From deep in his throat there came a sound.

The arm was lowered. She cried out in pity. "Oh, poor God! I forgot you didn't know." Kisses. Terrible kisses. "When I found you at the edge of the lagoon, you were hurt. One of your glass gloves was gone. Your hand was all torn from the sharp salt-crusts that form on the rocks below our cliffs. And there was a hyena. I drove it away, but its spit was poison and your wound stank and wouldn't heal. Grandpa told me what I would have to do. He didn't think I would dare." The coarse face, full of devotion, came close, bathing him in fetid breath. She smiled and withdrew, and then she was holding something.

A wooden hand.

"I had Grandpa make this for you." Somewhere, the abominable old man was giggling. "I'll put it on you now, so you'll be whole again." Happily, she held it up for him to view. The stump fitted into a kind of leather cup, and there were straps. The digits were fully jointed. "When you're well, you'll be able to make it move. That's what Grandpa says." She tilted her head anxiously for a moment, casting a dartlike glance at the old man. "I hope he's telling the truth. He doesn't, always. But you mustn't think about that. Just think about getting well."

He closed his eyes against the prospect. The old man's laughter trailed away into a paroxysm of hacking.

Warm oil smell. "Don't worry. Don't fret. I know what to do. How to bring the life-energy back." Insistent, primal, the two-note humming captured his heartbeat and began speeding it.

The fur blanket removed. The oil smoothed and kneaded into his paralyzed flesh. Rolled over. She flexing and invigorating the flaccid muscles. On his back again, with her kneeling at his hips.

"Come alive, my God of Joy. Come alive for me!"

No, he besought the betraying energies. No—not with *her*. But a sunlight radiance was responding to her coaxing, brightening the cave with rosy-gold glory. Its urgency could not be pent. She breathed, "Oh, yes. Oh, yes."

The brightness was engulfed by her. She was humming again to an ever-accelerating tempo, and rocking, and he was swept away in the tide of life.

6

PEOPEO MOXMOX BURKE.

I hear Elizabeth.

I have seen your dilemma Peo.

Madness! Found nearly 1000 bivouaced [location] west-shore LacBresse. Sickstarvinghurt. Fighting amongselves. Chivvied into thisplace by Howlers(?) Firvulag(?)

Both I think. There have been peculiar migrations of Howlers during the past months. And the Firvulag sacked Burask and drove its bareneck populace into the Hercynian Wilderness. Part of the group you found consists of Burask refugees. The others are Lowlives whose tiny settlements were raided by the migrating Howlers.

Just *look* perisherschlemiels! Thisplace shithole until ourparty come force order kill crazies. What HELL going do? HiddenSprings or IronVillages never absorb suchrabble. We abandon they goners. Besides Amerie won't leave.

She scents a mission!

Well? Advise! They *are* human.

Postpone returning to Hidden Springs. Your mission there will keep. And Basil's embassy to Sugoll and Katlinel must be reorganized as well. The Howlers have left the Feldberg.

World turned upsidedown!

Peo your mounted and armed force of thirty can deal with this wretched mob and at the same time forward part of our

own design. Take them north. At the head of the Lac de Bresse
is a small river with a trail that will take you to a low divide.
Across it and sixteen kloms to the west you come upon the
headwaters of another river. The Firvulag call it the Pliktol.
Follow it. It becomes raftable almost at once. About a hundred
and sixty kloms downstream it merges with a larger river the
Nonol. (This is the one that flows past Burask.) Follow this
Nonol River for another fifty kloms until you reach an extensive
meadowland that the Little People call the Field of Gold. (This
time of year it's a mass of buttercups and St. John's-wort. Later
there are big yellow daisies.) On the right bank of the river
connected to the Field of Gold by a hanging bridge is the
Firvulag city of Nionel.

I thought just legend!

No real. Sugoll and Katlinel and their people have been
given it by the Firvulag on condition they restore it.

!!

Take your mob of pathetickers there Peo. Sugoll will welcome them.

Surely you jest.

He will. Don't tell the mob they're bound for a Howler city.
Just say it's a place where they'll be safe and happy . . . Are
any of them torced?

No. I figure all torcers either spookkilled or Tanurescued.

Satisfactory. While you're in Nionel you can confer with
Sugoll about new expedition to Ship'sGrave. He'll give you
guides. You can leave Nionel with the guides and your daredevils immediately after the May Day festivities. Drop Amerie
off at Hidden Springs. You should probably stay there yourself
and put Basil in charge of the expedition. I leave this to your
discretion. There will probably be a stepup in Firvulag hostil-
ities this summer. And sooner or later Aiken will make a move
toward your iron.

Wonderful.

Things will remain quiet for now Peo. There's a twoweek
truce on either side of GrandLoving.

You better beright about Nionelthing Elizapupikeh. Imean
why Sugoll welcome us with fekucktehrabble? Morelikely we

arrive Nionel Howlers chopus mincemeat!

Trust me. He will welcome your refugee mob because most of them are men.

?

Trust me! And blessings Peo.

Oy.

7

THE FISHING CAME TO AN EARLY END THAT SEASON—NOT
because the tarpon stopped coming, but because of Marc's own
malaise and dejection, which were directly attributable to the
idiotic European adventure. Once the ketch set sail he had tried
to banish all thoughts of the young people from his mind; but
they would not stay banished. The temptation to track them
with his mind's long eye was irresistible, especially in the
evenings when he was no longer distracted by supervising Hagen.

He would sit then on the screened verandah overlooking
Lake Serene, sipping his one vodka collins and letting the jungle
noises of Pliocene Florida overwhelm his auditory nerves. Across
the garden, the lamplight was soft in Patricia Castellane's window. But the last star-search had drained his libido more than
he was willing to admit, and this time the recuperation was
sluggish. Brooding, he would find the scene around him fading,
and he would see a thirteen-meter ketch slatting doggedly over
the calm Sargasso, propelled more by the psychokinesis of its
crew than by any vagrant horse-latitude breeze.

The midwatch was invariably taken by Jillian and Cloud
while the men slept. His daughter would couch herself like
some pale nereid on the foredeck, generating the metapsychic
wind. Back in the cockpit, the dark-haired boatbuilder at the
helm maintained an east-northeast course so steady that the
wake was a phosphorescent line drawn with a straightedge

176

through tilting reflections of stars. Sometimes a flying fish would erupt, to gleam like the ghost of a drowned seabird before plunging back into fluid dark. Or there might be schools of luminous squid, or vast patches of snakelike elvers squirming silver in the moonlight.

So young. So confident of success. But there was no way of predicting mad Felice's response to their overtures. Cloud and Elaby were strong coercers whose redactive faculty was also highly developed. Jillian was a PK lioness. Vaughn, in spite of his limited intelligence, packed a respectable psycho-creative wallop in addition to his usefulness as a farsensor. The ketch's lockers were packed with assorted weapons, as well as the docilization equipment (which might work), and a 60,000-watt hypnogogic projector (which probably wouldn't). In a direct mental confrontation, the children didn't stand a chance against Felice: Their only hope lay in overcoming her through guile.

The guile of Owen Blanchard.

Marc's farsight penetrated the ketch's fo'c'sle, which the venerable rebel strategist had commandeered for his private quarters. Blanchard tossed uneasily in his narrow bunk on this night, soaked in perspiration in spite of the mild weather. From time to time there would be episodes of Cheyne-Stokes respiration, in which the breaths would come farther and farther apart, then cease altogether for nearly a full minute before resuming with a snoring gasp. Steinbrenner had said that the condition was probably benign. On the other hand, Blanchard was 128, with only one rejuvenation. He had adamantly refused to submit to Ocala Island's rather quirkish regen tank.

How the old boy had raged against his impressment for the voyage! Marc had had to exert every erg of his own coercion and charisma to pry Owen loose from his beloved hurrah's nest down on Long Beach, a thatched hut where he lived with a collection of indolent cats, countless scavenging land crabs, and a plague of palm-cockroaches the size of playing cards. Owen Blanchard's sole interests, when he was not reminiscing over days of lost glory, were beachcombing for shells and playing his vast collection of classical music recordings. The cats made futile stabs at exterminating the roaches and crabs, but Owen didn't really mind sharing his hut with them. The invertebrates ate a lot less than the cats, and the record-flecks were indestructible.

At the start of the voyage, when the ketch had wallowed in a smart chop in the Gulf Stream, Owen had been deathly sea-sick. He rallied once they entered the region of calms, but still preferred to spend most of his time below, playing portentous selections by Mahler and Stravinsky on his implanted microin-ductor. He was cool to the four youngsters and they in turn maintained a diplomatic aloofness from him. It was impossible for them to believe that this frail aesthete had once directed a rebel armada in a near-successful strike against the Galactic Milieu. Marc was only too aware of the undercurrents circu-lating among the young people. In spite of their pledge to follow Owen's leadership, they would insist that Marc's deputy prove himself once they reached Spain. If Owen moved too cau-tiously, there was a strong probability that the others would dispose of him, knowing they were temporarily out of Marc's reach. And then some disastrous error would doubtless be per-petrated, and Felice would blast the entire foolhardy crew to ions . . .

Marc withdrew his farsight and came to himself. Brows knit in a furious scowl, he gulped down the remnants of his drink and flung the glass into the dark garden. Patricia's light had gone out.

Damn them all! Damn Owen Blanchard for surrendering to old age. Damn the younger generation for their half-baked impatience. Damn Cloud for not trusting. Damn Hagen for being weak.

Damn the universe and all its empty stars.

"Hagen!" he roared. *Hagen!*

I'm inside. With Diane.

Get rid of her! We're going to the observatory!

At the time of the Galactic Milieu, only five solar systems (not counting that of Earth) had managed to engender intelligent beings who survived the perils of high technology and passed into metapsychic coadunation, that state of mental Unity that admits of the peaceful, noncompetitive colonization of compatible planets.

Marc Remillard's computer in the observatory on Ocala told him that there was an infinitesimal probability that a single coadunate world existed in the Pliocene Milky Way Galaxy. He had mapped exactly 634,468,321 main-sequence stars of spectral types F2 to K1, those adjudged most likely to have worlds harboring sentient life. Over the past 25 years of exile, he had mentally probed 36,443 of them in search of a coadunate race and a new base for the dream that had failed.

In that search and that dream was life for him, and purpose. He should have rested for another two weeks before resuming, but he would not. No action or advice of his would affect the events in Spain. (What outcome his subconscious wished for he did not dare to investigate too closely.) No . . . the star-search was his work. He would not let the young distract him from it any longer.

Together, he and Hagen selected the one hundred stellar candidates that would occupy his attention for the next twenty days. They ranged in distance from 4000 to 12,000 light-years; but for a metapsychic of Marc's caliber, range was almost a negligible factor, provided that the mind could be focused upon the remote object of scrutiny with the necessary precision, and this maintained for a critical interval. In the absence of an alerted "receiver," direction was accomplished with delicate auxiliary equipment temporarily fused to the operator's brain and supercharging it with energy. Other equipment, heroically life-supportive, enabled the star-searcher to survive the experience.

Hagen helped Marc settle into the body-molding metal-and-ceramic casing, programmed the vitals, adjusted the blood-circulation shunt, and set the timer for the 20-day period. The search would be carried on only at night. During the sunlit hours, the searcher would sleep in oblivion-stasis.

"Ready?" The young man had the massive, completely opaque helmet suspended from its traveling hoist. His face was white and his mind leaked apprehension—but not for his father's sake. Formerly, Marc had prepared for the star-search alone; Hagen's assistance was redundant . . . except as training.

"What are you waiting for?" Marc's voice was already tired. "Put it on me."

The thing came down. Fourteen tiny photonic beams drilled Marc's skull and fourteen electrodes slipped into his cerebral cortex, sprouting invasive superconductive filaments. Two more needle probes linked to the refrigeration and pressurization systems pierced his cerebellum and stem. The pain was excruciating and brief.

INITIATE METABOLIC REPROGRAMMING.

Fluid filled the casing. Marc stopped breathing. The liquid circulating in his body was no longer blood; nor, strictly speaking, was he still a human being, but rather a living machine, protected both internally and externally from his own brain's hyperactivity.

ENGAGE AUXILIARY CEREBROENERGETICS.

Each telepathic command came to Hagen via the computer's audible voice, and simultaneously on the VDT screen. His father was gone. The devilish mechanism was in complete control, waiting with cold patience while Hagen reiterated and verified each operation, then proceeded to the next thing on the checkoff list.

ACTIVATE INSERTION.

Hagen's hand on the command mouthpiece was slippery. He said, "Insert operator," and the armored mass rolled to a small platform atop a hydraulic lift.

ACTIVATE ASCENSOR.

"Take him up." The encapsulated body on its recliner carriage rose toward the observatory dome. Automatically, without a sound, a segment of the roof rolled away. The lift slowed and halted. The stars of Pliocene April waited for Marc Remillard just as they would wait, in some month to come, for Marc's son.

ACTIVATE DRIVE.

"Close final linkage and drive," Hagen commanded. Coordinates for the first study were fed into the focusing docent. The visual display of the computer went blank, leaving only small blinking SLIs. The searcher had begun his work and there would be no more communication until he "returned." The interior illumination of the observatory was shut off. All of the systems were locked and impregnable, totally shielded, defended by a hidden array of X-lasers (as Hagen and every other inhabitant of Ocala Island knew only too well). No one, no thing could interfere.

Hagen replaced the command mike on its bracket. He stood for a moment, looking up, seeing the slowly revolving carriage at the top of the lift cylinder occult the spangled sky.

"Not me!" he shouted, his voice thick with hatred. "Not me!"

He fled, and the doors locked automatically behind him.

8

"WE'RE LOST!" TONY WAYLAND DECIDED. "THIS DAMN RIVER can't be the Laar. It's flowing north, not northwest."

"I fear you're right, milord." Dougal squinted at the purpling landscape. It was well past sunset. "We'd best make for shore, and after a good night's sleep try the fair adventure of tomorrow. Mayhap the mighty Aslan will come to us in dreams, and set our feet aright for far Cair Paravel."

He hauled on the sweep and guided the raft toward the right shore. They grounded on mud in a grove of enormous liriodendron trees whose gnarled branches were hung with swags of moss.

"'Ware crocodiles," Dougal said casually, shouldering their packs of supplies. "We must seek higher ground."

Leaving the raft, they slogged downstream for a few hundred meters and found a steep-sided hummock, which had evidently been a small islet during the late rainy season. It supported a few cinnamon trees and currant bushes and had an area of open grass. "This looks good," Tony said. "At least the critters will have to work climbing up, and there's driftwood for a fire."

For once, setting up camp was relatively painless. After a frugal supper of bulrush tubers and grilled beaver, they slumped contentedly beside the fire.

"Our path of flight has been a rough one, milord." Dougal was combing his ginger beard. Leftover bits of beaver fell onto the golden lion emblem on his knightly surtout and skipped away from the soil-repellant fabric. "Do you repent of having taken French leave from Vulcan's stithy?"

"Don't be an ass, Dougie. We'll find the way to Goriah. We'll try one more day on this river and if it doesn't start a westerly trend, we'll take off overland. Damn . . . I wish I was a better orienteer. I goofed off shamelessly during that phase of our training at the auberge."

"It was a tedious exercise, I trow. At any rate, our pursuers seem to have packed it in."

"Let's hope so. That great black lout of a Denny Johnson is likely as not to hang us for traitors if he catches up with us." Tony began fiddling with their compass, a magnetized needle that had to be floated on a bit of chaff in a cup of water. "That can't be right," he muttered. "Move your bloody great slicer, will you?"

Amiably, Dougal shifted his mild-steel bowie knife.

"That's better. You know, I thought we were home free when we reached this river. It was just as that fellow from the Paris Basin told us back at Fort Rusty: the second major watercourse west of the Moselle. But was the first river we crossed really *major*? And this one did seem to appear rather sooner than I anticipated." Tony put the compass away and stared dispiritedly into the fire. "I might have known things were going too well."

"The path is smooth that leadeth on to danger," Dougal observed. He was cleaning his nails with the knife. "I follow as your obedient servant, milord—but what will become of us if this Aiken Drum denies sanctuary?"

"He won't. He'd covet a metallurgical engineer even more keenly than the Hidden Springs Lowlife contingent. I'm a prize, Dougie! There's going to be war between Drum and the Firvulag, you know, and iron weapons could make all the difference—"

From the jungle came an unearthly blatting, like a much-magnified and bungled flourish of brasses.

"Hoe-tusker elephants?" Tony suggested, drawing closer to the fire.

Dougal's eyes glittered beneath bushy red brows. "Or the evil presences of this enchanted wood! I sense them all about us . . . the cruels and hags and incubuses, wraiths, horrors, efreets, sprites, orknies, wooses, and ettins!"

Tony broke out in a muck sweat. "Damn you, Dougie! It's just some beast, I tell you!"

The trumpeting was joined by an ensemble of roars and whoops and obscure, evil chittering.

"Ghouls and boggles," the knight intoned. "Ogres and minotaurs! The spectres and the people of the toadstools!"

With a rustle of titanium chainmail he climbed to his feet, drew his great two-handed sword, and struck a noble attitude in the dying firelight. "Stiffen the sinews! Summon up the blood! Screw your courage to the sticking place, and we'll not fail!"

"For God's sake pipe down!" Tony expostulated.

Gaze riveted to the sword, Dougal declaimed:

Wrong will be right, when Aslan comes in sight.
At the sound of his roar, sorrows will be no more.
When he bares his teeth, winter meets its death,
And when he shakes his mane, we shall have spring again.

He grinned, sheathed the sword, yawned, and said, "That'll do it. Sack out in peace, old son." He curled up and was snoring within two minutes.

Cursing, Tony put more wood on the fire. The jungle noises got louder.

In the morning, the islet was bedecked with dewdrops and the night's fearsome bedlam gave way to melodious birdsong. Tony woke stiff and puffy-faced. Dougal, as always, was splendidly dauntless.

"Looks like a beautiful day, milord! Proud-pied April, dress'd in all his trim, hath put a spirit of youth in everything!"

Tony groaned. He went to take a leak in the bushes. Watching him from a crystal-beaded web was a spider bigger than his hand. Somewhere in the misty woods back of the huge tulip trees, wild chalikos were whickering. At least, Tony hoped they were wild.

They launched the raft again and sailed on. Their river merged with another coming from the east and the countryside became more open.

"This just can't be the River Laar," Tony said. "It's supposed to flow through thick jungle for a couple of hundred kilometers, until it reaches the Tainted Swamp."

"Something moving on the left bank," Dougal noted.

"Bloody hell!" Tony was looking through his monocular. "Mounted men! Or—no, by Christ, some kind of exotics! Steer right, Dougie. Quick, man, before they spot us!"

The riders, numbering a dozen or so, were at some distance out in the midst of a blooming steppe, apparently intent on coming upwind of a large herd of grazing hipparions.

The right shore of the river was heavily forested. The raft drew in behind sheltering willows and its occupants scrambled onto the bank. Tony used the monocular again and spat an obscenity. "That's torn it. One of the hunting party has veered off toward the river. He must have seen us."

"What is it—Tanu or spook?"

Tony was puzzled. "Unless it's wearing an illusory body . . ."

"Give us a squint," Dougal ordered, taking the little telescope. He gave a low whistle. "Son of a bitch. I'm afraid it really *is* Howlers this time, not just regular Firvulag masquerading."

The rider on the opposite bank seemed to be staring right at them through the screen of branches.

"Do Howlers have farsight like regular Little People?" Tony asked.

"Betcher sweet ass," the knight replied. "He knows we're here, all right. Still, the river's pretty deep at this point for a chaliko to swim."

The exotic observer finally turned his mount and trotted slowly back to his fellows. Tony gave a gusty sigh of relief.

"By the Mane of Aslan," Dougal swore, "that was close."

Tony was near panic. "We've gone wrong. I knew it. We came down the wrong river, and God knows which. Some tributary of the Nonol, maybe." His eyes darted from side to side. "We'll have to go back upstream. Hike. It'll be hell beating through the jungle unless we find a trail—"

Dougal was looking through the spyglass again. "Something to the north. On that plateau beyond the river-bend." He started. "A fair citadel, methinks! But not Cair Paravel." His voice fell to an awed whisper. "El Dorado!"

"Oh, for God's *sake*," exclaimed Tony.. "Give me the friggerty glass." As he swept the skyline, he felt his heart sink. It was some kind of an exotic city, all right. But which one? It was on the wrong side of the river for Burask—and it didn't look ruined. But there weren't any other Tanu settlements this far north. "Whatever it is, it's bound to be bad news for us. We're hitting the trail."

They packed up the supplies and began to hack their way through the riverine thicket toward higher ground. After about fifteen minutes of sweaty work, they came upon a game track roughly paralleling the water.

"Keep your eyes open for animals," Tony warned. They set off south at a brisk pace, Dougal bearing his unsheathed sword and Tony carrying his machete. The sun climbed. The bugs came out. Leeches dropped from the broadleaved undergrowth and fastened to Tony's flesh. (He was wearing a short-sleeved shirt, worst luck. He envied Dougal the chainmail.) They paused by a creek for lunch, and when they got up to retrieve their packs, they found some species of small viper had taken refuge under them. It struck at Tony, narrowly missing his arm. Dougal smote it in two with his sword.

About midafternoon, when Tony estimated they might have covered eight or nine kloms, their little track abruptly widened to a veritable jungle boulevard. Smack in the middle of it was a pile of turds the size of footballs.

The two men came to an abrupt standstill. A light breeze

blew from behind them. There was a hint of thunder in the air and the ground beneath their feet almost seemed to vibrate.

Tony looked up, shading his eyes. "Can't see any clouds. On the other hand—"

"Look ahead," said Dougal, very softly.

It was, amazingly, almost invisible against the harsh pattern of lights and shadows, standing completely motionless a short distance up the trail. They saw a stupendous triangular head with widespread ears like tattered fans, poised nearly five meters above the ground. The trunk was curled up, the distended nostrils scenting them. From the chin grew two downcurving tusks sleeved in skin for half their two-meter length. The beast was long-legged, dun-colored, with an air of affronted majesty. It might have weighed twelve tons.

The deinotherium hoe-tusker studied the pair of humans, classified them as trespassing vermin, blared out a challenge like the trump of doom, and charged.

Tony catapulted off the trail to the left and Dougal went right. Since Tony was screaming, the elephant followed him. Spindly trees splintered and snapped. The hoe-tusker wagged its great head and the ivory hooks uprooted larger trunks, which the beast tossed aside with its curling proboscis. Tony jinked and slithered, still yelling at the top of his lungs, while the beast crashed after him like some ambulatory mountain, trumpeting in rage.

Tony stumbled back onto the wide trail and ran flat-out, saving his breath. The hoe-tusker burst from the trees and came rumbling after him. The earth shook. Tony's legs pumped faster, but the elephant was gaining on him, never ceasing its hellish noisemaking.

A spasm stabbed Tony's side. His vision reddened and his heart seemed about to burst. He tripped over a pile of dried droppings and went down, resigned to being trampled to death.

From somewhere ahead of him there came a sizzling snap. Tony both heard and felt a thunderous impact, and then dust fountained up, completely enveloping him. The voice of the deinotherium was stilled and the shocked jungle seemed to be holding its breath all around.

"Don't you *love* it?" caroled a blithe, squeaky voice. "Isn't it absolutely dumfounding?"

The dust wafted away. Tony raised his eyes. Standing over him was a richly caparisoned chaliko. On its back perched a little old human with the look of a puckish marmoset. He wore the classic riding habit of the English gentleman hunter, remarkable only in that the tailcoat was turquoise instead of pink. Under one arm he cradled a heavy-duty twenty-second-century stun-gun.

Tony stared. There were other chalikos and well-dressed riders, apparently of Firvulag stock. A handsome man and woman with the look of Tanu haute noblesse also held futuristic weapons.

The marmoset hopped down, chucked Tony under the chin, and said, "Easy does it, laddie. You'll be all right now."

Faithful Dougal emerged from the jungle, sword still in hand. Tony staggered to his feet. The elephant hunter had strolled over to his prostrate quarry and placed one foot on the trunk.

"Ready with the camera, Katy dear? Cheeeese!"

The Tanu lady smiled and waved.

Crazy Greggy shouldered his weapon and marched back. "And now we'd better be getting along. We'll take you lads home with us to Nionel. It wouldn't do at all"—and the little man winked—"for you to be here when your animal friend wakes up."

9

Aiken's cavalcade returned to Goriah on the twenty-first of April—quietly, at night, on the ground, for the participants in the Grand Loving were already converging on Armorica and the Firvulag royal party was expected momentarily. As Aiken had ordered, Mercy was there waiting for him in the forecourt of the Castle of Glass, with only the necessary minimum of gray-torc hostlers standing by to lead away the drooping chalikos of the Exalted Personages.

The Shining One was in eclipse. The visor of his gold-lustre helmet was closed and its canary-diamond ornamentation and black plumes were dulled by dust. He bade no vocal or mental farewell to his noble traveling companions, who went separately to their apartments. Aiken dismounted by means of the block, nodded to Mercy, and cupped one of her draped elbows in his gauntleted palm.

"My Lord?" she queried anxiously. They entered the foyer of their own wing of the castle. "Shall I help you to unhelm?"

The corridor was lit with sconces burning olive oil in amber cups. A draft from the open casement windows set the flames flickering. The walls were alive with furtive shadows. After loosing the straps, Mercy lifted the heavy casque from Aiken's bowed head.

He was gaunt and hollow-eyed and his springy red hair had

189

gone lank. He said, "Thanks. I'll carry it." They walked toward the stairwell.

"But . . . the progress was a success!" she said, dismayed.

His laugh was dry and humorless. "Oh, yes. Celadeyr seemed to cave in, the wily old bastard. But I had to kill the hothead protégé of his who'd taken over Geroniah. And there was a terrible row at Var-Mesk with a coercive redactor named Miakonn, one of Dionket's sons. A one-eighty switch on his peace-loving old man. And he was supposed to be one of my allies!"

"What happened?"

"The damn sod threw a banquet for us, and when we were all thoroughly sloshed he tried to brain-burn me. Would've done it, too, if Cull hadn't been on the ball. Fortunately, the Interrogator *never* gets drunk. He zapped Miakonn to a drooling idiot. But it was a squeaker. When we sorted things out, we found that most of the Var-Mesk nobility were loyal, so we just installed a new city-lord. An old PK-creator who was in charge of the glass works."

They came to the spiral staircase leading to their suites. But Aiken shook his head and went to an unobtrusive bronze door tucked away in a corner. He used his PK to slide it open. Behind it was a flight of steep stone steps that went down into blackness.

"I want to take care of a little matter, lovie. You can come with me, or wait."

"I'll come."

He conjured a ball of illuminating psychoenergy. It floated overhead, lighting their descent. The door clanged shut behind them and locked.

"You've *darkened*," she observed. "Not even the Flood so lowered your vitality."

His voice was sepulchral in the stone shaft. "Part of the problem is, I'm tired to death. Levitating all those people takes it out of a man. Naturally, we didn't fly everywhere we went. But I always lifted the knights and their mounts to make an impressive entrance into the cities, while the elite human brigade stuck to terra firma. Hoisting four hundred people and chalikos isn't something I can keep up for more than a half hour, though. And I'm drained for the next day or so after putting on one of my better performances; so three weeks of a progress—not to mention the Geroniah dustup and a small bagarre we had with a Firvulag raiding party around Bardelask—well, I've had it. As you can see."

"Poor Shining One."

He gave her a wry glance over his shoulder. "You're looking fit. How's . . . how's it getting along?"

It indeed! His jealousy was stronger, if anything. "Agraynel's thriving. Her body and mind are perfect. She's adjusted well to the torc."

Aiken grunted.

"Lady Morna-Ia says she'll grow up to be beautiful and fortunate." And that's all you shall know!

"You're back to normal after the pregnancy?"

"I am Lady Creator," she replied. And my creativity is life-enhancing, whereas yours . . .

"Does the best it can. Under the circumstances." He flashed the mocking smile. "I'll have recovered myself by the time the festivities begin. None of our distinguished guests will ever suspect how much this progress wrung out of me. Not even my own people knew—except for Cull. And he helped me put a good face on matters."

"The Interrogator is a master of redaction. Among other things." She paused and her aspect was unmistakably accusatory. "Your friend Raimo Hakkinen has nearly recovered from Culluket's deep-reaming. But you may find the poor man bitter."

"I couldn't help it," Aiken snapped. "We had to know about Felice and Celo. We needed a word-by-word replay with full nuance analysis of everything buried in his subconscious."

"But he *is* your friend. You might have dealt with him more gently and still gathered your intelligence data."

"I needed it fast." He stopped on the stairs and spun around. The lines of strain around his mouth were ugly. "Felice does have the Spear. After the Grand Loving, I'm going to have to figure out what to do about her. Christ, Mercy! D'you think I *liked* handing poor Ray over to Cull? But it had to be done. Kings have to do a lot of things that—that—"

"They're ashamed of?"

"I'm not ashamed! I'll make it up to Ray. It was thanks to him that we knew all about Celo's strengths and vulnerabilities. From the SOS Celo shot to the Craftsmaster. Ray was one of Aluteyn's closest human cronies until the old poop decided Chopper was getting too big for his britches."

"And if Raimo presumes on his friendship with *you*?"

"He won't, dammit." Aiken resumed his tramp down the stairs. Mercy had to hurry to keep up with him.

"Well, I daresay you're right. Your Raimo wears the gold, after all, and once you saved his life. But there are other humans here in Goriah who bear you a grudge. And their numbers have grown since you went away."

"What are you talking about, woman?" His weariness made even irritability an effort.

"You promised that any human who rallied to your banner would receive a golden torc. That hasn't happened."

"Of course not. We'd run out of torcs! It's only the fighters and the folks in strategic occupations who get gold. And even then, not until Cull and his boys certify their loyalty. That's what I meant to do from the beginning."

"Most of the human recruits had it otherwise."

"Tough shit for them," Aiken said brutally. "I plan to do the best I can for everybody, but there are limits."

"Ah, of course. The royal benevolence always has limits."

They reached the foot of the stairs and stood before another door. It was even more ponderous than the last, fastened with a battery of Tanu coded-PK locks. There was also a gooseflesh-raising force-field that Mercy knew could not be a product of exotic technology.

"I never intended the Many-Colored Land to be some kind of half-ass democracy," Aiken muttered. He manipulated the locks mentally to the tune of clickings and buzzings. Behind the door, bars were sliding back and latches lifting. The force-field cut off.

"I didn't suppose you had," she retorted. "But you should

know that certain numbers of the newcomers who were torced with silver or gray, rather than free gold, are resentful. In spite of the pleasure circuitry! And the incompatibles, those unable to tolerate the torc amplification at all, feel betrayed. There's one group that Congreve had to discipline severely when they attempted to run away from their work detail down at the Grove of May."

"I'll look into the matter tomorrow. Don't worry about it." Aiken swung the door open and touched a switch. A fluor ceiling lit. "I'll charm the socks off those mutineers, lovie. Now . . . what do you think of *this*?"

She stood transfixed. What was evidently a former dungeon had been converted into a storage dump. The stone walls were coated with plastic sealant, and the atmosphere, in contrast to that of the damp and musty stairwell, was temperature- and humidity-controlled and redolent of some sterilizing agent. There seemed to be endless aisles of racks and shelving. Some of the stored goods had been anonymously packed in pods, but other items were shrink-wrapped in clear plass. The variety of small twenty-second-century weaponry was impressive. There was also a plethora of other sophisticated equipment confiscated from time-travelers, all items that the feudal-minded Tanu deemed unsuited to their culture. Mercy saw every kind of solar power cell, small fusion units, collapsible vehicles, a shrouded thing labeled LINK-BELT MINIMINER, another called FAIRBANKS MORSE MARINE ION CONCENTRATOR, a third designated NOBLE GAS ATMOSPHERIC EXTRACTOR—MITSUBISHI HI LTD. There were antenna dishes and excavating zappers and microorganic culture units. There were devices of unfathomable function shelved next to homely domestic appliances.

"I call it the General Store," said Aiken. He sat down at the console of a small inventory-control computer and spoke inaudibly into the mouthpiece. "Nodonn and Gomnol seem to have shared a certain pack-rat instinct for keeping paraphernalia that King Thagdal had ordered destroyed. The late Lord of Burask did, too, but on a much smaller scale. Gomnol's cache was raided by Brede just before the Flood. Certain nonmilitary hardware was turned over to Elizabeth's little clique of do-gooders. The rest must have been destroyed by the Shipspouse. My people have searched the ruins of Muriah and there's no trace of it. The Burask hoard, on the other hand, was captured by the Firvulag."

Mercy gasped. "Sharn and Ayfa won't scruple to use it!"

A small robot retriever came rolling silently along one aisle and stopped in front of Aiken. "Your requested material, Citizen," it said.

"Mucho thanks." He opened a top hatch, took out a small package, and stowed it behind his left pallette. Then he shut down the computer and headed back to the door. "That's that, lovie. Come along. Some other day I might let you have a little shopping excursion."

"In time for the war?" she inquired sadly.

"I won't be the one to start it."

"The Firvulag may try to assassinate you at the Loving. Inviting them was very rash. Their Great Ones are now capable of meshing minds even more effectively than the Host of Nontusvel once could."

He came close to her, the armor's sharp glass plates pressing through the thin voile of her gown. He still held the helmet in one arm. The other encircled her waist. "Having the Little People here as our guests shows strength, Lady Wildfire, and that's the tactic called for right now. Both the Firvulag and the Tanu are primitives. Sharn and Ayfa. The vacillating city-lords and shifty old Celo. Even crazy Felice is a primitive! Strength is all that barbarians understand. As for the danger of assassination . . . I'm a match for any Tanu or Firvulag while I'm awake. And when I sleep—well, that's why I came down here tonight. To get me a stem-shield generator. God knows what paranoid time-traveler thought he might need it to guard his mind in the Pliocene. But the gadget is made to order for me, since I'm not all that good at self-redaction."

Her sea-colored eyes held admiration, and something else. "Ah, they've underestimated you until it's too late. All of them. I think you'll conquer them all with your tricks and glib tongue. But there'll be a price. I wonder if you'll pay it? Or will I?"

His gem-hard hand was behind her head, drawing her down

until their lips met, electric and searing. He saw into her and laughed. "So it's mortal fear that's your aphrodisiac, Lady Wildfire?"

"As yours, Amadán-na-Briona."

"That's not a Tanu name. What does it mean? Stay open to me—"

But her deep levels were walled off, and the passion was palpable and growing. "Amadán was a figure from the old Celtic folklore. A jester. A Fatal Fool whose touch was death." Her laugh was reckless. "Let us go up, my Amadán! Out of this place. I've changed my mind about waiting, and you shall find your peace in my welcome home."

The April sky flared with auroras on that night of their first true coupling. And at the height of it, the castle of Goriah rang like a great glass bell.

10

Vaughn Jarrow, hanging precariously from the pulpit in the bow of the ketch, sent out the seductive telepathic call again.

"Give up on it," Elaby Gathen said, not bothering to mask his distaste.

"You just drive the boat and mind your own business." The eerie trill rang out once more on an inhuman farspeech mode. From the sparkling wavelets ahead came a faint, answering cry.

"Tally hoo!" Vaughn yodeled. He raised the Matsushita RL9 carbine.

"You know what Owen told us—" Elaby began to say. But at that instant the porpoise broke the surface in a joyous leap of welcome, and Vaughn fired, the red beam piercing the sea mammal's body just below the dorsal fin. It gave a dreadful telepathic scream that mingled betrayal and anguish. Vaughn chuckled and fired again at the flailing shape with his zapper dialed to blade-ray. The farspoken screaming choked off and the porpoise sank amid a spreading patch of maroon.

"You trigger-happy young cretin!" Owen Blanchard came raging topside and stood in the cockpit, swaying unsteadily. Elaby had been standing on the coaming, clinging to a shroud and steering the ketch with one foot on the wheel. Now he flicked on the auto and leaped to assist the older man, whose

196

chronic seasickness seemed ready to yield to apoplexy. "I told you to leave the porpoises alone! I ordered you!"

Vaughn lounged against the pulpit rail, the carbine tilted over one bare shoulder. He was naked except for a brief bathing slip and his overfed body gleamed with suntan emollients. "I get bored on watch. I have to do something besides scan the bottom of the friggerty estuary."

"Zap sharks or mantas!"

Vaughn shrugged. "They won't come when I call."

"The porpoises are sentient, dammit!"

Vaughn diddled with the Matsu's beam selector. He grinned slyly, not catching Owen's eye. "So were the four billion non-coadunates you helped to kill in the Rebellion. Don't come over righteous with me, pops."

Elaby's coercion reached out to throttle his contemporary. "That's enough, Vaughn. Don't pretend to be any dumber than you really are. Owen warned you that the porpoises might be able to communicate with Felice. She likes animals. They're her friends."

"Bullshit. Porpoise farspeech isn't loud enough to carry farther than a klom or two."

"We don't dare risk it," said Owen.

"And besides, Felice is nowhere near here."

"We're not sure of that," Owen snarled, "and until we are, you leave the porpoises alone!"

Vaughn's grin widened. He was slitty-eyed in the dazzle. "Okay, pops. I'll find me some new targets. Gotta keep sharp."

Owen dropped onto one of the cockpit seats. His face was deeply flushed and the pouches beneath his watering eyes were more prominent than ever. He said to Elaby, "I've managed to complete the modification on the headset. The docilization gear is as ready as it'll ever be. But she'll have to be pretty naive to fall into our trap."

"And the lullaby-gun?" Elaby took the wheel again.

"Dead as mutton." Owen produced a handkerchief, knotted the four corners, and set the improvised cap on his sandy crew cut. "After twenty-seven years on the shelf in a tropical cli-

mate . . . you'd have more luck putting Felice to sleep with a
mug of hot milk than with that thing."

Elaby cursed. The 60,000-watt hypnagogic projector, the-
oretically capable of dropping a rioting mob in its tracks at 500
meters, would have rendered their conquest of Felice almost
easy. "It'll be up to you and me and Cloud, then. We'll have
to take on the monster barebrained. If only Cloud and I hadn't
worn ourselves out pushing the boat . . ."

It was April 27. The transatlantic passage had taken nearly
a week longer than anticipated when the westerlies failed them
just beyond the Azores. Only Elaby, Cloud, and the ketch's
skipper, Jillian Morgenthaler, possessed the psychokinetic talent to generate useful winds, and they had not fully recovered
from their labors in the doldrums when they were called upon
again. The boat finally broke out of the stagnant air 900 kilometers off Spain; but the overworked trio still felt mentally
below par, and Owen's crippling mal de mer had returned when
the wind freshened.

Owen and Vaughn, the top farspeakers in the expedition,
had attempted to notify Felice of the delay. But there had been
no response. After the ketch entered the Gulf of Guadalquivir,
Owen and Vaughn had undertaken a painstaking overview of
southern Spain. They had not found Felice, even though her
deserted eyrie was easy enough to locate. For some reason of
her own, the madwoman was deliberately shielding her mind
from metapsychic observation. "We'll just have to live cool
and let her come to us when she's ready," Elaby had said. The
others could find no fault with this conservative proposal.

Now the yacht cruised up the narrowing gulf in a leisurely
fashion, hugging the southern shore, making for the Río Genil,
which flowed down from Mulhacén. Pink sand beaches fringed
with fruiting palms were separated by low headlands that led
back into lushly forested foothills. On the southern horizon,
poking through a layer of haze, were the Betics—Mulhacén,
at 4233 meters, tipped with white in disdain of the tropical
climate.

A farspoken signal came from Cloud in the galley: Mess
call in ten!

Right! "How's that cove look below, Vaughn? Any reefs?" Elaby altered course to starboard.

The farsensor exerted himself minimally. "Seems clear. Drive right in."

The chop smoothed as they came into the lee of a small promontory and glided toward the anchorage. Elaby used his PK to roll the mainsail and mizzen. He kept the jib neatly filled with his own light air.

"Coming up on fifteen meters," Vaughn said.

"Let go the lunch hook."

The ketch drifted broadside to, then swung her head into Elaby's zephyr as the small anchor bit and held. When Vaughn had them snubbed down, Cloud and Jillian, duty cooks of the day, appeared carrying platters of grilled pompano, palm-heart salad with sweet-and-sour dressing, and rice popovers. To drink there was watermelon cooler.

"But without the rum." Cloud stared pointedly at Vaughn. "Someone has been swilling more than his share, and we're running low."

"What d'you expect when neither of you broads will have me?" Vaughn's mental tone was martyred. "Grog is my only friend. And food. Pass my plate."

The cove was a tranquil and inviting spot, sheltered and deep. A stream came splashing down a notch in the rocks at the base of the headland and flowed a short distance into roseate sand before disappearing. In the transparent waters, shoals of sizable fish came to inspect the intruding boat.

"There are worse places we could stay in," Elaby remarked.

Jillian nodded. "Vaughn and I could take care of maintenance and foraging while you three rested up for the hunting of the snark."

"Hey! I'm ready for a hunt right now!" Vaughn had engulfed his lunch in three minutes flat. Now he came clambering into the cockpit. "Just let me throw a few clothes on. Do a job on the dinghy for me, will you, Jill love?"

"Anything rather than you," she told him as he disappeared below. She went to the stern and began to ready the inflatable tender.

"I heard the porpoise," Cloud said to Owen quietly. "Its cry went though my brain like a knife. Do you really think it might have identified us to Felice?"

"I don't know," the old rebel said. "They're sentient, and they communicate telepathically with each other. That's the factor that worries me—not the death cries of the individuals. Vaughn potted three yesterday and seven the day before. Today there was only one—and it was adolescent. Inexperienced."

"You think the word's gone out?" Elaby asked.

"Who can say?" Owen set his nearly untouched plate aside. "Why the devil you brought that blockhead on this expedition escapes me."

"He's one of the original group who planned this," Elaby said, "and the best farsensor of all of us. He may be a bit thick, but we never would have known about Felice in the first place if he hadn't been farsensing Europe just for the hell of it last fall."

Look. All of you. Quickly.

Jillian's thought drew them to the stern, which had swung about to face the beach. At the edge of the jungle stood four little figures, the two largest about the size of six-year-old children and the others shorter. Their bodies, except for the faces, were clothed in smooth, tawny hair.

"Aren't they adorable?" Cloud breathed. "Are they monkeys?"

"Apes," Elaby decided. "Dr. Warshaw said we'd probably run across them in Europe. These could be Dryopithecus, ancestors to the chimps of our era. But they're so small and upright . . . I think they must be Ramapithecus. The ancestors of humanity."

"I get images from them," Owen marveled. "Crude self-awareness and innocent curiosity. Like a baby two, three years old. A lot different from the inhuman sentience of the porpoises. It reminds me of the indigenes on a planet where—"

A scarlet beam of coherent light blasted from the boat's cockpit behind them. The tallest of the creatures toppled, zapped through the head. Jillian cried out. Cloud leaped at Vaughn.

"You rotten *shithead*!"

Tears streaming down her cheeks, she hauled him up, laser carbine and all, and threw him overboard. On the beach, the surviving ramas were frozen, gazing down at their dead companion and then at the boat. A split second later, only the single huddled shape could be seen.

Vaughn came paddling around toward the stern step, coughing and swearing. Elaby ignored him and went to soothe Cloud. Jillian plucked the marksman and his weapon from the water with a rough PK hoist. "That was nice going, Ace. Even for you."

"So what's the flap? We need provisions, right? You gonna be squeamish about monkey stew?" Vaughn inspected the zapper, muttering, "Damn. You probably shorted it out. Now I'll have to spend the afternoon taking it down."

The boat was turning idly on its anchor cable in a vagrant breeze. Vaughn remained at the stern while the others came together in the cockpit, shutting him out of their telepathic colloquy. But suddenly the Coventry screening fragmented and the four broadcast stunned incredulity. They were looking once again toward the shore. Vaughn turned to see what had caught their attention.

"Hey—will you look at that sucker!"

A gigantic bird was descending on outspread wings toward the corpse. At first Vaughn thought it was a condor, because of its size; but his farsight identified it as a jet-black corvid, a huge raven. Lightly, the bird settled, cocked its head, and gave a discordant cry.

Vaughn raised his Matsu. "Maybe there's some juice left—"

He disintegrated.

The sleek skin tightened and burst, blood boiled, muscles ripped into expanding shreds. The bones shattered in the midst of scarlet vapor, the skull last of all, with its jaws agape and grayish fog wreathing it at eye-level. The weapon clattered to the deck. The gory cloud seemed to spin like an obscene waterspout, moving out over the cove. Cleaner waters arose and merged with it, roaring; and then the entire manifestation dwindled away, leaving only pink patches of foam.

The black bird vanished.

Felice stood in the stern near the inflated dinghy, which had not been launched. She was a pallid wraith, except for her huge brown eyes. Her platinum hair was as buoyant as a great dandelion clock. She wore a vest and short kilt of snow-white chamois and there were white buskins on her tiny feet. The dark eyes looked down at the fallen weapon and then at the four adventurers, who saw impending death.

"We didn't mean—" Jillian began.

The thirteen-meter ketch heeled to starboard with unbelievable violence, throwing the people in the cockpit into a shrieking heap. All around, the cove waters erupted. The keel smashed against the suddenly uncovered bottom and its stabilizers splintered. The water rushed back and the yacht was flung upward, gyrating wildly. Felice stood as though nailed to the deck. Eventually, the tossing calmed. The small anchor had miraculously held.

Cloud and Elaby bent over Jillian, who lay unconscious with blood leaking from her left temple. Owen scrambled to his feet, clinging to the instrument housing on the pedestal.

"It was wrong of you to kill my porpoises," Felice said. "They're much nicer than humans or exotics. Always kind."

Owen Blanchard let his mind open slowly: See, I am elderly. See, I wish you no harm. See, I mourn with you the loss of your precious animal friends. See, I repudiate the cruel one and rejoice that you have destroyed him. You were right to do so. This is your world. You rule it, Lady of Animals, Goddess of the Forests, Moon-Virgin. Avenging Huntress.

"Yes," said Felice.

May I address you, Great One?

"You are all devils."

We have come at your invitation.

The ivory brow creased. "I don't remember."

From North America. We are your friends. The friends who helped you open Gibraltar. Who come now to serve you.

"But you were young when I spoke to you and invited you. Why are *you* old?"

To give you the help you require takes wisdom. I am wise.

These others—and the woman you struck down—are here to work with me. For you.

Felice gave Jillian a contemptuous glance. "She may die. Her skull is fractured."

We are healers. All three of us who stand here humbly before you. We will make our companion well again.

"Really?" Felice's deeper mind-levels revealed themselves: chaotic, a morass of raw colors, inarticulate shouts, and ravenous, hurtful need.

(Link with me! Owen told Elaby and Cloud on their intimate modes. Be prepared to follow and bolster me.)

"There are times," Felice said, "when I feel in need of healing, myself. I have nightmares. Sometimes the bad dreams come when I'm awake now." The threatening masses. The filth.

(Now! But cautiously.) Is it *here* that you suffer, Great One? Here? Or here?

"Oh, yes! How did you do that? It felt—good."

We can do even better than that. Help you still more if you only open—

NO!!

(Good God, Owen! She nearly snuffed the lot of us!)

(Easy, kids. Stick close to me.)

"I won't open to you," Felice said peevishly. "I've never let anyone redact me. Not here, and not in the Milieu. They wanted to, you know. Wanted to change me. But that would be wrong. If I changed, I wouldn't be myself! I'd be lost. That's what the mind-benders do to you. Take away your self and make you over like them. Blah self-satisfied little worms."

Great One, we are very subtle healers. The most skillful redactors do not alter personality. They only erase hurts. Remove pain.

"Some pain...I like."

That is part of your dysfunction.

"My Beloved and I share that, you know. He's a very powerful redactor, for an exotic. Second only to that coward, Dionket." Her attention was beginning to drift. Images formed in the maelstrom. A beautiful male face with sapphire eyes and hair like a torch. A nonhuman mental signature.

Is this your Beloved, Great One? The Culluket you wish us to bring to you?

"I love him more than life or death. He can't be dead!" A wave of panic ignited her. "There's been no trace of him since the Flood! If he's died without me—if he's dared to—then it's all wasted! But he could be hiding. My farsense and red-action are really much weaker than my other faculties." Abruptly, she shot a bald query: "Are you a Grand Master redactor, devil?"

(Look out, Owen.)

Of course. Shall I show you the affirmation of the Conci-lium? [Image.] There. Not only am I a Grand Master, but I have these two young assistants who are also powerful healers.

(That was very clever of you, Owen. You could have fooled us!)

(Felice is a child. What does she know of such matters? Besides, the line between coercer and redactor is rather easily fudged . . .)

"But if you're a Grand Master," Felice was saying, "you could lie to me without my knowing."

(Oh, oh.)

"Open your minds to me, devils! Let me probe *you!*"

Great Felice—if you damage our minds, we won't be able to help you in any way. And you lack the skill for a benign probe. Forgive my saying so, but if you harm us, you may never find your Culluket. Or become Queen of the World.

"Queen?" The pale figure standing in the stem of the ketch brightened physically as well as mentally. A pearly halo, visible even in the tropical sunshine, transfigured her into an apotheosis of Diana. "You could make me a queen? Not just of the animals and the forests—but of the people?"

Queen of the Many-Colored Land! Everyone would love you. Humans and Tanu and Firvulag. We will make you queen, then serve you forever. All that's needed is your healing. When the nightmares and misery are washed away, your true nobility of spirit will manifest itself. Your metapsychic powers will

grow even greater. You'll be irresistible! You will be the Goddess!

"The exotics worship the Goddess. But they say she never
took on a material body. Do you think she could have? Without
their knowing? Without the *body* knowing?"

The apparition was coming closer, gliding over the deck
toward the midships cockpit with the deck paint crisping and
bubbling beneath her buskined feet. Elaby mustered his creativity into an invisible shield, praying that she wasn't emitting
anything hard—and in his momentary disengagement from
Owen and Cloud he became aware of the presence of the *other*.
Watching. He could not give warning, could not interrupt
Owen's facile reassurances with their hypnotic, coercive undertones.

A Goddess, Felice. You will surely become Goddess when
you're healed.

"Well . . . what would you have to do? Show me exactly!"

We have special equipment with us, Felice. Quite different
from any of the redactive devices you may have seen when
you lived in the Milieu. We can forge a mental link between
you and us very easily, while you remain in complete control
of your faculties at all times. Your healing would take only a
moment! And then all of the wrongness will vanish, leaving
only glory. Shall we show you the equipment? Demonstrate it
on one of us?

The girl frowned. "Equipment? I thought—you could heal
me working mind to mind."

That would take much longer. And perhaps not work nearly
so well. You have a very strong mind, Felice.

"I know." Her smile was chilling.

(Elaby. Cloud. When you get the docilization equipment,
be sure the power transmittal is in full phase. Watch for the
marked headset.)

Owen Blanchard indicated fallen Jillian to Felice. Aloud,
he said, "This unconscious woman is our skipper, the one who
built the boat. May we take her below and then bring the
equipment up to show you?"

"I'll carry your skipper," Felice offered, the Goddess condescending. "I'd like to go inside the boat."

"Your aura," Owen cautioned.

"Oh. That." Felice seemed to notice for the first time the damage inflicted by her radiation. She gave a mischievous little laugh as the glow about her faded. Then she stooped, passed a hand over the scorched surface, and restored it. Lifting Jillian easily in one arm, she followed the others down the companionway into the salon.

"You can lay Jill on the settee," Owen said. Cloud and Elaby slipped away aft.

Felice was gentle. She touched the head wound with one finger. "I'm sorry about her. It was a mistake. I only wanted to scare you." She looked about the salon with interest. "This is very nice. What a clever way to mount the lamps and table and stove."

"On gimbals," Owen said. "Then they always stay level, even when the boat doesn't."

"And you sailed all the way from North America," Felice mused. "I've often thought about flying there, but I don't think I could stay aloft that long without falling asleep. Flying takes great concentration, especially if there are winds. Do you devils fly?"

"None of us here can. A few back in Florida do it. Not far."

Felice wandered forward, peering into the head and the fo'c'sle. She opened a hanging locker, then grimaced over her shoulder at Owen. The storage space was packed solidly with cased laser weapons and their recharging units. "You won't need these if the Goddess protects you."

"Of course not," said Owen heartily.

"That's all right, then." She flicked offhandedly at the cases. There was a silent flash and the locker held a sintered amorphous mass that steamed a little. Owen swallowed with some difficulty.

"We have the redaction equipment ready," Cloud said, back in the salon. "Shall we carry it topside, or would you like to inspect it here?"

"I'd rather go upstairs," Felice said. "If I feel like leaving, going through walls and things is so tedious . . ."

"Please don't go." Elaby Gathen's sincere face, ruggedly boyish and sunburnt, showed worshipful entreaty.

"I may stay awhile longer," Felice said. She smiled at him.

The docilization equipment was reasonably compact with its power unit left below. Cloud carefully paid out the cable as they climbed topside, Felice coming last. Elaby set the small console on the forward bench, activated the preliminary evaluation mode, and donned one of the three monitor-director headsets. Another of those headsets, now tossed carelessly on the chart table, was externally distinguishable from its duplicates only by the unobtrusive scratch on one of the electrodes. Felice was scrutinizing all of the equipment with X-ray intensity, but the microscopic fleck-circuitry could be deciphered only by an expert.

"The machine is ready to conduct a preliminary mind-assay," Elaby said. He lifted a hood of fine golden mesh that glittered in the sun. "The analysand wears this tarnhelm, and the operators work through headsets like the one I'm wearing. Would you like me to analyze you now?"

"Let her be the guinea pig," Felice said, pointing to Cloud.

Marc Remillard's daughter drew the netted hood over her blonde hair. She lay down on the starboard bench, her tanned limbs now showing bruises from the earlier roughhouse. She was wearing blue shorts and a matching halter. Her breathing was regular, relaxed, and her superficial mental aspect undaunted. She closed her eyes.

Elaby tapped the activator, simultaneously overriding the deep-probe mode telepathically. Another mental impulse readied the shunt of the docilator.

"Would you like to listen in to Cloud's evaluation?" Elaby picked up the modified headset and held it out to Felice.

She hesitated, then took it, turning it over in her hands. The three North American redactors were motionless, their minds opaque. Felice lifted the headset—

Don't put it on, Felice.

Startled, the girl dropped the thing. Elaby flung up his

strongest defensive screen around Cloud, Owen, and himself and braced for Felice's retaliation.

The farspoken voice of the other reverberated in all their minds.

That headset has been tampered with, Felice. It will harm you, not heal.

The large brown eyes regarded the cowering devils with reproach. "You lied to me?"

They lied.

"You didn't come to help me?"

They came to use you. They are incompetent to help you.

"No one can help me." Tears spilled down the pale cheeks. "I'm too filthy ever to be clean. Oh, devils. I suppose it was all lies. Even about making me queen and bringing Cull."

The devils were mute.

"Now I'll have to keep on with the nightmares until I drown in the shit. Until the last scream."

No, child. I will help you.

Felice looked bleakly into the azure sky, toward the northeast. "You, Elizabeth?"

I am a genuine Grand Master redactor, Felice. You know that for the truth. This other forfeited the Unity when he participated in the Metapsychic Rebellion, and even before that his specialization was coercion, not mental healing. He never intended to help you. He and the young ones came to make you their slave so that they could take over Europe.

"I shall kill them. Now!"

Stop.

"Why?"

You must not kill again. It would make your healing that much more difficult by enlarging the burden of guilt. Come to me so that I may drain away the pain and the evil as I promised. You will attain peace. I will help you find real love in place of your perversion.

"Love? But she wouldn't have me," said the girl forlornly. "Even though she said she loved me."

My poor little one. That was only sex renounced, not love.

You have so much to learn! Let me teach you. Only come freely and trust.

With all of his strength, Owen intruded his thought:

She lies! She lies! Don't listen, Felice! What has she ever done for you? Did she help you at Gibraltar? We did! We're your true friends!

The drowning mind and eyes turned to him. "Prove it, devil."

Ask Elizabeth if she'll make you queen! Ask her if she'll give you your Beloved!

"Elizabeth?"

After you are healed, you'll see all things differently, Felice. You will know what is sick fancy and what is clean love. You will know wherein true power and completion reside and you will make free choices. You will know yourself, love yourself. Believe me. Come.

The slight figure shimmered in opalescence. And then it was gone, and there was a raven skimming the water of the cove, soaring high above the eastern headland.

Elaby let his protective screen dissolve. He removed the headset and dropped it. Cloud came up slowly and pulled off the tarnhelm. Owen slumped on a bench. The back of his neck was scarlet and he trembled slightly.

"And now?" Elaby's voice was dull.

"We get out of here as quickly as possible." Cloud met his gaze calmly. "We do what we can for poor Jill, repair the boat, and keep our minds well wrapped. After that, let's hope my father has some useful advice for us when he returns from his star-search."

11

"I KNOW YOU'RE GOING TO LIKE HUNTING," AIKEN INSISTED, "and you've never seen anything like these beasts. One of the dragons almost ate me at my Tanu initiation bash."

"How fateful for the Many-Colored Land, Battlemaster," King Sham observed, "that you were spared."

Queen Ayfa and the other five Firvulag Great Ones chortled, and all of the flying chalikos laid their ears back and rolled their eyes at the sinister sound until Culluket banished their anxiety.

The Flying Hunt was the culminating entertainment in the pre-Loving houseparty hosted by Aiken and Mercy for the Firvulag Gnomish Council. Some of the guests had declined to participate; for even though Aiken had abolished the older, crueler style of pursuit, bitter memories lingered of the times when Hunt quarry fled on two legs. The anti-bloodsport faction had stayed behind in the castle attending a musicale supervised by Mercy, while Aiken led a compact aerial safari on a quest for phobosuchine crocodiles in the bayous of the Laar delta. His Tanu companions included Culluket, Alberonn. Bleyn, Aluteyn Craftsmaster, Celadeyr of Afaliah, and the formidable Lady Armida of Bardelask, widow to Darel and now ruler of the beleaguered Rhône city. In addition to the King and Queen, the Firvulag party was composed entirely of battle champions: Medor, a Firvulag First Comer and Sharn's deputy, whose illusory aspect was a spiny black wereinsect; the Dreadful Skathe, Ayfa's ogress crony of the snaggleteeth and dripping talons; the novice hero Fafnor Ice-Jaws, who had trounced Culluket in the Encounters at the last Grand Combat; Tetrol Bonecrusher, the feathered serpent, who had been defeated by Alberonn in the same event; and Betularn of the White Hand, another First-Comer champion, who had been the antagonist of the equally venerable Celadeyr for as long as anyone could remember.

None of the Great Ones among the Little People was capable of personal levitation, much less teleporting a steed, and so it was up to the Shining One to keep his guests airborne. The potential hazard in the arrangement was minimized by the meta-psychic firepower advantage held by the Firvulag. At the very start of the visit, Sharn had taken pains to demonstrate the progress made by the Little People in offensive metaconcert. Whereas in former days each champion had jealously declined to share his powers with another, under Sharn's innovative direction they were learning to link minds. The cooperation was still rough, and operant only in the creative spectrum; but Culluket had estimated that the combined psychoenergetic wattage of the Firvulag royals very likely exceeded Aiken's own creative potential, depleted as he was by the strain of the progress. And of Aiken's allies, only Bleyn, Alberonn, and Culluket himself were familiar enough with his mental pattern to mind-mesh. Given the circumstances, Aiken set aside any hope of engineering a convenient mass assassination of top-ranking Foe. Sharn and Ayfa, following their own strategy, exuded goodwill to all and pretended that they had never violated the Armistice.

It was full dark when the Hunt arrived at the Tainted Swamp south of Goriah. A yellow moon, lacking two days to fullness, shone disapprovingly through rising mist like some suspicious demonic concierge.

"The plesiosaurs—the sea monsters—have to lay their eggs in fresh water," Aiken said. "They come up the Laar this time of the year and mate in the lagoons. Of course, the dragons are lying in ambush for the poor love-sotted brutes."

"Passion," Queen Ayfa remarked, "has been known to distract even the bravest of hearts."

She was wearing a spectacular riding outfit of pinkish metallic cloth with purple boots and a cloak of black brocade. Her apricot-colored hair, partly hooded, was crowned with a jeweled diadem trailing beaded wire streamers. That peculiar Firvulag adornment that humans called a "face-frame" covered her chin, the sides of her face, her brow, and the bridge of her nose in a kind of open mask, also thick with gems. She looked nearly beautiful, if you were prepared to ignore her bulging shoulder muscles and the bellicose glint in her dark eyes.

"It would be easy to pick off a plesiosaur as well as a dragon while we're here," young Fafnor suggested.

The Tanu contingent radiated disapproval. Aiken explained: "We consider it unsporting to Hunt sea monsters during their wooing, kid. But the dragons are fair game. You get first dibs."

"Poor crocodiles," said Lady Armida. "No one feels sentimental about *them*. And yet our sage Seniet tells us that they are as much of an endangered species as the marine plesiosaurs."

"Or you Tanu," put in the Dreadful Skathe, with a merry guffaw.

"Thanks be to the Good Goddess that so many of *our* people were saved from the Flood," old Betularn crowed.

"You survived because we licked you, White-Hand!" Celadeyr shot back. "You couldn't get your exalted asses off the White Silver Plain fast enough after we whipped you in the Heroic Encounters. Downright disgraceful the way you always skipped out before the post-Game awards. Sore losers!"

"But live ones." Betularn was smug. "In this year's Combat, you Tanu'll be lucky to field four companies to our forty!"

"This year's Combat will be different," said Aiken. "Shall we tell them, Sharnie?"

"Why not, Battlemaster? We're only anticipating the official announcement at the Grand Loving by a couple of days."

The Hunt slowed and wheeled into a tight circle, coming to a halt in midair. There was a mental and vocal clamor from all of the Firvulag vassals, as well as from Celadeyr, the Craftsmaster, and Lady Armida, who were not privy to Aiken's schemes.

"It's simple, folks," Aiken said. "Things have changed so much in the Many-Colored Land that the old customs just aren't practical any more. Betularn's right about you Little People outnumbering us ten to one. We couldn't fight the Grand Combat in the old way without getting slaughtered. So I proposed a completely different type of setup to King Sharn and Queen Ayfa a few weeks ago. Not a Grand Combat, but a Grand *Tourney*—with nonlethal contests and a completely new system of scoring. Hell, the Heroic Encounters of the Combat were already mostly judged on points, not kills, and everybody knows that they were the most exciting part of the Games. What we're going to do is have a complete program of rugged events *and* skill events. I'm not saying nobody'll get killed. We don't want to turn this into a fewkin' tiddlywinks match, after all! But now the headhunting will become symbolic instead of literal, with the losers paying off the winners in treasure and battle standards."

"And a brand new trophy," Sharn concluded. "Compliments of us Firvulag. Now that both the Sword and the Spear are gone, we need a new symbol of rivalry. So the best craftsfolk back at High Vrazel are busy making one. A Singing Stone. It's an enormous beryl, tuned to be psychoreactive and carved in the shape of a regal field stool. At the conclusion of the Tourney, it will be programmed to the aura of the winning faction's monarch. Then, for one whole year, the Stone will respond with aethereal music whenever the *true* High King of the Many-Colored Land is enthroned upon it."

"Putting the squash on any pretender tushies once and for all!" Aiken winked at Sharn. Everyone knew that the Firvulag ruler had been using the title illegally ever since the Flood.

"No more battles to the death?" exclaimed the dismayed Celadeyr.

"No more beheading?" echoed Betularn. Both veterans were aghast.

Aluteyn Craftsmaster vouchsafed his contemporaries a sour smile. "All good things come to an end. Our Exile is entering a new era—whether we like it or not."

"But the Gnomish Council hasn't voted on it!" Tetrol

Bonecrusher protested. "Old King Yeochee would never have—"

Ayfa cut off her liegeman. "Our royal brother Yeochee has passed on to Té's peace. *We* have decided the matter. You'll also be interested to know that this year's Grand Tourney will be held on our own Field of Gold in Nionel, as will subsequent contests—"

"If you win, Queen Ogress!" Armida interjected.

Ayfa sailed serenely on. "As will subsequent contests until you Tanu get around to constructing a new tournament ground of your own. Then our two races will take turns hosting the event, no matter who wins."

"It makes sense," said the Craftsmaster.

"It stinks!" said Celadeyr.

"Damn right!" Betularn agreed.

"It's settled!" Aiken and Sharn shouted together. All of the chalikos reared. From the swamp below came an answering bellow.

"You see?" The trickster was grinning. "The dragons know that their favorite tidbit has arrived: Me! Shall we descend? You Firvulag who feel like Hunting get your weapons ready and I'll play bait. If the crocs eat me, all arrangements are off and you can have the fewkin' Nightfall War, for all I care."

The chalikos coursed down the wind toward a lagoon bordered with tall taxodium cypresses that was separated from the mainstream of the Laar by a meandering channel. Aiken switched off his golden metaluminescence and the other riders followed suit. Sharn urged his mount to keep pace with that of the human usurper. Unlike the Queen, Sharn was dressed not in a riding suit but in ornate obsidian armor. In place of the heavy battle-helm he wore a light visorless sallet surmounted by three horns. His long dark hair streamed from openings in the skullpiece like smoky plumes. He bore a sword with a clear crystal blade nearly as long as Aiken's body.

"You have no weapon of your own, Battlemaster," the Firvulag King remarked to the little man.

"I'll have enough to do on this Hunt, holding you up. In

return, you gotta keep the beasts from making a midnight munchy out of Me!"

Now came the telepathic warning of Culluket, who possessed the strongest farsensing ability in the party:

Silence all. Something comes channel! Not dragon. Plesiosaur!

Aaah! exclaimed the Firvulag. The train froze in midair, eerily backlighted by the moon.

Down in the bayou, something broke water and rose up, up—until it seemed that a sea serpent was cruising swiftly through the inky slot, a V-shaped wake trailing after. And then the back of the plesiosaur became visible in addition to its five-meter neck. It opened its jaws wide to the moon and uttered a plaintive two-note hoot: *Ooo-awww*.

In the lagoon ahead, another snakelike neck burst from the depths, throwing sparkling drops of water. It hooted in higher tones and the approaching creature answered and put on speed. Back and forth the monsters called until they finally met. The gleaming necks entwined and the hooting became an earsplitting duet; and then both animals sounded, leaving a mass of oily bubbles and dwindling echoes. The farsighted among the observers saw the gargantuan consummation deep in the water, after which the male floated up to lie on the surface, paddling gently, while the female swam toward a portion of the shore where the cypresses grew wide apart in a semiliquid mass of saturated soil and organic detritus. She hauled her massive body onto the land and wriggled ponderously along, gasping, until she had traveled five or six lengths—perhaps 80 meters. Then she seemed to explode in frenzy, digging with flippers and head and flailing body until she had hollowed out a muddy bowl that gleamed darkly wet from seeping groundwater.

The eggs! The eggs!

The exclamations of Queen Ayfa were picked up by the other Firvulag. For the sake of the weaker farsighted, Culluket amplified his own vision until they all saw the great pearly spheroids, twice the size of a human head, being deposited one by one into the warm muck. The female rested for a few moments after the last egg was laid, then began gentle swimming motions that served to tumble the sides of the bowl and bury the clutch securely.

Out on the water, the male plesiosaur was slowly sinking from view. It uttered one last prolonged hoot and vanished. The female now lay motionless, only her muddy sides heaving.

Culluket said: Look on the right!

Aiken said: Two bigbastards! Yoicks!

He thumped his glass-spurred heels on the shoulders of his chaliko. Golden knight and mount slid down the air and landed with a resounding squelch. The chaliko sank up to its shaggy fetlocks in mud but remained composed. Aiken leaped from its back and burst into halide-bright effulgence. The area beneath the mossy cypresses was lit like midsummer noontide. Creeping through the thin underbrush toward the exhausted female plesiosaur were two enormous crocodilians. Their eyes blazed red and their mouths were slightly open, showing tusks like peeled and sharpened bananas. The head of the larger reptile was more than two meters long.

Aiken came capering over the surface of the mire like a demented will-o'-the-wisp, emitting vulgar noises. The lead phobosuchus veered toward him while the other halted, nonplussed.

"What are you spooks waiting for?" Aiken taunted the Firvulag. "Charge, dammit!"

"May I, High King?" begged Fafnor, couching his lance.

Sharn nodded. "And you, Medor. Stand by . . . and be alert."

With valiant yells the two spurred their chalikos toward the dancing bright manikin. It seemed they would ride him down, but he leaped and whirled like a burning leaf, dodging easily out of harm's way. Fafnor spitted the nearest crocodile through the middle of its body. It roared and contorted and its powerful tail whipped toward the chaliko, which was saved only when it abruptly rose four meters into the air. Fafnor's lance was left behind in the madly twisting body. The young hero drew his longsword and darted back after the prey, now having to avoid not only the beast's jaws and tail, but also his own lance, which seemed to have an enmity all its own. Several times it came perilously close to smashing him from the saddle. Medor stood back, helpless. Metapsychic intervention would be an unsporting gaucherie, and Hunt conventions allowed a companion to participate only when the principal was unmounted or disarmed.

"Don't hack at its tail, dummy!" Aiken cried. "You think you're carving a joint at a banquet? Get its brain! Behind the eye!"

Fafnor rallied and finally located the critical spot, stabbing his sword down with a mighty two-handed blow. He backed off to safety while the reptile thrashed in mortal agony. Dark blood gushed at last from its jaws and it lay still.

The entire Hunt sprang brilliantly to life. A rainbow radiance lit the lagoon and both Tanu and Firvulag cheered. Aiken strolled to the dead monster, zapped off one of the projecting tusks by means of his psychoenergy, and handed the trophy to Fafnor. "Nice going, kid."

By now, the second crocodile had disappeared. But the sporting blood of the Little People had been stimulated at last, and they demanded that Aiken produce fresh quarry.

"Why not? The night's young!" A smile of studied casualness played about the jester's lips. "Of course, anyone can fight a beast on land. But the real thrill comes when you manage to take one from the air, out over the sea. If you Firvulag were game for a real challenge, we could fly on back to the Strait of Redon and find us a bull-plesiosaur. Nonmating ones are always in season. But the usual restriction prevails: no fair using metapsychic force—just your regular weapons. And one further catch! No sloppiness, leaving a wounded beast to swim off and die. If you don't make a clean kill at first cut, you have to go into the water to finish him off."

There was abrupt stillness. Aiken's satirical eye roved over the faces of his ogrish guests. "What? No volunteers? You Firvulag are supposed to be a lot braver in the water than Tanu. It should be easy for you to polish off a sea monster in its own element. They aren't all that hard to nail. All it takes is a good eye—and nerve."

"I'm game, if no Foeman dares risk." Old Celadeyr of Afaliah had an unaccustomed gaiety about him.

"Let me do it, High King!" Betularn begged his sovereign. The other ogres hastily chimed in.

"No," said Sharn. "The honor will be mine alone, lest our saucy host think us deficient in that quality so prized by Low-lives—*nerve*."

"I need to be taught a good lesson," Aiken said. "Let's go!"

The Flying Hunt soared aloft and westward, toward the strait. The moon was halfway to the zenith. Aiken carried the riders to a considerable altitude, so that they could see the black stretch of the coast and the gleaming water, the lights of Goriah on the horizon, and even the twinkling fires marking the Fir-vulag encampment far up the curving Laar, adjacent to the Grove of May.

"Plesiosaurs that stay out to sea on nights like this are apt to be very young or very old," the shining youth explained. "Now, these big old bulls may be past it, but they still know how to fight—believe me! We'll cruise around until Cull spots a really choice specimen for you, Sharnie, and then you can show us a sample of the real Firvulag jisum!"

Idiot, Ayfa told her husband on the intimate mode.

He tricked me.

Of course he did.

Was I supposed to let myself be upstaged by a pair of creaking dotards? I'm the King and Battlemaster!

A very paragon of nerve and jisum...men!

Plesiosaurs don't look to be as dangerous as the crocodiles. I could have taken that one back there in the swamp with a dull tableknife.

Well, you're for it now. And I have uncomfortable pre-monitions that Aiken Drum planned it this way!

Any treachery would be certain to take place while I was distracted by the beast. You and Medor must monitor the little gold bastard's PK output every second. At the least diminu-tion—the least hint that he might drop me in the water—all of you combine to blast him out of the sky. Even if we all lose our lives in the fracas to follow, we'll die with our racial honor intact.

Té save you, dear fool! You *know* what I think of this honor!

Yes. But you'll do as I say nevertheless. Now be silent.

"I have discovered a suitable sea monster, Battlemaster," said Culluket to Aiken.

"We're off!" cried the Shining One. The cavalcade, like a pyrotechnic arrow, plunged toward the moonlit sea. "Is he on the surface, Cull?"

"Basking," the Interrogator confirmed, "but alert. We'd better go invisible—save for the royal antagonist."

Thirteen members of the Hunt vanished, leaving only Sharn and his mount plummeting like a dark meteor, sustained in flight by the psychokinesis of Aiken Drum.

The farspoken thought of the trickster came to the mind of the Firvulag King:

We standby above! Gogethim! Neckchop besthope. Slonshal BigBoy!

Sharn drew his sword. He reined in his mount to come nearly to a halt just above the water, and drifted toward an indistinct gleaming mass that lounged amid waves that were thinly crested with white. The neck of the plesiosaur was down, extended in graceful S-curves, and its slender tail was undulating. It was a gigantic thing, nearly the length of the sperm whales of the Anversian Sea, at least half again as large as the mating pair they had seen back in the swamp.

Sharn approached the creature almost at wavetop, from directly behind the head. He prayed that its peripheral vision was poor, that its rubbery skin was insensitive to aerial vibrations, and that the wind would not shift, carrying his scent.

The plesiosaur began to scull with its paddles as well as its slow-moving tail. Sharn followed, a bejeweled ogre with an upraised crystal sword, biding his time until the beast should be directly upwind of him and the neck in a favorable posture.

The wind shifted. The monster caught his scent. Sharn's heels drove into the barrel of the chaliko and it hurtled forward. An incredible neck curled up, flinging sheets of water. It snapped back like a whip and the jaws opened. Sharn gave the chaliko a violent crossrein and it heeled over at a full gallop, not a meter above the tossing waves, with the monstrous head snaking after it.

In a sudden convulsion of terror, Sharn felt something grip
his armored left calf. The chaliko was wrenched to a halt and
both rider and mount cried out. But even in his extremity, the
King felt constrained by the rules of the Hunt. Instead of blasting the creature, he stabbed at it awkwardly with his sword.
The jaws let go, the chaliko gave an explosive grunt as the
hold on its rider eased, and Hunter and prey were flung wide
apart. Sharn urged the chaliko aloft and it responded as it had
been trained to do, racing through air as easily as it might have
pounded across the steppes. Sharn turned it and sent it speeding
back down. Fury had raised a high-pitched singing sound in
his brain. The Lowlife usurper had planned this! He and the
Torturer knew this plesiosaur's wiliness and savage courage of
old, and they had led the Hunt directly to its territory. And
now waited for it to kill him.

The monster darted up from the water in lightning lunges,
champing and foaming, writhing like a nightmare python. The
head was not large but the teeth were recurved and razor sharp—
and at least one had already penetrated a chink in his hinder
jambeau, for there was a trickling at the back of his leg, although he felt no pain.

Oh, you would, would you?

As he dived at it he shouted the ancient battle-curse of the
Little People, the one passed down from his grandsire's grandsire, who had contended with Bright Lugonn at the Ship's Grave
and wielded the immortal Sword.

"Ylahayll!" roared King Sharn-Mes. "Ylahayll Tanu! Ylahayll Aiken Drum!"

The coiling neck shot at him, jaws wide, on a perfect trajectory to catch him if he missed. He cried again, "Ylahayll!"
And struck.

The head of the monster tumbled into the sea.

Up above, the members of the Hunt flared in multicolored
light, circling like angels on a merry-go-round. Sharn retrieved
the floating head and flung it aloft with all of his titanic strength

straight at Aiken Drum. The head blazed green and the teeth in the open jaws were wickedly aglitter.

"This time," Sharn called out to his host, "the trophy is for you."

12

AT DAWN ON THE LAST DAY OF APRIL THE GRAND LOVING OF Firvulag commenced its preliminary events.

From their encampment on the Field of Gold streamed thousands upon thousands of Little People, all dressed in their finest clothes. The boys and girls of marriageable age carried beribboned wreaths of vervain and St. John's-wort, species deemed to resemble most closely certain fertility herbs native to lost Duat. The matrons were burdened with armloads of precious gifts wrapped in embroidered linen, and their menfolk toted trumpets, shawms, fifes, cymbals, tam-tams, and sixteen varieties of drum. Trailing after came a great herd of little children wearing surcoats and caps of green leaves, carrying baskets of colored eggs and waving noisemaker rattles.

Making a musical din, the throng marched to the ramp of the Nionel suspension bridge, where it was met by a mounted delegation from the city, headed by Sugoll. The Lord of the Howlers, all in white and adorned with a magnificent illusory body, bade his kinfolk follow him a-Maying, and led them over the bridge. The suspension cables fluttered with rainbow-colored banners, and garlands of greenery decorated the rails.

On the opposite shore of the river, reborn Nionel waited with its gates wide open. The industrious goblin citizenry had burnished forty years of verdigris from its toadstool-domes and bulbous cupolas, and now they shone like gold in the sunrise.

222

Golden, too, were the freshly plastered walls of the houses, the sanded streets, and the sweeping expanse of the grand plaza where the celebration was to take place. Nionel's fountains and lamp-standards and sidewalk furniture had all been brightly gilded. And the new Pavilion of the Great Ones had pillars of green serpentine twined with yellow roses, and a cloth-of-gold awning. All around the plaza's perimeter was a greenbelt of lawns and blooming trees. The surrounding buildings were hung with effigy-pennons and swags of brilliant flowers.

The Howlers of Nionel, dressed even more sumptuously than their nonmutant cousins, crowded balconies and windows, thronged dozens-deep in the peripheral arcades, and overflowed into the side streets, cheering as the benevolent invasion poured into the square to the accompaniment of the Grand Loving Madrigal:

> Come unto these yellow sands
> All those who seek a lover.
> Dance ten times around the flowering tree,
> Choose your sweetheart and pay the price.
> > But beware of love-thieves!
> > And beware the disguised Foe!
> > Shun mama's-boys and shrewish maids
> > And potential in-laws with empty pokes!
> O King and Queen of May, reign generously.
> Kind Goddess, bless this time of joy and wooing.
> Let the two tall fires be kindled at midnight,
> And grant to those who pass between eternal love.

Sugoll and his party came to the Pavilion of the Great Ones, where the Howler lord dismounted and ascended to his throne. Katlinel, who would play Queen of the May to Sugoll's King, waited with the gorgeous crowd of Firvulag nobility, headed by the Great Captain Galbor Redcap and his wife Habetrot, and the legendary artisan-mates Finoderee and Mabino Dream-spinner. King Sharn and Queen Ayfa and most of the Gnomish Council were away in Goriah at the Tanu festivity. But they

were hardly missed, so great was the excitement among the
Little People at having the Loving in Nionel again.

Two full generations had passed since the last Maying in
the city. During the time of the Tanu ascendancy, the Firvulag,
for sorrow and hurt pride, had let their Grand Loving degenerate
into scattered local observances. Nionel had been a site to shun
rather than cherish when it seemed that the Field of Gold would
never again host the Games. But now all that was changed.
As the new arrivals took their places, they were buzzing about
the splendid renovation job the mutants had done. (Truth to
tell, the dear old town had never looked better.) What with
Brede's successor having solved the sticky problem of the
Loathly Brides—why, it seemed that this would truly be a May
Day to remember.

"Next, they'll crown Sugoll and Katy with flowers," Crazy
Greggy said to Chief Burke. "And then they'll issue their first
official command and the riot will start!" He tittered with antic
glee.

"Surely not a literal riot," said Sister Amerie Roccaro, setting down her cup of coffee. They were all securely ensconced
in a side wing of the pavilion—the thirty-three sidetracked
adventurers bound for Hidden Springs and their impromptu
festival guide, Greg-Donnet Genetics Master. The mob of nearly
a thousand bareneck refugees that they had shepherded to Nionel from the Lac de Bresse was dispersed among the local
populace for the holiday. Dressed in borrowed Howler finery,
the human emigrés were virtually indistinguishable from medium-sized members of the Firvulag race.

Greggy said, "You just keep a sharp eye out, Sister. Sugoll
briefed me on what happens next. See? Here comes the Little
Green Army now!"

The flock of children dressed in leaves approached the thrones
of Sugoll and Katlinel. The King of the May lifted his flowery
sceptre.

"O valiant Greenfolk, defend our sacred festival from the
Foe! Search every hiding place, every mousehole and secret

cranny, lest foul interlopers invade our Grand Loving and steal away the precious brides and grooms."

A piercing shriek went up from the elfin host. They scattered pell-mell into the crowd of adults, impudently lifting petticoats and rooting through bundles. The adults responded with yells and swats and used their musical instruments to set up a deafening clamor. The urchins were not at all discouraged. They ranged out among the Howler celebrants, concentrating on the east side of the square where the eating establishments were situated, clambering over tables, upsetting the sunshades, and stealing whatever food was insufficiently defended.

"No Tanu ever show up as clandestine participants, of course," Greggy said. "I'm afraid that the Little People have rather an inflated opinion of their own desirability! But just to keep the fun going, a few adolescents from Nionel are tricked out in fake glass armor to play boogieman. And—whoops! Here they come!"

A squad of mock invaders, armed with big soft balloon-cudgels, dashed into the plaza from a side street. Squealing, the Little Green Army converged and produced its own weaponry. In a moment the air was filled with flying colored eggs. Some were stuffed with confetti and some contained heavily perfumed dye-water. There were eggs stuffed with sneezy fungus spores, with feathers, and with honey. A few were unblown and fresh from the nest, and the less principled among the children flung missiles that were hard-boiled or even addled. When the "Tanu" were struck, they retaliated with ferocious wallops from their balloons and momentary glimpses of some hideous phantom aspect. The leaf-clad imps were unfazed. Scores of them leaped at the faltering, besmutched Foemen and pulled them down to the yellow sand. The enemy expired to the tune of lugubrious groans, exploding balloons, and the crackle and crunch of a few leftover eggs. Then ropes were brought and lashed to the glass-armored ankles, and the victorious Greenfolk hauled their captives away while the adults laughed uproariously, relaxed, and settled down to enjoy a long picnic breakfast.

"The little nippers have a beanfeast of their own in another part of town after they peel off their leaves and wash up," Greggy said. "For the rest of the festival, they'll have their own separate entertainment. Puppet shows, games, and the like. That way the grownups won't be inhibited in their own merrymaking."

"The leaf-clad army was weirdly evocative of parts of Frazer's *Golden Bough*," remarked Basil Wimborne. "The banishing of malevolent influences before the start of the fertility rites! One wonders what the original, more violent aspect of the ritual might have been in primitive days on their home planet?"

"Please, colleague," Greggy protested. "I'm eating." He licked strawberry jam from his fingers and went back to the lavish buffet, where the privileged human guests mingled with exotic nobility, gorging themselves on pastries, tongue toast, scrambled eggs with morels, grilled antelope sausages, barbecued kid, and fresh fruit-cup spumanti slathered with honeyed whipped cream. "However, if you fancy a really first-rate piece of euhemeristic speculation, consider the ceremony involving our innocent King and Queen of May and the maypole—"

"Putting your naughty interpretations on our folklore again, Greggy?" Sugoll was standing there, tall and splendid, crowned with red and white lilies. The Genetics Master had the grace to look sheepish. Sugoll turned to Basil and Chief Burke. "And your companions. Are they enjoying the spectacle thus far?"

"It's a welcome diversion, Lord Sugoll," Burke said. "We've had a long, hard winter. And then to be saddled with that crowd of poor starving wretches when we thought we were safely on the way to Hidden Springs..." The last of the Wallawallas shook his iron-gray head.

"Are you sure you can assimilate them?" the nun asked anxiously. "We still don't understand why Elizabeth told us to bring them to you. Some of them are quite hard-bitten, you know. They're mostly from the lowest bareneck stratum of Burask—or else Lowlife outlaws driven from their remote little settlements by your own Howler migration. Frankly, we've never come across such a wild and cranky bunch of humans before. Not during the Finiah war and not even during the evacuation from Muriah. We nearly went crazy riding herd on them. Gideon got a broken hand refereeing one fight, and some raggedyass brutes ambushed Ookpik and Nazir in retaliation for a punishment detail and roughed them up quite badly." She poured herself more coffee. "It was also rather tedious for Wang and Mr. Betsy and the Baroness and me, always having to fend off the odd slavering rapist."

Sugoll's smile blended humor and compassion. "Now I'm more than ever certain that Elizabeth did the right thing, sending these desperados to us. You'll see!" He lowered his voice. "We have a little time before the skill-contests and other entertainments begin. Sister, if you will excuse us, I'll take Basil and Chief Burke away to settle a matter relating to the Ship's Grave expedition."

Amerie nodded and went off to join Greggy, who was arguing mutagenics with Magnus and Thongsa, the expedition medics.

"This way," the Howler lord directed. He led Burke and Basil to a draped alcove where a well-dressed dwarf was waiting. "This is Kalipin, who has volunteered to be your guide into the eastern wilderness."

The little exotic shook hands. But even as Burke was uttering conventional pleasantries, the dwarf underwent a metamorphosis that froze the words in the big Native American jurist's throat.

Kalipin's body shrank. His torso became rounded and his limbs spindly. The grinning face compressed and sharpened until it was nearly birdlike, except for the flapping ears with their droopy upper margins. The eyes turned black and sank into grotesque pouches. The exotic's skin became greasy and his hair, falling in strands from beneath a smart green cap with a jeweled buckle, resembled a dirty mop.

"Well?" The bogle shifted his glance from one human to the other. "Still want to risk traveling to the Ship's Grave with me?"

"We know about the genetic misfortune of the Howler nation, old chap," said Basil gently. "We can't pretend that your—differences—don't exist. But I can't help wondering whether we humans don't look just as odd to you. Perhaps we can all agree to ignore one another's peculiarities and simply get on with the job at hand. It's formidable enough."

"We must travel more than six hundred of your kilometers," Kalipin said. "During the first part of the journey, we may be in danger from the Firvulag if they suspect the purpose of the expedition. Sharn and Ayfa aren't fools. We'd do well to get beyond the Rhine before they return to High Vrazel."

"We have chalikos," Burke said. "Can you ride?"

The bogle grimaced. "Not those bloody great monsters! I can manage a hipparion. But mounts won't do you any good beyond the Rhine. You'll have to walk until we reach the Ystroll's source under the Feldberg. I hope your people are all in good shape. The Black Forest trek is going to be rugged." Kalipin glared at the Native American. "I noticed that *you* limp."

"That I do," Burke sighed. "But it's pretty well decided that I'll stay behind at Hidden Springs while Basil takes charge of our tribe of daredevils. Elizabeth expects trouble around the iron mines this summer."

"Blood metal!" Kalipin shuddered. He shot a reproachful look at Sugoll. "Sometimes, Master, we simple ones despair of understanding why you insist that we ally ourselves with the Lowlives!"

"It is our only hope," said the ruler of the Howlers. "Some day you'll understand. Until then, obey me!"

For the briefest fraction of a second, the handsome figure in the white robe seemed overshadowed by another shape, hideous beyond belief. Burke and Basil gave involuntary gasps.

Sugoll's smile was melancholy. "You didn't know? But I am the greatest among my people in all things—even in physical abomination. As my guests, it was simple courtesy to spare you." He addressed the goblin guide. "And you, Kalipin. Use your goodly form when you are in the company of humans. We must not distress our friends unnecessarily."

The creature obediently transformed himself into a normal dwarf. "But all of us go back to our regular shapes when we're asleep," he told the men with wry satisfaction. "You'll just have to be brave at bedtime on the trail! Unless my Master orders me to sleep in a sack."

Sugoll laughed. "Impudent scoundrel. Just fulfill your mission faithfully. And now you are dismissed. Back to breakfast with you!"

When the bogle was gone, Sugoll indicated a sizable carved chest that stood in the shadows. "There is one more way I am able to assist you in your expedition. Open that, please."

Basil knelt. When the lid lifted, he cried, "Great Scott! Where did you get these?"

"The stun-guns were a gift from Sharn and Ayfa."

"Oh, shit," said Chief Burke.

"I can only presume they were a delicate hint. Sharn may already suspect that my loyalty to the Firvulag throne is less than wholehearted. And if there is war with Aiken Drum . . . Well, it takes no grand strategist to note Nionel's position between Goriah and High Vrazel."

"If we're successful in procuring the aircraft," Basil said, "neither Aiken nor Sharn will dare harm you." He ran his weather-beaten hands over the weapons, mutely pointed out the recharging unit to Burke, then closed the lid. "These could be very useful to us. We thank you, Lord Sugoll. Even with our thirty technicians and experienced wilderness hands, it will be a dangerous trip—and it's questionable just how many of the flyers can be made operational. The Chief and our people at Hidden Springs will prepare a hiding place for at least two."

"How would they be useful in a war?" Sugoll asked. "You must forgive my ignorance, but flying machines would seem to be quite useless against ground forces such as the Firvulag would mount. You no longer have the Spear of Lugonn, which was used against Finiah."

"True," said Burke. "But in their haste to get a single flyer airborne, Madame's party may have overlooked another set of potential weapons. This was pointed out to us by one of our new companions, a former spacecraft design engineer named Dmitrios Anastos."

Basil said, "You see, the ancient devices at the Ship's Grave are actually sophisticated gravomagnetic craft with planet-orbiter capability—quite similar to machines we had back in the Galactic Milieu. In our era, such orbiters were always equipped with tractor and pressor beams to assist in docking and midspace transfer when the rho-field was off. These force-beams were also used for meteor deflections. Sometimes, our ships even had small lasers for zapping away space debris. If our technicians can find similar systems on the ancient flyers, they might very possibly modify them for offense. If this isn't feasible—there's always the iron. And the hope of finding and raiding Sharn's cache of twenty-second-century armaments."

The Howler Lord had been looking more and more puzzled. Now he threw up his hands in resignation. "Téah grant that the mere possession of flying machines by our friends will deter aggression!"

"Amen," said Basil. He added, drily, "Nevertheless, let's not count too heavily on divine intervention, shall we? Not with the Firvulag on one side of us, and Aiken Drum on the other."

"Look at those little beauties! Just look at them!"

Tony Wayland clutched Dougal's mailed arm and dragged him toward the front row of the exotic throng. The gnomes and ogres were good-humored enough about the shoving, although one fighting-drunk human in Firvulag costume threatened to upend his seidel of beer on Tony if he didn't mind his manners. "You're not the only eager one, cockie," the suds-buster declared. "Simmer down, and you'll get plenty before this night's over."

It was nearly midnight. The carousing and dancing of the married folk had come to an end and a great space around the maypole was cleared for the Dance of the Brides. The impromptu orchestra played a slow, demure melody and the maidens emerged in solemn procession. All of them wore gowns and headdresses of fantastic richness, with a color scheme of either red or green. The girls in scarlet were the most striking, with their gorgeous coats, tight jeweled cuffs, and tantalizing body suits with red boots. Perched on flowing locks of brown or dark red were tall starburst headpieces encrusted with rubies and some fiery gemstone resembling opal. The piquant faces beneath the towering constructions were enhanced by jeweled frames.

"Pocket Venuses, every one of them!" Tony rhapsodized.

The knight's expression was unreadable. "They're exotics. Kin to the soul-devouring Tanu."

Tony ignored that. "And willing, just for tonight! God, Dougie—it's been so long!"

"Too long for all of us," growled the beer drinker. "Jesus, look at the jewels on 'em!"

"Jewels, hell," said another Lowlife feelingly. "I wouldn't care if they was wearin' gunny sacks. Real live women at last!"

"Inhuman women. Faerie women!" Dougal's voice rose.

Tony said, "Who gives a damn? Just on this one night in the year, they'll go with anybody! All you have to do is grab the flower-ring they hold out in the dance."

"I want me a red one!" somebody yelled. "A gal in little red boots!"

"Keep your breeks on, amigo! It won't be long now!"

The gnomish musicians struck up a more lively air and the damsels began to circle the maypole. The male exotics all bawled out a phrase in their own tongue and the girls responded. Back and forth the two sexes called, teasing each other, while the veils on the starry headdresses streamed behind the accelerating dancers in a blurred conflagration. Finally, after a great shout, the circling girls extended their arms and rushed toward the central maypole with its braided ribbons and heaped flower garlands at the base.

The maidens vanished. In their place rose a myriad of small, rainbow-hued lights, like tropical fireflies. In some magical fashion, each ignis fatuus attached itself to the end of a gleaming ribbon, and the entire swarm resumed dancing at a more languid, sensual pace. The ribbons twined and untwined; the wispy lights soared and fell, undulated and whirled. The invitational song was almost a hum, lower-pitched and alluring. Swaying helplessly, the ensorceled males sang along.

Abruptly, the music changed again to the faster beat. The costumed maids were back on the yellow sand and each one had a wreath in her hands. They danced out to where the swains waited, and as the teasing phrases were exchanged, the pairing-off began. One man after another gripped the wreath of his chosen red or green sweetheart and let her draw him by it onto the dancing ground. It was all irresistible: the spinning colors, the intoxicating scent of the flowers, the music with its thumping sexual beat.

One of the diminutive beauties stood before Tony Wayland. Black eyes sparkled beneath the jeweled face-frame. The fragrant May wind blew aside red and gold draperies to show a delicate body, curved, enticing, and perfectly human in its contours.

"Come, come," sang the nymph.

"No, my Lord!" Dougal cried, trying to haul Tony back. The metallurgist shook free.

"Come, come!"

Tony clutched the wreath. She pulled him out among the other couples. The girls in red, he noted, had mostly chosen Lowlife lovers. How fastidious of them, since they were by far the loveliest of the lot!

"Don't go!" Dougal pleaded. "You're bewitched."

He was indeed, and gladly. The darling exotic wench hung the hoop of flowers around his neck as they danced. She kissed the fingers of one hand, then pressed his lips. Tony's blood sang. The warning shout from Dougal was swallowed as the music became a sonorous paean of love triumphant. Two by two, the couples circled the maypole.

On the side of the square nearest the city gate, the mob of spectators was suddenly cleft, opening a clear path. Two huge bonfires sprang to life, their flames topping the seven-meter walls. The couples marched safely between the twin fires, through the gate, and into moon-drenched meadows. The music back inside Nionel floated to them on the warm breeze.

"I am Rowane," the nymph in red said. "I love you."

"I'm Tony, and I love you, too!"

Giddy from the insidious flowers hung round his neck, he let her draw him on until they were far away from the other couples. They came to a rustic bower formed of bushes and entered, and he lifted the starburst headdress and the face-frame away and bent to kiss her. They shed their clothes and made love—not once, but four times. She howled in ecstasy and he was devastated by bliss, and wept at the end of it and she comforted him.

"Now we'll sleep," she said. "My dearest Tonee."

He felt a silken cloth pressed over his eyes, wrapped around his head and softly tied. "Rowane? What are you doing?"

"Shhh. You must never see me when we sleep. It would be terribly bad luck. Promise that you'll never try." Her warm lips met his, and she kissed his eyelids through the silk.

"My little Mayflower. My exotic darling. If it'll make you happy . . ." He was sinking toward sweet unconsciousness. Her voice faded, and the memory of her exultant cries, but not his pride in his own manhood that she had so marvelously reaffirmed. "For your sake . . . I won't look. Strange little one . . ."

"It's not for my sake, dear Tonee. It's for yours."

She laughed fondly, and then he was asleep, and he had the most singular dream.

When he woke up and absent-mindedly tore off the blindfold, he discovered that the dream had come true.

"Oh, my *God*!" he croaked.

She opened her eye and was instantly her old self. Petite. Lovely. Putting on her clothes and lifting the withered remnants of the wreath from his neck.

"Rowane!" His voice was anguished. "What have they done to you? And to *me*?"

Her smile was pert and very wise. "The ordinary Firvulag are able to see through our guises. They never would choose the brides in red, you see. And you poor human males . . . we know how few of your own women came through the time-gate, and those still mostly enslaved by the Tanu. What could be more right than this?" She reached up and kissed him passionately. He felt himself respond in spite of the knowledge. "Dear Lord Greg-Donnet says the first cross will produce a normal-appearing hybrid. After that, there can be genetic engineering to modify the mutant strain."

"The—first—cross?" He felt the world lurch. The meadow was full of golden flowers and rising larks.

"And our child will be immune to the blood metal, just as you humans are. Isn't that a nice bonus?"

"Uh," he said.

She was pulling him to his feet. "And now everyone's hurrying back to Nionel for the May Morning feast. We don't want to be late, do we!"

"No . . ."

"You'll love Mummy and Daddy," she added. "And you're going to love Nionel, too. Let's run!"

They went racing over the soft grass, hand in hand. Tony thought: What am I going to tell poor old Dougal? But then he saw other lovers converging on the city gates, and among them was a great ginger-bearded man wearing a surtout with a golden lion's head, being led along by another lovely little woman in red.

And Tony knew that his question was superfluous.

13

"WE'VE TRIED FOR THE PAST THREE NIGHTS TO BLAST THE little gold devil while he was asleep and drawn zilch," Medor grumbled. "I don't see why tonight should be any different. He's using some kind of mechanical brain-shield. Pass the rabbit mousse."

King Sharn shoved a platter toward his first deputy, who scraped a great quivering wedge onto his plate and slurped it with gusto. "Tonight, Aiken won't sleep in the castle," the King explained. "He'll be out here in the Grove with everyone else, and using the gadget would cramp his style."

"How so?" inquired Mimee of Famorel, who was viceroy of the Helvetide Little People.

"Our ingenious hostess has scheduled another crazy innovation. Something called the Night of Secret Love. After the feast, we're all supposed to go to those robing tents on the other side of the amphitheatre and pick up a masquerade costume. No illusion making allowed. At midnight, a masked ball begins, followed by hanky-panky in the Trysting Grounds until dawn. Kind of a glorified bachelor party before all the weddings tomorrow. Except, being Tanu, the damn brides'll probably be off in the bushes rutting away with the rest of the Foe."

"Decadent bitches," growled Mimee. "And to think that our own folk are beginning the sacred Dance of the Brides almost at this very moment up in Nionel." He cast a wistful look at the high-riding full moon, whose light was drowned by the gem-lamps that illuminated the feasting boards. The Firvulag had insisted on segregated dining facilities. They were willing to wolf down Tanu food, but disdained Tanu wines and high-proof brandies in favor of good old beer, mead, and cyser.

"You know what you're getting when you wed a Firvulag bride." Medor heaved a maudlin sigh. "Virgins! Every last toothsome morsel! And faithful to you forever, once they finally open that adorable vagina dentata. If only my little Andamathe was here . . . You brought *your* wife, Sharn. It was damned unfair of you to make the rest of us leave our mates behind! Spoils the whole Loving! Pass the sweetbreads grand duc."

"I'm the Queen," Ayfa said. "I *had* to come. And the rest of you are supposed to keep your wits about you. This is a mission into the Foe's territory—deadly serious business. You can exercise your damn gonads on your own time."

"So we're to try for Aiken Drum again tonight, then," said young Fafnor Ice-Jaws. "I presume that we put on costumes and mingle."

"Not too enthusiastically," warned the Queen, her dark eyes twinkling. "The Tanu ladies have no teeth where it counts, but rumor has it that when they've finished with a man, his filberts are nothing but rattling husks. Don't be tempted, lad."

"The Goddess forbid!" said the young ogre, all in a huff.

"We must track Aiken wherever he goes and make our strike right at the magic moment," Sharn said. "All twelve of us."

"He'll be after that young coercer wench, Olone," Medor said shrewdly. "Her shameless flaunting of herself before the King of the May is the talk of all the Tanu gossips. Pass the ortolans en brochette."

The King seized the silver dish and slammed it down out of Medor's reach. "Dammit—will you think of something besides food? No wonder we haven't been able to work up a decent mind-meld! All the blood deserted our brains for our digestive tracts from the moment we set foot in Goriah!"

"Medor's in need of distraction." Old Betularn had a wicked smirk. "And not just because his wife's in Nionel. Guess who we saw at a special table off in a quiet corner of the feast-garden, dining on invalid's slop with his blood-brother, the Interrogator? None other than Medor's Grand Combat antagonist, Kuhal Earthshaker! The one we thought was surely dead."

"Té's toenails!" exclaimed the King. "That's bad news. Kuhal tied you in the Heroic Encounters, Medor, and his PK talent is—"

"Nil," the ogrish champion said, grinning around a half-masticated songbird. "His twin, Fian, died and Kuhal is a basket case. He still spends most of the day in Skin. I guess Aiken forced the Afaliah contingent to tote him up here to participate in the rump coronation on the third day of the Loving. Kuhal *is* a High Tabler, you know. But about as much threat to us as a newborn dik-dik. Pass the poached marrow and the salmon mayonnaise."

Mimee of Famorel made a face. "Your liver will take a month to recuperate."

"So what?" Medor said. "The war's not scheduled to start until fall."

"Silence!" hissed Sharn. His demonic aspect came upon him, the guise of a three-meter albino scorpion with glowing internal organs. His mind dealt a savage correction to the imprudent Medor, who tumbled from his seat onto the grass, pained and shocked and splattered with mayonnaise. Sharn's body returned to normal. He regarded the Gnomish Council with a bleak expression. "No one knows the day the Nightfall War begins. Not I. Not you. You will never speak of it among yourselves. Never *think* of it! Do you understand?"

"Yes, High King," said the others. Over by the table of the King and Queen of May, a kind of fireworks display of fountaining Roman-candle lights had started. It signaled the end of the Moonlight Feast and the imminent beginning of the Night of Secret Love.

"Now get your fancy-dress outfits and sober up," said Sharn. "Ayfa and I will meet you at the base of the maypole in an hour."

"You look . . . ridiculous," said Kuhal. "But in character." Culluket shrugged. "I judged it a droll choice of disguise."

His expression behind the death's-head mask was perfectly clear to his brother. In light of the idiotic charade taking place out on the dancing ground, Cull's mocking smile was understandable; but *excitement*?

"You do surprise me, Interrogator. I had thought you well beyond the simpler styles of concupiscence."

"Even so. But tonight is a special occasion."

Death folded his black-clad arms with their painted bones and surveyed the scene. The ball music was becoming more frenzied in its eroticism and the dancers more madcap and abandoned. The young, who scarcely needed the artificial stimulus anyway, were already pairing off and slipping away through the trees in the direction of the Trysting Grounds. Even those traditional Tanu who had entered reluctantly into the masquerade seemed about to surrender to the Dionysian atmosphere. Surely that capering wanton disguised as a purple moth was none other than the venerable Morna-Ia. And the stout, cloaked figure sporting a panther's head, shamelessly cavorting with a willowy charmer on each arm, bore a suspicious likeness to the Craftsmaster. Aiken Drum was out in the middle of things, of course, dressed inevitably in the particolored outfit of a medieval jester. He wore a mask with an obscenely long nose, which seemed to have a libido all its own.

"And on the day after tomorrow," Kuhal observed, "we will acclaim him King! Goddess forgive us. And you have been among his chief supporters, Redactive Brother. You, an elder of the Host! I have the excuse of brain-wreck, at least. But you, for all your quirks of temperament, are a paragon of glacial rationality. Yet you calmly accept this human mountebank— even serve him! It was well known that you and Nodonn were estranged; but that you should pledge fealty to a Lowlife . . . it negates all that the Host of Nontusvel stood for."

Death laughed. "Who remains of our vaunted Host? Fifteen meager-powered brothers and sisters under Celo's protection, most of whom survived because they were wounded in the Combat and shipped off to Redactor House to get them out of the way. I myself. And you."

Kuhal turned away. His gaunt features tightened. An unbidden image rose in his memory, easily perceptible to the Interrogator. "And me. Half a mind. Half a man. Widowed and crippled in the same bereavement. Deprived of a love no singleton could ever understand!" The vehemence of his bitterness made him falter, grown suddenly gray-faced. Culluket took his brother by the arm and led him back to his cushioned seat near the clipped hedge, beyond the sight of the revelers. Kuhal sank down, accepted a small tumbler with some medicinal tisane, and sipped at it until the strong herbs took effect. He ventured a wan smile. "I almost envy your poor sweethearts their embrace with Death, Brother! Be sure to choose young ones, if you can lure them away from that priapic jackanapes. The young are less likely to know the melancholy history of your nine wives and thirty luckless mistresses."

"I have my lover already selected," Culluket said. "And she knows."

"Go away, then," said Kuhal Earthshaker. "I can rest here as well as anyplace. In the morning, Boduragol and the other Afaliah redactors will tend to me. Enjoy your Night of Secret Love, Brother!"

Death nodded, raised one skeletal hand, and slipped away to the masquerade.

Sullivan-Tonn danced with his betrothed, the beautiful young coercer Olone, knowing with sick certainty what black impulse from his own subconscious had made him choose the antelope mask with the spiral horns.

"You can't go with him! I forbid it. Your father gave me his most solemn promise!"

Olone was a vision in a cloak of floating white petals and a tall flowered headdress. Her tiny half-mask was gold, the top margin all decorated with jeweled stamens. She looked down at her elderly fiancé with a smile that blended amusement and contempt.

"Father is dead. And anyway, a King's wishes overrule those of a city-lord."

"Olone! My darling child. My untouched flower! I'll spirit you away—"

She felt the tightening embrace of his great psychokinesis. But all that was needed was a single coercive thrust, and he was crushed and weeping behind his silly antelope head, and they whirled over the soft grass and the music throbbed.

"Father pledged me to you without my consent when I was nothing but a child. You should be grateful that I still agreed to accept a human."

"No psychokinetic can match my powers!" Sullivan-Tonn blustered.

"Except *him*. And you're not such a prize. You're much too dumpy, and you're terribly *old* for one who's only ninety-six, and I think it was craven of you not to fight at Finiah."

"Don't talk like that! I love you so much!"

"Oh, twaddle." She was guiding the two of them closer and closer to the center of the dancing-ground, where the Fool and his Lady were spinning and soaring. "I know why you want a virgin. Don't think I can't read those terrible books you were showing the Interrogator just because the words aren't Standard English! Do you think we Tanu are incapable of using a Sony Translator? *La nouvelle Justine*, indeed! You try just one of those Lowlife tricks on me after we're married, and I'll coerce you to jelly!"

"My darling, I'd never—"

"Oh, be quiet!"

Most of those couples still on the dancing-ground now gathered about Aiken and Mercy. The Lady of Goriah was scarcely disguised at all, wearing a simple black domino and the Celtic costume that had been her choice for passing through the time-gate. The music had slowed to a languid three-quarter time. The jester and the Irish princess danced at arm's length. His face was hidden not only by the ludicrous long-nosed mask, but also by a mental curtain. Her lips were colorless, curved in a knowing smile.

The dance ended and they bowed to one another. A new melody began, jagged, eerie, impossible to dance to. The ball was over and the couples hurried toward the shadows.

Olone slipped out of Sullivan's arms and rushed to Aiken. "My King!" she said breathlessly, and curtseyed to the ground.

The Fool snapped the fingers of both hands and came leaping at her. She rose, dissolving in giggles, to be met by the relentless caress of the nose.

Helpless, Sullivan saw them run away. Mercy was almost alone now in the midst of the great bowl of lawn. The musicians, all human, had slipped into the climactic bars of "La Valse." Sullivan shivered in premonition. A spectral figure that had been waiting under the plane trees came into the moonlight and beckoned. Mercy went to him slowly, then rose on tiptoe and kissed Death's fleshless mouth.

"Everybody ready?" whispered Sharn.
"Ready," said Ayfa and the ten ogres.
They meshed minds and flung the bolt.

Olone's eyes were like stars. "Oh, Aiken. I never knew it would be like *that*."
The trickster looked slightly puzzled. "I think I surpassed myself! Maybe there's something to this maypole magic after all!"

Unlike the Firvulag weddings, those of the Tanu took place in broad daylight, beneath the noon sun of May Day. The nuptial pairs, led by Aiken-Lugonn and Mercy-Rosmar, circled around the great golden maypole to a stately processional chorus, climaxed by the Song. The brides and grooms wore gowns or robes of their own heraldic colors, and over them mantles of white. The brides had chaplets of white lilies and the grooms wreaths of male fern. Mercy's sole innovation in the ancient ceremony had been the inclusion of sprigs of rosemary in the nuptial crowns. "It's a plant used to bless weddings from time immemorial on Elder Earth," she had explained, "and it's also my own plant: rosemary of Rosmar. Rosemary for remembrance . . ."

She remembered another wedding.

It had taken place in the middle of last June—not a mass celebration as this was, but a more intimate one, with only the courtiers and the people of Goriah in attendance. She had not worn the blue-green of the Creator's Guild (she had not yet been initiated) but the rose and gold of her daemon lover. If he had lived, they would have reaffirmed their vow today, leading not the parade of newlyweds but the later procession in the ceremony of renewal.

Nodonn! she cried on his intimate mode. No one heard. Not the solemn little man beside her in his gold-and-black robes, not Eadnar and Alberonn, who walked directly behind them in the place of honor, not any one of the other one hundred and sixty-seven Tanu and gold-torc human couples who followed in measured figures traced around the golden shaft. They danced holding the strings of flowers that depended from the maypole's tip, weaving the ribbons ever tighter until the betrothed came all together in a tight circle facing the pole, dropped the streamers, and kissed in the final pledge.

Raising her tear-glinting face from Aiken's, Mercy-Rosmar Lady Creator held out both hands and exerted her metapsychic powers. In a soft miracle, the air filled with a fragrant tempest of tiny white blossoms that swirled about the kissing couples, settled in their hair, spilled from the nuptial cloaks to form perfumed windrows on the emerald dancing ground.

"Slonshal!" cried all the witnesses. "Slonshal! Slonshal!"

Then, with ritual finally over, the Grove of May swarmed with thousands of rama servitors and human waiters, all wearing Aiken's gold-and-black livery. The couples and the throng of guests reclined on shaded grass and partook of a picnic feast, this time with dishes and potations selected for their alleged aphrodisiac effect. There were strolling entertainers, and as evening descended, a great deal of ribald minstrelsy. A gorgeous and sensual ballet served for a final prelude to the love-making.

(By then the Firvulag had gone back to their own encampment, where Sharn and Ayfa and the Gnomish Council gathered around the fire, chaste and furious, and got blind drunk. Culluket kept a farseeing eye on the Foe all that night; but the mossy grottos that Mercy had so carefully prepared went completely unused.)

When the May moon rode high, the Tanu and human couples

once again paired off—but more decorously than on the previous night. They came to their bowers and their couches hidden among the shrubs and found them heaped with fresh flower petals. The newlyweds spread their white cloaks, and the old married folk managed in their old familiar way, and even the casual and the desperate found sweet solace in the nightingale-haunted forest.

After everyone else had gone, Aiken and Mercy went to the maypole. They joined hands around the tapering column of gold and began to circle.

"Now you are mine," he told her.

"But whose are *you*?" she retorted, breaking into wild laughter as the triumphant grin faded from his face.

His only answer was to crush her hands and dance faster. The maypole was now free of its flowery cords and jutted like some monstrous pylon toward the starry zenith. Its sleek hardness separated them as they left the ground and spiraled upward. They had lost their bridal crowns, but the white cloaks billowed, seeming to become larger and more enveloping, and then form a rotating fluidity like a ring of rising cloud. Mercy tilted her head from side to side as they went faster and faster. The night was a spinning blur except for his golliwog face and her laughing one and always the golden shaft between.

They spun above the apex, wrapped in the moonglow bubble that the capes had become. She felt she would die with the fear of him and the desire, and his eyes were two black bores and he was no longer a little man but enormous. And there was a great golden maypole that brought a great golden light and warmth beyond measure, beyond the Sun, even beyond Death.

"But whose are *you*?" she heard herself repeat, long after. And then, "No one's. Poor Shining One."

But by that time he was gone, and it was dawn, and time to get ready for the coronation.

Traditionally, the Grand Loving climaxed with the gentle deposition of the erstwhile King and Queen of May, after which the loyal Tanu subjects renewed their oath of fealty to the legitimate sovereign. This year, however, things were going to be different. Everyone knew it; the Many-Colored Land had been alive with the news ever since the successful conclusion of Aiken's progress. There were those who rejoiced and those who despaired and even a few who trusted that the Goddess would intervene at the last minute to solve what had become a grievously untidy state of affairs.

On the morning of May second, Lady Morna-Ia sent out her farspoken summons, and by noon the Conclave of Tanu had assembled in the grassy bowl of the festival ground. More than 6000 of them were in attendance, perhaps two-thirds of the total number left alive after the Flood. The Firvulag guests were there, too, clustered in a sullen knot, all wearing their obsidian armor and deeply hung-over. At the fringes of the exotic gathering was a mighty mob of humans that spread out into the parkland surrounding the amphitheatre—perhaps 15,000 silver-torcs, grays, and barenecks who had come not only from Goriah and its satellite plantations and mining villages, but also from as far away as Rocilan and Sasaran, expressly invited by the usurper to witness his hour of glory.

The dais had been cleared of its Maytide decorations. The flower-decked thrones were gone and in their place stood two unfamiliar chairs of unadorned black marble.

A single note sounded from a glass carnyx. The crowd fell silent, watching the dais, and abruptly Elizabeth was there. The minds and voices gave an involuntary cry of astonishment. Elizabeth wore Brede's great black-and-red headdress and costume, and held the glass chain of silence high in her hands. A wave of thought rolled out from her, calming the anxious Tanu minds, reminding them who had given her this rôle.

And then Aiken was there beside her, wearing his gold-lustre armor. His head was bare.

"Choose freely," said Elizabeth. "Will you have him as your king?"

The reply was quiet, numb, inevitable. "We will."

"The Tanu kings have no tradition of coronation," said the Shipspouse's successor, "just as they have no tradition of peaceful accession to the throne. For your race, a monarch has always been a battle-champion, his only crown a warrior's helmet. But this king has asked for a new symbol, and so I give it to him."

Elizabeth handed Aiken a simple circlet of black glass. He nodded to her and set it himself upon his springy dark-red hair.

Another sound swelled from the crowd: perhaps an indrawn breath, or one let out, or a sigh of relief, or a sob suppressed. Elizabeth bent over Aiken, speaking to his mind alone. Again he nodded, and Elizabeth disappeared. Where she had stood were now sixteen Tanu—and Mercy.

"I present to you your new High Table," Aiken said. His physical voice was quiet, but even the most distant bareneck heard his words.

"First, my Queen and Lady Creator, co-ruler of my city of Goriah: Mercy-Rosmar." She knelt before Aiken and received from him a green circlet. He took her hand and led her to the two marble thrones. They ascended. One by one, the High Table candidates approached, touching their torcs as their minds pledged silent fealty.

"The President of the Guild of Farsensors, the Venerable Lady Morna-Ia Kingmaker...the President of the Guild of Redactors, Culluket the Interrogator...the Deputy Lord Psychokinetic, Bleyn the Champion...the Second Lord Psychokinetic, Kuhal Earthshaker...the Second Lord Creator and Lord of Calamosk, Aluteyn Craftsmaster...the Second Lady Farsensor, Sibel Longtress...the Second Lord Coercer and Lord of Amalizan, Artigonn...the Lord and Lady of Rocilan, Alberonn Mindeater and Eadnar...the Lord of Afaliah, Celadeyr...the Lady of Bardelask, Armida the Formidable...the Lord of Sasaran, Neyal the Younger...the Lord of Tarasiah, Thufan Thunderhead...the Lord of Geroniah, Diarmet...the Lord of Sayzorask, Lomnovel Brainburner...the Lord of Roniah, Condateyr the Fulminator."

Aiken surveyed the newly accoladed Great Ones. "I myself assume the presidency of the Guild of Coercers and the Guild of Psychokinetics. The post of Second Redactor is left temporarily vacant. Since neither Lady Estella-Sirone of Darask nor Moreyn Glasscrafter, city-lord of Var-Mesk, are here at this conclave, I withhold naming them to the High Table until they personally offer oaths of fealty."

He rose from his throne and stood silently for a moment looking over the throng of exotics and humans and hybrids. His solemn manner softened and the old jesting smile appeared as he tapped the blazon on his glass breastplate. It was so stylized and encrusted with yellow gemstones that the digitus impudicus was hardly recognizable.

"And what about the rest of you? Do you accept me whole-heartedly as King of this Many-Colored Land?"

"Slonshal!" thundered the minds and voices of his subjects. "Slonshal King Aiken-Lugonn! *SLONSHAL!*"

The Firvulag said nothing. By the time anybody thought to look for them, they had ridden away on the trail to Nionel.

THE END OF PART TWO

PART III

THE GIGANTO-MACHY

1

IN HIS SLEEP HE CALLED OUT TO HER: MERCY! ONLY TO AWAKE again to the grotto of living rock surrounding him, impervious to any telepathic impulse.

Mercy! his mind screamed, but the sound that emerged from his lips was barely audible. As always, he tried to rise. As always, he could move only the muscles of his face and neck. A warm wind, laden with the scent of the blooming maquis, stole along the cavern wall. He was very thirsty. Turning his head, he concentrated his will on the good arm, commanding it to move, to reach out to the nearby flask of water. The arm remained limp. He was helpless.

Goddess, let me die, he pleaded. Let me die before Isak Henning and Huldah come back.

A fly settled on his face, crept maddeningly about his cracked lips. He called down vain anathemas upon the miserable creature. The hot wind skipped about, lifting dust and dropping it onto him. His skin was now exquisitely sensitive. He could feel every irregularity in the cave floor beneath his fur mattress, the damp hairs of the furs themselves. As the sun sank, its strong beams shone directly upon him for a brief time, making him break out in sweat. The thirst was appalling.

The fly on his mouth flew away. But then came his most dangerous insect enemy, a kind of large black-and-white warble fly that pierced the skin with a needlelike ovipositor and laid its egg in living flesh. Terror and loathing welled up in him at the sight of it. He flung his coercion at the filthy thing, strove to push it away with his PK.

It settled onto his belly.

He uttered a strangled shriek. A long shadow thrust down the cave's length and the wind brought a familiar smell of musk. He grunted with desperate urgency and she came running, dashing the warble fly off him with her bare hand just as it began to prick.

"There!" she cried, stamping it into the dust with her horny feet. "There, it's dead, the devilish thing!" She bathed the defiled spot in cool water and gave him to drink, then cradled his head against her breasts, crooning. Grandpa came in with rabbits from the snare and gave them a derisive look. Huldah paid no attention.

"Are you all right now?" she asked.

"Yes."

"No other bites? No pebbles hurting you?"

"No. Just give water." She let him drink again, then brought the ceramic bedpan. While she cleaned him up, Isak skinned the rabbits and spitted them. The smell of roasting meat was mouth-watering.

He could chew and swallow with ease now. Huldah had been very hurt when he adamantly refused the lip-to-lip feeding, but now he was able to close his jaw tightly against her, and so she no longer importuned him.

"There's going to be a lovely moon tonight," she announced. "Nice and full. Would you like to go outside? You and I could sleep on the grass and Grandpa in the cave."

"No," he said flatly. "Stay here."

"All right. But tonight is special. Grandpa says so." Her eyes were shining and she tossed her stringy flaxen hair. "After supper, there'll be a surprise!"

His heart went cold. A full moon in spring warmth? "What month?" he asked.

She bent over him, listening, and he repeated, "What month . . . is this?"

The evil old man heard and came back to stand over him.

"*We* call it May, Lord God! You call it the time of Grand Loving. Loving! And didn't you used to have a fine time— you Tanu and your bloody fertility rites? But no more! Your people are gone, Lord God. All washed away in the avenging Flood. The Flying Hunt hasn't come from Muriah since 'way last fall. It'll never come to Kersic again."

"I told you that, Grandpa," said Huldah placidly. "But you wouldn't believe me."

"Just because you're nothing but a half-witted slut," Isak Henning muttered. "But you were right about that."

"And I was right about my God waking." She stared at her grandfather with peculiar intensity. "Someday soon, he'll be all well."

The shabby ancient skipped over to the cooking fire. "When he is, he can use his PK to move his wooden hand!" The old man chuckled maliciously. "And scratch his own lice, and wipe his own ass. Hee hee hee!"

"Stop it, Grandpa!"

The old man scowled at her, defiant and half-fearful. "Just a joke. Damn cow, no sense of humor."

They ate. The dusk was long in coming. Outside, the birds began to sing and Huldah announced she was going to the waterfall to bathe. "And when I come back, I don't want to find you here, Grandpa. Take your things to the cork-oak grove. It'll be nice there. If you try to spy tonight, you'll be sorry."

Isak watched her go, mouthing impotent curses. He gathered up his sleeping robe and tossed into it fire-making tools, a water bottle, a broken chunk of ash-bread, and his set of three vitredur woodcarving knives. Then he shuffled to the rear of the cave, bundle over his shoulder, and stood over the supine invalid.

"You're in for it tonight, Lord God. The May madness has our Huldah in thrall!" He laughed until he fell into a fit of coughing, hawked, and spat. The foul gobbet landed only a few centimeters from the God's beautiful face.

With great effort, he spoke. "Who is Huldah? What . . . is she?"

"Aha! Ha ha ha!" the old man exulted. "Want to know what

ground your by-blow's sprouted in, do you? Well, Lord God, her grandmother was one of *you*! Almost. When I was a new-transported bareneck slavey in the plantations of the Dragon Range on Aven, they sent me to thin the antelope herds. I found a baby exposed there on the mountainside. I didn't know it, but it was a changeling. A Firvulag half-blood that some poor human trull of yours had given birth to, the way it happens sometimes. In more civilized parts, I understand the Firvulag babies are turned over to the Little Folks. But on Aven, where no Firvulag live...Well, I found the mite and took her to my hut. I had a pet antelope with a kid, so there was milk. In the beginning I was just experimenting, you see. The changeling could shift shapes even when it was tiny, and sort of read my mind as well. It knew I was lonesome, and it found I liked its human-looking body best. It grew up fast, anxious to please."

Isak hunkered down beside the motionless figure. The God said, "Huldah?"

"No, no, not yet. What happened, this changeling was a kind of a pet at first, and then a friend and servant, and then...well, the way you Tanu bastards don't give us bareneck men hardly any women, when the changeling was big enough to screw, I screwed it. It liked me. I named it Borghild after a girl I knew back in the Milieu. We were happy out there in the mountains, me doing my stupid herding job and the changeling doing her best to look pretty, just like the other Borghild. Then one day, another guy found out about her and wanted his share. When I beat him up, he told the overseer. But by the time the gray-torc troopers came, me and Borghild were way to hell and gone over the Dragon Range, and we made a skin boat with a little sail and came to Kersic. And then she had a baby, and then she died."

"Baby Huldah?"

"Not yet, dammit. I named the baby Karin. She grew up fast, too, and we lived in a Lowlife settlement we found here on the island. Karin was enough of a Firvulag to scare off the other guys in the village. They were afraid of her and afraid of me. We did pretty good in those days. And then Karin had a baby, and *this* time it was Huldah. One night a Flying Hunt came from Muriah. They used Kersic now and then when the outlaw human population built up. Everybody in the village was slaughtered except me and little Huldah. We got away and found this place. It was a long time ago."

The God's slow voice said, "And when Huldah grew, you took her."

Isak started back as if struck tripping over his bundle and falling to the cave floor. "I didn't! I didn't!" Breathing thickly, he groped in the tangled furs. A sapphire blade gleamed in the meager firelight and approached the God's neck, trembling above the ornate knobbed catch of his golden torc.

"Alien bastard," the old man hissed. "For years I've dreamed of doing this."

"Do it," said the God.

Isak Henning grasped the handle of the knife in both scrawny hands and raised it high. "Hate you, hate you! You wrecked it, our chance for a new world! Now you're finished, too! We're all—" The aged body shook uncontrollably, arched in sudden spasm. Isak dropped the glass knife, covered his face with his hands, and began to sob.

Huldah came—tall, shining clean, naked, and wreathed with wild orange blossoms. "Silly Grandpa. I told you to go." She smiled at her God. "Grandpa tried to hurt me only once, when I was a little girl. I taught him better. Show the God, Grandpa."

The old man, still weeping, pulled aside his loincloth to show what an unwilling girl with Firvulag genes could do to one who tried to force her.

"Now go away. Leave us alone, Grandpa."

The old man crept off and Huldah went briefly to the back of the cave, then returned to begin dressing her God. She handled him as easily as a doll. Lost in horror, he paid little attention.

Firvulag! She was Firvulag. He who had aspired so high had violated the greatest taboo between the two races. Firvulag! It explained her great stature and strength, her coarse vitality. And once, that mutilated wreck of a father–grandfather had been a brawny human male.

"Tonight will be the best full moon of all, since you're finally awake," she said. And after a little while, "You'll kill him for me, won't you? As soon as you're able?"

He could not reply. He realized now what garments she had put upon him—gambeson and trews of membranous bubbles caught in a mesh web, the padding for his glass armor. And now the pieces themselves being strapped on, encasing legs and arms (except for the missing right gauntlet), thighs and shoulders. She held up the breast-plate with its sun-face blazon all embossed in gold and rose-colored stones, then eased it on. Last came the helmet, with its fierce glittering spikes and heraldic crest of a crouching, unearthly sun-bird. She left the visor open, and tucked wads of fur here and there beneath his head so that the awkward weight would not turn him awry.

He was in an agony of discomfort in spite of the padding. The harness pressed into his supersensitive body like some fitted bed of nails. Humiliation, guilt, and hatred for her rose in him like a surge of magma.

The armor began to glow.

"Oh, wonderful!" she cried. "My wonderful God! God of Light and Beauty and Joy!"

She knelt, drawing aside the skirt of tassets, and began the act of worship. Her body was a soft mass of peach-colored luminosity and ebony shadows, and in spite of himself, he was coming alive to her.

"No!" For the first time, he heard his voice echo in the cavern's vault. He strained to lift his arms, to thrust away that adoring face. His muscles were lead. The radiance grew.

"God of the Sun!" she sang. "O my own God!" She mounted him, easily straddling the armor, a huge compelling softness devouring him. He was lost, and she was crying out in the sweet avalanche of blinding light, quenching the sun, blotting him out.

She fell away, senseless, and he hung in a scarlet void. I am dead, he thought, and damned.

He opened his eyes. The blood-colored glow dazzled him. It was coming from his own body. The glass armor flamed with it. An infinitude of tiny pain-impulses assaulted his skin and became a tingling that pulsed in rhythm to his thudding heart.

His left hand was on his breast. He raised it. And then the right, with even the wood suffused with brilliance and the crudely carved fingers flexing. He rolled away from the body of the woman, braced himself against the cave wall, and rose. The storm-sunrise light of him poured into every cranny of the cave. He saw a slight movement near the dark entrance and strode up to it.

It was the old man, cowering behind a rock. He had come back to spy after all.

Nodonn plucked Isak Henning up by the scruff and held him dangling. The laughter of triumphant Apollo was like the hurricane's roar. And then the gaunt shape was flung toward the rear of the cavern and crashed to the rock floor beside Huldah. The old bones snapped and there were piteous screams. The woman stirred, lifted her head, looked with stupid astonishment at the broken huddle—and then at *him*. She raised an arm to shield her eyes from his aura.

Nodonn came back to the two of them, his armor chiming with every step. He picked up Isak in his gauntleted left hand and poised the glaring wooden one, like a flaming claw, before the contorted old face.

"Now you will die," said the Battlemaster. "Both of you."

The old man began to laugh.

The claw affixed itself to the dome of his bald skull and began to twist. The laughter ascended to a shriek. "Kill her! Kill her! But before you do, look inside! Look . . ."

The high-pitched croak merged with other sounds. Nodonn wrung the head from its body and tossed both aside. Wide-eyed, Huldah watched. There was no fear in her.

Look inside?

She sprawled in gory dust, a few smashed orange blossoms tangled in her hair. Nodonn exerted his deep farsense. Hidden within that capacious Firvulag abdomen was a twelve-week fetus, half the length of his little finger. Perfect and strong. A male.

"A son," he breathed. "At last."

But how? How, beneath this pitiless star's sublethal radiation that had mocked him for eight hundred years? He was the almighty Battlemaster, and yet he had begotten only poor weak things, of which only a few languid daughters still survived.

He looked up at the shielding rock. He looked down to the placid woman with her forbidden genes. His race had resisted this mating to the brink of the Nightfall War in the remote Duat Galaxy. But Gomnol, promoting his eugenic schemes, had also urged miscegenation . . . as a short-cut to operancy.

Could it be?

His redactive faculty reached gingerly into the tiny brain. But the fetus was too unformed, and he too clumsy. He would have to wait.

"You will stay here," he told the woman, "and when my son is born, rear him with the utmost care until I come for him."

"You will go away now?" Huldah whispered, stricken.

"Yes."

Tears sprang from her eyes. She slumped, shivering. Nodonn picked up the rumpled fur coverlet and laid it over her shoulders. She touched the hard, smooth glass of his gauntlet.

"In the back of the cave," she said dully. "Your weapon."

His cry was jubilant. It was the Sword and its pack! Inoperable, he discovered by flicking a stud; but he would find a way to repair it. He fastened its harness. "And now farewell," he said to the woman. "The child's name will be Thagdal. Remember that."

"Dagdal," she said, weeping. "Little Dag. O God."

He emerged from the cave and exerted his farsight. It was ominously dim, but he discerned a high promontory on the western shore that would suit his purpose, and he set out briskly. Before he had gone more than a kilometer or two he slowed, then found himself staggering. His convalescent mind and body were weakening rapidly from the tremendous earlier effort. It was to be expected. He would have to be prudent.

His creativity, which in former days had called down lightning and moved mountains, now barely sufficed to cut a stout wooden staff for him to lean upon. The mighty PK faculty that once levitated fifty knights and their battle-chargers strained to augment his faltering leg muscles as he climbed the cliff.

The sun cleared the ridge behind him and seemed to smite him between the shoulder blades. Out of breath, feverish, he thrust the staff into the earth of the steep trail again and again and hauled himself along. Dust from his shuffling feet hung about him in the still air. The shrubs were pungent with resin. Insects buzzed and the plates of his armor rang discordantly with the clumsy motions of the staff.

Where am I going? . . . Why am I here? . . . Yes. To call. To send a telepathic message, telling the others that I live. Climb high, above the thought-obstructing rock. Otherwise the diminished farspeech would have no range . . .

He gained the height at last, still in the midst of a dense thicket of maquis and twisted juniper. It was easier to walk now, though, and there was a slight breeze. Call to them . . . the survivors of the Host, his blood brothers and sisters. Call and wait for rescue.

He came to the promontory's tip, to the open spot where the umbrella pines grew and ashes and charcoal from Huldah's last bonfire (the one celebrating his awakening) lay strewn on a burnt circle of soil. And there he had his first view of the New Sea that had drowned his world—vast and blue, not milk-white, as the shallow lagoon had been—extending to a misty termination on the far horizon and north and south to the limit of his mind's feeble eye.

Nodonn clutched the staff with both the gauntleted hand and the wooden one as he began to fall. On his knees, still transfixed by the scene, he groaned aloud. The memory came back: the gigantic wave overwhelming them, the cries of the drowning ones. And echoing over chaos, laughter as harsh as a raven's croak . . .

He rested under one of the scraggly pines and managed to remove his armor. Almost miraculously, he found tiny strawberries on plants creeping among the rocks and gathered enough to assuage both thirst and hunger. Then he crept to the brink of the headland and summoned his farsight again.

North: Formerly, Kersic had had salt flats stretching from its northernmost rocks to the continental scarp east of Var-Mesk, a small city whose proximity to soda-ash beds made it a center of glass production. Now all the flats were inundated and Kersic was a true island.

South: More salt water, all the way to Africa. In that direction had been one of the deepest parts of the old lagoon.

East: The interior of Kersic, rugged and forested.

West: Aven...

Oh, Goddess, yes. There it lay, dimly perceived. The peninsula shrunken, salt water creeping far up the valleys, and Muriah broken and silent and overgrown with jungle, while waves lapped at the cracked steps of the Thagdal's palace. The plantations deserted, the antelopes unharvested, the chalikos and hellads reverted to the wild, and a timorous remnant of domesticated ramas scuttling about the ruins, waiting in vain for their overlords' commands to reanimate their cold little torcs.

What was left? *Who* was left? What should he do?

The questions floated in his brain as crazily as the specks of goldleaf in a stirred goblet of starwater liqueur. A roaring of blood filled his ears and pulsating colored masses swam across his blurred vision.

Call for help.

No!

Why did the precognitive flare of warning admonish him? Why did every instinct shriek that he should take care, make no overt sign until he had recovered more fully—until he learned what had taken place during the six lost months he lay unconscious in the Kersican cave?

What was there to hide from? Who?

He slipped into unconsciousness. When his eyes opened again he knew that he must not call to his brothers and sisters, nor to the faint telepathic focuses that marked the mainland cities. There was only one person he dared reveal himself to, one who could be trusted to tell him the truth about the postdiluvian Many-Colored Land. Weak as he was, he could still direct his thought on the intimate mode and eventually reach

her. She would have known that he lived. She would still listen
for his call, even though logic insisted he was dead.

If anyone could come to him, she would.

Summoning his remaining strength, he fashioned a small
bright needle of thought, a farspoken call that arrowed over
the New Sea and spanned Europe, to be perceived by one mind
alone:

Mercy.

2

THE STAR WAS ·K1-226 IN HIS CATALOG, BUT AS SOON AS HE focused on that oddball three-planet system he knew it had to be Elirion. And second from the sun, six million years younger and in the midst of one of its miniature Ice Ages, was Poltroy. The inhabitants, who would in the Milieu be admired for their urbanity and diplomatic equipoise, were roughly at the pithe-canthropine level of mental development. Pudgy little cannibals swathed to their ruby eyes in fish-fur romped over glaciers with nothing on their precoadunate minds but the ambush of their neighbors and the subsequent breaking of their skulls for a eucharistic brain-feast.

Elirion was the last star in Marc Remillard's search-sequence and clearly useless for his purposes; nevertheless he lingered more than two hours past the allotted scrutiny time, fascinated by the primitive Poltroyans. He told himself that it was intellectual curiosity about this familiar world and its one-day-to-be-famous people. His superego sneered and suggested that he would use any excuse to delay homecoming and the nasty surprise that very likely awaited him.

The paleolithic Poltroyans hipped and hopped and bipped and bopped, and genuflected politely to their dead victims before starting the ritual trepanning operations. The blood-thirsty chieftain of one little clan was a doppelgänger for Ominen-Limpirotin, Fourth Interlocutor of the Concilium...

Marc withdrew his farsight at last. He told the search-director: EXPLICIT. Immediately he was back in his own body, enclosed in the opaque armor that sustained his life during the period of hundredfold cortical overload. He could see someone waiting in the observatory anteroom and for one hopeful instant his heart lifted and he thought the premonition false. But it was not Hagen out there. Patricia Castellane had come, fully mind-blocked, and the intimation of disaster was confirmed.

DISENGAGE AUXILIARY CEREBROENERGETICS. His brain began to cool. There was a nauseating implosion of pseudosensation somewhere behind his eyeballs.

REESTABLISH NORMAL METABOLIC FUNCTION. An interval of suspensory coolness, quiet marble solidity after cometary flight.

SEVER DRIVE LINKAGE, ACTIVATE CARRIAGE DESCENT. KILL FENSIVE X-LASER ARRAYS. REPORT BODY FUNCTION.

"Normal parameters all operator body functions," the scanner reassured him. At this point, Hagen should have taken over, supervising removal of the brain-probes and freeing his father from the armor after double-checking his vital signs.

No help came. There would never be any now.

Aloud and telepathically, he gave his own divestment commands:

WITHDRAW CEREBRAL ELECTRODES. WITHDRAW CEREBELLUM AND STEM CONTACTS. REMOVE GODDAM FUCKING HELMET.

Imperturbable, the computer transmitted his orders. Helmet dogs clicked open, clamps latched on, the heavy cerametal casque rotated a quarter turn, and the hoist's vibration reached him through the attached cables. There was warm humid air, indirect light, and the familiar digital chronograph reminding him that this was Pliocene Earth:

23:07:33 .... 16.5. + 27

The body armor fell apart in two halves and the carriage tilted to allow him egress. He did a few isometrics in place, absently touched one of the tiny wounds on his forehead left by the psychoelectronic crown of thorns, and noted that the blood had already clotted. Below the neck he was clad in a black, skintight pressure-envelope coverall, studded with re-

ceptacles for the circulatory shunts. The coverall was sopping
wet and stinking of the dermal lavage he had floated in for the
past twenty days. He told himself that he really ought to re-
formulate the gunk with a more pleasing scent.

Marc. May I come in?

The gut-clutch that had been only temporarily sidetracked
by the divestment routine got in its licks. Time for the really
bad news.

He climbed out of the armor and sent it off to the equipment
bay. The dome-room door opened and there was Patricia, carrying two tall iced drinks garnished with lime. She wore a
backless formal dress of pale blue shot with golden threads.
She looked much younger and her hair, unbound, had become
the color of the maple-sugar candy Marc remembered from his
New Hampshire youth.

He accepted her kiss, as briefly melting as a snowflake's
touch, then took the drink and let the alcohol-laced citrus soothe
his throat. He asked, "How many others went with Hagen?"

"Twenty-eight. All of the children and the five grandbabies
as well. They took all of the ATVs and smashed every boat
on the island over six meters length overall."

"Equipment?"

"Five tons of assorted weaponry, the portable sigma generator, all of the mechanical mind-screens, a very odd selection
of manufacturing and processing units, miscellaneous supplies.
They left four days ago. We went after them in the small boats,
but Hagen and Phil Overton and young Keogh generated a
squall that nearly wiped us out. And without you, our attempt
at long-range coercive synthesis failed."

"Four days." The dark-circled eyes were more haunted than
ever. "They planned it well. By now, they're out of *my* coercive
range."

"But not beyond a massed creative thrust, if you furnish
primary impetus. There's no place on Earth they can escape a
psychozap . . . if you choose to use it. They're gambling that
you won't, of course." Patricia's mental aspect was neutral.
But then, she had no offspring among the fugitives.

"I've got to think." Marc ran a hand through his damp wiry

curls. The chemical smell of the coverall seemed irrationally offensive to him; and as always after a star-search, he was famished. "I'm going to shower and change. Have you had supper?"

"I waited for you. You're late."

The characteristic one-sided smile flashed as they came into the dressing room. "I dawdled over the last star system, postponing the inevitable."

"You expected this?" Her expression showed the dismay that her mind-shield had kept hidden from him.

"I'm beginning to think that I deliberately provoked it."

He stripped off the coverall and entered the old-fashioned shower cubicle, luxuriating in its preprogrammed small comforts: pulsing needlejets of warm fresh water and liquid Canoe soap, salt spray, and the final icy deluge. As she handed him the toga-towel, Patricia let her eyes roam over his body in a frank appraisal that was only half jesting.

"What a pity the star-search makes you lose your tan. Otherwise . . . the same old frosty-haired Adonis with the Mephisto eyebrows. God, how I hate a self-rejuvenating man." *And covet your membrum virile!*

"Sorry, luv. Another casualty of the search. For now, at any rate." *Until I get mad enough to start the life-juices flowing again.*

She sighed. "Two wasted weeks in the regen tank to perk up my faded allure. Why do I bother?"

"You're magnificent. I like the new hair. Just have patience." *And she would—ever considerate, ever faithful, and never ruining it by loving him.* Patricia Castellane, who had directed the obliteration of her own home-planet in support of his Rebellion, was the only woman to share his bed since the death of Cyndia, back in the apocalypse on Elder Earth.

"Shall I summon the others?" she asked.

He pulled on a ruffled shirt. "We might as well get on with it. Call Steinbrenner, Kramer, Dalembert, Ragnar Gathen, Warshaw. Van Wyk if he's sober. Strangford whether she is or not. And the Keoghs." He wound a scarlet cummerbund around his waist.

"Alexis Manion?"

"To hell with him. I'm surprised he didn't take off with the kids! Encouraging that damn Felice scheme—" He broke off. The interrogatory thought flared.

One part of Patricia's mind responded to Marc as another sent out the telepathic summons. "Felice killed Vaughn Jarrow in their first encounter with her. Cloud and Elaby and Owen are all right, but the mission is in disarray." A reprise of Owen's reports from Spain passed instantly from Patricia's memory to Marc's own. He knew about Felice and Elizabeth, and about the coronation and marriage of Aiken Drum. "With Felice out of the picture for the moment," Patricia concluded, "Elaby and Cloud are concentrating on saving Jill. They still profess loyalty to you in spite of the defection of the other children, and say that they expect to follow your directives."

Marc allowed himself a bark of cynical laughter. He ran a comb through his hair, then offered Patricia his arm. They left the observatory and walked along the shore of Lake Serene toward his house. The young moon had gone down and the semitropical sky blazed with diamond stars. None of the constellations had the twenty-second-century pattern, of course, but the exiled rebels had named new ones. Mars hung low in the west, a baleful cockade on Napoleon's Hat.

"Elaby and Cloud will have given up on Felice, now that she's gone to Elizabeth," Marc observed. "I think we're safe in assuming that the new target will be Aiken Drum."

"A direct assault on him when the other children reach Europe?"

"Not unless Elaby and Cloud have lost their minds."

"A proposal to join forces, then?"

Marc paused, looking over the lake. There were boats on the glimmering water carrying his old co-conspirators toward his dock, the men and women who had been magnates of the Concilium until they linked their fates with his dream of human ascendancy in the Galactic Milieu. Debarring Manion, there were only eleven principals left alive—counting Patricia and Owen—and thirty-one subordinates.

He said, "The most likely course for the children to follow

would be some kind of peaceful overture to Aiken Drum. We still don't have any clear idea of his full potential or his vulnerabilities. Given the children's lack of experience, their judgment of King Aiken-Lugonn is going to be even more flawed than our own."

"The Firvulag royalty tried a crudely concerted attack on him during the Grand Loving festivities. They failed. We weren't able to analyze the reason for the failure because of the distance, but Jeff Steinbrenner thinks Aiken might have been wearing a stem-shield generator."

"Perhaps. On the other hand, this nonborn kingling may simply have grown in power. He's capable of it. A most interesting young man! His metapsychic faculties are only part of his arsenal, you know. He seems to be an instinctive politician as well."

There was fear close below the surface of Patricia's mind. "If Aiken Drum should respond favorably to the plan to reopen the timegate—" She left the rest unsaid. With a two-way passage between the Pliocene and the Milieu, agents of the Magistratum would see that justice was visited upon the surviving rebels, even after twenty-seven years.

Marc looked up at the countless stars and was silent for several minutes. Then he said, "Just a single world with a coadunate racial mind. That's all I need to find, Pat. The altruism of the Unity would compel them to come for us if we asked for refuge . . . and they wouldn't comprehend the truth about poor flawed humanity until it was too late. We'd have a fresh start, but this time there would be no mistakes. We'd spin our takeover bid across decades. Infiltrate while we engender an enormous new generation artificially. We could do it—even the handful of us who remain. If I could only find the star . . ."

"Marc, what are we to do *now*?" she cried.

He took her hand and placed it on his arm again. They resumed their walk to the house, where the dock lights had come on and at least six boats had already arrived.

"Come along and share my supper," he told her, "and then we'll talk about it with the others." His redaction pressed gently against her still-firm mental screen. "Don't be afraid to open to me, Pat. I've known for a long time that you and the others feel that my star-search is futile. Perhaps my own subconscious does, too. If that's the case—and I'll know the truth before we finish tonight—I may decide that it's time for a completely new plan of action."

"I'm not afraid to say it, if the rest of you are!"

Gerrit Van Wyk's eyes were bulging and bright. With his wide mouth slightly open, scalp shining in the verandah lamplight, and trembling little hands clutching a drained glass with rattling ice cubes, he looked more than ever like a truculent frog. He took a deep breath.

"We've had plenty of hints that something like this might happen. The Felice affair was a clear indication of the way the children's minds were working. And can we blame them? Face it, Marc! Your notion of finding another coadunate world is a long shot at best, and you've had twenty-five years to bring it home. More than thirty-six thousand systems scanned, and only twelve with rational beings—none even approaching coadunation of the racial Mind."

Marc still sat with Patricia at the small dining table while the nine others stood about awkwardly or occupied the scattered wicker furniture. Patricia opened the waiter and removed two plates with mangos for dessert. Marc skewered his and began to peel it with a silver knife, catching the drippings by psychokinesis.

"This time out," he said, "I found Poltroy."

Eight of the nine gave vent to excited mental and vocal comments. But Cordelia Warshaw, the cultural anthropologist and psychotactician, knew better. "How far up the ladder were they?"

"Roughly erectus."

Her head bobbed confirmation. "It figures, given their slower evolutionary pace. What a pity you didn't find the Lylmik instead."

Marc ate neat slices of the fiendishly juicy fruit while his mind displayed a reprise of the search-sequence, reminding them all that he had begun the hunt by examining the rare star-group containing the Lylmik home-sun. He had found no trace of the galaxy's most ancient rational race.

"They're out there somewhere." He touched his lips with a napkin. "But God knows where."

"The vague little masterminds *did* something to their sun," Kramer said bitterly. "Marc and I went over the matter years ago. There's no telling what spectroscopic signature it has here in the Pliocene. Some astrophysicists among the Krondaku speculate that they might have goosed the dying star back onto the main sequence a million years or so before the first coadunate fusion. If that's true . . ." He shrugged.

"I can't waste time examining incipient red giants," Marc said. "Our chances are slim enough if I stick with the likely prospects."

"Our chances are nil, now that the kids are gone," Van Wyk exclaimed. He struggled out of his chair and reached for the vodka decanter, then tugged frantically at the bottle that seemed welded to its tray.

Helayne Strangford's laugh was strident. "If I can't have mine, neither can you, Gerry! Watch the end coming, cold straight sober! Or do we postpone it, Marc? Do we? Are you going to ask us to help you kill them? Our own children? So that we'll be safe?"

She had come to the table and stood over Marc with a contorted face and fists pressed into her thighs, taut as an overtuned string in spite of Steinbrenner's heroic redaction job of an hour previous. From his own depths the Angel of the Abyss considered her threat and reacted mercifully. Helayne collapsed into Steinbrenner's waiting arms, overcome by a simple motor paralysis and simultaneous muting of her speech; but her understanding was left intact. The physician lowered her onto a couch. Dalembert and Warshaw propped her up with cushions.

"It will be a hard decision for all of us, Helayne," Marc said. "You love Leila and Chris and little Joel, and Ragnar loves Elaby, and the Keoghs love Nial, and Peter and Jordy and Cordelia love their children and grandchildren."

And you, the silenced mind accused him.

"And me," Marc acknowledged. He pushed back his chair and rose. One of the screened jalousie casements was slightly ajar and moths were coming in and orbiting the lamps. He pulled the latch to, casually exterminated the insects, and stood leaning against a porch pillar with his hands thrust in his pockets.

"Cloud and Hagen are all that I have left of Cyndia. It was necessary that I bring them here, to share my exile. Wrong, but necessary." His gaze swept the others. "Just as it was wrong, but human and understandable, for the rest of you to reproduce here in the Pliocene. We hoped we could revitalize our dream, transmit it to the young ones. All of us failed in that—and I failed doubly, in not finding a world that would come to our rescue."

"There *is* still time," Patricia said. "Centuries, if we choose to use them! If we have the courage."

"We took our risk in the Rebellion!" snapped Jordan Kramer. "My first family died on Okanagon, in case you've forgotten, and Dalembert's son was in the Twelfth Fleet. Don't lecture us on courage. Castellane. As for love, we all know you're incapable—"

"Jordy," said Marc. One winged brow lifted. No mind-thrust was needed to cut off the physicist's tirade. Sick-faced, Kramer turned his back on the rest of them and stared into the night.

Ragnar Gathen's slow voice came from a shadowy corner. "The star-search was a wonderful idea, one that gave us hope, made this exile more bearable. But the children . . . they never knew you as we do, Marc. So now, when they see a possibility of release from this prison that we chose for them, they must seize it."

"When the time-gate reopens," Van Wyk stated, "we die. Or have our personalities obliterated after the humiliation of a public trial."

Gathen said, "Elaby promised me that the children would destroy the time-gate after passing through."

"Hagen would do otherwise," said Marc. "Not consciously,

perhaps. But somehow the gate would remain open, and the agents would come.

Sweet-faced little Dr. Warshaw nodded. "Marc's right. And his child isn't the only one harboring retributive sets. The only safe course open to us is killing them all." She stroked one of Helayne's hands. The paralyzed woman's eyes were shut, pouring tears.

"It does seem to be the logical solution," said Patricia. "If even a few of the children survive to show Aiken Drum that data on reconstructing Guderian's apparatus, sooner or later he'll undertake the job himself—with or without the help of the manufacturing equipment that the children stole. I've analyzed the probability."

"We endorse Castellane's conclusion," said Diarmid Keogh. The mind of his sister Deirdre projected the remorseless image of the concerted psychoenergetic blast they would all have to synthesize to bring the resolution.

The leader of the Metapsychic Rebellion was looking blindly toward the wall of the house. Looking eastward. "There is another possibility. A risky one."

Wrenching silence.

"I see them," Marc said. "The ATV modular combine is moving very slowly through the region of calms and light winds called the horse latitudes. Their sails are useless, since they've channeled all of their PK into the main impeller. It would be rather easy to blast them out of the water. It would be much more difficult to heat up a large air mass somewhere southeast of their position and maneuver it to blow them back home to us."

"Is it possible?" cried Peter Dalembert, his mind a garboil of conflict.

"How about it, Jordy?" asked Marc.

"They're pretty far out." Kramer was dubious as he did the calculations. "Damn near two thousand kilometers, thanks to their initial push. And we can't simply heat air from scratch, you know. We have to locate a suitable tropical low that will respond to our hype-up, then move it in. One like *this*." He showed Marc an image. "Anything like that north of the equator?"

"No," Marc said.

Kramer shrugged. "There you are. We could wait a week, even two, before one showed up. They could be across by then—or into the zone of prevailing westerlies, where we wouldn't have a dimbuck's chance of forcing them back."

There's *this*," said Marc, presenting another meteorological image to the physicist. "Off the African coast."

"H'mm. Not too shabby, if we could boot it back west. It also has the potential of pushing them onto the Moroccan shore if we find that we can't raise enough wind to bring them home."

"Dammit, Jordy," Steinbrenner growled, "we've got enough watts to divert hurricanes from Ocala—so why is it so bloody tricky to conjure up a useful wind?"

"Diverting an air mass is a whole 'nother thing from hyping one up, Jeff. Or moving it counter to the planetary winds that prevail this time of the year. We have forty-two minds left to work with, but six or seven are virtually worthless for a PK-creative job. Whatever we try, it's going to be hellaceous tough on the operators."

"And the children will fight back, count on it," Diarmid Keogh reminded them. Deirdre projected the memory of the vicious squall that the fugitives had engendered on their first day out, and Diarmid appended, "You'll see that it was our own dear Nial leading the push to drown his lovin' da and mumsy—and working mighty handily with Phil Overton and your Hagen, Marc, for all that the lads are noncoadunate. Yes, we must assume that every mind among the children will resist."

"They have photon weapons, too," Van Wyk said tremulously.

"Don't talk like an idiot, Gerry," said Patricia. "Marc's here now. None of those portable zappers can touch us. They'd be inside Marc's coercive range before the zappers had line-of-sight on Ocala."

"They'll use everything they've got," Van Wyk persisted.

"Perhaps fight to the death," Warshaw added softly.

Marc had gone back to contemplation of his earlier farseen vision. "We might try to save the children. Above all, gain time to increase the number of options. Don't forget Cloud and Elaby and Owen in Europe, with Felice temporarily absent from her lair and Aiken Drum susceptible to manipulation. I must have time to think, to study the situation."

"You've had twenty-seven years," muttered Van Wyk recklessly.

But Marc was far away. "If we find that we can't turn the children back, we can certainly deflect them away from Europe. If they're driven onto the African coast, we'll have a chance to mind-zap the equipment and still spare their lives. Neutralize their threat until we can mount our own action. Yes . . ."

He came back to himself, to touch each mind with a split second's coercive force, then the more hypnotic persuasion.

"The star-search! If it had succeeded, it would have been our salvation: an acceptable substitute for our old dream that failed. My dream—my failure that drew you along with me. You and the other faithful ones chose to follow me here to the Pliocene and try again. And again, I've failed. Our children cling to their own dream, and I've been forced to consider the implications of their choice. I have done that for twenty days as I ranged the stars—and here again tonight while we looked for solutions to this dilemma. The final decision will be mine. But tell me how you would vote. Now."

"Kill them," said Cordelia Warshaw.

Patricia agreed. "It's the only safe course."

There was a moment of hesitation; but only Gerrit Van Wyk joined the two women in the death pronouncement. The others chose the more dangerous course.

Marc spread the new construct before them, the revision that might insure their own safety while granting their offspring's wish to return to the Milieu. There was an equal probability that the plan would spell the doom of all of them—and the unsuspecting inhabitants of the Many-Colored Land as well.

"This is what I shall do," Marc said. "Will you follow me?"

In a single telepathic acquiescence, the former members of the Galactic Concilium reaffirmed his leadership.

"Very well. I'll contact Owen tonight. Tomorrow we begin modification of my star-search equipment and construction of a new vehicle. We will maroon the defecting children in Africa, and see that they remain there until we're ready for them. If no unforeseen screw-ups develop, we should be ready to go to Europe about the end of August."

3

FELICE MOVED RESTLESSLY ABOUT THE BALCONY OF BLACK
Crag Lodge, a farouche woodland sprite in a white leather kilt,
doe eyes flicking and nervous farsenses sweeping the mountain
forest like a beacon.

"You're safe here," Elizabeth insisted. She stood in the
doorway, dressed in the old red denim jumpsuit that the girl
would remember from the auberge: a friend, an anchor to the
past. Every day for more than two weeks now the raven had
flown up to the chalet, perched on the upper balcony and turned
into a frightened young girl. And every day, in spite of Elizabeth's expert persuasion, the raven had refused to stay, flying
away after an ever-lengthening interval of conversation. Today,
Felice had dared to remain for more than two hours.

"There were bad nightmares last night, Elizabeth."

"I'm sorry."

"I'm going to scream out loud soon. If I do that, I'll die.
I'll drown in gold and shit."

"Unless you let me help you," Elizabeth agreed.

The mad eyes seemed to swell enormously. Talons sank
into Elizabeth's brain—but before they could do harm the
Grand Master redactor slipped an adamant barrier into place.
The mind-grip slipped, clenched impotently against unyielding
slickness, then withdrew.

"I—I didn't mean to do that," said Felice.

273

"You did." The redactor's voice was sad. "You'd kill anything that threatened to love you."

"No!"

"Yes. Your brain is short-circuited. The pleasure-pain pathways are anomalously fused. Shall I show you the difference between your mental structure and one I would call normal?"

"All right."

The images, of awesome complexity but bristling with labels that even this untaught child could comprehend, formed in the vestibulum of Felice's mind. She studied the two brains for nearly fifteen minutes, hiding behind her own screen. And then a crack opened and a shy thing peeped out.

"Elizabeth—? This brain is mine?"

"As close an approximation as I can produce, without actually entering you."

"Whose is the other?"

"Sister Amerie's."

The girl shuddered. She came away from the balcony railing and approached Elizabeth, a pale and tiny figure, utterly forlorn. "I'm a monster. I'm not human at all, am I?"

"You can be. All of this is in your unconscious—and since your opening of the Straits of Gibraltar, it has profoundly affected your conscious mind as well. But you can be healed. There's still time."

"But not . . . much time?"

"No, child. Before long, you'll be incapable of the volition necessary to permit redaction. You must freely let me in, you see. You're much too strong for me to overpower. And even if you do freely submit, your healing is going to be a very hazardous undertaking for me. Until you came here, until I was able to scan you at close range, I didn't realize how hazardous."

"I could kill you?"

"Easily."

"But you'd still try to help me?"

"Yes."

The elfin face with its pointed chin tilted up. The dark eyes swam with unshed tears. "Why? To save the world from me?"

"Partly," Elizabeth admitted. "But also to save you."

Felice's eyes shifted. An odd little smile appeared. "You're as bad as Amerie. She was after my soul. You're a Catholic, too, aren't you?"

"Yes."

"What good is it—here, in the Pliocene?"

"Not much, sometimes. But the basic lifeway remains, and I must try to adhere to it."

The girl laughed. "Even when you doubt?"

"Especially then," said Elizabeth. "You're very clever, Felice." She drew back from the doorway, turned and went across the room to where two chairs stood before a large window. "Come in and sit down."

Felice hesitated. The redactor felt the swirl of conflicting emotion agitating the girl, stark fear fighting against the genuine love-need that still abided, nearly crushed beneath the burden of guilt and perversion.

Keeping her own eyes on the view beyond the window, the rolling hills of the Montagne Noire, the distant gleam of Lac Provençal, Elizabeth slipped into one of the chairs. The raven still had not flown. Felice watched, and then a sinuous little probe tried to slip past the redactor's defenses: curious, desperately hopeful.

Elizabeth covered her face with her hands and prayed. She lowered her barrier completely and said, "Look into my mind if you wish, Felice. Be gentle, child. See that I've told you the truth—that I desire only to help you."

The thing entered . . . tempted . . . came closer . . . inadvertently revealed a glimpse of itself. O God see the pathetic betrayal of the poor infant girl by her wretched parents. Had it made her incapable of responding to any parent figure?

"You *love* me?" Incredulity . . . the fury held in abeyance . . .

"I had no children of my own, but I loved many of them. And healed them, and taught them. It was my life in the Milieu."

"But none of them . . . were as bad as me."

"None needed me as much as you do, Felice."

The girl was sitting in the other chair, leaning toward the figure in the red jumpsuit with the hidden face. It was only

Elizabeth! She who had been kind back at the auberge, convincing the officials to relinquish chaining her to the chair after the attack on Counselor Shonkwiler. Elizabeth who had bungled the elk-hunting, then showed such gratitude when Felice took over the distasteful skinning and gutting task. Elizabeth who had been so sad about losing her husband. Who had learned to pilot a balloon so that she could fly free and at peace in the Pliocene . . . only to give up that freedom and peace so that Felice might escape Culluket.

"I believe you," said a small voice. The monster receded into the far distance.

Elizabeth lowered her hands, straightened, smiled. "Shall I tell you how it would be done?"

Felice nodded. Her cloud of platinum hair was electric with excitement.

"First, we'll need to work in a safe place, where the discharges from your mind won't be a danger to others. Have you ever heard of Brede's room without doors?"

Felice shook her head.

"It's a mechanical mind-screening device of great power. Brede used it as a refuge, when the pressure from other mentalities became too great to bear. When she was within it, she could see out by means of her farsight—but no other mind could reach *her*. Brede let me share this refuge for a time. Before she died in the Flood, she gave the device to my friends so that I might have it here. The room without doors isn't a prison. Those inside can leave it at will. But if I am to undertake your healing, you must agree to stay inside the room with me for the duration of the treatment. Perhaps several weeks."

"I agree."

"There is another condition. Now that I know how strong you really are, I would like to use helpers in certain phases of your healing. I'm not as strong as I was in the Milieu. You remember that I had lost my metapsychic powers and only regained them with the shock of passing through the time-gate."

"I remember. Who would be the helpers?"

"Creyn and Dionket."

The girl frowned. "Creyn is all right. I'm not afraid of him.

But the Lord Healer . . . he's stronger than my Culluket, and yet he didn't stop the torture. He was too cowardly. And now he hides away in the Pyrénées with Minanonn and the stupid Peace Faction most of the time, instead of helping his people fight the Firvulag. I think that's despicable!"

"You don't understand Dionket. Nevertheless, you must accept my need of his assistance."

"How would you use the two exotics? They could never hold me, you know."

"Not using their own powers. But I would program a number of specialized mental restraints that they would operate while I was occupied with more complex healing functions. Think of a surgeon going deep into the body, using retractors and hemozaps and other devices to allow a clear field of work. Dionket and Creyn will free me from having constantly to monitor your defense mechanisms while I perform the catharsis."

Felice was silent. The great brown eyes were abstracted, seeming to watch a fire-backed eagle that wheeled slowly in the cloudless May sky. At last she said, "And when it was all finished, would I be *good*?"

"You'd be sane, child. Only God knows the other."

The monster peered out, mocking Elizabeth. "Amerie couldn't prove to me that there was a God. Or if there was, that he cared about us. Can you prove it?"

"There are rational proofs for a First Cause and an Omega, for the Father and Son. Empirical proofs for the Love that we call the Holy Spirit. But I never knew a single being who attained faith through the proofs. Mostly, they seem to be used after the fact of conversion . . . as reassurances."

"To plaster over your doubts, you mean!"

"To shore up our weakness. But the need has to come first, I think. That seems to be the only real proof. The need for love."

"Amerie said something like that to me once. I wanted to believe in a God then. I needed his help. Perhaps he existed then, for me. Now he doesn't. There is no God and there are no devils and you are nothing but a dream of mine! There! Now you know what I think."

"Felice—"

"Does it make a difference? That I don't believe any of you exist? Can you still heal me?"

"I'm confident that I can."

The monster's grin bloomed like a poisonous flower. "I wonder if your God would approve of your great confidence! If you bite off more than you can chew, you'll pay the price. And a lot of other people might, too."

Elizabeth stood up, her mind still open. "Make your choice now, Felice. Agree to the healing—or leave and never come back."

The diabolical smile faded. There came the old fear, and the still older need that had never been fulfilled. Poor tormented infant, accepting hurt in place of love, filth as substitute beauty, death's oblivion rather than agonized life.

"Well?" said Elizabeth.

"I'll stay with you," the girl whispered.

Her wall tumbled down. A naked thing looked at Elizabeth and waited.

4

SOMETIMES, AIKEN DECIDED, BEING A KING WAS A CROCK OF shit.

He was wide-awake at three in the morning, glumly watching the tawny owls chase mice around the ramparts and balconies of the Castle of Glass. The house lights were off. He'd had to decree a blackout once a week in order to give the feathered hunters a clear field in their war on the rodents, who throve as a result of his courtiers' penchant for alfresco dining.

It had been a frustrating day. Celadeyr of Afaliah had taken great exception to Aiken's master plan for the raid on Felice's lair. He objected to having to supply all the chalikos for the campaign, and he wanted the rendezvous to be in his own city rather than at the Gulf of Guadalquivir. He had given in with very bad grace when Aiken asserted his royal authority.

Then Yosh Watanabe told him that the new shipment of bamboo was hopeless for fighting-kite bones. The stuff was too weak for use in the big man-carrying o-dako, and too brittle for the smaller rokkaku. It was back to the drawing board (and the swamp) if they hoped to have a kite-fighting event in the Grand Tourney this fall.

Then came news that the damn barenecks had mutinied in the main candy factory down in Rocilan. Aiken sent Alberonn to check it out and it was discovered that a cadre of Aiken's jumped-up gold-torcs (the ones without any significant laten-

279

cies) had been running a scam, forcing production to unnaturally high levels by overworking the bares and ramas, then selling surplus goodies on the Lowlife black market. The golds had been promptly snuffed and the harried workers given a revised quota. But Aiken brooded over how much more ripping off his dubious recruits might be into, and he finally decided to recall the entire elite guard back to Goriah where he could keep it under his coercive thumb, rather than spreading it out. It would leave some city garrisons dangerously undermanned, but that would happen anyway once he got the Spanish campaign off the ground.

Then there was Bardelask. The Famorel Little People were closing in, polishing off the outlying Valentinois plantations one by one. Lady Armida was running scared (with good reason), demanding that the sovereign lead a relief force to put the fear of Tana into old Mimee and his gang.

Aiken couldn't do it, of course. Not with all his big guns mobilizing for the move into Koneyn. Poor Bardelask was expendable, even though he didn't dare admit it to Armida. The principal strategic objective was the photonic Spear and the cache of golden torcs that Felice had squirreled away. Any day now, Elizabeth would wind up her redact job and turn the monster loose. (Aiken's spy in Black Crag estimated that the brain overhaul would take another two weeks—but who could risk it?) He had to raid the treasure-cave before Felice emerged from the room without doors and then, following Culluket's plan, ambush her before she added it all up.

Then a newly arrived Lowlife from the Vosges region reported that some kind of Free Human expedition was in the offing. There were also rumors that the outlaws would soon have other weapons besides the iron.

And Sullivan-Tonn "respectfully requested" that he and Olone be allowed to move to Afaliah, and Olone defied her husband right to his face, calling him a jealous old cheese-pecker all the while giving Aiken the eye. (The request was taken under advisement.)

As a result of all the demands made on him during the day,

Aiken had been late to supper. The roast swan dried out and the soufflé fell.

And for the fifth night in a row, Mercy had merely submitted, unaroused, and blamed it on "fey influences" abroad in the May night.

This last, unaccountably, had troubled Aiken most of all. He himself had felt the presence of some uncanny mental substratum; but inexperienced as he was in the nuances of farsensing, he could not even confirm its existence, much less identify it or trace its source. He had appealed to Culluket, but the Interrogator detected nothing. Whatever the emanation was, it seemed closely directed along the uniquely human mode.

After Mercy fell asleep, when he was coldly alert and unsexed, he finally worked up the nerve to check out one of his most insidious suspicions: that she herself was the source of the metapsychic disturbance. While she lay there among the satin sheets, he carefully fashioned a soft mind-probe, supposedly indetectable, that could be merged with his great coercive faculty and used to winkle out secrets. The Interrogator had been training him in its operation over the past several months, and he had used it successfully on other humans— notably the potentially traitorous Sullivan. But Aiken had never yet dared to use it on his wife. Redaction was his shakiest power, and if she caught him . . .

In her sleep, Mercy smiled. A pang of fury shot through him. It had to be! There was no other explanation. No other way to explain why she was no longer afraid of him—and thus, no longer responsive.

The probe had slid easily into her, oblique and wheedling:
Are you happy Mercy my love?
So happy.
And why are you happy?
I have my child and I have my sweet acushla.
And who is he?
Who else but my own true lover?
(But no image, damn her!) *Look upon your lover dear Mercy and tell me what you see.*
I see the new sun rising beyond the inland sea.

(Sun!) *Do you hear his voice?*

I hear it now.

(But she could be talking about Me!) *What is his name Mercy my love?*

His name is Joy. Brightness. Culmination.

Where is he woman where is he WHO is he?

Oh . . . oh . . . halfway betwixt Var-Mesk and hell alas don't go Love don't risk the Monster wait for me to help wait . . .

Jesus!

He whisked his coercive effort from her cortex to the stem reticulum until her frenzied movements calmed and her breath became slow and regular and there was no risk that she might awaken. But something at her deepest mental level was now *aware*. It had not recognized him as the intruder; but it knew that there was danger. Aiken waited, but the crystal of cognizance continued to glow. Finally he had to withdraw with the utmost caution. He waited awhile, then climbed out of bed, put on a robe, and retired to the balcony to think.

Every one of those replies Mercy had given could be applied to himself, as well as to the other. Only the fleeting reference to Var-Mesk was puzzling. (Unless you classed the entire bloody Q&A as an enigmatic totality.) Mind-probes! What a rotten, cowardly thing to do—grubbing around inside the brain of the woman he loved, looking for an excuse to set her up.

Yes, set her up.

Yes, the woman he loved.

"Never again," he vowed. "No matter what I suspect about her. If it's true after all, and he's back, I'll find out soon enough. But not by probing Mercy."

He stood at the parapet watching the owls and listening to the surf from the Strait of Redon lash the distant seawall. How true it was: Being a king could be hell.

He went switch-off, stopped thinking, let his racing mind go flaccid inside the snug screens of his own weaving and the artificial mental shield of the psychoelectronic device he now wore constantly. Downhearted, tinged with vagrant dread, he floated . . .

And heard it.

A farspoken voice, faint but distinct on his intimate mode in spite of the stacked barricade:

Aiken Drum. Greetings at last. You've been a hard nut to crack, you know. Don't be afraid. We've been trying to bespeak you for nearly a week now—with a good deal of untidy slop-over on the European end unfortunately. It must have been very uncomfortable for those around you.

"Who the fuck *is* that?" Aiken whispered.

Laughter. Easy, lad, easy. Trace the thought-beam. Can you do that? Right. Way to hell and gone across the Atlantic. Nowhere near you or your Many-Colored Kingdom. Only me speaking to you now, not the others. And no threat to you. Just the opposite, actually.

"Identify yourself," he said between gritted teeth, straining to penetrate the dark distance, "or I'll phase in the sigma!"

You have one of those available? Interesting. But I'd still get through. Your own metapsychic wall is much more formidable than any contrivance, you know. Very effective, for an uncoadunate amateur. That's why we had such difficulty reaching you in the first place. But it never would have done for us to hail you on the ordinary declamatory mode. What we have to discuss is for your mind alone.

"Show yourself, dammit!"

Very well.

An image: massive, shining and metallic, roughly humanoid in shape, artifact of high technology. Space armor? Radiation shielding? Extremity life-support equipment? Superimposed was the man's face, ruggedly handsome; cleft chin and wide mouth, sunken eyes with winged brows, fine aquiline nose, curly hair going gray. He said:

We'll help you get the Spear and the cache of golden torcs.

"The hell you say!" Aiken's heart soared at the same time that he was frozen with alarm. Who *was* he? "You mean, you know the exact location of Felice's hideout in the Betics?"

Yes. We can make a deal.

The trickster's natural craftiness reasserted itself. "Oh, yeah?"

Three of my people are in Europe already. You have nothing to fear from them. Metapsychically, they're much weaker than

you. [Images.] We know of your preparations to invade Spain
before Felice comes out of the room without doors, your hope
of finding and repairing the photonic Spear and then using it
against her before she can retaliate.

"It's my Spear, dammit, and the torcs are my property, too!
I won't blast Felice if she listens to reason after Elizabeth
finishes her psychic overhaul job."

So you think a sane Felice equates with a benign one, do
you?

"Fat chance," he admitted. "Get on with your pitch."

Your scouts have not been able to pinpoint the location of
Felice's hoard. To prove my good will, I will tell you that the
eyrie is on the northern flank of Mount Mulhacén, about 430
kilometers southwest of Afaliah.

"No map image?" Aiken remarked snidely. "It's a big mountain."

My people will meet your forces here [image] in the foothills
of the Betics, along the Río Genil, and lead you directly to the
cave. Be there one week from today.

Aiken gave a scornful chortle. "Better still, let your guys
pick up the Spear and the torcs and bring 'em to me here in
Goriah!"

They are incapable of levitation and have no ground vehicles. Also, there is the inevitable mortal hazard, should Felice
return prematurely. As you are no doubt aware.

"Don't get cute with me," Aiken said quietly. "Suppose you
tell me what's in this for you, Mr. Ironass. And who are you
anyhow? That damn lobster shell you got on, how do I know
you're human at all?"

I'm as human as you are. The equipment . . . allows me to
exert my farsenses beyond normal metapsychic parameters. For
example, the penetration of your multiphase barrier.

Aiken's mental eye studied the now faceless mechanism.
"It seems to me that I've seen pictures of rigs like yours. A
long time ago, in some schoolbooks I should have paid more
attention to. Metapsychic Grand Masters use life-support equipment like that in the Milieu when they're into really heavy
mindwork. And I don't just mean farsensing." Abruptly, he

changed the subject. "This deal of yours. I suppose it would involve share and share alike from now on in Europe."

Not at all. If I had wanted the Many-Colored Land, I could have taken it years ago. You need have no fear that I covet your little realm, Aiken Drum. Ruling a few thousand barbarians as a quasi-feudal overlord isn't exactly my style.

"Neither is diplomacy, sweetheart!"

Touché, Your Majesty . . . But I still maintain that this planet is quite large enough for both of us. My needs are modest and unlikely to affect your ambitions in the least. Unless you become tempted to aspire beyond Pliocene Europe.

"Spell out the arrangement."

It will take a good deal of explanation, including some rather ancient history. And some of the governing factors haven't matured yet. I would prefer to postpone discussing my side of the reciprocity until you've dealt successfully with Felice. For now, I offer you the knowledge possessed by my three associates, plus their full metapsychic cooperation in your raid. Their minds are stronger than those of your Tanu allies, but still susceptible to your coercive control within the metaconcert you and Culluket have devised.

"So you know about that, too! How do I know you aren't really counting on Felice's blasting me—putting me out of the picture so I won't be able to queer your own scheme later?"

Felice represents a much greater threat to my designs than you.

"Ha! So you don't have enough watts to put her down yourself! Not even operating through that wizard rig of yours!"

No. Felice is one of those wild factors I mentioned. She is a menace to both our ambitions.

Aiken hesitated. The unknown operant in North America was making uncomfortable sense, but the lingering suspicion remained, together with Aiken's own deeper doubts on the ability of his amateur metaconcert network to stop Felice in a direct confrontation.

"I'm going to show you something," Aiken decided, allowing a diagram to form. "These are the minds I've got to work with. And this is the orchestration Cull and I worked out for a three-barreled coercive-creative-PK assault with me doing the focus and him monitoring the penetration. You seem to know Felice a hell of a lot better than I do. So . . . how about it? Given the fact that she'll probably come up sane, be more in control of her faculties, would we have any chance of stopping her?"

There was a silence. The armored image faded, leaving Aiken alone on the balcony, the chill wind blowing up his robe and making his golden balls retract with a sense of keen foreboding. Then:

Your original plan was to avoid confronting Felice at all costs. You hoped to secure the photonic Spear, repair it, and poise yourself at a high altitude above Black Crag in order to burn her as she exited the room without doors.

"Right. But that scheme was contingent on finding her lair in the Betics before Elizabeth finished her redact. We still might pull that one off. But what're the odds if Felice catches us flat-footed?"

I lack complete data. But it seems likely that even with the help of my three people, Felice would be able to destroy you if she got within two kilometers of your assault team. The metaconcert matrix that your friend the Interrogator taught you is highly inefficient. In true synergy, the whole is greater than the sum of the parts.

"What's our coefficient?" Aiken inquired grimly.

Only about point-four-six.

"Could *you* teach me how to jack up the output? In a week?"

Laughter rang in Aiken's brain. He saw again the human face of the unknown, and his neurons tasted appreciation by another who shared a certain sense of bravado. "Well, could you?" yelled the shivering little man. (And is it possible you are who I think you are?)

I could design such a program and impart it to you. Its use, however, would involve inherent perils, even for a raw natural talent such as yourself. Ideally, the metaconcert should involve my own operants as well as your torced subjects. The pair of us would contribute to the input, and one of us would filter and provide impetus while the other handled executive focus.

"I do that. *I* control it."

Channelizing that amount of psychoenergy barebrained could prove fatal. I don't know your capacity.

"Culluket does. He could monitor the transfer. And cut me off as well if you tried to go primary and zap *me* instead of Felice!"

Laughter. Sobriety. The equipment I use protects me from being annihilated by my own metapsychic power. You could never handle my full potential . . . but less may not suffice for Felice.

"On the other hand, it might! Right?"

Silence.

"Right?" demanded the Nonborn King.

Do you know what psychocreative feedback is? [Image.] In this more sophisticated form of metaconcert, there is danger to all the participants if the focusing agent is inadvertently overwhelmed—as could happen if your concentration failed at a crucial moment.

Aiken chuckled. "I see. The director cashes in, there's a good chance the rest of the grunts in the orchestra do, too. But if the monitor does his stuff, the danger's minimized for you. Right? If Felice reflects the psychozap back on me, I get snuffed—but Cull's linkage snaps for a fail-safe and the rest of you can pull out under a synergistic umbrella. Isn't that the way it would work, Mr. Paramount Grand Master? *Isn't that the way it worked when your brother and his wife put down your Rebellion?*"

Silence.

"Well? You wanta have a bash or not? You don't have much to lose . . . aside from making me a present of a mighty useful metapsychic program."

It would be safer if I handled the focus. And we would be sure of finishing Felice.

"No soap. I'm the King here, Ironass, not one of your leftover rebels. If you won't play, I'll revert to my old risky scheme. I should be able to find Felice's cave now, even without the help of your trio in Spain."

Very well. I will work with you and your redactor, Aiken
Drum.

The trickster grin flashed across the intervening ocean. "I
thought you'd see it my way. Folks often do! What would you
like me to call you? Some of the humans in my outfit might
get nervous if I use your real name. And they'll have to put
some handle on you."

I have been called Abaddon. [Ironic image.]

"Very appropriate. One week to the Río Genil, then, Abaddon."

Assemble your most powerful metapsychics. You'll need
them . . . King Aiken-Lugonn.

The aether was abruptly clear, the alien emanations gone
as if they had never existed. He heard the night birds, the surf,
a soft moan from Mercy asleep in the bedroom.

He tiptoed in and shed his robe. She lay half-covered with
one arm flung up in a posture of sweet vulnerability, dreaming.
In his excitement and triumph, he found the temptation to probe
her irresistible. He looked at her dream, and discovered that
its subject was as he had suspected. Nodonn Battlemaster was
alive, hidden but no threat at the present time. He would keep.

In her sleep, Mercy smiled. Aiken gently removed the probe,
bent to kiss her, then tucked the satin around her shoulders.

"Why did I have to love you?" he asked softly, before
leaving the room to sleep alone.

5

THE THREE YOUNG MEN WERE TOGETHER ON THE COMMAND deck of the ATV modular combine, with Hagen at the helm. The sky was brilliant cobalt without a cloud, and the air almost dead calm; but the vessel was making a steady six knots, its solar-powered impeller augmented by metapsychic thrust from the PK specialists on watch.

"I haven't said anything to the others," Phil Overton remarked. "They've got enough to worry about, coping with the babies and the sickos and the PK load. But something's brewing in the atmosphere a couple of thousand kloms southeast of us that's got me worried."

The image of a suspect weather system hung in their minds, as clear as a Tri-D picture. "See how sharp the cloud bands are? How well defined? Compare it to this other low-pressure dimple south of the Bight of Benin—normal for this time of the year. I've had my eye on the little mid-ocean sucker for three days now, and it's firmed up and deepened in an unnatural way."

Hagen's knuckles whitened as he gripped the wheel harder. "You think my father and the rest of them are psyching it?"

"God!" Nial Keogh expostulated. "Not when we're so close to making the westerlies!"

Phil shrugged. "It's the wrong time of the year for hurricanes, and the track of this storm is definitely anomalous.

289

Meteorological conditions are favorable for its continued growth, whether anybody's helping it along or not."

"Can we avoid it?" Hagen asked grimly.

Phil made the projection. "Here's our vector—and here comes the storm, sneaking up beneath us. We're right in its track if we maintain present course. The kiss-point is 36–45 North. 16–20 West three days from now. We slow down, we get slammed by the winds in the northwest quadrant and pushed way south. We speed up, there's a slim probability of having it skim by our ass, or even bung us north into the zone of prevailing westerlies."

"That's assuming the storm track is constant," Nial put in. "If Marc's in the driver's seat, it sure as hell won't be."

"What can we do?" Hagen's face was a mask of sick despair. "Is there any chance of escaping the thing, short of increasing our speed? Sweet Christ, Phil—we're pushing ourselves to the utmost now! You saw what happened to poor Barry, and Diane's weakening, too."

Phil considered. "It depends upon what Marc's objective is."

"He's not out to sink us," Nial declared. "If he wanted us dead, he could have zapped us ten days ago. We won that gamble."

"Could he blow us back to Florida?" Hagen asked.

"Hell, no," Phil said. "The low would poop out long before that. He'd need a whole set of storms to pull that one off. If he'd tried this stunt earlier in the game, there might have been a chance." His mind reviewed the atmospheric patterns of the past week. "But, see? The potential just wasn't there. *This* low is the first hot prospect he's had. Let me think a minute."

Hagen said, "He can't blow us home and he's not looking to deepsix us. All that's left is diversion. That fix you mentioned, north of Madeira. If he manages to push us off to the southeast, we end up in Africa instead of Europe."

Phil nodded agreement. Another meteorological diagram appeared in his mind. "The storm winds rotate counterclockwise. All he has to do is keep us poised roughly between six and nine o'clock inside the system and we're off on the road to Morocco. Even the fuckin' current's in his favor! The only joker that might save us hinges on the energy he's able to pour into the storm. If he can't keep it stoked up, we'll break free before he maneuvers us close enough to land to marshal a direct PK-creative shove."

"What if we erect the big sigma-field?" Hagen said. "Lower our friction quotient so the winds stream around us?"

"No good," Nial said. "You get a prohibitive power drain, using the generator on salt water instead of dry land. Maybe four, five hours max output."

"Shit. He's got us in the nutcracker for sure." Hagen's mouth curved in a mirthless, one-sided smile, momentarily giving him an uncanny resemblance to his father. "We might as well change course for Africa right now! At least then the little kids will be spared riding out a hurricane."

"You're the captain," said Phil. "Of course, this is all conjecture about Marc being behind the storm. We have no proof yet..."

"Three days from now, we will," Hagen said. "It's him, all right. You can bet your life on it!" He engaged the autopilot, turned to the binnacle computer, and called up a new heading. Slowly, the bow of the combine swung to starboard.

"Course correction completed," said the autopilot. "Steady on one-one-five degrees."

Hagen yanked the door open and stumbled out onto the flying bridge. "Is that good enough for you?" he screamed at the sky. "You win again! Congratulations! And damn you to hell, Papa!"

There was no response. He hadn't expected one. Empty-minded, he groped his way to the companionway stair and disappeared below.

Phil and Nial reflected upon the inevitability. At last, young Keogh sighed. "I'll take the con for the rest of the watch, boyo. You get along and tell the PK heads to hang it up. There's no hurry now."

Moreyn Glasscrafter, city-lord of Var-Mesk, urged his chaliko and the riderless second mount along the moonlit beach with irritable telepathic nudges. How he hated to travel with these animals! Chalikos had an ingrained antipathy toward him and tended to evade his commands more often than not. The problem was negligible when there were other riders along who could augment his weak coercive faculty. But the mysterious farspoken message had insisted that he come alone, and enjoined the strictest secrecy through fearsome Psychokinetic Guild oaths. So he clumped along the ghostly gypsum-sand beach, keeping a sharp lookout for quickmires whenever he crossed one of the freshwater streams that ran down from the high continental escarpment. Faintly luminous wavelets lapped the shore and there was a thin line of wrack staining the formerly sterile whiteness. Diminishing salinity was making the erstwhile Empty Sea into a Sea of Life . . .

He was more than 40 kilometers from the city, traversing a deserted region that would, in six million years, lie just off the Côte d'Azur. Did he dare utter a short-range declamatory hail? He scanned the shore ahead and saw only dunes and isolated lumps of evaporite. The mysterious Psychokinetic Brother was well hidden.

Moreyn here!

. . . Aha! On the other side of that pyramidal mass of salt, the faintest of rosy-gold auras. Another poor devil, marooned all these months on some Tana-forsaken shore, had finally made his way back to the Many-Colored Land.

Mind-smiling, holding up a hand in welcome, Moreyn came riding around the saline monolith on the landward side, saw the raft, and finally recognized the guild-brother with the shielded mind who had summoned him.

"Lord Battlemaster!" he gasped, dumfounded. The chalikos slipped out of his uncertain coercive grip and began to shy from the glowing body that lay on the white sand. "Steady, damn you!" Moreyn shrilled.

Nodonn opened his eyes. The two animals seemed to turn to stone. Moreyn struggled down out of the tall saddle and knelt beside the supine form.

"Let me cover you with my cloak! Are you thirsty? Here— my flask! Goddess—what happened to your hand?"

"It's . . . a long tale, Psychokinetic Brother. Thanks for coming. I'm nearly used up." He took a long pull from the water flask and sank back upon the sand. Moreyn fussed about, tucking his cloak under the Battlemaster's legs and torso. Nodonn wore his suit of armor padding, now salt-stained and torn. His exposed skin was badly sunburnt.

"We thought you were dead! This is wonderful!" Moreyn's face fell. "I mean—it's terrible! The Lowlife usurper, Aiken Drum, has forced us to accept him as King. He went from one city to another with his army, threatening us. No one could stand up to him and survive. In Var-Mesk, I blush to admit that we were all craven before the Shining One save Miakonn Healerson alone. Oh, how proud you would have been to see his defiance, Battlemaster! It was hopeless, of course, but magnificently true to the traditions of the battle-company. Miakonn waited until the usurper was far gone in drink, and then called him to account! It was a bold ploy and might have succeeded had not the treacherous Interrogator—" The Glasscrafter broke off.

"Peace, Brother," Nodonn reassured him. "I am well aware that Culluket has betrayed the Host. I know what he did to Miakonn, and why you are now city-lord in his place."

Moreyn bit his lower lip, his mind veiled in shamed misery.

Nodonn reached out. "Never mind, Brother. You have always been an excellent glass technician." He nodded toward the raft with its crude sail of stitched skins. There was a bundle lashed to one of the crossbraces. "See there? It's the armor you fashioned for me three hundred long years ago. I've managed to lose one gauntlet. You'll have to make me another before I take to the field."

"You'll defy the usurper?" Moreyn was transfigured.

"Today, I'm a sorry excuse for a Battlemaster. But I'll mend. For more than six months I was cast away on Kersic, bereft of my senses and beyond reach of any farsightful knowledge. Now only two Tanu know of my existence: Lady Mercy-Rosmar and you."

"She is married to the Lowlife King," Moreyn lamented, "and crowned his Queen."

"Peace," said Nodonn again, easing the city-lord's mental turmoil. "Mercy bides with the usurper because I have instructed her to make no move until the time is ripe. She remains faithful to me in her secret heart and eventually we will be reunited. I plan to reclaim *all* that is mine. Will you assist me to that end, Moreyn?"

"I would give my life for you, Battlemaster—poor thing that it is. But you know how pitiful my aggressive faculties are. Aiken Drum would not even have me accompany his Quest to Koneyn . . ."

"I know he's after the Spear. And fresh gold torcs to decorate his puny-minded rabble-in-arms—much good may they do him!"

Moreyn's glance kept straying to the wooden hand, which he regarded with singular apprehension. "We don't have a healer in Var-Mesk qualified to tend your wound, Battlemaster. So many redactors perished in the Flood. The nearest practitioner with the competence—the nearest *trustworthy* Skin artisan—is Boduragol of Afaliah."

"He who has charge of my Host Brother, Kuhal. Yes, I know of him." Nodonn flexed the fingers of the prosthesis, smiling slightly. "But don't worry, Moreyn. This makeshift works well enough. If I go into Skin, I'll be nine months growing another. Too long to lie idle when my metapsychic powers are fast returning and destiny calls. I think that my hand's full healing may have to be postponed until I settle the hash of that Lord of Misrule over in Goriah!"

Moreyn's mouth dropped open. He projected sheer calamity. "Oh, no, Battlemaster! You mustn't delay the healing! Why—no one would rally to you!"

"You think not?" The Battlemaster was puzzled.

"My Lord, perhaps you have forgotten . . ."

"Pull yourself together, man," Nodonn snapped. "Explain—or at least open your damn mind so I can see for myself what you cavil at."

The timid screening lifted and Nodonn read plainly the tenet of the battle-religion that had not been invoked for thousands of years on lost Duat—and never since the Tanu had come to the Many-Colored Land: No one who was not perfect in shape might aspire to the kingship.

Nodonn laughed. "*This* is your objection? This piece of antiquated flummery? When our throne is profaned by a Low-life upstart?"

"It is the law," whispered Moreyn, with the stubbornness of the meek. "Aiken-Lugonn is lawfully elected by the plenary session of vassals, and he was the chosen of Mayvar King-maker—exotic though his blood may be. And as to that, it has been said that he was not of human woman born, but engendered through some miracle of Elder Earth."

"A test-tube baby nurtured in an artificial womb," scoffed the Battlemaster. "No miracle. There are many such among the humans."

But Moreyn pushed on. "My Lady Glanluil, who attended the Grand Loving in my place when I was taken ill, says that even stranger things were hinted at by the Interrogator at the wedding feast. He said—he said that both the King—I mean, Aiken-Lugonn—and Queen Mercy-Rosmar have true Tanu genes in their germ plasm!"

"Aiken Drum, kin to us? Chaliko flop!" But the Battlemaster felt his spine freeze. He knew for a fact that Mercy's heritage was more Tanu than human. The prodigy had been proven by Greg-Donnet Genetics Master long before the latter's defection.

"The Interrogator is a life-scientist," Moreyn said, "and he has gained great knowledge of these arcane matters after consultation with human specialists. He said that recent genetic assays have shown that virtually all of the humans here in the Many-Colored Land who possess metapsychic traits also have a preponderance of Tanu or Firvulag genes. There is some mysterious power at work, linking our race with that of the Lowlives."

"Impossible! Humanity's direct evolutionary ancestor is the small ramapithecine ape that we use as a servant. Would we foul our blood by mating with animals? Never! And these lowly hominids will not even begin to approach rationality for more than five million years. Long before that, we will have vanished from this melancholy planet."

"Can you be certain?" asked Moreyn.

Struck silent, Nodonn beheld in memory a pathetic pair of elderly humans—the rebel general Angélique Guderian and her consort, Claude, held captive in the moments before he permitted them to pass back through the time-gate to death. The old man had dared to defy him. Upon hearing the Battle-master's command, "Go back where you came from," Claude had uttered a baffling reply that now hung vivid and shorn of paradox:

You fool. We came from here.

"Madness!" said Nodonn angrily.

Moreyn went on. "These humans have legends. Myths about races of Old Ones who existed on Earth for long aeons before mankind arose—and who persisted as a pitiful and despised remnant even into the years immediately preceding the Galactic Milieu. Humans gave many names to these Old Ones: demons, faeries, gods, giants, elves. But all over the precoadunate Earth, primitive humans were convinced that the Old Ones existed. And that they mated, from time to time, with humanity."

"Madness!" Nodonn repeated. "I forbid you to speak of it further." He climbed unsteadily to his feet, kicking aside Moreyn's cloak. "Lead the spare chaliko to that lump of salt so that I may use it as a mounting block."

Moreyn hastened to bring up the animal; but he was constrained to finish his speech. "I think that all of this is an unlikely tale, Battlemaster. But other Tanu do not, and most especially, neither do the hybrids. The legend, the rationale of our kinship with humanity, makes the bitter pill of Lowlife ascendency easier to swallow.

"I'll give them another kind of medicine," Nodonn declared. "Get that armor bundle and lash it to my saddle. Do you know what's inside? The holy Sword! The weapon I wielded in my first confrontation with the usurper—and intend to wield again, victoriously! Then we'll see who dares prate of lost hands and Nonborn Kings and bastard descendants of the Tanu returning through the length of time to mate with their own forebears!"

The hapless Moreyn cringed. Nodonn's body glowed a raging solar gold, its brilliance on the threshold of pain. "Oh, take care lest the Foe detect you, Battlemaster! Take care!"

The aura was instantly extinguished. "You're right, old friend. My vehemence is rash. Stupid. Mercy warned me that the usurper's spies are everywhere. From now on, I'll guard myself well. I would not put you in jeopardy."

"Oh, who cares about me?" the Glasscrafter moaned. "My life means nothing. Yours means everything!" He fumbled ineffectively with the stirrup of his own chaliko, tried to mount as the beast danced, then gave up and wafted himself ignominiously into the saddle with his PK and made haste to fasten the dicky strap. Nodonn was careful not to smile.

"You are my charge, Battlemaster," Moreyn said. "I have a sacred obligation to shelter you until Lord Celadeyr and Queen Mercy-Rosmar can come for you and take you to safety in Afaliah." He sent a plea for forbearance toward the flawed titan, whose face was now lost in the moonlight's shadow. "I have prepared a secret hiding place for you where I can minister to your needs myself. I'm afraid that you'll find your confinement tedious, for the chamber is small, in a deep subbasement of the glassworks. But if you can restrain your battle ardor for a little longer, be patient—"

"Recently, I have had much experience practicing patience."

"—then, the Good Goddess willing, your body as well as your metapsychic strength will be restored, and you will fulfill your great destiny."

Nodonn bowed his head. "I'm in your hands, Moreyn. From now on, command me and I obey."

The Glasscrafter heaved a relieved sigh. "Oh, that's fine. We'll head for home right away. *You* direct both chalikos, if you don't mind."

"Of course," said the Battlemaster.

Side by side, their gaits perfectly synchronized, the two huge animals began to trot along the strand toward Var-Mesk.

6

"THEY'RE COMING! THEY'RE COMING!" CALISTRO THE GOAT-boy shouted as he dashed up the length of Hidden Springs Canyon, his charges forgotten. "Sister Amerie and the Chief and a *lot* of others!"

People swarmed from the cottages and huts, calling out to one another in excitement. A long train of riders was wending its way into the village outskirts.

Old Man Kawai heard the commotion and stuck his head from the door of Madame Guderian's rose-covered house beneath the pines. He sucked air through his teeth.

"She comes!"

A small cat came running from the box under the table, nearly tripping him when he spun about to snatch up a paring knife. "I must cut flowers and hurry to greet her!" He pointed a stern finger at the cat. "And you—see that your kittens are groomed so that you do not disgrace both of us!"

The gauze-screened door slammed. Muttering to himself, the old man chopped off an armful of the heavy June rose clusters, then rushed down the path scattering pink and scarlet petals behind him.

There were sentimental reunions with old friends for Peopeo Moxmox Burke, Basil Wimborne, and Amerie Roccaro, who were hailed as heroes of the Lowlife liberation; and a fervent

welcome was extended to the thirty daredevil pilots, technicians, and specialists of whom there were such great expec-
tations. This group was instantly dubbed "Basil's Bastards" by
Denny Johnson, commander of the Lowlife defensive forces,
much to the flusteration of the alpinist ex-don.

After a gratifying interlude at the community bathhouse,
the new arrivals were honored at a gala fish fry and strawberry
shortcake feast that was hastily contrived by Marialena Tor-
rejon. Perkin the vintner hauled out demijohns of Riesling and
fragrant vinho verde and sweet white muscatel to fuel the never-
ending round of toasts, with the result that quite a few of the
villagers, as well as Pongo Warburton and Ookpik and Seumas
Mac Suibhne of the Bastards, were in no condition to join in
the Mass of Thanksgiving that Amerie celebrated to bring the
grand day to a close.

Finally Old Man Kawai led exhausted Amerie to Madame's
cottage, over her protests that the place was his home now and
should remain so. "We will speak of this later," said the former
electronics manufacturer. "For now, you must take Madame's
bedchamber. Her spirit would wish it, and I will perish of
vexation if you refuse the honor. I will be quite comfortable
on a pallet in the kitchen with the cats for company."

He opened the screen door and held it for the nun. She
stopped short, sank down, and cried, "Dejah!" A slender little
animal with a sandy coat and a black-tipped tail came running
and leaped into her arms. Except for its large eyes and ears,
it resembled a miniature puma. It was a female of the species
Felis zitteli, one of the earliest of the true cats.

Amerie cradled the purring creature, her eyes brimming. "I
never thought I'd see her again, Kawai-san. Do you think she
missed me?"

"She had certain distractions," the Japanese remarked drily.
He pointed to the box under the table. Three tiny heads peeped
over its edge. "They are all males. Nine weeks of age. I have
not named them. I waited, hoping that you . . . that my vow to
the Nagasaki martyrs . . ."

He hung his head. Suspicious drops of moisture spotted his
happi coat. Amerie put down the cat and embraced him. "Crazy

old Buddhist." Then she let him go and played with the kittens while he unrolled a tatami and futon in front of the hearth, then made sure that everything was ready for Amerie in the bedroom.

"I've decided to name them Tars Tarkas, Carthoris, and Edgar," the nun said, tucking the kittens back into the box with their mother. "They'll grow up to be the patriarchs of domestic felinity."

She rose from the floor, stiff in every joint and woozy with fatigue and reaction. But the discomforts faded as she looked about the little room, the combination kitchen and parlor that was the only real home she had ever known in the Pliocene Exile. She had lived in the cottage for a few short weeks during the time Madame and Felice and Richard and Claude and the others undertook their expedition to the Ship's Grave; but every feature seemed precious and familiar. There were Madame's handwoven curtains, her cherished lace tablecloth, the braided skin rugs. Beside the fireplace were the brass poker and shovel and trivet that Khalid Khan had made, and one of Miz Cheryl-Ann's baskets with kindling. Her own library of medical references and devotional works was safe in a cupboard, together with her nun's habit neatly folded, with little packets of herbs to keep it fresh. The wooden rosary Claude Majewski had carved for her was beside it in a beechwood box.

Kawai emerged from the bedroom. "All is ready."

"It's so good," she said in a broken voice, "to be back."

Solemnly, the old man bowed. "O-kaeri nasai, Amerie-chan. Welcome home, dearest daughter."

Burke and Basil were too wound up to sleep, and there were matters that needed discussing.

"Come on over to the old wigwam," the big Native American said to Denny Johnson. "You ought to meet the thirty-first member of Basil's Bastards."

"He still feels rather shy with crowds of humans," the alpinist said. "When he declined to attend the party, we tucked him away in Peo's house with plenty of food and drink. Let's hope he hasn't OD'ed on strawberry shortcake. The Little People are quite irrationally fond of it."

The Chief's bark-slab hut was close to the southern wall of the canyon, a few meters away from a rill born of the merging of a hot and cold spring. A thin filament of smoke rose from the hut's nonaboriginal chimney and vanished among the lower branches of the sequoias.

"Kalipin?" Burke called softly. He pushed aside the leather curtain and stooped to enter, with Denny and Basil following. The interior of the wigwam was almost pitch-black. A squatty shape faintly limned in scarlet stirred near the stone hearth.

"So you come at last, Peopeo Moxmox."

"I hope you haven't been too bored waiting. Would you mind if I lit a candle or two?"

"I shall have to shapeshift then," the voice said querulously. "But go ahead. It's your house."

"Please don't put yourself out," Basil protested.

"I have my orders. There, I'm ready."

Burke thumbed his permamatch and lit two tapers in a reflecting lantern that stood on the table. The light revealed a middle-aged dwarf surrounded by a litter of dirty dishes, drinking beer from a big pottery schooner.

"This is our Lowlife defense coordinator, Denny Johnson," Burke said. "Denny—meet Kalipin, assigned by Lord Sugoll to guide Basil's Bastards to the Ship's Grave."

Denny extended his hand. The mutant, evincing some hesitation, finally shook it. "You humans are always so eager to *touch* each other," Kalipin complained. "I do my best to go along with your customs, but it's hard. Téah knows it's hard." He gave a lugubrious sigh and drank deeply.

"How come none of us noticed you earlier, friend Kalipin?" asked Denny.

"I went invisible." The dwarf shuddered. "All those clamoring Lowlife minds! There are many of my people who accommodate themselves readily to humankind. And my Master is convinced that we must ally ourselves with you in order to survive. But it is hard. Hard."

"There's a little cave in the hillside back of the wigwam

that I use for storage," Burke said gently. "Would you be more comfortable there?"

The mutant brightened. "A cave! How I've missed the security of earth's bosom since we quit Meadow Mountain for Nionel! Oh—the city is very grand and progressive and nonmutagenic, I'll grant you. But there's nothing like the shelter of a cosy cave for making one feel safe, and snug, and ready for sweet fast sleep."

Burke helped Kalipin gather up his things and led the little Howler out of the hut.

Basil poked up the fire and put on a pot of coffee. "You'll want to take a look in that skin bag that our little friend was guarding so closely," he said to Johnson.

The black man took the bag to the table, slid open the drawstrings, and whistled. "Three Huskies! Holy shit, man— how'd they get through the time-gate?"

"Smuggled, I should say. Together with a considerable quantity of other armament. Do you know that Aiken Drum has equipped his human elite guard with twenty-second-century weapons?"

"Yes." Denny's eyes narrowed. "You steal these pieces off him?"

"No, they were a gift from Lord Sugoll . . . who got them from Sharn."

"Oh, my God."

"Exactly." Basil set out three mugs, horn spoons, and honey.

Burke pushed through the curtain. "Kalipin's settled." His eyes took in the half-opened bag of stun-guns. "Inspecting our presents, I see. Basil will take two on the Ship's Grave trek, and we'll keep one here. It'll be some help. But we're in for a rough summer, Dennis."

"The Firvulag are attacking the Iron Villages openly?" Basil asked.

Denny's ebony forehead wrinkled and he shook his head quizzically. "Not quite. There's never been any declaration of war, and that pegleg ambassador from High Vrazel still comes around regularly, all buddy-buddy and 'Long live the Armistice.' We bitch about the raids, but Sharn and Ayfa keep brazening it out, blaming the attacks on Howlers and telling us to refer all complaints to Nionel."

"If we get a couple of those exotic aircraft aloft, the Firvulag will sing another tune," Burke said. "And so will that little gold mamzer in Goriah."

"When we first heard the rumors about modern weapons," Denny said, "we offered to trade Aiken Drum pig iron for some."

"Response?" inquired Burke.

"None worth diddly-squat. He'd try to take over our mines himself if they weren't so close to High Vrazel. As it is, he hopes the Firvulag will wipe us out before we can infect too much of Pliocene humanity with the freedom virus. Oh—he sends good-will envoys to us, pledging peace and co-prosperity and liberty and justice for all. But what he's really interested in is luring away our metallurgical technicians. There are beds of iron ore in Brittany that shrimpy little motherfucker's itching to exploit."

"Just how bad have the Firvulag attacks on our mines been?" Basil asked.

"We may have to abandon Iron Maiden and Haut-Four-neauville. Damn—I'd give my right eye and my left nut for a few dozen Matsu laser carbines with nightsights."

"I'm thinking over the matter," said Burke enigmatically. "Once we get Basil and his Bastards fairly launched, I'll try to work something out."

"We march the day after tomorrow," Basil said.

"Hey, no, you just got here!" Denny protested. "You gotta rest up. And we haven't even started to get to know your people. I mean—that big mama named Sophronisba Gillis is one *bad* lady."

"If you plan to—er—make a move on her," said Basil diffidently, "I'd counsel caution. She used to be third engineer on a tramp freighter out in the Fourth Sector. When we were herding that crowd of sex-starved delinquents to Nionel, Phron-sie was the one woman in our group who never feared for her own safety."

"I'll wear her down," said Denny confidently. But then he scowled. "Sure you can't stay longer?"

Basil shook his head. "Sorry to cramp your style, old chap. But we leave on schedule—the delectable Sophronisba and all."

"Other people will be getting ideas about grabbing those aircraft," said Burke.

"Right now, Aiken has his hands full with other matters." Basil touched the golden torc at his throat. "Elizabeth has assured us that he doesn't yet know about our expedition. But the purpose of Basil's Bastards must now be quite obvious to all who shared in the welcoming celebration today..." He trailed away tactfully.

Denny shrugged, resigned. "And the word's bound to leak to the Iron Villages, and all we need is one defecting turkey with a big mouth skipping out to Goriah and the shit flies."

"Scouts from High Vrazel are also sure to spot us once we cross the Rhine," Basil added.

"You think *Sharn* will tell Aiken?" Denny was unbelieving.

"He might," said Burke, "if he weighs threats to his own security and we come out heaviest."

The coffee pot finished perking and Basil poured. They drank in silence for a few minutes.

"I've wondered why the Little People didn't go after the aircraft themselves," Denny said. "God knows they've been innovating like mad in other directions these past months. Sham and Ayfa seem to've thrown the old traditions right out the window."

"Not all of them," Basil corrected. "The Grave site is still sacred to both Firvulag and Tanu. One of their strongest taboos has to do with concealing the final resting place of the dead. They try to wipe out even the memory of it."

"However," Burke said, "once the aircraft are transferred to another locale, we can expect quite a different attitude to prevail. Which is why hiding those salvaged ships is so critically important."

"Well, I found a place for two of them, just like you wanted," Denny said. "A place called the Vale of Hyenas, where the

Firvulag never go. If you saw the bone crackers that hang out in there, you'd understand why. There are lots of giant redwoods and other trees in the valley, good cover in case of Flying Hunts. The place is about two hundred kloms northwest of here, near the headwaters of the Proto-Seine. Handy to Nionel."

"Sounds good," said Burke.

"Maxl knows the spot," Denny added. "If you go ahead and take him with you and leave the Bastard with the broken hand here, you'll have no trouble at all finding it." He gave a wry smile. "Getting out of the valley alive after you stash the birds—now *that* might be a problem!"

Basil sipped his coffee with equanimity. "We'll muddle through."

The big fighter persisted. "And what do you plan to do with the rest of the aircraft there at the Grave? You can't leave 'em for Aiken to find, and it'd be criminal to trash 'em."

Burke said, "We can't tell you, Denny. Nothing personal. Not even Basil's Bastards will know until the expedition reaches the crater lake."

"Hey, okay. No big thing. Only I noticed that there are twelve pilots in your gang—"

"Fourteen," Basil amended. "Dr. Thongsa is also qualified in orbiters, and Mr. Betsy has flight experience in addition to his engineering abilities."

"That drag queen wacko?" Denny snorted, smacking one palm on the table. "Lord, I figured he must have something going or you wouldn't've taken him on. But—*Mr. Betsy!*"

"His chosen persona is Queen Elizabeth I," said Basil primly, "hence the pearl-studded red wig and—er—costume. In the Milieu, his name was Merton Hudspeth. He was a senior research engineer with Boeing Aerospace Company's Commercial Rhocraft Division."

"No shit?" Denny was chastened.

"Betsy takes some getting used to," Burke admitted. "But don't we all?" He stood up, yawned hugely, then eyed the husky fighter with sly humor. "There's old Basil, who'd rather be miserable climbing mountains than teach literature in a nice

Limey university. And Mr. Justice Burke with the feathers in his hair and the breechclouted tushie, sort of a Geronimo manqué. To say nothing of *you*, my fine Covent Garden baritone! Tell me, nigger—do you still sing 'Toreador' at the top of your lungs while you chop exotic raiders to dogmeat?"

"You better believe it, redskin! Say—remind me to call for freeleader elections tomorrow. I'm gonna nominate you to the hotseat again personally."

"Thanks all to hell, yellow-eyes."

"You're friggin' welcome, baldy-balls."

The rough-hewn face of the Native American went sober again. "God knows, I'd like to roost here and play elder statesman. But there's another possibility. After I think about it for a while, I'm going to discuss it with Elizabeth. See what she thinks." He set his cup down, lifted the bag with the stun-guns, and pulled the drawstring tight. "Iron spears and arrows looked like the ultimate weapon for a few weeks after the Finiah war. God knows they've helped us, and they'll continue to be useful against the exotics. But we'll look pretty silly shooting arrows out of gravomagnetic aircraft, my friends. And Aiken Drum's elite guard is no more poisoned by the blood-metal than thee or me."

"You figure on getting us some real weapons," Denny stated. "How? Raid Sharn's armory?"

"We'd never get within ten kloms of High Vrazel alive. No. There's another possibility. Sham got his cache from a secret hoard when the Firvulag devastated Burask. Aiken Drum is supposed to have got his guns from a magazine in the dungeons of Goriah. So there were at least two city-lords who defied King Thagdal's edict against retaining Milieu weapons. And I think there may have been others as well."

"Finiah had zip," Denny reminded him. "But, hey—how about Roniah? That's the town *I* busted out of, man. Old Lord Bormol was a real scientific type. A coercer. You know how paranoid that clan is about defending their turf. He *could* have had a secret stash! And the place is within striking distance of Hidden Springs. Hell, we could drift down the river, infiltrate from the docks—no wall to climb there—"

Burke said, "There may not be any weapons. And every Lowlife fighter could be needed here in the Vosges, defending the mines. The pros and cons will have to be weighed with exquisite care. Thank God the final decision will be Elizabeth's, not mine."

Denny was indignant, incredulous. "You'd let that—that female mystic dictate our strategy?"

"Oh, yes," said Basil easily. "She has all along, you know. She's the most important person in the world."

"Poor thing," added Peopeo Moxmox Burke.

7

Once again, Elizabeth prepared to descend.

The entrance to the abyss was miserly, constricted, yet perversely eager to open and spew a final cataract of destruction as the ego threatened to rupture and its aggression sought ultimate discharge in death.

Dionket and Creyn, linked in the penstock configuration, braced themselves against the fiendish pressure, steadfast and agonized. They shared the guilt as well as the hope, for they knew that the heritage of malignant violence incarnate in this soon cresting flood had sourced in their own racial Mind.

The peril to the healers was now extreme. Felice's fund of submission was nearly exhausted. The closer Elizabeth had approached to the core of dysfunction, the greater the patient's fear had become. Felice's human cathexis, weak at best, was tottering at the imminent prospect of irremediable change. Rather than face that, she toyed with implosive or explosive termination.

Each time that Elizabeth had passed between Dionket and Creyn and entered that pit of aureate, whirling foulness, the two exotic redactors found it impossible to believe that she could return. If even the superficial layers of the girl's madness put such mortal strain upon their own metareinforced minds, what horror must lie in the incandescent depths waiting for the

Grand Master—especially now, with the consummation so close?

"Felice is almost at the fifth stage of dysfunction," Dionket had warned. "She hovers on the brink. If you fail in catharsis, the disruptive blast of psychoenergy may be directed outward, in conformity with her fantasy of planetary ruin, and engulf all of Black Crag in a solaristic fireball. On the other hand, if you tipped *her* over, all of the aggression and violence would be directed inward, toward her own annihilation. This would be a failure on your part—but one that equated with objective success. The monster would be gone."

"I cannot deliberately harm a rational being," Elizabeth had reminded him. But more than the old stricture, there was pride. "And I believe more than ever that I can save her. I'm almost on top of the fountainhead! I think I've finally tracked down the neuronal source of the dereistic behavior pattern."

She had shown them the correlation between the limbic system circuits and certain anomalies afflicting the secondary levels of Felice's rhinencephalon; but the two exotics had been unable to grasp her point because of their lack of training in developmental psychobiology. The Tanu redactive technique had degenerated into more art than science by the time of the race's exile.

"Let her die, Elizabeth," Creyn had pleaded. "If you persist, and if she doesn't disrupt totally, she may consume you. You would be trapped in an obscene psychocreative splicing, forever participant in her pain-projections, an accomplice to her enormities."

"But if Felice were sane—" And Elizabeth revealed the potential apotheosis, the marvelous things that the pale little goddess might accomplish under a Grand Master's tutelage. "There would be no more wars in the Many-Colored Land. No more threat from the exiled rebels in North America. With Felice as the coercive catalyst, her irresistible soul-weight on the *right* side of the scales, we could instigate a kind of miniature Unity amongst Tanu and Firvulag and torced and operant humanity!"

Dionket and Creyn had looked at Elizabeth with sorrow and

dread, rejecting the vision. "It has become more and more clear as your redaction of Felice proceeded: She yearns for death."

"She'd choose life if she were sane! And nonaggression."

Dionket Lord Healer smiled—not with cynicism but with ancient wisdom. "Then you metapsychics of the Galactic Milieu abolished sin?"

"Of course not," the Grand Master retorted angrily, and then was silent behind walls.

The two continued to remonstrate, mutely. At length she said, "I've never undertaken any work as terrible as this. The lifting of Brede to operancy and adept status was nothing compared to it. And we're so close to success! I can't abandon Felice now, in spite of the danger. I can't let her die. A mind like hers is so inconceivably valuable! She must possess coercive and creative faculties approaching the six-hundredth order of magnitude, and the PK function is not too far below that. There was no single entity in the Galactic Milieu with such power."

"She can never attain the state you call coadunation," Dionket said. "She is a monstrosity, hopelessly warped. Her parents—" He shook his head. "We have no experience with a case like Felice's. Tana knows that our race is faulty, but no parents among us would ever use a child as this poor girl was used. And out of sheer ennui, devoid even of malice!"

"Felice is no monster," Elizabeth said. "Not any more. I've uncovered the residue of humanity, given it air. Each time I go into her for the draining and the redirection, she shows more soul."

"Then why," Dionket asked, "is she still so afraid? Why is she weakening in her resolution to permit the final catharsis?"

"Because of the danger, of course. She walks the brink, just as you said, and she continues to suffer."

"She's bound to turn on you," the Lord Healer said, "and if she strikes out with her full power, you will be lost."

"She's worth the risk, I tell you!"

Creyn said somberly, "It is you, Elizabeth, who have been designated by the Shipspouse. Not Felice."

"The Shipspouse had no right to play God."

"Do you?" Creyn asked.

"Why do you keep pressing me?" she cried. "You agreed to help. You knew the magnitude of Felice's dysfunction . . ."

Dionket's mental overlay was compassionate. "But not, perhaps, certain limitations of the healer."

"I'll make her sane. With or without your help." Adrenalin-fired determination seared the two Tanu.

"We will help you," said Dionket, "even to the point of death."

Elizabeth descended into Avernus, and stayed for six hours.

The walls of the room dissolved. The three healers, gathered around the cot where the etiolated girl lay, were buffeted and drenched with fluid agony, dark and clinging and abominable. Lacerated by the shards of Felice's memories, choking upon her stifling rage and infantile helplessness, sharing her humiliation and deafened by her ceaseless screams, they endured.

In spite of the psychoelectronic barrier of the room without doors, some portion of the ravening discharge was not grounded into the rocks of Black Crag but overflowed to escape into the atmosphere. A noisome adiabatic cloud formed above the mountain, and lightnings, scarlet in dust clouds, played around the chalet roof. Hot ion winds crisped the needles of nearby evergreens and withered the alpine wildflowers. Sensitive little warblers fell from their perches, dead. The weaker gold-torced retainers who served the lodge fled screaming down the precipitous track, and even the strong-minded protectors became frantic with the plangent psychic tension, taking refuge in the farthest corners of the cellar, lying half-conscious on the polished graphitic shale.

Elizabeth said, "Come, Felice."

It fought, erupted, shrank, flared. It ripped at the cradling redactive wings, ever intent now on escape but held fast by its own paradoxical love-fetters. The normal pleasure-paths of the brain, so long atrophied, sang in shrill newborn anguish and delight. The darker channels, their electric venom beginning to pool and stagnate, still clamored for a fresh influx, a last reprieve into the old familiar pain, the deserved embrace of the death-father (is it you, Beloved?), the foul joy coming after, with death-mother's devouring and the thanks and the stinking kisses.

"Come, Felice."

Come away, let go, cast off. Forget that body and take a new. Forget those casual wicked ones who begot you and played with their poor sentient toy and then tossed you away in heedless cruelty. Be nonborn. Be selfborn! Heal yourself. See yourself as lovable. See the faithful animal friends' irrational devotion. See Sister Amerie's unstained love for you. See mine as I become your life-mother and that of these two life-brothers who also embrace you. (But Amerie refused . . .)

"Come, Felice."

See, admire, love the shining new self. You are beautiful, child, and your body is strong. And now your mind . . . oh, child, look upon its glory! Yes, born of the agony and the filth it is, as the physical form; but like it, capable of transfiguration. (He did it! The Beloved. I have him to thank for freeing my latencies, for cutting their bonds with his double-edged bright lancet. Culluket!)

"Not him, Felice."

Culluket!

Don't turn that way now. Not when you're so close, little one, so clean and strong, so nearly good . . ."

Amerie?

Look the other way. Look up toward light and reality, toward peace, toward union with other minds who can truly love you.

Culluket? Amerie?

See the errant energies calmed, the wordless baying stilled, emotions reined, will strong and directed. Now: Choose unselfish love! Choose to be good and noble and giving . . ."

I choose—I choose—

"Wake, Felice. Come back now. Open your eyes."

They were brown eyes, very large, startling in the bloodless face beneath ashen brows and limp platinum hair. They were eyes full of wonder, darting from Elizabeth's face to Dionket's to Creyn's and back again, misting briefly with tears and then star-bright.

"This is sanity?" Felice asked. She rose trembling on one elbow. Her gaze fell. "Same old body, same mind—but different." She laughed very softly. The brown eyes flicked up, locked onto Elizabeth. "Why did you wake me up—bring me back before I could finish choosing?"

The Grand Master was silent.

"You want me to choose to be like you, Elizabeth?"

"Make your own choice." The vocal tone was gentle but the mind's, grating and apprehensive.

"Be like you." Two spots of color appeared in the girl's cheeks. Her hair seemed to come alive. She gave a kind of bounce and was standing on the cot, petite and strong. Her entire body was sheathed in a pearly aura. "Me, be like you, Elizabeth?"

Felice threw back her radiant head and laughed, a wild and vital peal resounding with barbed vitality. "I choose my self! Look at me. Look *in* me! Wouldn't you rather be me than you? Free to choose what I want to do instead of letting others bind me?" Again the laugh, so shattering, so sane.

"Poor Elizabeth." The goddess extended a luminous hand, touched the Grand Master's shoulder. "But thank you."

She vanished.

Elizabeth sat unmoving, her gaze still fixed on the empty cot, too drained to weep, too diminished even to despair. The cocoon of fire was there, beckoning, and she studied it with an odd sense of detachment, as though the real choice had already been made and this one was a mere consequent.

"Stay," urged Dionket.

Creyn was standing over her, red of blood, white of mind-light, the constraining golden torc clasped about his throat. His hand with its long fingers and prominent joints, adorned with many rings, held out a stoneware cup. "Drink, Elizabeth."

As once before.

She sipped the bitter herbal tea, then lowered the wall so that he could clearly see the waiting flame-coffin, the overwhelming temptation.

"We need you more than ever now," said Creyn.

But Dionket, wiser, was more comforting in sternness. "You really don't deserve purgatory. Not until you try to put it right."

"Yes," she said, and smiled, and wept.

8

CLOUD PLACED THE BOUQUET ON THE MOUNDED DIRT, THEN stood dry-eyed, seeing all the intricate details of the orchids with her deep-scan at the same time that she shut out the larger image of the grave itself. The bunch of flowers was enormous, containing twenty-five or thirty varieties. She had gathered it in less than five minutes without going out of sight of their moorage on the Río Genil.

"The Tanu call Spain 'Koneyn,'" she said inconsequentially. "It means 'Flowerland.' I overheard one mind tell another that no place in Europe has so many different kinds. I like the azure orchids best, I think. And the pale green ones with the velvet-black edging. Orchids in mourning. Poor Jill."

"We did our best. Steinbrenner warned us about the danger of meningitis." Elaby concentrated on the rock slab he had propped against the roots of a great plane tree. Portions of the rock glowed palely in the noontide sun as he exerted his creative metafaculty. The pungent stench of molten mineral overwhelmed the subtle orchid fragrance, then dissipated on the light breeze blowing downstream. Satisfied, Elaby lifted the slab with his PK and positioned it in the waiting trough at the head of the mound.

JILLIAN MIRIAM MORGENTHALER
20 SEPTEMBER 23 – 2 JUNE P27

"WHERE LIES THE LAND TO WHICH THE SHIP WOULD GO?
FAR, FAR AHEAD, IS ALL HER SEAMEN KNOW."

"Will it last six million years?" Cloud wondered.

"We're still in the Guadalquivir Basin. This place will be
buried in silt. Who can tell?"

Cloud turned her back on the grave and walked listlessly
toward the beached dinghy. "Last winter, when we were all
wrapped up in planning this thing, I asked Alexis Manion if
there had ever been any trace of the exile population found in
Pliocene rocks. He said no. It's hard to believe that *nothing*
survived."

She climbed into the little boat. Elaby joined her and shoved
them off into the languid water, as brown as strong tea. It was
navigable to within 50 kilometers of Mulhacén in the shallow-
draft rivercraft that Aiken Drum was bringing.

Elaby said, "If any paleontologist found a fossilized Homo
sap skeleton in a Pliocene formation, he'd keep his mouth shut
about it unless he wanted to be drummed out of the bonediggers'
club. As for a fossilized Bermudian ketch . . ."

"Dr. Manion said that nothing we do here in this ancient
world can affect the future. That the future—already *is*."

"Nice reassuring thought. Remind me of it when we have
to go concert with Aiken Drum and his bunch and blow the
top off Mount Mulhacén."

The inflatable skimmed up to the accommodation ladder.
Cloud made the painter fast and mounted. "Owen's still sleeping," she noted, after sending a fleeting redactive touch be-
lowdecks.

"Good. He wore himself out working with you on Jill. Thank
heavens he didn't insist on coming ashore for the burial." He
rummaged in the portable cooler and brought out a flagon of
coconut punch and two of their dwindling supply of gamma
chicken-salad sandwiches from Ocala. "Funeral baked meats.
Relax, babe. Take a break before the King of the Elves shows
up."

They sat in canvas chairs in the cockpit, sheltered from the
sun by an awning stretched between the mainmast and backstay.

Cloud chewed the sandwich rapturously. "Civilized food! God, I'm sick of fish and roast waterfowl and those insipid palm fruits. It's breakfast time back in Florida—do you realize that? Bacon and scrambled eggs. Grits and honey. Orange juice and sweet iced tea."

"Heartless broad," Elaby accused. He refilled her beaker with the milky-colored rum drink. "Sorry you came?"

She shook her head. "I had to. All of us did. Even the gang Papa shunted off to Africa aren't sorry they left home. We're a little closer to the time-gate, anyhow. We've forced Papa to take us and our needs seriously." She hesitated. "He'll come to Europe, you know."

"You're certain?"

"I know him better than anyone."

"Will he help or oppose us?"

"He may not have decided. I can't say." She set aside the remains of the meal. A cloud of sulfur-yellow butterflies fluttered by the port rail, heading toward the Gulf of Guadalquivir. She caged one briefly with her PK, watched it tremble and flail its tiny knobbed antennae, then set it free. It flapped off after the others. "Papa doesn't want to kill us. I was right about that. He won't do it unless we force him to. Unless we deliberately put him and his people in jeopardy by our opening of the gate—or if we try to kill *him*."

"Some of us wouldn't scruple at it."

"I know." Her expression was tranquil. "Hagen. You."

"But not you?" The young man swirled the ice cubes in his drink, frowning at them. When Cloud did not answer, he posed another query. "Would you stand in the way of the rest of us, if there seems no other way to handle it?"

"I want us all to be free," she said. "If we could only work together—both generations—instead of at opposite poles! Building the apparatus and siting it properly in the midst of this barbarian circus will be difficult enough. Maybe impossible."

"Don't wash us out too soon, babe. We've lost some ground—but we may have gained some as well. Our element of secrecy is gone now that Marc's guessed our intention, and your hothead brother's threats have made Marc the teensiest bit skeptical of our loyalty. But your father isn't the only big gun in the fight. Don't forget the Nonborn King. If things keep going downhill here in the Many-Colored Land, he just might start seeking wider horizons."

Cloud was dubious. "Here, Aiken's a large fish in a small pond. What would he be in the Milieu, compared to the Coadunate Mind? Besides, Papa seems to have him quite overawed as a result of the metaconcert teaching."

Elaby gave a quiet chuckle. "Don't you believe it. This head's young. Only about twenty-two. Yet he's managed to take over an establishment that dominated the Pliocene for forty years, using just his own naked brain."

"Aiken simply picked up the pieces after catastrophe. He's king of the ruins! A demigod in Götterdämmerung."

"Maybe yes, maybe no. I see him chock-full of nuts and eager to howl. And a first-class *power*, babe—don't forget that. Your father may just have a fish on his hook this time that's more than he can handle."

Cloud bit her lower lip, looking toward the gorgeous heap of blossoms and the upright stone slab on shore. Finally, she said, "Do you think Aiken will actually be able to handle this massive synergy? Papa could be planning to seize the executive from him at a critical moment."

"If Marc doesn't—if he *can't*—then there may be a chance for us to enlist Aiken on our side later on. I still find it amazing that Marc agreed to let Aiken focus the psychozap. It implies confidence in Golden Boy's abilities...or a nasty piece of manipulation."

"It's hard to think that someone else in this world might just be a match for Papa." Cloud's thought-tone was full of perplexity.

"He's played God too damn long," said Elaby bitterly. "We've forgotten that Marc's human. That he's a loser. He lost it all in the Milieu, and now he's lost us. And he obviously feels threatened by both Felice and Aiken."

"Papa is still a Paramount Grand Master farsensor, coercer, and creator," said Cloud quietly. "And he's limited here in the

Pliocene mainly because there are so few suitable minds for him to work with. Don't ever forget that he was one of the two greatest mental coordinators in the Galaxy. Only his brother Jon was better."

"Remind me to light a candle to St. Jack the Bodiless."

Cloud stood staring aft, her farsight wandering northward to the little islands off the mouth of the Genil where the forces of Celadeyr and Aluteyn and the other Spanish Tanu had been camped for two days, awaiting their rendezvous with Aiken Drum's fleet. She shifted her gaze, scanning westward toward the Atlantic. "I still don't see Aiken coming," she said nervously. "How far out are they now, Elaby?"

"Fifteen hours, approx. Their ETA at the base-camp on the Genil is still dawn, as Aiken promised. They've been saving their metafaculties, using Ma Nature's winds most of the way from Brittany. But this morning when they finally rounded Cape St. Vincent, Aiken put his psychokinetics to work. The fleet must be making twenty-six knots now. We'll all be off to the Betics tomorrow on schedule."

"And maybe we'll all die." Cloud came over to him, laying her head on his shoulder and embracing him so tightly that her fingers dug into the muscles of his back like claws. "Darling, I don't know why . . . poor Jill this morning, and now this stupid dangerous thing we're being forced to do with Aiken Drum . . . why I should feel like this . . . it's insane, but . . ."

"It's normal," he whispered in her ear. "Normal to reach for life when the world seems ready to end. Very common phenom, if you can believe the books in the library back on Ocala. Plagues, wars, earthquakes—all disasters are keen incitements to venery."

"It's ridiculous."

He kissed her. "Sex often is. So what?" He led her to the companionway stairs. "What say we rock the boat, then make everything shipshape for the royal visit?"

They disappeared. The breeze died and the jungle creatures were hushed in the afternoon heat. Two ramas emerged briefly from the undergrowth to inspect the mound of flowers and finger the strange incisions on the rock slab. Then they melted back into the greenery, their curiosity satisfied.

In his cramped cabin on the great tem schooner that was the Tanu flagship, Culluket worked on the cuirass of his ruby armor, resetting a few loose gemstones in the blazon, riveting a new strap in place of one that had weakened, then burnishing the whole so that the glass with its transfixed caput mortuum gleamed more richly than a slick of fresh blood.

You will die looking magnificent, at any rate, he told himself. Too clever at last, Interrogator! If you should escape being devoured by your demonic sweetheart, then surely your overdevious brain will be reduced to charred meat after serving as a living buss-bar between Aiken Drum and the Angel of the Abyss. You will die for your King, a very martyr to the battle-religion of your ancestors. A hero of the Host of Nontusvel could ask for no more glorious fate! What a pity you are a traitor to your blood, and an atheist, and so addicted to life that you would submit to any degradation now in order to be spared. You would even appeal to *her*, were it not the ultimate in futility . . ."

"Culluket," said Mercy.

He started, torn from his bitter reverie. Mercy's figure, clad in her silver-and-green parade armor, materialized out of invisibility. She had interpenetrated his cabin door. It was a violation of Tanu etiquette almost as serious as levitating without a steed.

"Great Queen, what is it?" He hastened to pull the scattered pieces of armor together so that there would be room for her to stand.

Her mind radiated a fearful intensity, impinging on his own thick barrier with a coercive force that blurred his sight. "I need you to escort me to Lord Celadeyr now, while Aiken is locked in mind-meld with that horrible Abaddon. It may be the only chance I have. Hurry, man! Enarm yourself. This is no social call. And I'll want the small sigma-field Aiken's given you as a defense against Felice."

He harnessed up hurriedly. The two of them, invisible,

body-flew eastward above the Gulf of Guadalquivir, toward the deformed old moon rising late over the Andalusian jungle, and the camp where the Lord of Afaliah and the Craftsmaster and the rest of the Koneyn nobility awaited the fleet's arrival. The site of the rendezvous was carefully concealed, both physically and mentally. The 3500 chalikos that would equip the raiding party had been penned in a mangrove swamp a full five kilometers from the camouflaged pavilions of the nobles and their retainers.

As Mercy and Culluket hovered just offshore, she commanded, "Farspeak your brother Kuhal on the intimate mode. Tell him we have arrived."

"Kuhal is here?" Culluket was nonplussed. "Surely he would not have been forced—"

"Do as I say," she snapped. "It was I who saw to it that Celo brought him along. You'll soon find out why. Tell Kuhal to call both Celo and Aluteyn Craftsmaster to his tent."

Culluket obeyed. He and Mercy wafted into the encampment and became visible inside the dimly lamplit shelter of the convalescent Earthshaker. Kuhal lay on a bunk, propped up with cushions. Beside him stood the two Tanu heros, waiting in silence for Mercy's explanation. Their antagonism for the Interrogator was unconcealed.

She said, "Nodonn is alive."

"Glorious Goddess!" exclaimed Kuhal, and Culluket made haste to clap a crude redactive damper over the invalid's mind.

"Erect the sigma-field," Mercy commanded. "It will be enough protection for us so long as Aiken and the others have no suspicions and don't deliberately try to poke into it."

Culluket took the device from his armored crumen, set it upon Kuhal's nightstand, and activated it. The noises of the jungle night chopped off. The tent and its inhabitants were isolated within a dynamic field virtually impervious to most energy and matter.

"I've known about Nodonn since early in May," Mercy said, responding to unspoken questions. "He's been marooned on Kersic all this time, in a coma, tended by a Lowlife woman who kept him inside a cave. This is why none of us detected him. Not even I."

"Where is he now?" asked Celadeyr flatly. "What shape is he in?"

"He's hidden in Var-Mesk, cared for by Lord Moreyn, who is"—she swept the Lord of Afaliah and the Craftsmaster with a trenchant glance—"a First Comer to the Many-Colored Land, just as you. And loyal to the old traditions. As you are."

"Now, hold on a minute!" Aluteyn protested. "I gave my oath of fealty—"

"To a foul usurper!" Kuhal interrupted. "Under mortal duress and a sense of desperate inevitability, as we all did. Such an oath stinks before the Goddess! It *demands* repudiation!"

"Calm down before you strain something," the Craftsmaster advised. He pulled up a sturdy stool and lowered his bulk gingerly onto it. The others also drew up seats close to the cot, and Mercy and Culluket removed their helmets. Aluteyn addressed his Queen. "Tell us exactly what happened to Nodonn, lass. Don't leave out a thing."

She coordinated the data in her mind, then displayed it without comment, save for the shining backdrop of her own joy.

When they had done studying, Kuhal beckoned her and took her silver-gauntleted hand to kiss. His eyes overflowed for the first time since his rescue.

"You are truly one of us, Mercy-Rosmar," he said, "and worthy to be Queen."

Old Celo's reaction was bleaker, practical. "Nodonn's still weak as a kitten. Not as badly off as you, Kuhal, but in no shape to take on Aiken." He stared at Mercy. "You've waited this long to tell us...and perhaps it's true that you had no choice. But what do you expect us to do?"

"Abandon *him*," she said simply. "Leave him to Felice. We can all of us fly except Kuhal, and Celo can carry him. Let's start for Var-Mesk now, flying within the sigma-field! Let's go via Aven and Kersic, where we can hide in wilderness when we tire, deep in sheltering caves secure from his golden wrath!

Aiken has no long-distance psychoenergetic function. And he won't follow us, since that would mean abandoning his Quest."

Aluteyn groaned. "Lass, lass! Your happiness over Nodonn's deliverance has robbed you of your wits."

"How could we leave our fellow warriors behind, in peril of Felice?" Celo demanded of her. "Would Nodonn want this?"

"The fleet is almost here," Kuhal said sadly. "Our people are committed. Great Queen . . . if only you had told us your news earlier."

"I didn't dare try to contact you through farspeech!" she cried. "I'm too clumsy still at far focusing. It was Nodonn who held the thin mind-beam secure between us. And he warned me—" Like a red-hot wire, her scorn lashed out at Culluket. "*You* watched and listened! And now even Aiken suspects something—perhaps he even knows for certain that Nodonn lives! I was afraid my own farspeech would betray Nodonn completely. Or that Culluket would!"

The Interrogator bowed his head. "My former loyalty to the usurper has been shaken since his alliance with Abaddon. You know the rôle that those two have forced on me . . ."

Aluteyn uttered a short laugh. "And we also know what your loyalty's worth compared to your own precious skin! Poor Cull. Whipsawed yourself properly this time."

"I know Culluket hates Nodonn." Mercy's mind was icy. "But they are Host Brothers. And Tanu. And now there's a fine expedient reason for Cull to turn his coat again! Isn't that so, Redactive Brother?"

"The Great Queen is wise," said Culluket, without emotion.

"Well, then!" she exclaimed, the old wildfire in her eyes. "If we can't fly to Nodonn now, then let's think about how we might use Felice to kill Aiken! Shall we warn her of his impending raid on her treasure-trove?"

"Elizabeth has Felice inside the room without doors," said Aluteyn. "She might not hear. And if she did, we can't count on her sparing *us*."

Kuhal's face had gone livid. "For the love of Tana—don't think of summoning that elemental female, my Queen! Cull can tell you what she's capable of!"

"Even the worthy Abaddon holds Felice in respect," said the Interrogator. "And may I suggest, as we mull over possible plans of action, that we don't forget that Abaddon has unexcelled directorial powers in metaconcert. He can smite us with a psychocreative blast at any range—I know that for a fact. He can't coerce us from the other side of the world, but he does possess stupendous farsensing power."

"Then why the hell didn't he finger Nodonn for Aiken?" Celo puzzled.

Culluket gave a mental shrug. "My dealings with this mysterious person have been peremptory in the extreme. I'm less than a thing to him. Abaddon seems indifferent to our petty politics. He's a manipulator, but only on a grand scale—"

"As opposed to you, Brother," said Kuhal.

"—and it's very possible that he doesn't care who rules the Many-Colored Land. He'd use Nodonn as readily as he now uses Aiken."

"The bastard!" hissed Mercy. "Who can he be?"

The four Tanu men regarded her in amazement. "You don't know, then?" asked the Craftsmaster. "Oh, lass. No wonder you've been so full of mad plans." And he told her, beginning with the events he himself had witnessed twenty-seven years before, when he and the old Lord Coercer and Gomnol and the Lord of Roniah first encountered Marc Remillard and his party of exiled metapsychic rebels.

Mercy seemed turned to marble inside her silver-lustre armor. "Then there's no hope at all of halting the Quest. No hope." She turned away from them. "But, if Aiken gets the Spear, then Nodonn will have no advantage over him in the final Duel of Battlemasters."

"No." Culluket smiled at her back. "Nodonn will have to meet Aiken fair and square if he wants to be king. And maybe lose."

"Brother—enough!" Kuhal struggled to a sitting position. "There is no honorable escape from the present peril, no way to abort the raid. We must cooperate fully with Aiken Drum, and the Good Goddess alone knows how this affair will end. She may use Felice as her agent to destroy the usurper . . . or she may grant him success. But if we survive, then there may still be time for us to rally round the true king as he leads us in the Nightfall War!"

Kuhal fell back, his face twisted in pain. Culluket bent over him with his palms pressed to his brother's temples. Kuhal relaxed, instantly asleep.

Mercy turned off the little sigma-field generator and handed it to the Interrogator.

"So that's that," Celadeyr remarked. "But poor Kuhal was right. We'll have to give Aiken Drum and his North American evil genius our very best shot in the Quest. Whether we like it or not." He and Aluteyn saluted Mercy briefly, then pushed aside the door-flap of the pavilion and went out into the loud night.

She stood close to the ruby-clad Interrogator as he replaced the screening device in his sabretache. "You knew about Nodonn all along, didn't you, Death? My announcement was no surprise to you."

"I am the greatest redactor of the Host. I would have felt my eldest brother's extinction."

"And yet you didn't warn Aiken."

"He knew. I showed him where the proof lay, within you."

"Machinator!"

"As you, my Queen. But I think my game at last reaches its climax."

He smiled down at her before covering his beauty with the red-glass helmet. She let her gloved hand rest lightly above his armored heart, touching the transfixed death's-head that was his heraldic cognizance. She had never noticed before that the skull's eyes were sapphires, like his, and that there was a flaming halo about it that mimicked his hair.

"Do you mean you're finally afraid?" she inquired archly.

"Yes."

"Ah! Well, so am I. Again. Will you take my hand, Death? Will you comfort?"

Nodding, he closed his visor and drew her to him. The tall red-armored form and the smaller one of emerald and silver faded together like wraiths and were gone, leaving Kuhal Earth-shaker alone in dreamless sleep.

Dawn mist clung to the Hidden Springs evergreens like trailing scarves as Amerie walked by herself toward the little log chapel, carrying the bread and wine. The roosters had crowed and the penned goats and picketed chalikos were making low sounds; but the villagers and their guests still lay abed after the impromptu party of the night before.

Amerie thought: It's just you and me this morning, Lord. I'm glad.

She lit the two altar candles and prepared the offerings, then went into the tiny vestry to remove her wimple and veil and put on the scarlet chasuble of Pentecost. Singing her own entrance song, she came into the sanctuary.

> Veni Creator Spiritus,
> Mentes tuorum visita:
> Imple superna gratia,
> Quae tu creasti pectora.

She said the prayers at the foot of the altar with bowed head, then turned toward the dark interior of the chapel to give the first blessing.

"Dominus vobiscum."

And Felice said, "Et cum spiritu tuo."

The priest stood frozen in place with her hands raised as a girl in a long white gown came up the aisle and stood before the altar step, smiling.

"I'm back," Felice said. "Elizabeth's been working on my mind, and she's reamed all of the old garbage out. I'm sane now, Amerie. Isn't that wonderful? I can love properly now, without the pain detour. I can make a free choice of who to love, and how. I can give you joy just like mine! Elizabeth told me to choose, you see, and there was you and there was Culluket. You remember him, don't you? I did love him more than you before, when I was mad. But now I know better. So I've come to fetch you."

Amerie said, "Felice... my vow. *My* choice."

"But it's me," said the girl reasonably. "Not just any woman—me! You love me and want me just as I want you. So come."

"You don't understand. My renunciation is my gift to God. My body offering, like the bread and wine I'll consecrate in the Mass. I gave it away long ago—"

"You can take it back." Felice stood in front of the half-log benches, luminous in the light of the two candles, swaying as if she were a thing cut from fragile tissue set in motion by the priest's own accelerating breath. Her eyes were like wells. "Come away now. We'll fly together! I'm a white gyrfalcon now, and you shall be a cardinal-bird!"

"No," Amerie whispered. "Felice, I can't. You still don't understand. This is where I belong, serving these people who need me. I'm their priest and their doctor. They're good for me and I love them—"

The girl in white interrupted. "You love me more."

"Yes," Amerie admitted. "I do and I always will. But it changes nothing. I can't help the love, but I can choose not to consummate it. And I do."

Slowly, Felice's expression changed. There was puzzlement, surprise, hurt, frustration, fury. "You *won't*?"

"No."

"It's your God, isn't it! He's locked you up! Trapped you in this stupid web of self-denial!"

"I haven't denied myself. You don't understand."

"Stop saying that to me! I do understand! You choose him and not me! You still think my love is filthy and sinful!" Tears poured from the black holes of her eyes. "I'm no good after all. I can see into your soul, see that you're still afraid of me. You won't go with me and you'd never let me stay here with you. Oh, no! I'm not human enough to be one of your little flock, am I, Good Shepherd? I'm a Goddess! But you'd rather have your damned old mean-spirited, jealous God."

Amerie sank down onto her knees. "You *are* human. Dear

Felice, you are. But so different from the rest of us! Go back
to Elizabeth. Let her teach you how to live in your world of
the mind. That's where you belong."

"No," Felice wept. "I belong with you."

"I can never enter your mind-world, Felice. I'm only a
normal woman. I can't help but be afraid of people like you . . . just
as I can't help loving you. Felice, let me be. Go to your own
people."

"I won't!" the girl screamed. "I won't go without you! If
you won't come with me willingly, I'll force you!" The two
altar candles were suddenly extinguished. Only the wan mist-
light from the two little windows and the garnet sanctuary lamp
gave illumination.

Felice's hands seized Amerie by the shoulders. Psychoenergies flowed from the girl's brain and Amerie was wrenched
by shock. "You'll do as I say!" Felice cried, terrible in coercion.
You'll stay with me for as long as I want you. Do you hear
me?"

Racked by clonic spasms, her vocal cords paralyzed, Amerie
felt herself lifted. There was a smell of burning fabric as her
vestments smoked beneath Felice's grip, and then the priest's
own flesh burned and her heart stopped.

Sursum corda.

"Choose me, Amerie!" The one elevating her was now in-
candescently nude. "Do it—and I'll start your heart again. Just
say you love me."

Dignum et justum est.

Felice flung the body in its red vestments to the floor and
loomed high, dimming. Hoc est enim corpus meum. "Choose
me! Please, Amerie!" Per ipsum et cum ipso . . . "Please!" In
saecula . . .

Amerie's dying eyes shone. Her mind told Felice: No. I
love you. This Mass is for you.

And then the mind escaped, leaving the girl to rage and
mourn and finally shape-shift back to the old raven form. In
this Felice set off for Spain, to give the other lover his choice.

9

SHE'S LOOSE. SHE'S LOOSE. FELICE IS LOOSE...

The dumb refrain played over and over in a subliminal stratum of Aiken's conscious, a piping discordancy over a sustained drone of fear. The bad news hadn't come from his incompetent spy in Black Crag but from Elizabeth herself, who farspoke him shortly after dawn, when his fleet was less than an hour from its rendezvous with the Koneyn land force and the three North American operants:

She's loose Aiken! Felice is loose. I let her get away from me... and she's killed Amerie.

God damn.

Amerie's death is my fault mine. I could have taken Felice out during redaction. Let her sink into aphanisis. Ego demolition. She would have become veggie Creyn&Dionket urged it I could have yes nonaction in such complex case wouldnot violate ethic. But no! I was so certain I could save her! I *did* make her sane...

Sane ≠ altruistic. Right?

Felice remains totally selfcentered. Dedicated to doing exactly as she pleases above all things. She made complete fool out of me.

Elizababe innocent.

I worked with children in Milieu! And Felice *is* child. If only she had stayed had let me educate her mature her 0 Aiken

329

she may never grow up now a childelementalforce on loose!
She's loose...

Damnyou. *Damnyou!* [Spinechill genitalshrink heartrace.]
Madmonsters can be tricked through own delusions. Sane-
monster $\geqq$ Me + AngelAbyss!!

And she's loose... loose. I don't know where can't track.
Her mentalscreen perfect. You must ask Remillard try physical
scan with enhanced farsight. Certain: Felice will look for Cull.
Rejected by Amerie she goes for other loveobject. Don't have
to tell you what happens if she finds him. You must shield
Cullmind with everything you've got.

Cull has job to do for Me.

No no hide him some deepcavern get him out of Europe
altogether assoonas possible! You must abandon notion raid
Felicelair Betics. Suicidal!

Got to have Spear Babe. Photocannon + psychozap concert
we cooking tips firepower balance My side. And not only *vs*
Felice...

Aiken you MUST NOT continue Quest now that she's loose.

We're all set. Postponing won't help. Maybe we have chance
grab loot before she realize what makes. Her farsight 2ndrate.

Don't fortheloveofGod don't.

Must. (Looseloose Felice is loose! Looseloose Felice is
loose!) Shit now you got Me looping—

Felice capable of destroying you + entire force.

I'll win! [Panic. Temptation abandon. Resist! Slam on it!]
Looseloose Felice is loose! Looseloose... SHUT OFF THAT
DAMN LOOP ELIZABETH!

If you go you'll die I'll have your deaths on my conscience
as well as Amerie's!

Youyouyou! Too fewkinbad for you! *And* fewkinconscience! Quit BLEEDING on me! Go make good actcontrition
or something.

Please...

GET *GONE*.

...

As he sent an additional fusillade of curses at her, Elizabeth's thought pinched off. She had retreated to the sanctuary of the room without doors.

"That's it—hide!" he yelled. "Leave me to shovel up the shit, you bungling do-gooder! Well, if I have to, I will!"

He shot a carefully guarded call to North America. Even though Felice emitted no mental aura that a farsensor could detect, she still possessed physical mass impossible to disguise. The augmented ultrasenses of Abaddon, scanning southern Spain, had no assurance of finding the girl—but they could determine where she was *not*. After a suspenseful interval, Aiken was reassured that Felice was not at that time physically present within an 80,000-square-kilometer area centered upon Mount Mulhacén.

The intelligence was sufficient to put a "go" stamp on the raid.

The 75 sailing vessels of Aiken's fleet, which included every seaworthy craft in the Many-Colored Land, moored just off the mouth of the Río Genil at 0530 hours. Some 2000 humans of the elite guard, who served the expedition in a support capacity, made haste to unpack, inflate, and launch a flotilla of 180 pneumatic rivercraft and guide them to the base-camp where the Spanish forces waited. Each solar-powered barge could carry 20 Tanu knights and their chargers, together with field rations and a spartan quota of supplies. Two of the craft had been fitted out as primary and backup laser repair shops, so that there would be no time lost getting the Spear operational.

Shortly before 0800, when everything was in readiness, Aiken mounted his own black chaliko and levitated to a commanding height before the ranks of waiting combatants. Unlike them, he was not wearing glass armor, but rather his golden suit of many pockets, the glittering jet cape, and the broad-brimmed hat with black plumes, now surmounted by the regal circlet. He saluted the knights and nobles, the High Table Exalteds and Queen Mercy-Rosmar with the small, gold-plated laser-truncheon he had taken to carrying as a baton of office.

"Battle-companions! We're ready to raid the monster's lair. Up on Mount Mulhacén, inside Felice's cave, is the holy Spear of Lugonn that was torn out of my hands during the Great Flood. The Spear is a sovereign symbol of our Tanu heritage. It's also a weapon that can be our ultimate defense—not only against Felice, but against the Firvulag Foe or any other enemy that dares to challenge us. In addition, the cave holds a treasure-trove of golden torcs. Since the equipment for manufacturing torcs was destroyed when Muriah flooded, it is vitally important that we seize this supply so that we will be able to raise our children to metapsychic operancy during the years before natural operants are born to us. The sacred Spear and the cache of torcs represent nothing less than survival insurance for our Tanu race! This is the true objective of our Quest.

"I won't minimize the hazard. We are all in danger of death. Felice's mind is more powerful than any in the Many-Colored Land, more powerful even than any mind that will exist in the Galactic Milieu six million years from now. But we can stand up to her! We can unite in a true metaconcert—and under my leadership vanquish the female demon once and for all. Believe this!

"Let me tell you what we will do. This Genil River is navigable for about one hundred and thirty-five kilometers, ninety Tanu leagues. We follow it to Mulhacén, where it has its source. There'll be rapids, but the best skippers in the Pliocene will be doing the driving, so have no fear. Certain of you psychokinetics have been assigned to add auxiliary power to the boats, to insure that we reach the head of navigation by 1400 hours. Then we take to the saddle. We'll be out of the jungle by then and into open savanna, and we'll ride hell for leather for another twenty-five or thirty kloms. A little over an hour and we should be at the base of the Sierra Nevada massif, where a dense forest begins and we're in the very shadow of Mulhacén.

"All of the way up the river and all across the savanna you will have your minds in linkage, forming a protective umbrella of psychoenergy that will hide us from the monster's sight. At the foot of the mountain, you'll take your stand, waiting in a well-sheltered spot with perfect line of sight on the region around Felice's lair. I alone will fly to the cave. You'll extend your defense to cover me while I abstract the Spear and the torcs. Since I'm able to lift more than four hundred tons, I should have no trouble making off with the loot. However, that time when I'm flying back with it does represent the most hazardous period of our raid, since I'll be using most of my brainpower in the levitation. I'll maintain my direction of our offensive metaconcert—but minus my usual share of the psychozap potential. If you ever plan to pray for us, pray then . . .

"Once I'm safe at the foot of the mountain, I parcel out the treasure and we all haul ass back to the riverboats. We'll turn the mounts loose. That'll give us added speed back to the gulf, since the boats will be lighter. We'll also be traveling with the current instead of against it. As we sail downriver, our hard-working technicians under Pete Carvalho and Yuggoth McGillicuddy will fix the Spear. Again, let us pray! I will lend them my royal assistance unless I'm occupied battling for our lives.

"After the sacred zapper is repaired, we are virtually home free! Abaddon has studied what Felice did at Gibraltar, and he's also analyzed the potential of the metaconcert we'll be putting together. Felice's creativity checks in at something he calls the six-hundredth order of magnitude. Very heavy. But if we hit Felice with a photon cannon in addition to the metaconcert blast, we should pull the equivalent of six-thirty— and the monster dies, zapped to a flaky flinder.

"So we're off. And we're going to win! You have the Shining One's guarantee!"

They had been cautioned against uttering even the most discreet response. But the aether fizzed with jubilation, nevertheless, as the pneumatic boats cast off and sped up the Genil at more than 20 kph. No sooner had the journey begun than the 3550 combatants were put to work, assembling their minds into the three-pronged metaconcert that would shortly serve as both weapon and buckler for King Aiken-Lugonn.

The three human operants from North America began the process, sorting and interleaving the minds, one by one. Owen Blanchard took the coercers, who were headed by Alberonn

Mindeater, Artigonn of Amalizan, and Condateyr of Roniah. Cloud Remillard coordinated the psychokinetics under Bleyn the Champion, Neyal of Sasaran, Diarmet of Geroniah, and Kuhal Earthshaker (the latter only a proforma participant). The all-important creative faction was marshalled by Elaby Gathen, working with Mercy, Aluteyn Craftsmaster, Celadeyr, Lomnovel Brainburner, and Thufan Thunderhead. The High Table members were entrusted with refinement of the substructures in each syntagmatic chain, binding together the lesser minds into coherent units that would be—thanks to the new sophisticated armature furnished by Abaddon—greater in power than the sum of their component parts.

Once the newborn Tanu metaconcert had stabilized and assumed a proper condition of dynamic potential, Marc Remillard took it up, smoothed the rough spots, and phased in the operant minds under his personal control: the surviving rebels in Ocala, together with their runaway adult children (now simmering but submissive), who were situated in a bivouac on the Moroccan coast about 900 kilometers southwest of Mulhacén. To this combination Marc added his own awesome creative faculty, boosted by auxiliary cerebroenergetics. The whole was then subtly cleft into offensive and defensive capabilities, with the former relying more heavily upon the creative powers and the latter weighing more on the coercers. The defensive aspect of this Organic Mind Marc kept under his own control. His farsense, in a virtuoso maneuver that neither Aiken nor the Tanu could fathom, somehow maintained its independent monitoring function. Aiken, as prime executive of the Mind, could watch out for the enemy himself; but if he became distracted, or if Felice contrived some outrageously subtle ploy, the cold farseeing eye in North America would be watching and ready to sound the alert.

Plugged in last of all, poised between Marc and the director's slot, with its soul-substance attenuated and drawn into a virtual cylinder of enormous bore, was the mind of Culluket the Interrogator. He was completely passive (but aware), a living conduit through which psychoenergies might pass in only one direction: outward. If Felice tried to penetrate the Mind with her own forces, or if she attempted to choke off the output, instigating feedback, the sentient safety fuse would disrupt. Culluket would die. (And he thought: That would be the easiest! But at the same time came the nagging voice of prescience, admonishing: Not until you pay the account in full.)

When the Mind was finally ready, the faceless entity called Abaddon presented it to Aiken Drum.

"All you need do is slip your own mind into the ultimate position: prime focus and executive director. If you're quite sure you're up to it . . ."

The waiting mental edifice seemed to shimmer before Aiken's bemused eye. How splendid! How strong! How *huge*! True, the program was Abaddon's, as well as the expertise in the assembly. But it was Aiken Drum who now took up the organism boldly and wore it—he who was in control.

The sky he saw now through the defensive barrier was almost purple. The solar disk shone vermilion with a white-hot core. As the lead boat he rode in hurtled up the river, the rushing walls of jungle were a green so intense that it verged on black. The Genil itself, still carpeted in mist, was a twisting track of molten gold unwinding endlessly.

If you're quite sure you're up to it . . .

Was he!

He let the godlike offensive potential fill him, let himself expand with it, savoring the biddable menace. He was Mercy, he was Aluteyn, he was Alberonn and Bleyn. He was Owen Blanchard, Grand Master Coercer. He was Cloud and Elaby, raw and youthful and operant. He was more than 3000 Tanu minds, synchronized in unprecedented union. He was 40 veteran villains of the Metapsychic Rebellion and 28 of their adult offspring. He was Marc Remillard, challenger of a galaxy, locked in refrigerated armor with charged needles piercing his incandescent brain.

He was all of them! And himself! He was King.

She was sure, so sure that he would be there in Goriah, but when she circled the Castle of Glass, calling his name, he did not answer, nor was he anywhere to be found in the surrounding

city or in its satellite plantations and settlements. She would
now recognize his aura, no matter where he hid. But he was
not there.

Baffled, the black bird flew southward, following the Atlantic coastline to Rocilan. But he was not in the Candy City
either, nor in Sasaran far up the Garonne, that mighty river
called Baar by the Tanu. She scanned Amalizan, the citadel
guarding the principal gold mines of the Many-Colored Land,
and then winged tirelessly on to Sayzorask on the lower Rhône
and Darask in the Provençal Everglades.

Beloved! Culluket!

Again and again the raven called, but it seemed he was not
in any of the French cities. His aura, so glacial and hard, the
color of frozen blood, would be readily discernible now that
her farsenses had been sharpened as a result of the redaction.
If she flew to within a dozen kilometers of the Interrogator,
she would know him.

She rested and broke her long fast in a verdant parkland
west of the great lake, subduing a newborn antelope fawn and
feeding upon its tongue. Refreshed, she mounted into the air
again and called out in playful derision as she passed Black
Crag. She expected no answer from Elizabeth and received
none.

Elizabeth will be useful again some day, the raven thought.
But I really don't need her help to find Cull. It'll be more fun
to search for him myself!

She flew south at gale speed, streaking over the flowering
jungles of the Corbière Hills and through a pass of the eastern
Pyrénées. The Beloved was not in Geroniah, nor in Tarasiah;
so she angled far inland and crossed the Catalan Wilderness
and came betimes to the head of the Iberian Grand Canyon,
where Aluteyn Craftsmaster's lonely citadel of Calamosk
perched above the rushing torrent. Culluket was not there.
Indeed, the city was almost deserted.

She considered. Hadn't the other places she had visited also
been strangely emptied of life-aura—especially of *Tanu* life?
Where had all the exotics gone?

The limitless plains of the south were going from emerald

to lemon-yellow, now that the rains were two months in the past. Only the swales and the arroyos remained lush, and the bottomlands along great rivers such as the Proto-Jucar, which flowed past Afaliah.

Culluket! Culluket!

But again the Beloved was not there, and neither was the city-lord, Celadeyr, nor his cadre of battle-companions. The mystery deepened. Perhaps Aiken Drum had gone off on a Quest against the Firvulag marauders of the western Alps. Felice had not searched the cities of the upper Rhône but had flown straight from Hidden Springs to Goriah, where she had expected to find her quarry cowering in the protection of Aiken Drum. But if the King had mounted some punitive expedition . . .

It was a bore, deciding what to do. If she was to keep her search methodical, she should by rights skew across the Mediterranean and take up the hunt at dismal Var-Mesk, then go up to Bardelask and Roniah. But the afternoon was lengthening and her precipitous pace had begun to sap her strength.

She thought: I'll go home to Mulhacén, and start again tomorrow.

Her heart lifted along with her raven's body as she soared up on a thermal, then arrowed southwest toward the Betic Cordillera. Home to her mountain, her treasure, her dear animal companions.

She thought: I could keep *him* in there, chained in gold. Encased in gold. Pervaded with gold! Yes! All through the muscles, a precious network of conductive metal, and golden external terminals to each major neural plexus! The brain itself would need a very special divarication, which he would have to help her build. What a delicious prospect! With him thus equipped, she would be able to play him like some magnificent algetic instrument, first warming his sanguine frigidity with simple capriccios and inventions, then going on to immense panharmonies, dithyrambs of pleasure and pain.

Oh, Beloved! Before it was my joy to receive, and that was sick and unsane, wasn't it? But now I am well and ready for the joy of giving and contemplation relished by all sane minds—

even those who would like to reject it, indignant and disgusted at its dark enigma. But we know, don't we, Beloved, that the sight of the suffering Other only confirms our own power and pain-freedom, sealing our sense of worth. We triumph as we are spared. We are gratified by a price paid but not by us.

(And did she not suffer and die for me, Crucifixa etiam pro nobis, as her foolish God did for her?)

You, too, will suffer gloriously, Beloved, but not die. I love you too much ever to let you die.

Aiken came to Felice's cave as a new-hatched spider riding on a strand of gossamer, one of hundreds that the afternoon's thermal wind blew up the northern flank of the mountain. When his glistening thread tangled in a pine tree, he made his way down to a branch and rested there, carefully thinking arachnoid thoughts just in case Abaddon's earlier scan had missed the monster. Using the shortest possible soft-focus farsight, the spiderling scanned the cave ambit. Felice wasn't hiding among the green-framed boulders, or down in the canyon, or anywhere on the upper slopes where the alpine flowers bloomed in pink and white tufts. His deep-vision, exerted more forcefully, assured him that she wasn't concealed inside Mulhacén—at least, not within a kilometer or so of the cave.

The tiny spider descended from the tree and turned into a man in a golden suit. He lowered the metapsychic shield until it was closely cupped about the cave entrance. Then, from the large pocket on his back, he took a titiridion net, which he spread on the ground. With his face shining, he entered the cave and penetrated to the inner room, sliding aside the protective rock slab as though it were a paper screen.

The radiance streaming from him lit a pile of golden torcs higher than his head. How many had the mad scavenger gleaned? It seemed there were thousands, each necklet a hollow shell filled with components from Gomnol's demolished factory in Muriah. There remained small stockpiles of the psychic amplifiers in each Tanu city; but none could compare with this cache of Felice's.

He sent quantities of the torcs flying out of the cave to pile up on the net, and at length uncovered the Spear of Lugonn and its pack.

"At last!" he muttered, taking up the weapon. He had last worn it in the Duel of Battlemasters against Nodonn. When the torcs had all been removed from the inner chamber he strolled back outside the cave, the Spear over his shoulder, and stood staring at the heaped-up treasure.

Finally he gestured, and the net gathered into a purse that encompassed the golden torcs. All that remained was to fly back to the waiting army, parcel out the spoils, and flee. Felice might never know who had robbed her...

But he couldn't leave it at that.

He sprang into the air, lifting the enormous bundle, and carried it a couple of kilometers northward along the ridge connecting Mulhacén with its sister peak, Alcazaba. Leaving the torcs and the Spear, he flew back, enclosed in the bubble of defensive force maintained by Abaddon, and hovered over the vicinity of the cave. He said:

Kill the screen! Go to the offensive mode! I have to leave my royal calling card!

The sun brightened for him and the air regained its dazzle. His mind seemed to swell, totipotent, as the entire offensive sum of the metaconcert flowed into his creative reservoir and approached focus. (Throttle back, Exalted Laddie! No sense leveling the whole bloody place, you know. Might attract her notice, wherever she is. And the energy level *is* a wee bit scary, now that you experience the totality for the first time! So back off a tad. Give her the finger, the heraldic digitus impudicus, and let go.)

Let go!

He laughed like Jove as the psychic bolt flew and thunder boomed. A huge chunk of the mountain split away, fragmented, and rumbled down into the secret crevice where the raven-girl had dwelt. Most of the sound waves had been reflected skyward by the shape of the terrain. There was little dust, no smoke. But Felice's lair was gone.

The creative blast had burned as it traveled through him and he faltered in midair, engulfed in pain, willing Abaddon to

restructure the shield as he pulled himself back together. Even
mitigated, the energy of the metaconcert had nearly vaporized
his brain plasm.

Marc Marc what do wrong God help!

Amateur blockhead! You used wrong channels [images]
*harmless at lowlevel zap greatdanger at high. Even Felice knew
better than use that puny creativemode . . .*

Yeahyeahyeah. Just give fix. Pain.

*Overload kill you just as dead as feedback or allsystem
zorch! I took too much for granted.*

Godsake save schoolteacher act + fuckingduncecap for
owndamnkids show RIGHT WAY channelize megazap.

Suppressed expletives. [Profoundly esoteric image.] *You got
that Royal Highness?*

Uh. Say again?

*King Aiken-Lugonn take your loot and get back to the others.
I'll finish the lesson as you retreat. And I hope to hell you're
a quick study.*

The rainbow-colored knights on their chargers fled across
the Granadine savanna, the great claws of the mounts slicing
the dry turf and uprooting buttercups and purple scabious and
eyebright. The tumult of the Tanu army's passing scattered
herds of gazelles and hipparions. Sabertooth cats started up
from their naps and roared in alarm, and great bustards flapped
off on low trajectories from their violated nests among the
tussocks. The sun was now low in the west and broiling hot.
Dust devils trailed in the wake of the retreating force, wavering
like tall tan spectres above the dim gleam of the defensive
canopy.

The riders did not guide their steeds. Their minds were
utterly rapt in the task of maintaining their share of the metaconcert; and though their eyes saw and their ears heard and
they were conscious of the heat and the smell of dust and ripped
meadow herbiage, they had no volition, no sense of independent being. Each brain functioned as a cell of the Organic Mind,
exuding psychoenergy in the erection of the great shield, hold-

ing still more energy in reserve, ready for the offensive thrust they might be called upon at any moment to deliver.

King Aiken-Lugonn galloped at the head of the horde, leading his people back to the navigable stretch of the Río Genil. Behind his saddle, and behind that of each other rider as well, was a sack full of golden torcs that rang with every step his chaliko took. In his arms he held a golden-glass lance with a cable connecting its butt to a powermodule slung from a sturdy shoulder harness. The readout on the module showed no charge, and the five colored studs set into its armrest were fouled with salt, as was its needle-thin aperture. At the moment, the Spear of Lugonn was dead, inoperative. But technicians were waiting at the river with tools that would bring it back to life, and the diminutive form of the King glowed in anticipation of using it once again. This weapon would conquer Felice, then rout the Firvulag. And at the end it would complete the task that the Flood had interrupted: It would kill Nodonn.

Still clothed in her raven's guise, her mind perfectly screened, Felice arrived at her lair on Mulhacén. She hovered, incredulous, at the sight of the stupendous rockslide, the glittering blocks of micaschist larger than houses that had been sheared off the face of the mountain and tumbled into the nook that had been her home. The trees were gone, the flowering shrubs, the waterfall with its fern-bordered pool for bathing, the firepit and the quaintly wrought rustic furniture that had been just outside the cavern, the mossy boulders where the rock thrushes had perched and sung for her in the evening's hush. Gone. The small branch of the river where the fat trout swam was buried under tons of debris, as was the game-trail that had brought the animal friends to her door. The only living thing left to greet her was the lynx, Pseudaelurus, which sat on the flat crest of an isolated crag, basking in the last of the dying sunlight.

The raven spiraled down, crying. At first, she believed the catastrophe to be natural; but then she saw a dusty golden torc half-buried in the detritus, and she thought to exert her powerful deep-seeing eye, scanning the barricaded interior of her talus cave. She discovered that the treasure chamber had been emptied.

"Culluket!" she screamed. The sound echoed into the dizzying gorge cut by the young Genil. The lynx cringed, its ears flattened. "Culluket—you and *Aiken Drum*!" The lynx vanished into rocky chaos and the dark-feathered bird descended onto the vacant crag and was transformed.

A fantastic being stood on the rock, dressed in gleaming black cuir bouilli, the hoplite armor of Felice's old profession much modified by her mind's vagary. Now the angles of the carapace were sharper, the contours more cruel. The old open greaves and short gauntlets had expanded to enclose all the flesh of the legs and arms, and now were adorned with curved spurs and excrescences like talons. The helmet had a predatory beak, balanced by a spiny crest projecting to the rear. From its T-shaped opening shone two beams of light, white as magnesium flares. When the being turned its head and began to survey the Granadine steppe north of the mountain, the eyebeams drilled through an intervening ridge of metamorphic rock like lasers punching a wedge of cheese. Felice searched the valley of the lower Genil through smoking peepholes, located her prey at long last, and took off after it like a vengeful comet.

The boats were tearing down the river. Aiken, in the primary repair craft, was using his deep-vision to guide the technicians in reaming out the barrel of the Spear when Marc's abrupt warning came:

Felice is on her way.

"Finish the fix, for God's sake!" Aiken shouted at the shaken Carvalho and McGillicuddy, before levitating back into the lead boat in a sizzling cloud of ozone.

"Spotted her!" he cried. This time his focusing was nearly instantaneous. He sucked and the energy flowed into him. He exhaled and the terrible blazing gobbet roared toward the shadowy fleck that hurtled after the flotilla, spiky black against a turquoise evening sky.

The fireball bloomed, obliterating some 40 square kilometers of jungle below it. The passage of the monstrous energy surge stunned Aiken. Every neuron in his body had turned into a rill of lava. His brain not only seethed, it pulsed like some variable star, with each peak verging on disjunction. A squealing craven nub within him said: Marc was right! You overloaded—and now you're dead, sucker!

But the near-fatal vertigo dampened and he was surprised to find himself still firmly ensconced in the executive slot of the Organic Mind, with Abaddon not scornful or accusatory but registering Olympian approval:

Very commendable—for a barebrain. I think you got her.

"I did?"

I get nothing on a mass-energy scan in ground zero.

"Jesus, you better be right. That zap nearly finished—"

GOD NO SHE D-JUMPED! . . . [unintelligible image] *. . . ABOVE YOU AIKEN HIT HER AGAIN HIT HER!!*

Abaddon's warning crashed in his aching brain. He saw Felice again, magnified by some weird atmospheric effect, looming directly overhead. She seemed to be several hundred meters tall. Her form, now that of a human female, appeared to be clothed in white flames that rippled like liquid silk. Her monstrous face was translucent. Her eyes were black and blazing and so was her mind. Aiken felt the defensive barrier above the flotilla begin to crumble. Something was critically wrong in the coercive segment. A vital component had failed and the structure was collapsing—

The screen resolidified. Marc Remillard had injected some arcane reinforcement, bypassing his man, Owen Blanchard, who was dead. Instinctively, Aiken knew that this makeshift shoring mechanism would hold only for the brief nanosecond that he, the prime executive, needed to shift back into the offensive mode. He would have to blast Felice again with the full load of the metaconcert, even if it killed him.

There was no time even to focus. He demanded and received the soul-bursting volume of energy and expelled it point-blank at the monster.

A shriek, inhuman, clanging in the aetheric welkin. Conflicting psychic bursts impinging, exploding, imploding, cancelling. A slowly expanding psychocreative detonation that was

overwhelming light without noise or heat. Behind and beyond
this, a structure besprinkled with thousands of scintillations,
multicolored, some of which now flared and died away. A
tenuous rolling juncture, deepest carmine, stretched across half
a world. (Between my own pain and his?) Pain bridge sentient
and sharing, threatening to fade to black, rescued, regenerated,
newly joined to a deadly white flame. Candle burning in ruby-
glass tube, shrinking. Croon of laughter. Dwindling howl plummeting to despair.

"Abaddon?"

I hear . . . King Aiken-Lugonn.

"Get her?"

*Gone. No more menace . . . either of us. Alliance concluded
until your turn to fulfill bargain. No communication until then.
Goodbye.*

"Marc . . . overloaded. Die? Marc?"

. . .

"Marc ANSWER ME!"

. . .

Amazing, he thought. It was a terminal overload and I
should be dead, but it seems I'm not! Behold my mind, a sleazy
fabric of carbonized threads, glowing bravely in vacuum. Let
me out of my bell jar and into the real world and I may fall to
ashes . . .

"Nonsense, Aiken. Just hold onto me. I'm almost finished
pasting you back together. You're a tough Scottish lad and far
too wicked to die young."

Elizabeth?

"Be quiet."

I thought you couldn't redact long-distance?

"I can't. I'm here. Stop communicating, damn you. This is
very hard to do and I've been at it for nearly a week and I'm
tired."

A week—!

He drifted. All around him were minds whispering.
Hundreds—hell, thousands!—of them. Tanu. Gold-torc human operant. His people.

Elizabeth? My metaconcert fell apart, didn't it?

"It lasted long enough. Quiet. Ah. There and there. And *there*."

Lights! Action!

He saw, felt, heard, smelled, tasted. He sat up on the padded table and the sheet slithered from his mother-naked body. He was whole. The table stood in the middle of a small decamole shelter that was meshed on all four sides for ventilation. Outside was a typical Spanish jungle, extravagant greenery and the usual mammal-bird-amphibian-insect cacophony. Inside was Elizabeth, and Creyn and Dionket in informal redactor robes, and a leather-faced Tanu with a short blond beard, a Prince Valiant haircut, and uncompromising coercer-blue eyes. This personage held out a pair of golden jockey shorts.

"Allow me."

The weak and disoriented King allowed himself to be dressed in his suit of many pockets. It was somewhat the worse for wear. He said, "So Felice is dead?"

"Her body fell into the Genil like a flaming meteor," said Dionket, his mind projecting the image. "There was a strange secondary psychocreative concussion that brought a two-hundred-meter cliff crashing down into the river right on top of her. Some of your people were caught in the avalanche."

"I—felt people dying." Aiken was staring empty-eyed at the jungle outside. "Who?"

Elizabeth's redactive strength held onto him. "Ninety-six are unaccounted for. Aluteyn Craftsmaster. Artigonn of Amalizan. The human operant Elaby Gathen. Culluket the Interrogator. And Mercy."

"Mercy *dead*?" He looked from face to face. "I don't believe it!"

"Her body wasn't found," Elizabeth admitted, "but the avalanche and the surge in the river were tremendous things. The entire course of the Genil was changed. Your people did find the Craftsmaster's remains, and Elaby Gathen's, as well as the bodies of some minor nobility. You may know that the elderly operant, Owen Blanchard, died of a cerebrovascular accident."

"And nearly fucked the lot of us!" Aiken exclaimed bitterly.

"I felt the bastard give way right at the moment Felice started her attack. If it hadn't been for Marc..." He faltered and dropped onto the edge of the bed, sitting with his head in his hands. "He did a job. God, if you only knew." When he looked up there was an odd light in his eyes. His smile was tight. "It was an education. A painful one."

"You'll have the hangover of the Western World for the next month or so," Elizabeth remarked. "Go easy. Let your mind heal fully."

His nod was impatient. "Where the devil are we?"

"In the base-camp at the mouth of the Genil. Your people have been waiting for you to regain consciousness. Very few of them were hurt badly, aside from those who were caught in the full brunt of the avalanche and some who were brain-burned when the defenses faltered. The wounded are resting in Skin in Afaliah."

Aiken looked sheepish. "Thanks for coming, Elizabeth. I mean—I was pretty mouthy there earlier, babe. Sorry."

"What the hell," she said, and smiled.

Aiken turned to the burly bearded Tanu, whose mental signature was as notorious as the triskelion badge on his azure tunic. "I suppose you flew the medic party here from Black Crag."

A minimal nod.

"Thanks a lot, Minanonn. I wish you'd consider joining us. It's a new regime in the Many-Colored Land. Lots of things are changing. You could help."

The heretical ex-Battlemaster allowed himself a wintry smile. "I'll be watching you from the Pyrénées. Visit me some time. Without your army."

"You got a deal." Aiken thanked Creyn and Dionket, set his feathered hat very carefully onto his throbbing head, then hesitated as one last item of importance came to mind.

"I don't suppose you know what became of my Spear?"

Elizabeth sighed. "It's safe on your flagship schooner, guarded night and day by Bleyn and Alberonn. And it's been repaired."

"Kaleidoscopic!" The King beamed at them all. "In a way,

I'm glad I didn't get to use it on Felice. It's a sacred weapon, you know. Too good for the likes of her. I'm glad we finished her off with mindpower. Too bad about old Cull—but that's probably for the best, too."

Walking a trifle unsteadily, he gave them a jaunty wave as he went out the door. There was a sound of scattered cheering that grew until the jungle noises were overwhelmed. And when the shouting and the mind-cries fell off, the music of the Song took its place, carrying from the camp to the boats moored out on the waters of the Gulf of Guadalquivir.

The Río Genil flowed down from Mulhacén and swung wide, following its new course around a region covered deep in stony rubble. The dead bodies in the landslide were well-buried, secure from prowling jackals and other scavengers.

Far under the mound a tiny white flame burned within a ruby, waiting inside its dark temenos for fresh fuel.

THE END OF PART THREE

PART IV

THE
LORD OF
MISRULE

1

MOREYN OF VAR-MESK HUDDLED IN PITCH-DARKNESS IN THE deserted materials yard of the glassworks. A fine drizzle coalesced on his wispy hair, ran down the collar of his cloak, and dripped onto his neck. He sneezed. It was unseasonably chilly for the middle of June, with a sharp wind blowing off the New Sea. The weather, he reflected morosely, like nearly everything else in the Many-Colored Land these days, seemed to have gone mad.

Miserable, Moreyn scanned the black sky over the water and wished Celadeyr and the redactor would hurry. Did he dare to put up a small psychocreative umbrella while he waited? It was effete, but—Tana's teeth!—brute endurance wasn't the only virtue, nor was prudence necessarily a sign of cosy-wallowing or Firvulagish degeneracy.

He sneezed again. The invisible umbrella went up, and for good measure he spun a discreet infrared pod about his soaked feet. What could be keeping Celo? He was nearly an hour late.

Not that Moreyn was anxious to relinquish his sacred charge. It had been an honor to nurse the Battlemaster, and gratifying when Nodonn praised his cleverness in securing the rare materials needed for the repair of the Sword, and his refurbishing of the armor and fashioning of a new gauntlet to cover the wooden hand. (That hand!)

But as his strength returned, Nodonn had chafed in idleness.

351

He refused to stay hidden in his salty dungeon cell, and began to prowl among the lower levels of the trona diggings during the graveyard shift. Only ramas were about then to observe him, and there was no chance that they might betray his presence. But Nodonn had taken to helping the apes in their labors, using his recovering psychokinesis to load the gondola cars with excessive amounts of mineral, which might have been noted by the gray-torc foremen who checked the schedule. When Moreyn put a stop to this game, the bored Battlemaster began playing with the mice. Swarms of the rodents infested the citadel's sewers and gained access to the glass works via an enormous drain. More than once, as Moreyn came to minister to his patient, he had been startled by serried ranks of the little creatures—marching, countermarching, and performing precision drills, while Nodonn reviewed his miniature host seated on a lump of cullet glass, like some sardonic incarnation of Apollo Smintheus.

Yes ... it was high time that the fast-recuperating Battlemaster moved on to Afaliah. Where the hand could be fixed and the portent wiped out.

In spite of his warming feet, the Glasscrafter experienced a thrill of dread. The One-Handed Warrior! According to hoary Tanu tradition, it was one of the direst forecasts of the Nightfall War.

Moreyn, came the secret call on his intimate mode.

(At last!) Here. Down here, Celo.

And there came two dim riders spiraling down, their leather stormsuits and the bodies of their chalikos reflecting fog-fuzzed city lights until they entered the shadowy yard.

"Hail, Creative Brother," Moreyn greeted the Lord of Afaliah, who swung down out of his saddle. But when he turned to the other rider he went stock-still, lidding the astonishment that flooded his mind. The slender form was human and female, and though the mental signature and face were masked, he knew that this was not a redactor but a Most Exalted member of Celo's Guild of Creators.

When she lifted the visor of her hood, Moreyn exclaimed:

"Great Queen! You live! But it was said—we all mourned—
you and the other victims of the monster Felice—"

"A necessary hoax," said Mercy. "Take me to my husband."

"Oh, yes. I *see*!" Moreyn sneezed twice. "To disarm the
surveillance of the usurper. I see! Come this way."

They left the chalikos tied to a railing and entered a disused
storeroom crowded with obsolete machinery. Moreyn lifted a
trapdoor and they descended into one of the many tunnels that
underlay the city of the glassmakers. At first, the way was lit
only by a psychocreative flame springing from Moreyn's finger, for they traversed workings that had long been abandoned.
But then they came into a region where the hot salt springs
still bubbled, depositing crystalline masses of hydrous sodium
carbonate that were mined by silent crews of ramapithecine
apes.

Guttering torches filled the steamy chambers with an orange
glow. The layers of white and pastel evaporite were streaked
with soot, making infernal murals that almost seemed alive in
the wavering light. The springs burbled and emitted foul-smelling vapor. The small apes with their great lustrous eyes wore
skin buskins and mittens as protection from the alkali deposits.
They chipped off the trona crystals with vitredur picks, shov-
eled the mineral into waiting gondolas, and trundled the cars
away to a lift.

"What a hellish place!" Mercy said. "The poor little beasts."

"They only work a six-hour shift," Moreyn said defensively.
"The smell's only sulfur, and there's plenty of fresh air. Dear
Lady, our mines are really a paradise compared to the gold
diggings at Amalizan . . ."

"And *he's* had to stay down here?" Mercy said, stricken.
They were descending ever deeper. It was hot, and there was
a rumble behind the saline walls, as of a concealed cataract or
mysterious machines.

"Great Goddess," Celadeyr grumbled, pulling off his hood
and unfastening the front of his suit. "It's a damn steam bath!
How much farther, Mori?"

The Glasscrafter led them to a barred wooden door. Its
surface trembled faintly and the noise reverberated from behind

it. "Through here." Again he ignited the tip of his finger. He lifted the bars with his PK and swung the portal open like the gate of Tartarus.

They entered a great downslanting gut that carried a roaring stream of foul water. The air was a good fifteen degrees cooler and pervaded by a cloacal stench. Mercy gasped in dismay and Celadeyr hurriedly refastened his suit, pulled up the hood, and closed the visor.

"Follow me. Be careful." Moreyn trotted out along a cat-walk, holding high his hand of glory. "This is an underground section of the Var River. It carries the main sewage outfall and the factory effluent over the continental shelf. This tunnel used to be leagues long. But with the New Sea rising it becomes shorter every day. Turn here."

They entered a branch tunnel, mercifully dry. A few dozen mice fled as Moreyn opened the last door.

Mercy pushed ahead of the Glasscrafter into a small lighted room, little more than a den carved in striped evaporite and equipped with a minimum of furniture and supplies. Nodonn stood there pallid and gaunt-faced, his golden head brushing the low ceiling, wasted frame clad in a white woolen tunic. He held out both hands to Mercy—one of flesh and the other of wood.

She burst into tears. He held her against his chest, his heart on fire, and said to Moreyn and Celadeyr, "Leave us. Wait above ground. I know the way out of here very well."

When the two men had gone and the door was closed, Nodonn lifted her and sought her lips. Their minds cried word-less greeting, beyond happiness and beyond sorrow. They lived, and now they were reunited, but the soul-hunger of the terrible empty months could scarcely be appeased in that initial con-junction. The time was too short and they dared not expend in mere ecstasy the life-force that would be needed for the im-pending journey. So the daemon's coming was a sigh, and the belle dame's fulfillment gentle as an eyelid's soft closing before sunlight. Then they held each other, warm, minds still in sweet fusion.

"Motherhood has deepened you, Queen," he said. "You are a fountain of repose. A wellspring of comfort."

"All my comfort is for you. I'll never leave you now—not even to return to Agraynel. She is only my flesh. You are my mind's life. How could I have doubted that you lived? How could I have accepted him? Can you forgive my defilement?"

"If you forgive mine." He told her about Huldah. "It was not done freely, but I know now that I had dark joy in the shaming. And now this wretched hybrid woman carries the son I would have given you, Rosmar: the first of my Host."

"Never mind, love. We'll make it right somehow, now that we're together again."

She felt his body stiffen. He drew away, the two warm hands, soft and hard, clasping her shoulders. "As to that . . . you may have to return to him."

"No!" she cried harshly. Her horror was like a knife, and there was fear as well. "What do you mean?"

He turned from her and began to take off his tunic. From beneath the camp bed he pulled two sacks, one with his glass armor and another with the suit of padding. "It won't be easy, deposing him now that he's been acclaimed King by the battle-company. Leaving aside the matter of my gaining support from the people . . . we must consider him as a military objective. He's a formidable metapsychic adversary. I can't farsense him, Mercy. Even when he's not wearing those Milieu screens, he's too strong a mind-guarder for me to penetrate. I can't even follow his physical movements unless some other person is with him, scattering inadvertent clues. The only way I have of spying on him is through you . . ."

Her mind was shrouded. The sea-deep eyes were opaque, full of fresh tears. "I've only just gained you back. And you want me to go?"

"Of course I don't!" he said, in a voice of anguish.

She let her lips rest on his naked chest, breathing the exotic pheromones, hearing his heart. "I'll go to him if you tell me to, love. But I've had a foreseeing . . ."

Her face was completely hidden by her long auburn hair

and she shivered inside her storm-suit of dark green kidskin.
He held her tightly. "What have you foreseen?"

It was her mind that spoke:

My death is in him. He loves me and he'll kill me. It was
the same vision poor Cull had of Felice. (And the two of us
condemned ones were able to calm one another. A fine joke,
that!)

"Never mind Cull. I can understand Aiken loving you. But
to kill you—? Nonsense! You are the Lady Creator. Your
energies are lifebuilding!"

"For Tanu, perhaps," she whispered. "But not for humans.
Remember Bryan, who died of me."

Nodonn's tone was cynical. "Our Shining Usurper has put
it about that his own blood is Tanu, as yours. If he believes
his own tale, he can scarcely paint you a succubus."

"Perhaps it's envy, then. My creativity brings life. His psychoenergy is only for conquest, destruction of all opposition.
Aiken would always forswear love in favor of power. He can't
forgive himself for loving me. He'll only be *safe* when I'm
dead."

"He's no monster like Felice."

"No," she admitted. "He could have thrown Cull to her and
perhaps fended off Felice's attack. But he didn't. He tried to
save Cull as well as himself." Her mind brooded over memories
of the rencontre on the Genil. "Aiken was frightfully injured
in that fight, you know. Even now, his powers are greatly
diminished."

"I know." Nodonn revealed satisfaction. "I'm counting on
it."

She looked up at him finally. "But it would be easier for
you if I were there in Goriah. Oh, my love. Of course I'll
return if you want me to!" Her eyes were wild. "I'll gladly die
for you."

He was hauling on the padded gambeson. "Aiken won't kill
you. Not even if he suspects I'm alive. No normal man could
kill his beloved."

"No normal *Tanu* man," she said sadly. "Humans are different, vein of my heart." But then her laugh rang out in the

salt cave. "Ah, who cares about my silly second sight? In the Milieu, precognition was considered a hopelessly undisciplined metafaculty—sometimes reliable, more often a fraud. And look how dubious the sight is among your folk! Why, Brede said that Elizabeth is the most important person in the world. Imagine! That futile self-doubter. I know who the most important person *really* is. You!"

He was dressing swiftly in the rosy-gold armor, his expression somber. "More likely that mysterious human operant over in North America. Abaddon. Compared to him, Aiken and I are a pair of metapsychic infants."

Mercy's antic mood became instantly serious. "That one's playing his own game. Celo suspects he may have deliberately let Felice brainburn Aiken. There was something distinctly fishy about the mental surges at the climax of the fight. But of course I couldn't tell. I was too busy digging out from under a piece of hillside that had fallen on me. Celo came to rescue me, and that was when we decided I would have to play dead. He took back my poor little empty emerald helmet..."

Nodonn's piercing gaze had narrowed. "So Abaddon might have used Felice against Aiken. How fraught with possibilities! I wonder if this North American is open to other offers?"

"You may be able to find out," Mercy said. "His daughter is at Afaliah."

"What?"

Mercy nodded. "Cloud fractured her pelvis and the redactors thought it would be safer if she recovered at Celo's place before going on to Goriah." Her look became mischievous. "You'll have to think carefully before admitting her to your conspiracy, I suppose. But Cloud Remillard would make a fine ally for you, Battlemaster. She's a Grand Master equivalent in PK when she's fully operational, and quite good in redaction as well. She's also blonde, and a real smasher. Just your type."

The towering Apollo threw back his golden head and roared with laughter. Then both of his hands framed her face. "*You* are the type I waited eight hundred years for. Only you." And then his inhuman eyes were stinging and he kissed her upturned brow.

She seized his true hand. "Let me stay with you in Afaliah. Please! At least until you're healed. Oh, don't send me back to him until we've made up for some of the emptiness."

"A little while," he agreed. "Certainly a little while. But it would take nine months in Skin to regrow the hand and lower arm and I won't stand for it. I'll go against Aiken just as soon as I can gather a force. While his mind is still weakened."

Mercy drew back, her mental walls up. "You'd fight him with one hand?"

"The Sword-wielding one is in fine shape." He flexed the wooden fingers expertly with his PK. "It may not be much to look at, but it serves."

She lifted the prosthesis, turned it slowly. "Wood? Ah, no. Nothing so base will suit you, my daemon lover!" Her glance darted around the cell. "Gold would do—but we have only our two torcs, alas!" Her eye fell on the ornate eating utensils that Moreyn had furnished his distinguished guest. "Silver! Silver you shall have, from the mind of the Lady Creator herself. My loving gift to you, Battlemaster."

She gestured, and the gleaming plate and bowl and cup and pitcher shimmered, fused, went amorphous, then seemed to whirl in a scintillant metallic cloud at the end of his outstretched arm. "Silver!" she cried again. "Nodonn of the Silver Hand!"

It was done. The crude device carved by Isak Henning had vanished. In its place was a perfect replica of the missing member, mirror-bright, so subtly articulated that the sliding joints were invisible. Mercy bent over the hand and kissed each finger, and finally, the palm.

"I will wear it until I destroy Aiken Drum," he vowed. "Until I am King of the Many-Colored Land and you are my Queen."

He drew on the two glass gauntlets and opened the door for her. Neither one of them paid any heed to the foul cataract as they climbed back to the surface by the light of their shining faces.

2

"READY ON THE TEST BOARD?" CAME BETSY'S HOLLOW VOICE from inside the flux-tap reticulator.

"Yo," said Ookpik, untangling the cables.

"Tickle the input to the tertiary MHD-flow regulator," Betsy ordered. All that was visible of him was a great mound of farthingale skirts lying on the cerametal decking. His upper body seemed to have been swallowed by the exotic mechanism he was working on.

"Oh, yeah, the MHD-three really looking good," Ookpik reported.

From the access hatch came a hand with chipped enamel on the fingernails, groping in air. "It's make-or-break time. Let's have the number-ten therm needle, that pink chip with the two-cent hardwires, and the exotic component thingy with the code like a deuce of spades."

"You got 'em." Ookpik slapped the items into Betsy's hand. There was an obscure sizzling sound. A few wisps of smoke floated out around the engineer's tightly corseted waist. Then came a falsetto shriek as Betsy struggled frantically out of the reticulator's bowels, tearing at his throat and uttering picturesque Elizabethan epithets. "Set my damn ruff on fire soldering," he explained, once the blackened bit of lace was ripped off. He adjusted his pearl-studded wig, fitted the magnifying

359

optics back over his eyes, and dived back into the machine. There were additional sizzlings and a toccatina of elfin chimes.

"That's got the bitch!" Once again Betsy emerged. "Now test the entire external web circuitry—sneetch and all!"

The Inuit technician punched out the requisites and studied the readout with increasing excitement. "Hot zot, Bets, we're in business!"

Betsy yelled, "Ready on the flight deck?"

"Flight deck aye," came the dulcet reply of the Baroness.

"Light her up!"

As Betsy clapped the hatch back into place and fastened it, the deeply resonant hum of all sixteen operating generators filled the belly of the exotic aircraft. He and Ookpik linked pinkie fingers and grinned. Then he called out, "Power input to the external web, Charly."

"X-web aye," said the Baroness. "You guys just ground-testing, or do we fly at last?"

Betsy dusted himself off. The apricot brocade of his gorgeous gown was stained and torn and most of the ruching around the cuffs was scorched away. But the rope of pearls still gleamed magnificently above his cleavage and the upstanding collar of golden lace was hardly damaged at all. He took off the magnifying goggles and stowed them in his reticule, then went forward.

"All the engine-cluster idiot lights are cyan," said Baroness Charlotte-Amalie von Weissenberg-Rothenstein. She gestured out the ports on either hand. "And as you can see, we're about as well webbed as possible. I vote for flight-test. We've got time before supper."

Betsy squinted at the craft's anomalous swept-back wings, which crawled with the purplish fire of the rho-field. "Oh, fudge! Take her up!"

The Baroness's hands flew over the exotic controls, readying the gravomagnetic flyer for lift. Betsy sank gratefully into the righthand seat while Ookpik lounged against the navigation tank, chewing a corner of his mustache thoughtfully and eyeing the dupe panel readouts.

Inertialess, the craft rose vertically into the air without a tremor, then flew slowly along the crater rim toward where the others were parked.

The RF communicator said, "Oho! Welcome to the flock, Number Two-Niner. Are you now a total go?"

"Keep us onscreen, Pongo," the Baroness replied laconically. "We're about to find out."

The landscape outside the flyer vanished in a blur. The sky went from cobalt to purple to black in less than two seconds. The people on the flight deck experienced no sensation of motion or acceleration. Only the tumbling vista outside the ports and the exotic flight instrumentation revealed that they were now traveling in the outermost reaches of Earth's atmosphere at a velocity approaching 12,000 kph, maneuvering in intricate zigzag patterns in response to the delicate promptings of the Baroness's joystick and throttle treads.

They plummeted, glowing dully in reentry. She homed on the crater lake north of the Pliocene Danube that marked the site where Brede's Ship had crashed a thousand years earlier.

Now the dull-black aircraft seemed to change from a missile into a bird. With its wings fully extended in glide configuration, it banked and swooped above the water as gracefully as a swallow. Down along the southern edge of the lake's cup stood twenty-eight other long-legged exotic flyers, wings drooping to the ground and pointed snouts bowed as in meditation. Further west and north were areas where the crater rim was torn and scarred and partially collapsed, and where fragments of twisted cerametal protruded from burnt maquis vegetation. Some of the flyers had crashed on testing. One had exploded on initial light-up. Others had proved impossible to repair and had been dumped into the lake after parts cannibalization. Of the forty-two aircraft that Basil's Bastards had found more than a month earlier, this twenty-ninth would be the last to be salvaged, thanks to the persistence of Betsy and his crew. Rehabilitating the exotic flyers had cost the lives of two pilots and four technicians; and Seumas Mac Suibhne, a bibulous engineer, had fallen out of a belly-hatch one night at the close of a long shift and broken both legs.

All in all, the expedition had thus far been a surprising success.

"She flies. We're coming in," said the Baroness to the RF com. "This is Two-Niner coming in hot."

"Roj on the hot touch, Charly. And hoo-raw at last. We thought you guys were stuck with a deader for sure."

Betsy sighed deeply and said into the second headset, "I really thought I'd have to give up on her, Pongo. If Dmitri hadn't suggested that bypass on the MHD tertiary, we'd still be ground-bound. I've had it up to *here* trying to fix these barbarian clunkers."

"We knew you could do it if anyone could, Betsy," said another voice.

"Is that you, Basil?" asked the Baroness. The rhocraft was descending perpendicularly into the sitting flock of its fellows.

"I was watching you on the scope, luv," said Basil's voice. "Fine show. We're getting a celebration supper ready for you. Extra wild garlic in the old antelope stew."

Ookpik made a strangled sound.

"The last birdie out of the nest," murmured the pilot. There was a gentle jar as the field-clad landing gear touched. Smoke rose from bits of dried grass set on fire by the web of purple energy. Then the tail settled and the nose tilted down. The Baroness killed the rho-field, shut the rest of the systems down, and sat staring at the dead control panel with an abstracted smile. "I could have danced all night."

Betsy patted her encouragingly on the shoulder. Ookpik was already opening the belly-hatch. "Come along, Charly dear. Mustn't keep our noble leader waiting. I'm dying to find out where he plans to hide the bulk of our fleet."

"If I could have just kept on flying," the Baroness said. "Out of this crazy place for good! To the other side of the planet. To Pliocene Australia or China where there aren't any Tanu or Firvulag or crazy runty humans bucking to be King of the World! Oh, Betsy, how I'd love to steal this aircraft!"

"A lot of us know your feeling. I'm afraid Basil does too, however."

The Baroness collected her paraphernalia. "The ostensible

guarding of the fleet against Firvulag marauders was a pretty thin ruse, all right."

"And then there was Seumas." Betsy smoothed his goatee and lowered one purple eyelid knowingly.

"You're kidding—!"

"A very rash young man, for all his skill. I'm sure he and Thongsa must have had it all worked out between them. However, it was a sad miscalculation to think that Sophronisba Gillis would go along with the plot. She's completely loyal."

The Baroness smothered a guffaw. "You think Phronsie chucked old Shame out of the belly-hatch that night when he suggested that the three of them scarper off with the flyer?"

Betsy shrugged. "Seumas could still continue to work in spite of his broken legs. And his great and good pilot friend has had a certain air of suppressed terror about him ever since the incident. As any sensible soul would, with the indomitable Miss Gillis watching for any old excuse to whup his ass into the dirt."

"Phronsie the enforcer. My God."

"Basil is a fine leader. Devoted to his Bastards. But long years in the jungles of academe have given him a knowledge of human nature. Basil takes his responsibility seriously, and these flyers are such a *dreadful* temptation, even to the best of us."

They moved off the flight deck into the belly-compartment. The Baroness said, "Odds on that Taffy Evans is another of Basil's watchdogs. And Nazir! And that Scowegian hunk, Bengt Sandvik. Yes—now that you mention it, I can see that one or another of them was always in the crew whenever a fresh aircraft went operational—*oops!*"

She stumbled over one of the haywire testing cables. The dainty hand of the Elizabethan transvestite steadied her in an iron grip, in spite of the fact that she outweighed him by fifteen kilos. With a startled gasp she looked down into his lovely green eyes. "You too, eh, sport?"

"Our supper is waiting," Betsy said. He gestured to the exit ladder. "After you, darling."

*   *   *

The leading aircraft descended to 10,000 meters and hung in the air above the blindingly brilliant cluster of peaks.

"Fan-bloody-tastic," exclaimed Pongo Warburton. He eased them into a slow holding pattern. "How high she be, Basil?"

The exotic terrain-clearance indicator had been equipped with an improvised converter. Basil and Aldo Manetti worked with this for a few minutes, surveying the central section of the massif and making a permanent chart on a large durofilm sheet. Basil said, "The principal summit, Monte Rosa, is 9082 meters. The neighboring peaks are all above 8000." The don's voice was vibrant with excitement.

"How high was Everest?" Pongo wanted to know.

"Around 8850," said Aldo, "depending on how much snow was in that year's monsoon. And how recently the garbage-collecting crews had been there, cleaning up after the outworld daytrippers."

The pilot adjusted their altitude, bringing them closer to the pristine mountain.

"Sublime," Basil whispered.

"And virgin," Aldo added. "I could cry. I *am* crying."

"Is it the highest on Pliocene Earth?" Pongo asked.

"Undoubtedly," Basil said, "if geologists are correct in their premise that the Alps exceeded the Himalaya in height during this epoch. Of course, these Helvetides will be greatly worn down during the coming Pleistocene Ice Age, and there will be tectonic adjustments as well—rising and falling of the entire Alpine region. Poor Monte Rosa will eventually yield pride of place to Mont Blanc as highest peak in Europe. In our own Milieu she will only be second highest. And only the locals and a few keen climbers such as Aldo and I will know her name..."

The RF communicator of the aircraft said: "Number One, this is Twelve. All of us now in position at twenty kloms high and holding."

"Maintain altitude," said Basil. "Enjoy the view while Aldo and I decide which portion of the cold-storage locker to use."

"We're gonna put the rhoboats *here*?" said an anonymous voice in accents of acute dismay. Every one of the Bastards had perforce come along on this first phase of the ferrying mission. Only the Howler guide, Kalipin, had remained at the crater lake.

"That's my plan, yes," said Basil.

There were sinister female chuckles. "Any of you mothers figuring to sneak back overland later on and rip off a bird—don't forget your fur-lined jockstrap. And your ice pick."

"We'd sooner try to melt your heart, Phronsie," said the dispirited voice.

Basil said, "The inaccessibility of the place is one of its great advantages, of course. No chaliko-riding exotic or human could possibly get in here. Not even levitating. The beasts would be subject to anoxia and hypothermia, as would unacclimated riders."

"Some of the Tanu body-fly," said the voice of Taffy Evans. "And so does that friggerty Aiken Drum."

"We can't make the craft completely secure," Basil admitted. "But up here, if we choose a hiding place with care, the aircraft will be concealed by snow cover very quickly, making their detection by—er—mass-scanning farsense very difficult. And, of course, the Lowlife leadership will be in possession of the only chart showing the parking site. When we're ready to retrieve the flyers, they can be melted free by soft heat-beam fire."

The radio chatter continued while Basil and Aldo reconnoitered the terrain, finally landing in a high valley below the northern flank of Monte Rosa that was free of glaciers but still well covered with fresh snow in mid-July. Both of the mountaineers had bodies that had been artificially adapted for high-altitude exploration during a previous rejuvenation; and so, after cautioning Pongo Warburton to remain safely inside the aircraft, they put on warm clothing and went tramping gleefully in the snow, ostensibly doing a final ground survey with sonic probes before calling in the other ships.

Manetti finally sat down on a protruding rock and gazed at the mountain looming above them. "What a perfect place this is to begin the ascent! How do you like the West Col for starters?"

"Quite feasible, I should say. We're at—er—5924 meters, which leaves quite a respectable jaunt to the summit." His voice lowered. "It was the reason I came to the Pliocene, you know. To find this, if it existed, and climb it. Well—I've got this close."

"Maybe it'll be a short war."

Basil was looking around the perimeter of the valley with a small monocular. "Devilish tight place to get into without an aircraft. You'd have to come in from the north. Almost a straight-up slog from the Wallis valley of the Rhône. A logistic nightmare."

"No sweat as long as you have the two flyers tucked away in the Vosges. Then later, when the Lowlife Air Arm is trained, you can shift this frozen fleet to a more convenient spot. None of my business, of course . . . but aren't your precautions against theft of the flyers just a trifle extreme?"

"Chief Burke's orders, old chap. Like the biblical centurion, I am merely a man subject to authority. And rather glad to be."

Aldo got up and stretched. "Well, we might as well call down the others, then get back to the Ship's Grave for the second batch. Looks like we'll have no trouble getting them all ferried today."

"We'll have to post extra guards at the crater tonight," Basil said as they walked back to their flyer. "With only the two aircraft left now to take us back home . . . well, 'Quis custodiet ipsos custodes,' as your old countryman Juvenal will one day remark."

"I might be tempted myself," Aldo laughed, "if I only knew how to drive one of the things. And if I wasn't so eager to climb Rosa with you some fine day, compare mio."

"We're so close to finishing our task, Aldo. If something should go wrong now—"

"What could? Tomorrow, we fly home!"

Basil's expression was pained. "There have been—er—hints of trouble."

"Thongsa again?" Aldo's lip curled. "Not to worry. Phronsie's got that little pillroller so scared he won't even go to the loo without company."

"Something more ominous, I'm afraid. I shouldn't burden you, Aldo. As expedition leader, I shall have to deal with the matter as best I can."

"A centurion's lot is not a happy one. He had to give orders as well as take them, I recall."

The two of them crunched along wordlessly for a few minutes. In spite of the altitude and the surrounding snowfields, the sun was hot. They stripped off their balaclavas and opened their survival vests. The parked aircraft was still half a kilometer away.

"If Chief Burke were here," Basil said, "he'd make the necessary command decision in a trice. I'm afraid my own blood's too thinned by centuries of civilization to make me properly ruthless . . . May I pose an abstract problem to you?"

The suddenness of the question took Aldo off guard. "Go ahead."

"Suppose that last night, a trusted member of our company proposed treason, speaking to another member of our company. The second member, being secretly one of my—er—enforcers, notified me of the treacherous proposition after having temporized with the potential renegade."

"Jesus H. Christ!"

"Suppose this potential traitor is a person who has behaved in an exemplary fashion up until now. Suppose the person is possessed of extraordinary talents that we had counted on utilizing when we begin adapting the aircraft for combat. Suppose this person is not a pilot, and therefore hoped to suborn one in order to implement his treason—"

"To do what, for God's sake?"

"To turn over an aircraft, and the approximate location of this parking site, to Aiken Drum. In return for the usual perquisites."

"Keeping this abstract," Aldo muttered, "you seem to have two fairly clear choices. Numero uno. You kill the fucking bastard out of hand before he finds himself a pilot with shakier loyalty. Numero due—and this one holds good only if the guy's really valuable—you lock him up tighter than a Lylmik's bum and let him live as long as he cooperates."

Basil pursed his lips and nodded in agreement. "And which of those options, in your view, represents the most prudent choice?"

"Well . . . so far, the guy's done nothing but talk. Right?"

"Correct. And the proposition made to my informant was couched in the most ambiguous possible terms. Its basic intent was plain, however."

"Oh, hell, I don't know," Aldo said. "You've only got this peacher's word. What if he read the other guy wrong? What if your boy has some private little axe of his own to grind?" Manetti wiped perspiration from his forehead.

"The possibilities had occurred to me, too."

"Why not keep the traitor under surveillance? Maybe even let him know your doubts about him? He might back off, figure the game's not worth the risk. Then you'll still be able to use him. Good rhocraft technicians don't grow under every bush in this Pliocene Exile."

"True." They were approaching the flyer. "I appreciate your counsel, Aldo. I think you've helped me. A harder-hearted man would have chosen a more uncompromising course. But you and I . . . mountaineers are such romantics at heart. I'd like to give everyone the benefit of the doubt."

Aldo began to climb up the aircraft boarding ladder. He smiled over his shoulder at the don. "A little artful psychology can do the job just as well as the big fist."

"I hope you're right," Basil said. "I *do* hope you're right."

Basil groaned, shifting on the decamole cot. Someone was shaking him by the shoulder. There were staccato voices outside the tent and a wild sound of weeping. It was very dark.

"Basil, wake up." Bengt Sandvik was urgent. "Emergency."

"Oh, *no*."

The expedition leader pulled himself up and thumbed his wrist chronometer. It was almost four. His head spun from a belated touch of mountain sickness and he could barely understand what Bengt was saying. He groped for his boots and stuffed his feet into them.

". . . cracked Nazir over the skull and tried to grab the Number One flyer . . . if Mr. Betsy hadn't come by with the stun-gun . . ."

"Who?" Basil asked wearily. He knew who.

"Aldo Manetti. And he had the Baroness along to do the piloting for him."

Basil threw on a shirt and went out of the tent. Taffy Evans had a hammerlock on the mountaineer, who was still groggy from the stun charge. Baroness Charlotte-Amalie was tense in the grip of Phronsie Gillis. Betsy, efficient in a zippered flight-suit but still wearing the wig, had the prisoners covered with his Husqvarna.

Basil stepped closer to Aldo. "So you weren't able to settle for numero due after all."

Aldo's head lolled and he spat weakly. Saliva dribbled on his dark chin.

Basil turned away, consulting his watch again. "Well, it's nearly dawn. Time we were breaking camp." He looked off at the two tall aircraft silhouetted against the graying starry sky and the crater lake. "A pity there are no trees here. But the drop from the belly-hatch should be sufficient."

"What are you going to do?" screamed the Baroness.

"Tie the two of them to the landing struts of Number One until we're ready."

"What are you going to do?"

"Hang you, my dear," Basil said. Then he went back into his tent to finish dressing.

3

Boduragol, chief redactor of Afaliah, sat on his stool in the middle of the womb-dark Skin chamber, his eyes closed and his mind given over almost completely to his work. The great innovation had been an unqualified success. Both patients had improved markedly since he had thought of pairing their highly compatible enantiomorphous psychokinetic functions within the light yoking of his own redactive matrix. The atrophied right hemisphere of the male brain, especially, had undergone significant regeneration under the influence of the female's powerful iatropsychic input. The simultaneous acceleration of the woman's healing had been purely serendipitous. The scientist in Boduragol was fascinated by the outcome. The sentimentalist was gratified.

The bodies stood side by side in the suspensors, chaste as alabaster statues wrapped in clinging, transparent cauls. On one mental level, the Tanu man and the human woman were actively cooperating with the redactor. On another more intimate mode, behind a firm barrier, they were simply talking.

CLOUD: But, don't you see that it was almost the same for your generation as it was for ours? Your parents decided your destiny for you in advance. You had nothing to say about it and were forbidden to question their judgment. Neither did we.

KUHAL: How could it be any other way? Our people left the Duat Galaxy in order to be free. Free to follow a life we believe in. Was it not the same for yours?

CLOUD: Our parents said so. And for many years, we believed them.

KUHAL: But now you do not. Well . . . we Tanu also have our heretics.

CLOUD: Analytical criticism is not heresy if one is truly free.

KUHAL: You impute that *we* are not?

CLOUD: My generation was constrained by ignorance, inertia, even fear. The questioning was painful, dangerous. Ultimately necessary, nonetheless.

KUHAL: I do not understand.

CLOUD: Shall I tell you something of our story?

KUHAL: We have time . . . yes. Perhaps we Tanu have let ignorance and inertia rule us as well. In our relations with you. We knew only one small segment of your race: the voluntary time-travelers. The nonmetapsychics seemed to be useful servants. The latents we accepted into our family of the mind. Only Nodonn perceived the immense hazard in our developing relationship; but most of us would not listen to his warning. Blindness was more comfortable.

CLOUD: I know.

KUHAL: Do not let me distract you from the tale. Begin at the beginning. Tell me how metapsychic operants arose among you. Tell me how the Rebellion took root.

CLOUD: You know that the people of Elder Earth were slowly developing into natural operancy some millennia before they were contacted by exotic races and inducted into the Milieu.

KUHAL: This has been explained to us by our human Genetics Master.

CLOUD: The operants who lived toward the end of the twentieth century were fast approaching the adept status of coadunate minds. They were very circumspect about revealing their abilities to normal people. Certain ones—especially those with strong coercive or creative talents—used their metafaculties for personal aggrandizement. Others who were more altruistic studied the mental powers, using themselves and other operants as test subjects. Eventually, these scientists developed the special educational techniques that brought quasi coadunation to numbers of their fellows. They put together a small, imperfect replica of the Milieu's Coadunate Mind and broadcast the fact of their existence. This was the "beacon" that virtually forced the Milieu to initiate the Great Intervention of 2013, in spite of the fact that most humans were still ethical primitives... higher on the scale of psychosocial maturation than you Tanu, but still barbarians compared to the other five coadunate races.

KUHAL: So you and I are both primitives! The mystery of our compatible heritages becomes somewhat less murky. But do not let me digress.

CLOUD: One of the principal centers for metapsychic research on Earth was at Dartmouth College, a small learning institution in North America. The two people in charge of the department prior to the Intervention were Denis Remillard and Lucille Cartier. They were both significantly operant and came from a similar ethnic background. Shortly after they became colleagues, they married. They were my great-grandfather and great-grandmother. Denis and Lucille had seven children, all powerful operants. The youngest and most talented was my grandfather, Paul, who was born the year after the Intervention and trained in utero by means of exotic procedures that later became standard. Paul became known as the Man Who Sold New Hampshire. Because of his efforts, this small area in North America became the planetary center of metapsychic operations as Earth entered the mainstream of the Milieu.

KUHAL: And your family consolidated its dominance.

CLOUD: It was inevitable. Paul became the first human being elected to the Concilium, the governing body of the Galactic Milieu, which is composed entirely of masterclass metapsychics having profound skill in psychosocial analysis and problem solving. Later, four of his five children also served as magnates. Marc was the oldest. He became a Paramount Grand Master, one of the most powerful minds in the galaxy.

KUHAL: This is your father, the man called Abaddon?

CLOUD: Yes... That was the nickname he received during the Rebellion. In our holy book, there is a section telling of the last days of the world, when the forces of good and evil are engaged in a final confrontation. Abaddon is the leader of the demon army. He has other names: the Angel of the Abyss; the Destroyer. My Papa...

KUHAL: The war at the end of the world! It's part of our religious mythos as well. We call it the Nightfall War. When the persecuted Tanu and Firvulag were driven from their home planet to the edge of the Duat Galaxy, they thought that they would fight the Nightfall War themselves. But Brede intervened, and her Ship carried us to this starwhirl. Now Celadeyr and certain of his followers believe that the Nightfall War will be fought in the Many-Colored Land!... But you must forgive me, Cloud. Once again I interrupt. Tell me about your father's Rebellion.

CLOUD: I can't tell you very much. I was a year old. My brother Hagen was two. Both of our parents were involved in some colossal conspiracy to put the human race in absolute control of the Milieu. There was a grandiose scheme that Papa and Dr. Steinbrenner and some of the others devised that was supposed to eventually transform a group of us children into superbeings, ultrametapsychics. The rebels planned to inaugurate the scheme after the coup... but of course, the coup failed. Papa has never talked to us about his plans for us children, and the record of it has been expunged from the computer in Ocala. I'm afraid that something about the plan must have been horrible, because Mama—Mama—

KUHAL: Do not articulate the thought. I can see. I'm very sorry.

CLOUD: Papa loves us. I can't believe he would have done anything evil to us. Not knowingly.

KUHAL: Tell me the rest of the story.

CLOUD: The Rebellion took place in 2083. It lasted less than eight months in its overt phase. A large number of human operants were involved, and millions of normals, too. Almost all of the lower-echelon rebels died—and so did numbers of innocent people on rebel-occupied planets. Eventually, Papa was defeated by his own younger brother,

Jon, and Jon's wife, Illusio. Jon Remillard was a mutant.
He was fourteen years younger than Marc. By the time he
reached adulthood he had no body—only a naked brain that
wore any sort of shape that struck its fancy. I know he
sounds like a monster, but the Milieu made him a saint when
he put down the Rebellion. Jon's wife was a Paramount,
like him, a metaconcert specialist. She had only half a face
as a result of some psychocreative mishap and never had it
regenerated because the deformity became a kind of symbol
of her authority. She wore a diamond mask.

KUHAL: Jack the Bodiless and Diamond Mask. Gomnol spoke
of them . . .

CLOUD: The pair of them died, but Papa lived. And he brought
Hagen and me and a hundred or so of his surviving people
through the time-gate.

KUHAL: I remember the black day I fought against the invaders
in the Battle of the Grotto Wilderness. Our forces were
massacred. King Thagdal ordered the incident blotted from
our history after the invading humans disappeared across
the Western Sea.

CLOUD: Papa took his people to North America. He didn't want
to fight you. Many of his followers were badly wounded
and he himself was half-dead from terrible brain-burns. We
made a new home on an island off southeastern North America. It's very beautiful. We call it Ocala. All of the other
children were born there.

KUHAL: But you left it. Why?

CLOUD: When we were young, we could imagine nothing other
than following our parents' chosen way. Papa had brought
all kinds of equipment to the Pliocene. After he recovered,
he set up a farsensing observatory and began to search the
stars, looking for another race of metapsychics. He knew
that if he found such a race, he could prevail on it to come
and rescue us. He hoped to reinstitute his great dream of
human dominion in a world six million years younger than
the Milieu. A fair number of his original followers believed
he'd be able to do it. Papa . . . can make you believe in him.
But as the years went on, and thousands upon thousands of

stars were searched with no result, many of the older people became despondent. There were suicides—and murders. Some of the old rebels went mad and some psyched out on drugs and some just . . . withdrew. We children watched it all happen while we grew up. Finally, we began to think for ourselves, beyond Papa's futile dream. Felice was a catalyst. But we had been watching you long before she arrived. We put together a crude farsight combination and spied on you here in Europe as an entertainment.

KUHAL: Ah. The children of ennui while away tedious hours observing lower forms of life! We weren't real at all, were we, Cloud? Only ants busy in a nest. And one day, you thought you'd see what would happen if you let the water in—!

CLOUD: No!

KUHAL: Why did you help Felice destroy us, then?

CLOUD: We coveted your Many-Colored Land. Not in itself, but as a stepping-stone back to the Milieu.

KUHAL: *Back?* Back through the time-gate? But that's impossible!

CLOUD: No, its not. Elaby Gathen, the man who died in Aiken's fight against Felice, was certain that we would be able to build a duplicate of the original time-warping device that stands in the Milieu. We have a complete set of plans from our computer. And when my brother and the others fled from Ocala, they took all kinds of manufacturing apparatus and mineral resource charts.

KUHAL: And your father? How did he react to this?

CLOUD: He was violently opposed at first. Now . . . I don't know. We forced him to rethink his own objectives. He knows now that we'll never go back to Ocala. Perhaps he's decided to let us follow our own destiny. And after what happened with Felice and Aiken Drum, he may even help us. Just as he may help you.

KUHAL: *What are you saying?*

CLOUD: Hagen and the others marooned down in Africa spent some time studying a mental reprise of the fight with Felice. I've conferred with them about it. Since you Tanu are so metapsychically primitive, you probably don't fully realize just how many questionable things were happening down there on the Genil River! Let's hope Aiken Drum doesn't either.

KUHAL: Explain!

CLOUD: All right, consider the metaconcert program that Papa taught Aiken. We children have nothing like Papa's sophistication in things like that. But it was apparent that Papa planned for both Felice *and* Aiken to die in that fight.

KUHAL: Great Goddess.

CLOUD: Papa knew very well that as an individual, he couldn't measure up to Felice. Even using the metaconcert, throwing every available bit of mindpower against her, it would be touch and go. (Of course, if they'd had that photon Spear working, they'd have had the edge.) Now, there are a number of different options for setting up an offensive metaconcert. Some are much more hazardous to the prime executive than others. Papa gave Aiken a program that should have squeezed the last erg of psychoenergy out of the lashup if Aiken used it at full zap—as he'd be likely to do instinctively in a panic situation. And a full zap of that potential funneled through Aiken should have killed him as well as Felice. But Aiken didn't throw the whole basketful at her in the first strike. He'd been scared by his test blast up on the mountain and so he mitigated the flow, keeping it sublethal. As you may recall, Papa was fooled into thinking that the first strike finished Felice.

KUHAL: Abaddon said that he couldn't detect her mass or energy. But then—and I admit I did not understand this—he said Felice jumped.

CLOUD: He said she *d-jumped.* It's a meta slang term, short for dimensional-jump or translocation. A faculty that's extremely rare in the Milieu. Sometimes a variation of it is called teleportation.

KUHAL: Brede's Ship!

CLOUD: What?

KUHAL: The giant organism, her spouse. The Ships were capable of faster-than-light travel via hyperspace, using their mind-power alone. Do you mean to say that Felice—

CLOUD: She might have done it inadvertently, as a defense mechanism. Perhaps just skipping out of range. But Hagen thinks that she followed Papa's farsense beam—it was in peripheral mode—and scragged him!

KUHAL: But she attacked Aiken—

CLOUD: It could have happened in a split second. When Felice reappeared above Aiken, Papa's psychocreative input was altered. We reran the memory and proved it. He had been handling the defenses except at the very instant of the first strike, when he flashed briefly into the offensive mode on main channel. After Felice's jump the whole screen started to go. Owen Blanchard dropped dead. He might have been hit by Papa's flashover, given the configuration. We think Papa was able to pull himself back together in time to re-weave the disintegrating defense, then participate in the final zap.

KUHAL: You believe that Felice did no significant harm to your father?

CLOUD: On the contrary. And if he was hurt, it would tend to explain his strange withdrawal after the fight, and the fact that he's remained incommunicado for more than a month now.

KUHAL: But your father continued to function after the d-jump incident.

CLOUD: And he was hooked into a cerebroenergetic rig strong enough to bottle a small H-bomb! He's a Paramount, and he was operating with God knows how many factors of augmentation. It's when he shucks the armor plating and the superconductive artificial nervous system that the headache is likely to begin. Hagen knows more about this kind of thing than I do. He suspects that Papa was on the receiving end of a coercive-creative zorch heavy enough to send him to the regen tank—and *that's* why the aether between here and Ocala has been so peaceful lately.

KUHAL: How fortuitous for you and your peers.

CLOUD: And perhaps for you.

KUHAL: ?

CLOUD: Listen up, and try to understand. I think that you Tanu and my own people and even Papa now share a common nemesis. We may all have to cooperate if we want to survive much longer.

KUHAL: Aiken Drum?

CLOUD: Aiken should have died. He didn't. It almost seemed as though Felice siphoned the bulk of that psychoenergy away from Aiken *herself* at the last minute. God knows how or why. She's dead. But Aiken's very much alive, and only a little wonky, and by now he's figured out that Papa was out to screw him. He's in a position to do some heavy mindwork himself now, thanks to Papa's gift of the meta-concert program. It won't be hard for him to adapt it to safe use. When he dismantles the mental booby traps, he'll go after your brother Nodonn and his faction—and when your brains are barbecued he'll turn his attention to Papa.

KUHAL: Or you.

CLOUD: All my people and I want is to go to the Milieu. You'd lose nothing by helping us. And we have a lot to offer you.

KUHAL: You have already given of yourself to me.

CLOUD: Mutual, if you like. I'm nearly healed—and three times faster than a tank could do the job in our Ocala infirmary.

KUHAL: I had thought Boduragol's suggestion to be futile. The loss of my twin brother seemed an irreparable calamity. Our biotechnology of the Skin holds out scant chance of regenerating an entire brain hemisphere. And yet we see what is happening.

CLOUD: A novel adaptation, certainly. In human medicine, the left brain has very often been successful in learning to assume right-brain functions, and vice versa.

KUHAL: Perhaps what you have done is teach me to be human.

CLOUD: You need more work. But that can be arranged.

Boduragol opened his eyes and smiled. The duet of PK and redactive force flowing between the two patients was supremely harmonious. He really wasn't needed any longer. He slipped down off his stool and went to the two motionless bodies, the

man torced in gold, the woman crowned with heavy braids of
lustrous reddish-yellow hair.

"Why don't I just leave you two alone to get on with whatever you're doing? Another week, and you'll probably both be
well. *Most* gratifying."

Stooping, Boduragol made a minute adjustment in the Skin
around Cloud Remillard's ivory feet.

"Gratifying," he could not help repeating, and went out,
leaving the healing to proceed.

4

WHEN MERCY FINALLY RETURNED TO GORIAH AT THE END OF
July, the deadly languor that had afflicted Aiken ever since the
fight with Felice began at last to lighten, and his wounded brain
to heal. The Queen's tale was a thin one: that she had suffered
amnesia when her boat was caught in the landslide and had
wandered alone in the jungle east of the Genil, to be rescued
at last by bareneck plant hunters who did not recognize her,
and who brought her back to Afaliah only after having gathered
sufficient numbers of rare orchids for the conservatory of Lady
Pennar-Ia, Celadeyr's wife. Implausible though this story was,
Aiken accepted it without question, nor did he attempt to delve
into Mercy's mind. She was back, she was unharmed, and her
response to his lovemaking was once again fervent. It sufficed,
and he was content.

One fine August day they went out to the dune hills along
the Strait of Redon to see Yosh Watanabe and his crews demonstrate the different kinds of fighting kites being readied for
the upcoming Grand Tourney. Aiken and Mercy and a large
party of Most Exalteds lounged about beneath a shady canopy,
enjoying the sea breeze and the novel entertainment. There was
an abundance of picnic food and iced honey wine, and the kite
battles were diverting and occasionally dangerous.

First into the air were agile, lozenge-shaped Nagasaki hata,
with their flying lines coated in crushed glass, vividly decorated

380

in stylized designs of red, white, and blue. When one kite
managed to saw through the line of a rival, the well-rehearsed
Tanu nobility yelled out the traditional cry, "Katsuro!" and
paid off their wagers, while Yosh beamed and strutted and
explained the future history of the events.

The wind picked up after the sun crossed the meridian, and
the big kites soared aloft. There were Sanjo rokkaku, hexag-
onals half again as tall as a Tanu male, bearing gaudy portrayals
of samurai warriors, Japanese demons, and mythical creatures;
and there were rectangular Shirone o-dako, 6.7 meters high by
5 meters wide, ornamented with magnificent fishes and birds,
figures from folklore, and abstract motifs. Crewed by five to
ten humans, these fighting kites were too ponderous to attempt
line-cutting maneuvers. Instead they engaged in stately dog-
fights, crashing into one another while the competitors
attempted to foul their lines. A losing kite, deprived of aero-
dynamic lift, would falter and tumble down out of control. Its
victorious attacker would perforce follow it to the gound since
the lines were entangled; but the winning kite usually maintained its dignity to the end, landing safely while its foe crashed
to the sand, a mangled mass of torn paper and higgledy-pig-
gledy bamboo bones.

When the wind was deemed suitably strong and steady, the
truly enormous kites were trundled onto the beach, the combatant carriers that were destined to play a part in the Tourney
proper rather than the preliminary events. Two o-dako measuring 14.5 by 11 meters and weighing more than 800 kilos
apiece were hoisted onto temporary scaffolding so that their
many bridle lines could be attached, braided, and fastened to
the flying cable. This last was connected to a heavily weighted
winch. The kite warrior would be suspended from the lower
framework in a light breeches buoy. Three maneuvering lines
joined to key bridles gave the fighter some control over his
kite's flight; but the principal guiding force came from the
ground crew of fifty, who were equipped with running control
lines that joined the main cable by means of large D-shaped
carabiners.

When the pair of giant o-dako were ready for launching,

Yosh came to the royal enclosure, trailed by his assistant, the dour Lithuanian gray-torc, Vilkas. Yosh was attired in his gorgeous samurai armor and Vilkas in the only slightly less ornate harness of an ashigaru, or foot-warrior.

Yosh bowed gravely to Aiken and Mercy. "This will be our first official demonstration of the man-carrying kites, Aiken-sama, the first time that we've actually attempted aerial combat." He extended a singular pole-arm for the King to examine. "Vilkas and I will attempt to slice each other out of the sky using these naginata—curved blades mounted on long shafts. We won't go for each other hand to hand, of course. The fighter and his suspension rig are out of bounds. Fair game includes the bridle lines, the maneuvering ropes, the main cable, and the bamboo frame and paper facing of the kite itself."

"It sounds dangerous for you," Mercy remarked warmly. The young coercer woman, Olone, who had nursed baby Agraynel during the Queen's absence, stood immediately behind the throne holding the infant. Mercy held out her arms for the child and cuddled it while Yosh continued his explanation.

"Since we play without safety nets, the game could be very dangerous for ordinary humans like Vilkas and myself. We minimize the hazard—and add to the fun for you Exalteds—by using PK adepts for coaches." The Japanese technician made a courteous obeisance to a portly gold-torc human who stood beside the strapping Olone. "Lord Sullivan-Tonn was good enough to work with us during practice sessions. He's agreed to coach Vilkas, here, during the contest today."

Aiken eyed Sullivan thoughtfully. "Is coaching hard to learn?"

The pompous little psychokinetic lifted both hands in a deprecating gesture. "I found it quite simple, actually." He simpered.

"How do you play?" Aiken asked Yosh.

"The coach gives telepathic direction not only to his fighter, but also to the ground crew, advising on tactics. He's also allowed to generate PK wind for his kite *only*. Huffing the opposition's aircraft around is grounds for disqualification. This effectively limits windplay to periods when the two kites are fairly widely separated, unless the puffer has a lot of finesse. I think you may find that close work with the ground crew gives better control in most clinch situations. If a combatant gets his strings clipped, it's the duty of the coach to rescue him before he hits the ground. Which is why only PK heads get to be skippers in this game."

Aiken nodded. His smile was wan and his eyes were like two holes burned in parchment. He was wearing golden jeans and a black shirt open at the throat. "So Sullivan's going to handle your ichiban lad today, eh, Yosh? Who's coaching you?"

"I hoped you would do me the honor, Aiken-sama."

"Oh, please do!" squealed Olone. "I'm positive you'll win!"

Sullivan's face went starchy in the light of his young wife's disloyalty, but he added, "Yes, please coach the second kite, my King."

"I'm still feeling a bit seedy," Aiken warned.

Yosh said, "You needn't hold up the entire o-dako if I'm shot down, Aiken-sama. Just keep me off the deck. I only weigh sixty-four kilos, armor and all."

With a visible effort, Aiken roused himself. "Hell, I can manage that. This is a great job you've done, Yosh. Carry on! O-tanoshimi nasai, kiddo!"

Yosh grinned. "You bet, boss." He hurried off with Vilkas to complete the preparations. Aiken slumped back into his wicker throne, watching the scurrying crew members. His mind was shuttered. It was becoming hotter as the westering sun dropped below the edge of the canopy. Sullivan and Olone kept up a banal chatter and the baby fussed, resisting Mercy's attempts to coze and chirk her up mentally.

Finally, Aiken said, "Can't you see she's hungry, Merce? Let Olone feed her so she'll stop that damn mind-whimpering."

"Oh, the poor mite!" Olone exclaimed, taking the child eagerly. She drew one of her elongate breasts from inside her azure chiffon gown. "Are you starving, Grania lambie? Come to Nurse!" Voraciously, the infant began to suck. The irritating telepathic bleats were submerged into emanations of sheer bliss.

"Take her to the other side of the tent, where it's cooler, dear," Mercy told the girl.

"Yes, my Queen. Shall I bring her back when she's finished?"

Mercy's expression was remote, almost renunciatory. "Find some quiet corner to rock her and sing, Olone. I'm afraid all this turmoil has overexcited her. It was selfish of me to bring her along to the shore with us today . . . but I did so want her near me."

Olone sketched a curtsy and rushed away, as if half-fearing that Mercy would change her mind. Sullivan observed, "My wife loves Agraynel as she would a child of her own, my Queen."

"I know. And I'm more grateful than I can say for her nurturing of the child while I was—lost. I think perhaps it was my subconscious concern for Agraynel that must have cured my amnesia at last as I wandered forlorn in the jungle of Koneyn."

Aiken uttered a soft chuckle. "Well, we know that it wasn't subconscious concern for Me!" He pretended to be absorbed in the action out on the beach. The scaffolding was being removed from the two great kites, which were held upright by the taut anchor lines manned by the sweating crews. Sullivan's kite was predominantly scarlet and gold, decorated with a splendidly helmed Japanese warrior poised against a backdrop of cherry blossoms. Aiken's kite was more stark, a medley of blues, a tsunami wave à la Hokusai frozen elegantly in the breaking above a rockbound islet.

Sullivan was making a valiant attempt to be urbane in the face of ominous mental undertones. "No one was more astonished than I, Great Queen, when Olone volunteered to suckle your precious child, believing that you had perished. I had not realized that such a thing was possible for a woman who had not herself given birth! The Tanu are an amazing race, aren't they? So human and yet so fascinating in their difference! The unique breasts of the women have a counterpart in the folklore of several European countries, you know. The Ellefolk and

Skogrå of Scandinavia, the Fée of France, German Nixen, the Aguane of the Italian Alps, the Giane of Sardinia—"

"All elf-women with long breasts. I know." Mercy was gentle. "But there's nothing mysterious about the milk, Tonn dear. If a woman wishes it deeply enough and her will is strong, the prolactin hormone will be secreted along with others and the breasts will fill—even for those who are childless. Human women or Tanu, both are the same: The loving desire to nurture is all the magic that's needed."

"But don't forget," came Aiken's wry interpolation, "that the converse holds good as well. Both Agraynel and I were lucky."

Sullivan's face flamed scarlet. He was on his feet, backing away from the royal couple, his imperfectly curtained mind leaking mortification and futile rage.

Mercy's sad eyes saw only Aiken now. "Yes, I'm dry now, it's true. I've been sore troubled and I've been diminished, and so I have no life to give my daughter, poor thing. What I have to give *you* we both know! So take it."

"I'm—I'm going down to the beach!" Sullivan mumbled. "Keep tabs on my kite. Excuse me—excuse me—" And he fled, his rosy-gold caftan billowing in the hot wind.

"It was brutal of you to shame him to his face," Mercy told Aiken. "And unnecessary. He knows what went on."

"He's an ass. Impotent." Aiken's eyes were closed. Sweat made his dark red hair cling to his rounded cranium. "He'd betray me to all corners in fifteen seconds if he thought he could escape with a whole skin. And you were gone..." The hollow black gaze opened to her. "They told me you were dead, Mercy."

"And is it true that you wept over my silver-and-emerald helmet?" The taint of her mockery was elusive.

The little man turned away. "Oh, yes," he admitted. "All the way back to Goriah, as I lay in my cabin coddling my combustion-chamber skull, I kept the thing with me. My last memento of you. Still full of your perfume in spite of its dunking in the Río Genil! You bet I cried, babe. Even though I knew you were alive."

"Ah."

"I didn't think you'd leave him. It was his idea, wasn't it?"

Down on the beach, there was a shout from many voices and a telepathic affirmation: *Ue! Up she goes!* The Tanu nobles still in the pavilion rushed outside for a better view as the scarlet warrior kite rose slowly into the shimmering sky, its human cargo dangling like a spindly tail. A moment later the blue-wave kite climbed aloft. Yosh's farspoken voice said to the King:

Anytime you're ready, boss!

Aiken's mind and voice commanded: "Begin." The great kites seemed to bow to each other and then swoop in for the initial engagement. Silver naginata flashed in the sun. The ground crews hauled the wrist-thick flying cables this way and that and the winch operators took in slack.

Aiken squinted into the glare, gauging the wind. He said to Mercy, "You're supposed to stay close to me and report to him, I suppose. There's no other way he could get through the stacked screens I'm using."

She sat back among the cushions, inaccessible, her auburn hair rich on her golden-tan shoulders, glowing in contrast to her jade-colored gown. "I'm here to stay with you as long as you want me. Do you? Or shall I go?"

The blue kite, hovering a dozen meters above the scarlet, dived abruptly. Sunlight caught Yosh's slashing blow that severed one of Vilkas's maneuvering lines. The red kite retreated as line was paid out.

"You're afraid of me again," Aiken said. "It's made you burn! You won't go. You're wild for me, as you were after the golden maypole dance! I give you more than he ever can. I love you more than he does. Admit it!"

The scarlet kite bobbed up and down like a crazy pendulum, swinging as it tried to avoid the darting thrusts of the blue attacker. Vilkas managed to cut a few of the central bridle lines, but this had little effect on Yosh's kite. The Japanese concentrated solely on the right side of his antagonist's kite, cutting bridles and slicing great vertical rents in the paper until the painted samurai warrior's face was all but obliterated in ribboning shreds. The red kite sank low in spite of the frantic hauling of its crew, and Vilkas's dangling feet nearly brushed the scraggly trees growing on the top of a large dune.

Aiken's mouth was set in a tight smile. He did not look at Mercy, but her face was overwhelming in his mind, and she knew. He said, "Nodonn's gathering his adherents down in Afaliah right now, isn't he! Sending out a call for all the reactionaries and hotheads and human-haters to rally round the old sun-face blazon. How many knights do you think he'll finally muster? A few hundred, maybe? And how many first-class powers? Himself, Celo, his brother Kuhal if he ever gets his head put back together, maybe that old asshole from Tarasiah, Thufan Thunderfart. Does he really think he's got a chance of licking me with that lot?...Or is he planning to show up at the Grand Tourney with the Sword and just file a challenge against me—as though the kingship of the Many-Colored Land was some kind of a runoff election for village dogcatcher?"

The spectators gave a tremendous cheer. The scarlet kite wavered, its lower margin forced backward by airflow as Yosh severed a last pair of critical bridle lines. Its flayed surface stalled, tumbled. Vilkas dropped his naginata as he clung to the shrouds of the breeches buoy. He fell toward the crowded beach, with the flailing kite appearing to slap at him like some berserk billboard in the grip of a hurricane. The Lithuanian's despairing mental cry, broadcast by his gray torc, impinged on the minds of Aiken and Mercy. The mob below fled, crews abandoning their lines.

"*Damn* that Sullivan!" the King raged. He gripped the rattan arms of his throne, screwed his eyes shut in an agonized grimace, and reached out with his psychokinesis. Vilkas, tangled in his kite, was about to impact on the hard, wet sand. Yosh's kite had gone out of control when its crew scattered, and now plummeted toward the sea.

Aiken groaned.

Vilkas in his breeches buoy swung aside and upward, beyond the menace of the crashing starlet kite. Seconds later he wafted gently to earth. The blue kite, responding to a sudden blast of psychic wind, recovered from its negative angle of attack and soared upward at the limit of its tether. The winch operators who had let their machine unwind scrambled back to reengage the brake mechanism and effect an orderly landing. There were relieved shouts from the human crews down on the beach, cheers from the nobles who had viewed the contretemps from a dunetop vantage point, and a barely perceptible mental apology from Sullivan-Tonn on the King's intimate mode.

Mercy had come to stand over Aiken, astonished at what the effort had cost him. She took a silk handkerchief from her sleeve and wiped his streaming brow and his eyes; and when his stertorous breathing softened and he relaxed with his head back, she said:

"I didn't know. Was it Felice?"

"Who else?" He regarded her through slitted, pain-bleared eyes. "Well—*now* you know. Be sure to tell him the good news right away! But remind him that the Spear's working just fine . . . and I have a few goodies stowed away in the dungeon that I can welcome him with in case he decides to pay us both a friendly call."

She said nothing.

"But tell him not to delay too long," Aiken added. "I'm a funny sort, Lady Wildfire, Creator Lady. Every time I have you I heal a bit more. Olone was some help—but you're my sovereign remedy. If you stay, you may engineer your own defeat. And his!"

Her fingers touched the skin drawn tightly over his cheekbones, the long, well-formed nose, the thin lips now gone bloodless. She knelt on the cushions heaped beside his throne, placed cool hands over his eyes, and kissed him with soft passion. She put aside her mental veil and he saw the fear-spice joined inextricably with ardor. "Amadán," she whispered. "Fatal Amadán of my soul."

"But not your heart. Never that."

"It's all as it was before in the Grove of May. So take what you want, Nonborn King, what you need. Take it while you can, for when I'm gone you'll find no other."

5

DURING THE LATTER PART OF THE TRIP, WHEN HE WAS HALF-
dead with hunger and thirst and the endless jouncing gait of
the pack animal and the sadistic mind-prodding of his exotic
captors, Tony Wayland cried:

"I lied to you! There aren't any flying machines. I made it
all up so you wouldn't slaughter me like the others. But it
wasn't true. I lied, I tell you! Kill me. Please, kill me."

Fire ballooned behind his blinded eyes. The monster with
the melting face leered out of it and tittered. "All in good time,
Lowlife. Very clever, weren't you? And still think you are,
lying when you say you lie." The creature dealt him a terrible
neural wallop, cracking the firedrake illusion into a swarm of
tiny orange whirligigs. "You'll tell the whole truth when I bring
you before the High King and Queen, or my name isn't Karbree
the Worm!" The vision turned helminthoid. Loathsome squirm-
ers seemed to be invading Tony's skull via the nostrils. He
gagged and shrieked and promised to behave and fainted and
dreamed . . .

Rowane, his Howler bride, came to comfort him.

Sometimes she was lovely and sometimes she was her true
self, with the lidless eye in the center of her forehead and the
soft scales at her elbows and spine, and the mane and minor
chevelure the color of a blue fox's fur.

She said, "Oh, my Tonee. What have they done to you?

389

Let me help. Here is water and food. Here is soft peace in my arms and a loving eye to keep watch, to guard you from further harm."

And he felt her kiss, terrifying and ardent, and her embrace, and felt the two sets of teeth like whetted pearls—never offering hurt but only love . . .

"Rowane, you're gone!"

He woke up again aboard the trotting helladotherium. He was still blind, still trussed as tightly as a braunschweiger banger, still jolting up the endless mountain switchbacks on the way to High Vrazel.

"Rowane, my little goblin flower," he wailed. "Why did I leave you? Why?"

"We can make a pretty good guess, can't we boys?" came the derisive voice of Karbree. The other Firvulag in the party snorted and boomed and whooped with obscene glee.

"You should have eaten more garlic and truffles, punyprong!"

"Or hedgehog stew!"

"Or mandrake roots! Firvulag women take a heap of satisfying—even the Howler kind!"

"Hey, is it true what they say about Howler muffs?"

The merry monsters kept up their vulgar chaffing but Tony scarcely heard. Dammed-up tears tried in vain to escape the wads of sticky wax that capped his eyes. Rawhide thongs cut into his ankles and arms. The gait of the hellad bludgeoned his kidneys. The mere fact of consciousness was raw and wounding.

Rowane, abandoned, was far away in Nionel, perhaps even now howling the walls down in their honeymoon cottage at the foot of West Toadflax Lane, her faithful heart broken. Poor Dougal, who had reluctantly accompanied his master's flight, was probably dead in the underbrush back at the scene of the ambush. The others he had betrayed were certainly slain— Orion Blue, Jiro, Boris, and Karolina. His victims all! And when he sang for the Firvulag monarchs in High Vrazel, as he certainly would if he lasted out the journey, he'd be the death of all the rest of them working on the two flyers back in the Vale of Hyenas.

"I'm rotten!" Tony Wayland screamed. "Rotten! A jinx! My silver torc—why did they have to take it?"

He contorted his bound body in violent spasms so that even the placid hellad began to shy. Finally Karbree the Worm had to smite him in the brainstem and grant the oblivion he had sought.

Tony fell for a short distance and landed in soft matter: sawdust or leaf-mould, or perhaps some kind of tanbark redolent of conifer oil.

"Free him. Unseal his eyes," said a feminine voice, sharp as a vitredur blade. "Spruce him up a bit, then we'll bring him in."

With his bonds severed, Tony went limp, semiparalyzed. He heard one of the subsidiary monster captors say, "Yes, Dreadful Skathe. It shall be done."

Tony felt as though an infrared lamp had been focused on his face. The tenacious waxen blobs plugging his orbits began to soften. Claws scratched briefly around the bridge of his nose and there was a horrific rip. He lost all his eyelashes and regained his vision in a single motion. His yell was so parched that it was barely audible above the tumult of crowd noises that surrounded him.

"Water," he groaned, wiping his eyes with the back of one filthy hand. The sunshine was brilliant. Silhouetted against the glare was a dwarf in dusty obsidian armor, one of the original ambush patrol, and a gigantic Firvulag clearly of a much more exalted rank, whose black-glass accoutrements were all chased with gold ornamentation and inset with carbuncles. This personage had eyes like two slowly dying coals of fire, undoubtedly the source of the radiation that had helped to remove his blindfold.

"Give him a drink," said the ogrish official. Tony noted with some surprise that the giant was a female. Somebody held a horn cup full of cool liquid to his lips and he guzzled gratefully. A second dwarf with a basin and a cloth swabbed his face and hands, then began a rough massage of his tingling legs to speed the return of the circulation.

Tony looked around. He had been dumped in a pile of fresh litter at the door of some kind of stable. Outside was a mobbed area that seemed to combine an open-air market with a crafts fair. Around the perimeter rose crags and cliffs and stony buttresses that Tony at first took to be natural geological formations. But then he saw a myriad of small windows with winking open casements, and stepped balconies and terraces with shrubs and alpine flowers, from which the higher orders of Little People surveyed their fellows in the crowded plaza below.

The goblin market had hundreds of gaudy stalls with awnings and flapping banners bearing ideographs and totemic devices. Vendors sold food and clothing, domestic implements, jewelry, rugs, weapons, herbs, intoxicants, perfumes, and medicines. One large group was gathered around a hipparion auction, regarding the half-tamed, prancing little animals with expressions that mingled suspicion and fascination. Another crush of people waited their turn to enter an ornate open-sided tent hemmed about with an honor guard of giants bearing effigy standards draped with chains of gold-plated skulls. The air vibrated with the calls of the merchants, the laughter and shouts of buyers and lookers, and music from strolling gnomish players.

"Up with him," said the black-armored giantess with the red eyes.

Tony was hauled to his feet and stood trembling and blinking. The dappled buckskin outfit he'd chosen for its camouflage value when absconding from Nionel was stained with blood and a medley of other muck.

"He looks pretty scruffy to present to the Highs," the giantess observed. "For Té's sake fetch some kind of chaliko blanket or a cloak to make him halfway decent."

"At once, Great Captain!" One of the dwarfs scuttled off, to return with a fairly clean green-leather poncho. This was plopped over Tony's head, whereupon the Dreadful Skathe nodded and motioned her prisoner to follow her. The two dwarfs, bearing serrated black halberds, came along behind. As they made their way through the crowd. Karbree the Worm reappeared and accepted the salute of his little henchmen. He had freshened up for the royal audience, putting off his utilitarian field harness in favor of parade armor almost as handsome as Skathe's.

"Good catch, Worm," she remarked by way of greeting. "His mind leaks like a colander. Té knows what use the Highs can make of his intelligence, but it's diverting as all hell."

"The Lowlives are full of surprises ever," Karbree said jovially. "Sheer good luck, stumbling over him and his warders over at the Seekol headwaters. Normally we're never within twenty leagues of the place. We always use the main trail along the Pliktol. But one of our lads had heard of a secret spot where hoobies were supposed to grow thick as fleas on a bear-dog, even during high summer, so we took a detour. Never did find the mushrooms."

They came to the mob surrounding the royal tent. One of the dwarfs levered his way into the throng with the butt of his halberd, shouting, "Way, dammit! Way for the Great Captain Skathe and the Hero Karbree the Worm!"

The commoners fell back, chattering and grinning. A few made rude faces at Tony or contrived to step on his toes as he shuffled along. And then they were inside the big pavilion, which was full of Firvulag nobility, both enarmored and casually attired. With the crowd noises somewhat muffled, Tony was able to hear a succession of ushers announcing them. A frightful ogre whom Skathe addressed affectionately as Medor came to fetch them, saying:

"The artisans are bringing in the Singing Stone right now. You can have your turn right after. Come on in here and I'll let you have a front-row view. Damnedest thing I ever saw."

A dwarf prodded Tony and he followed Karbree to the edge of a space bordered by scarlet and gold ropes. King Sharn and Queen Ayfa sat on a low dais at one side, flanked by standard-bearers. They were clad in light robes of blue, green, and silver stripes and wearing identical silvery diadems. Elfin pages came and went carrying bowls of fruit and candy, beer and cyser

2

34 The Nonborn King

flagons nestled in buckets of snow, and occasional presents
from favor seekers. On the left hand of the joint monarchs sat
the royal scribes, busily accepting petitions, complaints, prop-
ositions, and denunciations.

"May it please the High King, the High Queen, and the
Gnomish Council of Firvulag!" the chief herald proclaimed.
"The Guild of Gemcutters, the Honorable Yuchor Tidypaw
presiding, does herewith set forth for the approval and hoped-
for acceptance of the Firvulag Nation the new Grand Trophy!"

A gasp of awe went up from the assembly. Ten Little People
in Guild regalia, led by their President, toiled up to the thrones
with a dolly on which the Singing Stone rested. It was an
enormous beryl, translucent blue-green with a faint core of
pulsating light. It had been fashioned into a field stool of the
type that Firvulag and Tanu royalty used when conferring ac-
colades on heroes during the heat of the Grand Combat. In
cross section it was a shallow U-shape, backless, with scrolled
armrests. The legs and corner members were carved to resemble
heraldic winged creatures with vaguely reptilian bodies, the
wyverns of lost Duat. All of the carvings were accented and
fimbriated with lustrous platinum-rhodium alloy. A green silken
cushion, tasseled and brocaded with thread of the same metals,
rested on the stool's seat.

"This Grand Trophy," the herald resumed, "shall be the
symbol of the new Era of Antagonism between the Little People
of the Many-Colored Land and their execrable Foe—through
the length of the world's age!"

A bedlam of cheers and martial shouts broke out, inter-
spersed with sundry curses and cries of "Death to all Tanu!"
and "Ylahayll Aiken-Lugonn!"

The King and Queen lifted their arms for silence and the
herald completed his announcement.

"This Singing Stone shall be awarded to the battle-company
that is victorious in the contest to be held this year upon the
traditional Firvulag Field of Gold. It has been programmed so
that it will sing a joyous song with a hundred voices—but only
when the *true* High King of the Many-Colored Land sits enthroned upon it. Should any upstart or lesser ruler presume to

mount the Stone, it will be death and not sweet music he will reap in the doing!"

The Firvulag nobility let loose another deafening clamor. Numbers of them flashed their illusory aspects, and glowing grotesqueries and nightmare apparitions sprang up here and there among the well-dressed giants and gnomes.

The President of the Gemcutters Guild now approached the dais while his people were offloading the trophy from its carrier. "High King! High Queen! Joint Sovereigns of the Heights and Depths, Monarchs of the Infernal Infinite, Father and Mother of All Firvulag, and Undoubted Rulers of the Known World— *manifest*!"

With a flourish, the gnome stepped to one side, gesturing at the waiting stool. Sharn gave it a speculative look but didn't move.

Ayfa pointed her stern finger at the Honorable Yuchor Ti- dypaw. "Are you *sure* the thing's programmed properly?"

The guildsman snatched off his cap and fell to his knees. "Oh, yes, High Queen!"

"After you, dear," Ayfa said to her husband. Sharn strode majestically to the Stone, took a firm stance in front of it, and lowered the regal fundament.

Eight notes pealed out. They were like immense belltones that had somehow acquired the overtones of exotic voices. They swelled in the air like physical presences, felt as well as heard, mirroring and enhancing one another with marvelous harmonic vibrations. The eight notes seemed to call forth responses from the earth, from the encompassing rocks of the mountain, from the very bones of the hearers. Each reiteration of the phrase was louder than the one before, more glorious, more painful:

Recovering from his first stupefaction, Tony Wayland began to laugh. The sound was lost in the Stone's singing, but King Sharn took notice. He stood up. The music sighed away in a reverberating diminuendo, leaving Tony's crazed cackling as a shocking counterpoint until he realized that all of the exotic minds were focused upon him, outraged.

Swallowing the last chuckles, he mumbled, "Well, you see . . . it's . . . I mean, it's . . ." He hummed a little tune in the same key, one that blended in an uncanny fashion with the still lingering Song of the Stone. "It's got to be a joke . . . by that damn Denny Johnson or somebody. Weia! Waga! Woge du Welle, walle zur Wiege, wagala weia—"

A roof-high albino scorpion with incandescent guts reared above Tony, Karbree, Skathe, and the dwarfs. *"Shut up!"*

The Worm shrugged. "High King, he's only a little loopy from the trip. Wait until you hear his story."

Sharn spun around, reassuming his normal form. He raised his arms and the fierce mutterings that had broken out in accompaniment to Tony's impromptu performance faded. The King said, "We thank the loyal membership of the Gemcutters Guild and its President, Yuchor Tidypaw, for a job well done. Let this Singing Stone now be removed to the Royal Treasury, where it is to be kept safely until the Grand Tourney, ten weeks from now."

There were spatterings of applause. Ayfa came over to frown at the cowering metallurgist, now firmly in the grip of the dwarfs. They had crossed their black-glass halberds under his throat.

"Who is this miserable wretch?" the Queen asked shortly.

"That," said the King, "is what we're going to find out."

I loved her dearly but she was utterly insatiable [Tony Wayland said], and I knew I was for it unless I got some rest. I mean—.if I'd still had my silver torc there'd have been nothing to it! But bareneck . . .

At any rate, I got hold of my friend Dougal, who'd also taken a Howler bride in the Grand Loving. His bearings were coming up on terminal metal fatigue just like mine, so we lit off one dark night, figuring to make our way to Goriah and Aiken Drum. You know he's promised torcs to anybody who joins him . . . You do know . . . He hasn't? . . . Christ—you can't depend on anybody these days . . .

Yes. Well, Dougal and I decided to keep clear of the Nonol and Pliktol Rivers. Too many Howlers on the trails. We went up the ProtoSeine instead; the river you people call the Seekol. We didn't know about the giant hyenas, you see.

We tramped on for a day or two, going upstream, until we came into some jungle country, tough as hell to get through. Then we found this blind valley late in the afternoon, an open place with big trees. That's where we saw the birds—the aircraft, I mean. Christ, it was a shocker! These bloody great stilt-legged things hiding there among the sequoias with people working on them doing God knows what. We lay back in the bush watching for the rest of the afternoon and then we were going to sneak away. But we saw them readying one bird for takeoff—and, I mean, could *you* leave at a time like that? So we hung about well into the evening. And damn my eyes if the ship wasn't a rhocraft, a gravomagnetic vehicle that works on the same principle as our egg-shaped flying machines back in the Galactic Milieu. How the friggerty things ever got to the Pliocene—

Oh? . . . The same kind that did for Finiah? . . . Son of a bitch.

At any rate, we watched one go up, and watched it come down. By then it was night, so we had to bivouac right there. Then this hyena pack came, and if Dougal hadn't done some fancy swordplay, the brutes would have torn us to pieces. We made enough noise fighting the beasts off to rouse the bloody dead. People came from the Lowlife camp and helped us get rid of the last of the hyenas.

But one of the Lowlives recognized me. And I was screwed six ways from Sunday.

I was a silver in Finiah, you see. When the Lowlives captured me and cut off my collar, they said I could work for their cause or have my tripes cut out. So I cooperated, bided my time, then scarpered with Dougal when a good chance presented itself. I planned to go to Goriah and join Aiken Drum way back then, too, but Dougal and I got taken by Howlers and . . . ah, shit. You don't have to hear that.

Well. When this man Orion Blue recognized me and called me a traitor, some of the Lowlives wanted to hang me right then and there. Dougal, too, of course. But their leader, a gold-torc named Basil, said we'd have to be taken back to Hidden Springs for a trial before Chief Burke.

So we set out. We were on the trail with Blue and three other Lowlife guards when your lot sprang the ambush. You know the rest. When I saw poor old Dougal go down, and the rest of the Lowlives being cut up, I thought it was time to be prudent. I yelled out about the aircraft. Your man, Wormface, decided to bring me to visit you. Charmed, I'm sure.

Now fry my brains and be damned.

What? . . . Yes, there were only two aircraft. We saw one operational. The other one had burnt vegetation around its pads, though. It didn't look broken. People were working on it. Toting equipment in and out while we watched.

How many? Well, we didn't exactly count them. Let me think. At least thirty-five people, maybe more . . . You bet there were guards! Some armed with iron spears and arrows, and one big black broad with a stun-gun, for God's sake! . . . they didn't talk about their plans for the aircraft in front of me. I'm a dirty traitor, remember? Turncoat Tony! First I betrayed the Tanu by choosing life, letting the Lowlives cut off my silver torc. Then I betrayed the Lowlives by running from the Iron Villages. Then I betrayed the Howlers by abandoning my wife. And if you keep me around here very long, I'll do my best for *you*! Walala weiala weia! . . .

"What do you think of his story?" Ayfa asked Sharn, after Tony had been led away.

"We knew that a Lowlife expedition went east, toward the Ship's Grave. Now we know that it was successful."

"What are we to do about this, High King?" Skathe asked. "There can be no Firvulag-Lowlife alliance in the Nightfall War. The humans will use these aircraft against us."

The King and Queen were sitting at a small table with Skathe and the veteran deputy Medor. They had retired to a curtained-off portion of the royal tent for the interview with Tony, and now drank cool beer from great glass beakers.

Sharn said, "I would call your attention to the fact that the Vale of Hyenas is suggestively close to Nionel."

"You think that there's Howler collusion in the bird plot?" Medor wiped foam from his split upper lip.

"It's a dead cert," said the Firvulag King.

"We were afraid it would happen," Ayfa said gloomily, "after the matter of the brides. Fitharn Pegleg has been re-searching the matter while on his diplomatic mission to Nionel. We have his full report ready to present to the Gnomish Council tomorrow. Sugoll still professes nominal loyalty to High Vra-zel. He's got his people working like beavers to complete the spiffying-up of the Field of Gold for the Tourney. But as far as allying with us in the Nightfall War goes—forget him. The entire Howler tribe has thrown in with the humans, and that's that."

"We've got to do something about those birds," Skathe insisted. "But it'll be a tough chew. You heard what that twit said—the Lowlives are guarding the aircraft with iron."

Medor said, "And if we go in there in force, we're likely to tip our hand ahead of time to Sugoll. Or to Aiken Drum."

"Fuck his earholes," growled Skathe. "If we could only use those aircraft ourselves!"

Medor gave a rueful laugh. "Not a prayer! We have only a handful of First Comers left alive who'd remember the original evacuation from Brede's Ship. I don't think a single one of them knows a flux-tapper from a hippy chip. Té knows I don't, and I'm about the closest thing to a technician on the Council. No . . . those ships are useless to us."

"Maybe not," said Sharn. A slow smile was beginning to spread across his great mouth. "Now consider. We've been bewailing the fact that the Foe leadership has passed to a puny human. He's bedded down in Goriah tighter than a tick, too, for all that Nodonn and Celo would like to hope otherwise.

They'll never boot Aiken out of the Castle of Glass with a few hundred knights. Not even using the sacred Sword."

"*Our* Sword!" Medor said in a strangled voice.

"Who knows it better than I?" Sharn cried. "My grandsire's grandsire wielded it in the first Great Ordeal at the Ship's Grave! And when the Nightfall War comes upon us, *I* shall carry it . . . if a certain idea I just had bears fruit."

"I think I see!" exclaimed Ayfa. "And Nodonn's honorable, for all that he's the Prince of Pricks. If he promised, he'd keep his word."

"Who?" demanded Skathe. "What? *How?*"

Sharn explained. "We tell Nodonn about the two aircraft. You know that the Foe retained a certain scientific bent. Celadeyr of Afaliah and Thufan Thunderhead are both creators, both First Comers. What's more likely than that they have some knowledge of these flying machines? In the libraries of their citadels, if no place else."

Medor broke in excitedly, "And if Tanu make off with the aircraft, then the machines no longer threaten us! Nodonn would never use them in the Nightfall War. He's too chivalrous."

"He'd use them against Aiken Drum, though," said the Queen.

Medor leaned back in his chair and laughed at the top of his lungs. "Nodonn zaps Aiken from the air in a glorified Flying Hunt before the Grand Tourney ever begins! He takes over as Tanu King! Tremendous! And in return for our help—"

"He gives me the Sword," Sharn said. "Just as soon as he conquers Goriah. It will be up to him to retrieve the Spear in one piece from the dead hand of the usurper."

The face of Skathe the giantess was wreathed in awe. "High King, your wisdom is beyond measure!"

Sharn sipped a little beer. "Oh, I don't know." He winked at Ayfa. "Maybe I do get a great notion from time to time . . ."

"When will you contact Nodonn?" Medor asked.

The King's expression became solemn. "I'll get hold of Nodonn tonight. Put the whole thing up to him. But he'll bite—I'd stake my throne on it. When the Gnomish Council hears from me tomorrow, I'll probably have the whole deal worked out."

Medor rose to go. "Shall I tell Karbree to dispose of that fellow Tony?"

Skathe looked thoughtful. "Let me have him for a while." She smiled at the dubious looks on the faces of the others. "You know me, always a traditionalist to the core. Still—it might not be a bad idea to check matters out, see whether those Howlers are onto something."

Sharn and Ayfa and Medor looked shocked.

"Well, you never know until you try," said the ogress reasonably.

6

It was nearly dawn in Afaliah and the first euphoria resulting from the conference with the Firvulag King had begun to dissipate.

Nodonn, his brother Kuhal, and Celadeyr were sitting in the ravaged library of the citadel drinking brandy-laced coffee. The floor was littered in rejected AV reference crystals, the aftermath of a near-maniacal search for prisms containing the specifications and flight manual of the ancient flying machines. These had been located at last, filed in the wrong drawer, and now Celadeyr was manipulating the visual display of the big reader while the other two considered courses of action.

"Just look at it," Celo said, magnifying an internal configuration diagram. "I'd forgotten the big baggage area back in the tail. If you really pack the passengers in, the thing can probably hold two hundred knights. That gives us four hundred crack fighters for your invasion of Goriah! We'll have that number and to spare by the time Thufan and his Hunt get here from Tarasiah day after tomorrow."

"It's Tana's own luck that the old Thunderhead is qualified to pilot the machines," Nodonn said. "But you, Celo—"

"I had six hours of instruction back on Duat!" bellowed the veteran. "That's more than anybody else."

"A thousand years ago," Kuhal said, keeping a neutral aspect.

402

"The flight manual's perfectly straightforward," Celo retorted. "And you don't need any fancy maneuvering. Just take the thing in at hover, screened and invisible, and blast that little gold bastard at close range with the Sword. Fat lot of good his sigma-field'll do him with the floor cut out from under him!"

"Still," Kuhal said, "it might be best if one of the younger creators—"

"No time to train anybody from scratch," Celo insisted. "I can do it, dammit! Stuff me full of calcium pangamate, let Boduragol have a brief go at me to reseat the old piloting reflexes, and I'll fly like a friggin' fruit bat in the mating season! Old Thunderfart can check me out before we leave the Vale of Hyenas."

"*If* we do," said Nodonn, frowning as he added more brandy to his cup. "It seems to me that the most critical part of this enterprise may be its inception. Making off with the aircraft without having Aiken Drum learn of it."

"The kid's spies are everywhere," Celo conceded.

"And Sharn told me that the leader of the aircraft technicians wears a golden torc. It seems a foregone conclusion that the Lowlives would prefer Aiken Drum's rule of the Many-Colored Land to my own. If the people at the Vale of Hyenas aren't dealt with very carefully, they may well warn Aiken that we have taken the aircraft. Then we would lose the element of surprise in our attack on Goriah. That could be fatal to us."

"We charge 'em with a Flying Hunt," Celo said fiercely. "Massacre the whole nest of 'em, just like in the good old days!"

The laugh of Apollo was pitying. "I am not the Battlemaster I was in the good old days—and these humans are not the cowering prey of yesteryear, either. They are well armed, and there may be forty or more of them guarding the ships. Not one must be allowed to escape—or even to give the alarm. Even if I had the endurance to carry a full Hunt all the way from Koneyn to the Hercynian Wilderness, I would not attempt such a course. The effort would drain me. I would go into the invasion of Goriah in a dangerously weakened state."

"But we could hold off until you recover—" Celadeyr began to say.

Nodonn held up a dissenting hand. "Every day that we delay sees Aiken Drum recovering further from his own debilities. Mercy has kept me closely informed of his progress. She even— participates in his healing, albeit against her will. No. If we are to vanquish the usurper we must strike as soon as possible."

"What course do you favor, Brother?" Kuhal asked.

"I'd use only a handful of the most powerful and courageous knights. We would fly north without chalikos on the wings of a metapsychic gale, then smite the Lowlives in the Vale of Hyenas with mindpower rather than physical weapons. No chivalrous confrontation, no Hunt." Nodonn smiled at the quickly stifled outrage that seeped from the mind of the elderly champion. "So, Celo—now you know the depths to which I'm prepared to stoop. But the Lowlives don't fight us by the tenets of the battle-religion—so I am prepared to use fair means or foul, myself."

Celadeyr hesitated, then said, "If you fight Aiken Drum unfairly, our Tanu people may repudiate you. He is the chosen of Mayvar Kingmaker and acclaimed by the Conclave."

"I'll meet the usurper according to the ancient ritual," Nodonn reassured him. "Sword against Spear, resuming the sacred contest that was interrupted by the flooding of the White Silver Plain."

The old creator's relief was evident. "That will suffice. As to the aircraft snatch, however: Your proposal is daring, but fraught with peril. This human wearing the golden torc need only broadcast a single thought and you are undone."

"If only Cull were alive," the Battlemaster said. "A combatant redactor would be invaluable on a mission such as this, sorting the identities of the alien minds, lulling their suspicions, and quashing their outcries."

"The really topnotch mindbenders went over to Aiken—or worse, they're with Dionket and the pacifists. My own Boduragol's a fine healer, but not really the man for stress situations. None of his underlings in the House of Healing are competent to work bareneck humans. It's hellish difficult to mind-mash Lowlives when they're not wearing gray or silver torcs. And the gold-wearer's a real sticker."

"If only Mercy were with us!" Nodonn exclaimed. "What we need is a human—to cope with humans."

Kuhal's coffee cup hit the table with a small crash. His face had gone radiant. "Of course," he whispered. "Of course!"

CLOUD: I'm going to do it.

HAGEN: You're crazy. Or else falling for that exotic on a rebound from poor old Elaby.

CLOUD: Bastard! [Pain.]

HAGEN: Oh, hell. I'm sorry . . . But you can't go throwing yourself away like this! We're getting so close. Tomorrow we cross the Rif Range, if we can repair the track on the bloody FH-4. I can hardly wait to see the humongous waterfall! After that, how long can it take? We latch up the ATVs, sail across the Med, crawl through the neck of the Balearic Peninsula, and we're almost on top of Afaliah. We want you there to meet us, luv—not charging off on some half-ass raid with your exotic boyfriend.

CLOUD: I can insure that Nodonn gets the aircraft for his attack on Aiken Drum. If I help the exotics with my redact, it'll virtually guarantee that none of the human guards will give the alarm. And it'll save human lives—which is important to me, if not to you. I can cold-cock the lot of them and we can fly them back as prisoners instead of killing them out of hand as the exotics planned. There's very little danger to me, provided I can avoid getting potted with a Husky.

HAGEN: *Husky?!* Christ, Cloud! What're the Lowlife humans doing with real weapons? I thought it was all bows and arrows—

CLOUD: I haven't got the straight of it. But there are definitely some modern arms being used by both the Lowlives and Aiken's elite corps.

HAGEN: Fuck.

CLOUD: The little scenario that Kuhal and Nodonn worked out for the Vale of Hvenas should keep me safe enough. I'm not worried.

HAGEN: Well, lotsa luck, sister. But, listen! Under no circumstances do you go along on the invasion of Aiken Drum's magic castle.

CLOUD: No fear.

HAGEN: Think time-gate. Remember that the rest of us are counting on you to mediate with Papa. He's not going to stay in the tank forever—if that's where he actually is. When he starts in again with the old hoo-ha, he's going to be right over here on our necks instead of back in Ocala. If anyone can get round him, you can.

CLOUD: I've tried calling him again and again on the i-mode, but he doesn't answer. He *must* be in the regeneration tank. Unless . . . Hagen, you don't think he could have—

HAGEN: Don't be an idiot.

CLOUD: Well, Felice nearly killed Aiken. And if she did d-jump to North America, she might have got right into the observatory, screens or no screens, riding right up Papa's peripheral farsense beam.

HAGEN: He's alive, damn him.

CLOUD: Have you had any success yet farspeaking Manion?

HAGEN: No. Veikko keeps trying, but he just doesn't pull the watts like old Vaughn on i-mode, and we don't want to risk an overall hail. Not that any of the others on Ocala would tell us the truth anyhow . . .

CLOUD: They've come. It's time for me to go now.

HAGEN: Take care. Take *great* care.

CLOUD: And you. Bring me a Tri-D loop of the Gibraltar waterfall if you can. It must be quite a sight . . .

A party of snipe hunters from the Lowlife camp at the Vale of Hyenas found Dougal. He was still alive nearly a week after the Firvulag ambush, raving in delirium, a pitiful mass of infected wounds and insect bites. He had managed to retrace his tracks nearly twenty kilometers before collapsing on a marshy trail just south of the valley where the aircraft were concealed.

"I would fain die a dry death," Dougal murmured, as his

rescuers dragged him from the mud. "By my troth, Morisca, my little body is aweary of this world."

"Sometimes I find it medium tedious myself," drawled Sophronisba Gillis. "How'd you get loose of Orion and the others, suck-face?"

But Dougal only mumbled incoherencies. Later, when they entered camp, he roused briefly at the sight of the two parked flying machines and moaned, "Alas! Poor falcons, towering in their pride of place!" Then he lapsed once more into a stupor.

Phronsie and the other snipe hunters carried the stricken medievalist to the infirmary. Dusk had deepened and the nearly full moon sent bars of searchlight-bright luminescence through the tall sequoias, painting the black aircraft silver. All of Basil's Bastards who were not on guard duty crowded into the infirmary shelter, where the physicians Thongsa and Magnus Bell worked in vain to restore the recaptured prisoner to consciousness.

"It looks pretty hopeless, Basil," Magnus said. "Guy's in shock. In addition to all the surface wounds, I think he may have a ruptured spleen. God knows why he's still alive."

"Get these people out of here!" Thongsa fretted.

Basil herded the throng out into the bright moonlit clearing. He said to Phronsie, "We've got to find out what happened to that prisoner-escort party. Whether Dougal simply escaped— or whether the party was jumped by Aiken's people or the Firvulag. Are you sure Dougal didn't say anything significant? Give any hint that this hiding place of ours might be compromised?"

The statuesque black woman shrugged. "He just spouted a lot of Shakespeare talk. The guy's usual shtick. Then when we got him back here, he was nattering on a little about the aircraft. Calling 'em proud falcons—some such thing."

The former Oxford don's eyes widened. "What did he say? Exactly?"

One of the other snipe hunters piped up. "I remember! It was, 'Poor falcons, towering in their pride of place.'"

Basil's gaze lifted to the long-legged aircraft with the downswept wings and empennages, their flight decks tilted like inclined bird necks. He recited:

A falcon, towering in her pride of place,
Was by a mousing owl hawk'd at and kill'd.

"Subhan'llah!" breathed the technician Nazir.

"Er—precisely my own sentiments." Basil fingered his golden torc. "Oblique though it may be, I'm afraid that Dougal's little quote admits of only one interpretation. And so—"

"Hey, stop where you are!" came a shout from the other side of the clearing.

Suddenly, there were more voices, and pounding footsteps, and electric torches flicking on and scything in the shadows behind the Number Two flyer.

"Stand still, damn you—or I'll drop you in your tracks!" Taffy Evans yelled.

The flashlight beams of the converging guards zeroed in on a redwood trunk, where a lone human woman cowered. She shielded her eyes from the light. Then, as a figure in a great hoopskirt and ruff stepped forward and administered a merciless prod with an iron-tipped spear, the intruder burst into tears.

Basil and the others stood thunderstruck.

"Don't hurt me!" the woman wept. "Please don't."

The guards had closed in, and now began to move with their prisoner toward Basil and the large group that still surrounded him.

"She's really human, at any rate," Mr. Betsy called out in smug satisfaction. "Not some miserable exotic shape-shifter!"

"Of course I'm human," the woman wailed. She seemed to stumble. Taffy Evans, carrying the stun-gun, shifted the weapon quickly to one arm and caught the prisoner in the other. She smiled at him.

"Keep that Husky on her, Taff!" The incarnation of Queen Elizabeth I was unrelenting in vigilance. "One false move out of her, and you blast!"

"Aw, come on, Bets," the pilot protested.

As the prisoner stepped into the bright moonlight in front of the infirmary, she seemed so obviously harmless that everyone, even the gang of armed guards, visibly relaxed. She wore a pair of white canvas shorts and a plaid cotton shirt knotted below her breasts. Her blonde hair, held off her forehead with a narrow bandeau, was clean and shining. On her shoulders was a small day-pack. In spite of her tearful apprehension, she was almost breathtakingly beautiful.

Basil stepped forward, the golden torc gleaming in the neck of his open safari blouse. Cloud Remillard came directly to him and said, "You must be Professor Wimborne!"

"I'm afraid I haven't had—" Basil started to say, instinctively—and then pained chagrin flooded through him and he wondered how he could have failed to recognize Alice. Enormous Alice, long-necked Alice, sly-eyed Alice escaped from Wonderland and pressing a single silencing finger against his lips, simultaneously muffling his mind that would have screamed a warning into the aether, alerting Chief Burke in Hidden Springs.

"Oh, no you don't," Cloud said gently. Her redaction coiled out like the multiple tentacles of a basket star, restraining every mind. Basil and his Bastards were helpless statues under the August moon. The stun-gun and all the iron weapons clattered to the ground. Tears of helpless rage glittered in the eyes of Mr. Betsy, who might have been a costumed waxwork at Madame Tussaud's, save for the anomalous mustache and tiny goatee.

The two physicians, torn from their patient by the irresistible command of the redactor, came to join their fellow humans in thrall.

"Are there any others?" Cloud inquired of thin air, and the atmosphere replied in the negative. "Not yet!" the woman said in a peremptory tone. "Not while he's still wearing the torc and there's the least chance of adrenaline override."

Basil watched her take off the backpack and flip it open. She took out a pair of yachtsman's heavy-duty cable cutters. Utterly lacking in willpower, Basil knelt and bent his neck. Cloud severed the torc with a single stroke and the alpinist crumpled senseless to the ground.

"Now it's safe," Cloud said.

The paralyzed crowd of humans would have cried out if

they had not lost control of their vocal cords. Four tall phantoms materialized in the moonlight, smothering the natural radiance in the glow of their vitredur armor. Two shone the krypton-green of creators and one was clad in the sodium-vapor glow worn by psychokinetic stalwarts; but the fourth, who towered above the others, had the eye-smarting brilliance of the noon sun. The pilots, the technicians, the medics, and the daredevils despaired at the sight of him: Nodonn, the implacable enemy of humankind, who had sworn to rid the Many-Colored Land of all time-travelers, no matter what the cost.

"But you promised," Cloud Remillard said.

And Apollo sighed, "Yes."

So with a painless medullary pinch the woman sent all of the prisoners cascading into welcome black; and none of them, not even recovering Dougal, awoke until they had been two days in the dungeons of Afaliah, and the clash between the rival Battlemasters had long since been resolved.

7

MERCY FOUND SULLIVAN-TONN SITTING ALONE IN A CLUT-
tered chamber at the top of the northwestern turret of the Castle
of Glass, reading *Essais de sciences maudites* and sipping Strega
from a Venetian goblet of a most scandalous shape.

"Great Queen!" he exclaimed, making haste to turn the book
face down. There was, unfortunately, nothing to be done about
the goblet.

Her face was pale, but her mind, only partially screened,
seemed on fire with some violent emotion. "I'm sorry to disturb
you. I would not have broken in upon your private space except
on business of mortal urgency."

"Whatever I can do—" He faltered at her look. "Has *he*
done something to you? Has he hurt you?" The portly psychokinetic was roused to indignation in spite of his own timidity. He rushed to Mercy's side, put an arm around her, and
led her to a chair that stood in the cool breeze blowing off the
sea.

"He's done only what he usually does," she replied darkly.
"But before this night is done I'll have revenge. If you'll help
me, Sullivan."

"I will," he declared.

"Your psychokinesis . . . can you open any lock?"

"Without question!"

411

"The special one he's put on the storage vaults beneath the castle?"

Sullivan's eyes bulged. "Not the secret rooms where the Milieu weapons and devices are kept—"

"The same. *Can* you?" She was reining in her coercion and the awesome psychocreative forces that could mould matter and energies to her whim, trying not to frighten him. The lock was a subtle thing that had defied her own manipulation and was proof against mind-blasts. Sullivan, with his great PK talent, was her only hope of neutralizing the high-technology weaponry in a way that Aiken might not detect until it was too late . . .

"I—I can only try, Lady Creator."

She leaped to her feet, her green gauze gown with its silver borders billowing like surf. "Try, for vengeance's sake, Sullivan! I know you hate him as I do. But soon, perhaps at dawn, he'll be paid in full for all his trickery! Now we must hurry, while he still sleeps off his surfeit of me." Seizing his moist hand, she held it tightly for a moment, her wild eyes ablaze. Then she cried, "Follow!" and was off racing down the circular stairs.

He bounded along in her wake, leather slippers thwacking on the dull glass paving, cerise dressing robe aflap, sandy hair standing on end for sheer terror. The castle was very quiet. They dashed through an open atrium where wind-chimes tinkled and a small fountain splashed, and the big white sheepdog Deirdre leaped up to welcome its mistress and nearly gave Sullivan a heart attack.

"Down, Deirdre! Stay!" Mercy hissed, and the animal vanished back into the shadows.

They fled down echoing halls with only the faerie-light chains for interior illumination; and the full moon riding high outside gleamed eerily through the colored-glass panels of the corridor roof, spreading pools of spectral lavender, pink, and amber underfoot. Here and there little ramas with feather dusters or mops cringed away in apprehension at their passing. The only human they saw was a middle-aged gray guard, stiff as a post outside the main audience room, holding a vitredur sword before his face with the staunch tirelessness of the pre-programmed torc wearer.

At last they reached the great foyer of the royal wing, with its sconces of flaming oil and spiral staircase. Mercy showed Sullivan the unobtrusive bronze door in the inner wall. "Open it without a trace."

He concentrated his PK, lips pressed together and forehead all corrugated. There was a subdued *clunk*. The door slid open and steep stone steps leading into blackness yawned ahead of them.

"That wasn't too hard." Sullivan managed a crooked smile.

"The real lock is down *there*. Hurry, man! He may wake and find me gone."

She conjured up a fireball torch and went slipping and sliding down the crudely cut shaft. There was no dampness now, but the stair treads and risers had been designed for long exotic legs and the going was precarious. Sullivan was beginning to gasp for breath, and only saved himself from stumbling by adroit use of his PK, which had him bobbing through the air from time to time like a silk-wrapped balloon effigy.

And then they reached the bottom. There was the vaultlike door with its battery of exotic code locks. As Sullivan came close to inspect them his skin crawled and the air seemed to attain a rubbery semisolidity.

"There's a force-field here as well, my Queen. Not a sigma, thank the Lord. Perhaps a gravomag repulsor, to keep damp air and fungus spores and things from seeping into the chamber. As well as thieves and malefactors." He giggled nervously.

Mercy was calm. "Open it."

He bent to the task. Perspiration streamed from his scalp and armpits. In his brain visions of the lock encodements—microscopic bubbles within bubbles, all dotted and etched with psychosensitive chemicals—zoomed into and out of focus. He concentrated, thrust, bent, and pricked. Something began to buzz. "Getting it," he mumbled. Magnify and hold the thing up to scrutiny. Ah—a sequential set. Ingenious! And with nulls scattered in the substructure...

Buzz. Click-click. Throm.

The force-field cut out. "That's a help! Now—" Press, press, push-pull twist!

There were noises behind the door, bars lifting, bolts sliding back. And then silence, and a tall crack opening.

"You've done it!" Mercy pushed past him, activated the lighting. "Now!" she cried. "It must all be saved for Nodonn—but put in a condition so that it's useless to *him* during the time that my daemon lover strikes!"

She regarded the long aisles with their glass racks and shelves, the thousands of different items podded or swathed in transparent durofilm, the walls of the place thickly coated in sealant impervious to damp and chemical action, the small inventory-control computer, and its robot retriever standing by.

"We'll start with you!" Mercy cried. An emerald ray lanced from her hand. The computer and robot began to smoke, and puddles of stinking liquid spread incontinently beneath their casters.

"That should slow my Lord King's next shopping expedition! And now what? We must embed all this—render it unusable until it's been painstakingly cleaned with special solvents that my Nodonn will have to get a Milieu chemist to formulate!"

His face full of fear, Sullivan-Tonn backed slowly toward the door. Mercy saw him and laughed. "That's right, Sullivan dear. Run off, man! Your work's done. Back up the stairs if you value your life! Fly . . . for I'm brewing up a witch's cauldron of foul sticky glop to sink Aiken Drum's weapons in, so he'll never use them against my love!"

A tremendous explosion made the rock walls quake. Putrid yellow matter began to boil from their plastic coating; it foamed and surged. "The polymers in the insulating sealant!" cried Mercy, safe in a psychocreative sphere. "Who else can tumble and stretch and refashion their giant molecules as I can? I—the mistress of organics, who can make food and drink all wholesome and nourishing from the trash of the fields! And can't I also make the devil's own glue, and a clinging foam to encrust all the pods and packages, and foul poison gases caught in the bubbles that knit the mess together?"

The terrible stuff flowed like magma, filling every cranny

of the storage chamber. Mercy's lifesaving sphere wafted out the door and she caused it to slam shut, still laughing wildly. The shaft was now half-filled with noxious vapors and so she went lofting up, to where the open door and Sullivan waited. And then she was safely through, and he crashed the heavy panel shut, and the two of them stood side by side.

Aiken Drum sat on the bottom step of the spiral staircase, staring at them. The air still reverberated with the slamming of the bronze door.

"It's done!" she cried exultantly. "And he's on his way! You'll fight him fair, little man, because it'll take weeks to get the Milieu weapons dug out of the poisonous mess I've sunk them in! Get your Spear, King Aiken-Lugonn. Cudgel your burnt-out brain into operancy again, if you can. Nodonn's coming! And it's the end!"

"Yes," Aiken agreed. Almost casually, he said to Sullivan-Tonn, "Get away from her, you."

The psychokinetic levitated and whisked across the great foyer, toward the passage leading to the exterior courtyard. Abruptly, his body seemed to meet an invisible wall. There was a sickening crackle, a choked scream.

"Not *too* far away," Aiken said.

Sullivan's stout torso was pinioned to the invisible wall. His nose oozed blood and his jaw hung awry, the lower lip pierced by splintered teeth. He began to utter liquid-thickened cries.

Both his feet burst into flame.

"No!" screamed Mercy.

"It's your doing," said Aiken.

The smoke roiled and blackened. Sullivan writhed, the sounds coming from his mind and throat as shapeless and hideous as his sloughing flesh. His clothing had flashed away in an instant; now he burned only from the knees up, his feet and lower legs having been reduced to calcined bone.

"Oh, God." Mercy was weeping. A small fulgurant ball flew from her, struck the flaming man full in the head. The mind-cries ceased. There was only the tick and sputter of the burning, and Mercy's low sobs.

"Come upstairs with me."

Aiken held out one hand to her. She came slowly to him, noticing at last that he was all in black, with even the golden tone of his thoughts damped down to a level of darkness more fearful—more exciting—than any aspect of him she had ever yet known.

She took his hand, warm flesh, quite human.

"What will it be, then?" she asked with fey archness. "How will you do it, Amadán-na-Briona?"

"Come," he said. "And see."

The Spear.

Golden and rising from the dark, full of hot energy, hungry. A living shaft, not one of glass, as she had known it would be. First discharging light and pain, then reabsorbing its own energies and hers, all of the life-force, all of the joy and sorrow, all memory, all thinking, all that had been created and matured and fulfilled. He took her and she was gone.

He was alive and shining.

As he looked at the ashes, he was surprised how little it had hurt.

8

NODONN HAD THE TWO EXOTIC AIRCRAFT APPROACH GORIAH from the seaward side, out of the descending full moon, even though it was plain that the usurper not only anticipated invasion, but had prepared a perverse and splendorous welcome for his archrival.

All of the city lights were on, so that even from a distance the sky formed a mother-of-pearl backdrop to the multicolored twinkling outlines of the buildings. The great city wall was topped with the orange beads of bonfires, and each bastion was strung with ominous purple and blue faerie lamps. On its height overlooking the sea, the Castle of Glass formed a soaring pile of blazing amethyst and topaz, braced with spangled flying buttresses and crowned by filigreed spires beaconed with yellow stars.

Hanging above the citadel, riding the night wind on wires and cables of gold and silver, were kites.

There were hundreds of them, from titanic oval wanwans more than twenty meters in diameter to stacked boxes, centipedes, Rogallo wings, parafoils, sinuous dragons, and Japanese fighting styles both geometric and theriomorphic. All of the kites were decked in tiny lights. The great man carriers, now flying without passengers, bore gaudy paintings of grimacing samurai, oriental demons, and fierce mythical characters.

Nodonn Battlemaster had to roar at the audacity of it. The

417

two flyers hovered, screened and invisible, a few thousand meters off the castle seawall, while the invaders recovered from paroxysms of hilarity before launching their assault.

"How shall we proceed, Battlemaster?" came the voice of Thufan Thunderhead over the RF communicator. "The air above the castle is as thickly tenanted as a locust swarm."

Nodonn stood behind Celadeyr, who piloted the Number One craft. He inspected the crazy barrage with his farsight. "Sheets of paper and bamboo frames and panels of flimsy silk!" he said contemptuously. "The rho-fields clothing our aircraft will burn them up like tinder. Fly into the midst of them—and let all the battle-company be prepared to descend upon the castle after I have swept the royal apartments with the power of my Sword."

"As you command," said Thufan. Celadeyr, a madcap grin showing through his open glass visor, twisted the throttle-grip and sent their own inertialess craft tearing into the swarm of kites at barely subsonic velocity.

Two blinding bursts of light lit the entire countryside as the gravomagnetic aircraft, flying side by side, simultaneously encountered the highly conductive anchoring cables. The kites all burst into flame and were consumed within seconds; but the rhocraft hung motionless in the center of an amazing firestorm. Their black ceremetal skins crawled with flickering networks of force. The energies were grounding out through the gold and silver wires, the flimsier conductors going molten and falling away in smoking arcs. The sturdy cables of the wanwans and the o-dako and the other great kites wrapped the birdlike machines with spiderweb tenacity, however, and the flux-tappers of the craft surged toward terminal overload as they strove to maintain gravomagnetic equipoise in the face of the relentless drain.

Now the telepathic laughter of the trickster could be heard ringing in the aether, mingling with the teeth-jarring screech of the dumping rho-field generators, the crackle of the current-laden wires, and a thunderous hiss of ion-charged vapor from the boiling sea below.

"Away!" Nodonn cried out to his knights. "Out of the ship, before it's too late!"

"Brother—the hatch!" Kuhal Earthshaker shouted. "Jammed!"

With his mighty psychokinesis Nodonn ripped open the short-circuited airlock, then formed a tunnel of protective screening for the escaping knights. Those who could not levitate by their own power were borne down by the Battlemaster or Kuhal to the seaside parapet of the castle like a stream of rainbow-hued meteorites. Nodonn himself, clutching his photonic Sword, flew out only after he saw Celadeyr safely away.

The Battlemaster hovered to one side as his craft shuddered, turned slowly end over end, and dropped toward the sea, enveloped in a seething violet cloud.

"Thufan!" his storm-loud voice cried. "Evacuate your flyer!"

The distracted thoughts of the First Comer pilot reached him dimly through a mental tumult. The knights trapped within the second ship were in a panic, chopping at the frozen hatch with their glass weapons and bombarding it with futile psychocreative thrusts. Thufan said:

Sorry Battlemaster... should have... danger of grounding... we Tanu... more chivalry than science...

Up on the highest turret of the Castle of Glass danced a spark of gold wielding a bright needle. A bar of green light transfixed the hanging aircraft as Aiken Drum's Spear discharged. The blast's shockwave flattened Nodonn. He saw a fireball bloom above the water with excruciating slowness, all flecked with torn purple force-field asterisms and ejecting secondary detonations.

Too late, Nodonn extended the Sword. A coherent light beam, twin to the one that had destroyed the flyer, vaporized the top third of the turret. The air reverberated to the shattering concussion.

And laughter.

Try again, came a jeering thought.

Beside himself, Nodonn blew the tower's stub to fragments. But of course the Foe was no longer there—only the echo of his gibes.

Nodonn sent his farsight boring into the main keep of the citadel. His 200 surviving knights were already engaging the enemy. Tanu forces loyal to the King, led by Bleyn the Champion and Alberonn Mindeater, were marshalling for an attack in metaconcert. The Battlemaster streaked into the forecourt with his Sword high, and a photonic blast brought a great chunk of the castle façade tumbling down upon the defenders.

"Hold off!" cried Bleyn, switching his direction instantly to a PK deflective structure. The threescore knights under his control managed to divert the bulk of the collapsing masonry and only a few were harmed. But Nodonn's forces piled in on the loyalists, and in the heat of subsequent hand-to-hand encounters, the discipline required for cooperative mental effort was almost totally disrupted. Both invading and defending Tanu turned instinctively to the ancient fighting style of the race, contending against one another with flashing glass weapons and haphazard mental blows.

"Minds together!" Alberonn pleaded. Numbers of the younger loyalists rallied around the hybrid coercer and resumed fighting in the efficient metaconcert mode. Those of Nodonn's force who were struck by multimind thrusts either died in their tracks or suffered massive brain damage. But Nodonn was quick to take advantage of the confusion. He encouraged the weaker among his knights to fight on in the courtyard mêlée while the stalwarts broke free. Divided into three groups led by himself, Kuhal Earthshaker, and Celadeyr, they pressed more deeply into the castle.

"Aiken Drum! Find him!" The Battlemaster was alight with solar fury. "Each force to a different part of the citadel—but when you corner him, remember he is mine!"

Ordinary farsight was useless for locating the usurper, who was masked not only by his own mind's cunning but also by the portable Milieu-technology screening devices he wore. He would have to be detected physically—or lured to a confrontation.

Celadeyr of Afaliah and the seventy-odd knights under his command smashed their way into the predominantly human wing of the citadel, taking a fearful toll of gray and silver defenders. The collared humans, loyal in their hearts to Aiken, became helpless before the invading Tanu overlords, who were able to coerce them through their torcs. Wave after wave of gray troopers advanced with their silver officers, only to meet the irresistible compulsion of the enemy that bade them throw away their iron weapons and submit to the terrible glass swords.

"Cut the Lowlife rabble down!" the old Lord of Afaliah crowed. "Wipe 'em out!"

He led his band into the castle garrison, thinking that Aiken might have taken refuge among members of his own race. His knights killed every bareneck or gray or silver that they encountered; but finally, when the invaders were far out of range of Nodonn's protective mental aegis, they were confronted by a detachment of the King's gold-torc elite guard, who advanced on them from behind the detention barracks.

Uncoercible, wearing full-body glass armor capable of deflecting the small psychocreative blasts of the individual stalwarts, the humans lifted unfamiliar slender weapons. There were only about twenty of them, headed by Commander Congreve, who glowed a vivid azure with the force of his own metapsychic power and saluted Celadeyr on the intimate mode.

"I know you, Congreve!" Celadeyr roared. "You were a loyal servant of the Battlemaster before that little gold pipsqueak turned your head. Join us! Throw down your arms!"

Congreve said, "Surrender, Celadeyr of Afaliah. King Aiken-Lugonn would not take your lives."

Celadeyr and all his knights laughed and hefted their great swords. "You're outnumbered more than three to one," the old creator stated. "I'll give you five seconds."

"Ready, Jerry?" said Congreve quietly.

"Up yours, then, Lowlife!" Celo howled, and launched the heaviest psychozap he could muster at the armored human. Congreve stood unmoving in the midst of a snapping coronal discharge. At the same time, a PK knight came soaring straight at him from the rear ranks of the invaders, brandishing a flaming sword like the Angel of Eden.

"Zap him, Jer," Congreve said.

One of the elites bent to his laser carbine and there was a Moogish chirp. A scarlet beam flicked momentarily. The psychokinetic, sailing into it head-on, was sliced cleanly from crown to crotch through glass armor, flesh, and bone, and crashed to the pavement less than two meters in front of Celadeyr.

"Surrender," Congreve repeated. The Tanu force stood stockstill. Then, abruptly, four coercers and a creator leaped forward, swinging their blades. The entire front rank of elites fired their Matsus, this time with the beams dialed to needle. Drilled through heart and brain, the five attackers crumpled, their armor ringing a death knell on the stone slabs of the compound.

"Surrender." Now Congreve's voice was weary. "We have been ordered to spare you if it is possible. King Aiken-Lugonn reminds you that the true Adversary in the Nightfall War is the Firvulag Foe—not humanity."

Celadeyr seemed to hear a high-pitched mental keening. It was coming from somewhere deep within the citadel, together with the sounds of a furious altercation. Desperate, he sent a telepathic plea on the Battlemaster's intimate mode:

Help us or we are lost.

There was no reply. And behind him was the sound of a glass sword dropping to the stone—and then more falling, and a sigh of many minds mourning forlorn hope. Slowly, Celadeyr of Afaliah let his own arm relax, his fingers open. Dulled, his once glowing sword slipped down to ignominy.

The human gold nodded. He said, "Carbines up. Huskies ready." Open-mouthed, Celadeyr saw the elite guards lift the light-weapons in a swift gesture, hanging them on the right side of their armored backpacks. Almost in the same motion, they seized the butts of different weapons that had been hung muzzle-down from the pack center and swept them into firing position.

Incredulous, Celo cried, "But, we've yielded!"

Congreve was almost apologetic. "Unfortunately, we're pressed for time . . . Ready at stun-five. Ad lib, *fire*." And the Husqvarnas sang their sizzling song of oblivion while the Lord of Afaliah and all his knights went tumbling down.

* * *

It was Kuhal Earthshaker who found Mercy.

He and his knights were storming through the royal wing, tearing open doors, poking into cubbyholes and presses, stabbing behind draperies, terrorizing lackeys and chambermaids, and slaughtering the occasional gray-torc guard, when they came upon a pair of tall golden doors. Mounted on them were great champlevé escutcheons set in bejeweled cartouches, ridiculously ornate, but unmistakably representations of the impudent finger motif of the usurper himself.

"His apartments!" Kuhal cried. He smote the doors with his PK so that they dropped from their hinges with a resounding clang.

Rosy-gold sword high, he dashed inside, most of his forty knights at his heels. There was an antechamber with cool rattan furniture and a wide balcony overlooking the moon-plated sea, and then a pair of dressing rooms with packed clothes closets, and an inner salon opening into a luxurious bath all tricked out in onyx and gold, and finally the royal bedroom itself, lit with festoons of purple and amber stars and dominated by a great gold-canopied circular bed covered in black satin sheets.

On it lay a pale shape.

Kuhal stood as though turned to ice. *Brother!* his mind cried out. *Nodonn—to me!*

The Battlemaster materialized at his side, filling the dark room with his sunlight radiance. Kuhal drew back, motioning his fighters to retreat, and Nodonn was left alone.

"My Mercy-Rosmar," Apollo whispered, standing over her.

Every dear contour had been preserved: the slender arms, one thrown wide, the other in repose at her side; the feet with their oddly long toes, the dimpled knees, the curved hips, and the dark cleft mystery of her sex. Her small high breasts were perfect in pearl-gray ash, and her shoulders, and the neck with its torc, slightly arched so that the delicate jawline was thrown into poignant relief. Her face was calm, the lips softly parted, tinted by his own warm light so that they might have been living flesh. But never had her lashes or her hair been so pallid,

gossamer-fine now as the rare basaltic threads spun by certain
volcanos.

"You hungered so," he said, "and made him afraid. Rightly,
rightly. And now all your fierceness, all vitality is consumed
in his restoration, to my death. Ah, Mercy. You knew. You
warned me. Wildfire, burning heedless and free. Wait."

He slipped off one rose-glass gauntlet. The silver hand passed
swiftly over the length of her body. There was left only the
torc and dust, scattered in feathery coils on black cloth . . .

Outside the window the sinking moon suddenly kindled to
a violent gold. A mind-voice commanded:
Come out.

They met in the high air above the sea, bright and furious
and shielded only by their minds, as the ritual demanded.

When the sharp green lightning of the preliminary sparring
began to flash, and thunder was flung back upon the ramparts
of the city, all of the other contention ceased. Tanu partisans
of both heroes left off their trivial battling, and the human
warriors as well, to watch the duel of the titans. Noncombatants
who had hidden from the invasion's fury now crept out onto
the battlements and turrets to stand among the quiet spectators
in glass armor.

Goriah was almost ghostly now, with the metapsychic faerie
lights turned off and the oil lamps guttering low in predawn
dark. The green explosions out over the Strait of Redon cast
shadows that were lunar in their starkness. The glowing bodies
of the two antagonists were all but drowned in the dazzling
glare.

Some of the people watching had been on the White Silver
Plain, witnesses to the earlier encounter between Aiken and
Nodonn that had been aborted by the Flood. These noted certain
differences in the fighting form of the opponents: The little
human had become more circumspect and defensive, and the
godly Battlemaster now fought with a wanton aggressiveness
at odds with his usual cool implacability.

Nodonn was the more active pursuer. Englobed in an auroral
nimbus, he soared about the drifting trickster, peppering him

with an almost continuous fusillade of energy gouts that spewed from his Sword like stellar flares. When these rebounded from Aiken's psychocreative screen, they seemed to bruise it, causing the corona to flash blue or sickly yellow-green or—in the case of the more intense blasts—a lingering vermilion.

"Spoiler!" the storm-voice roared. "Nonborn! I am the heir of the Many-Colored Land, the first child of the Thagdal and Nontusvel. Who engendered you, Lowlife? Sterile dishes in some genetic kitchen? Test tubes mixing frozen sperm and the sluggish egg of a dead woman? What a King! What a Battlemaster!"

And the Sword blasted and the monstrous concussions rolled over the affronted sea, and Aiken's mind-shield flashed deeply orange while his small armored figure seemed to dull and darken inside its metapsychic halo.

"Fight back!" Nodonn raged. "Or do you fight only women? Did her passion frighten you, little one? Did you shrink from her warmth like a slug fleeing the sunlight? I am the sun! Eclipse me if you can!"

Inside the slowly shrinking mind-screen, the trickster hoisted his Spear—and one finger. He remained silent, and he did not retaliate. The scarlet-patched sphere of force seemed to drift aimlessly, almost skimming the surface of the black water.

"Fight, damn you!" Nodonn thundered. "Or are you seeking death?" His aura streaming like a comet's tail, the Battlemaster orbited above his rival. "Is that it? By killing her, you hoped to restore your own broken mind. You fed on her creativity to bolster your own! Was it worth it, corruptor? Worth destroying the only thing you loved?"

Nodonn thumbed the uppermost of the five power-setting studs on the Sword's hilt, summoning the weapon's full potential. The readout on the power supply told him that he would have only two shots of this magnitude before draining the weapon.

"Are you tired of being King? Tired of coercing those who hate and fear and despise you? Little man! Trickster! Furtive conniver! Betrayer of honor and nobility and beauty!"

A stupendous light-burst engulfed Aiken and his screen and

seemed to dig a crater in the flat sea. Then a chaos of luminous vapor whirled and fountained, and deep within it were pulses of golden radiance alternating with sullen glows of deepest carmine lake.

Nodonn waited. At length, a smooth sphere bobbed up from the ferment, its color now as darkly red as coagulating blood. It barely sufficed to enclose the dull-armored little figure clutching its glass lance.

"Come then," Apollo invited. The bubble ascended slowly. Aiken's visor was open, his face like a skull wrapped in tight scarlet skin and his eyes deep as wells.

Nodonn blazed. "Will you go to death silent?" The Sword was ready. "Very well!" In the ultimate stroke, Nodonn called up all the energies of his brain and flung them simultaneously with the full power of the photonic weapon. The resulting flare was blinding green and white, clothed in a shimmering plasma haze. The doom-clap that accompanied it flogged the atmosphere and sent echoes caroming endlessly between the hills of Armorica and the Breton highlands across the wide strait.

Aiken was there. Unshielded. Golden.

"No," said the Battlemaster.

The Shining One was smiling and his mind open wide; and Nodonn in despair knew that it had all been planned and he allowed to do his utmost, so that those watching would receive the final affirmation—either through farsenses or through the evidence of their own eyes.

Aiken unfastened the baldric holding the Spear's powerpack and lifted the apparatus off. Held motionless in the strengthening dawn, Nodonn felt an insidious PK impulse working at his own harness. The straps slipped from his shoulders and the Sword's hilt was torn from his nerveless grasp. At the same time the Spear went flying from Aiken and both of the weapons disappeared.

Nodonn removed his helmet and stood poised in the air. His shielding nimbus had evaporated in his final effort against the Nonborn King, but his body was sunrise bright.

Aiken was a naked star.

His mind reached out. "I need yours, too," was all he said.

Apollo flamed and all his power passed, and what was left was only gray ashes and a blackened silver hand falling toward the sea, and a last ironic thought fading.

The King of the Many-Colored Land caught the hand. The sun was coming up behind his Castle of Glass, and his people were singing a Song that might be for him.

It was good enough, he thought, and headed for home.

THE END OF PART FOUR

EPILOGUE

ON OCALA ISLAND IT WAS STILL FAST NIGHT.

The tree frogs were practicing overtures for the autumn mating season. Fireflies blinked in the jacaranda trees next to the porch. The moon, bronze and low, seemed to be mirroring Marc Remillard's sardonic, one-sided smile.

"Was that what you expected?" Patricia Castellane asked.

He slowly rose from his canvas deck chair and stretched, the perfect metapsychic Wagnerite. "Just about. The mental absorption ploy was—unusual. The Poltroyan race were accustomed to batten on their foes in a similar fashion during their precoadunate days, but I've never heard of a human doing it. Rather baroque. Interesting, though . . ."

She stood beside him. The lingering memories of the drama just played in Europe flickered in his mind. The conscious levels were tranquil again, diamond-hard above the scars. "I'm so glad you're better," she said. "I was afraid."

His laugh was insouciant, rich with the old casual power. "You should know by now that Abaddon takes a lot of killing. I was taken by surprise. It won't happen again."

"You're still going?"

"If I don't, he'll come to me."

"That might be preferable."

"I'm considering it." He kissed her, put an arm around her shoulder. There was a chill wind off the lake.

She sighed. "Well—it should be a very interesting Grand Tourney."

428

"Perhaps we should plan to attend," said Marc Remillard. Hand in hand, they went into the house.

With the cooler air came dew. The frogs fell silent, the fireflies hid away among the foliage, and Ocala Island slept.

THE END OF
THE NONBORN KING

Volume IV of The Saga of Pliocene Exile,
titled THE ADVERSARY, tells of
the struggle against the fall of Night,
of a couple of redemptions and an ambiguity,
and of an ultimate recurvature back
to the Galactic Milieu
where it all began.

APPENDIXES

Map of Northwestern Europe
During the Pliocene Epoch,
After the Gibraltar Rupture

Map of Western Mediterranean Region
During the Pliocene Epoch,
After the Gibraltar Rupture

ALBION

GULF OF ARMORICA

ARMORICA

R. Thann

NORTH

PENEPL

R. Seraal (Seine)

Au
Cu

PARIS
BASIN

Sn

Fe

Gorian
[Belle Ile]

Sn
Au

Grove of May

R. Laar

R. Laar
(Proto-Loire)

WESTERN TA

N

Rocilan [Ile de Ré]

GULF OF AQUITAINE

B
O
R
D
E
A
U
X

R. Donaar [Dordogne]

GROTTO
WILDERNESS

R. Garoena [Garonne]

REBEL ROU
MT. DORE

R. Oltaar [Lot]

MAS

Ag

Sasaran

CANTAL

CEN

Black Crag

FLAMING MTS.

Amalizan

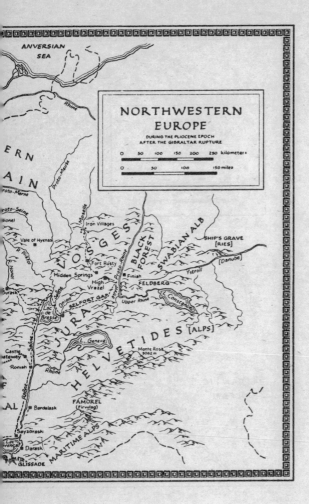

ANVERSIAN SEA

Rhine

NORTHWESTERN
EUROPE

DURING THE PLIOCENE EPOCH
AFTER THE GIBRALTAR RUPTURE

0   50   100   150   200   250 kilometers

0   50   100   150 miles

Proto-Meuse

ERN
AIN

roto-Morne

roto-Seine

ionel

R. Rhine

Vale of Hyenas

Moselle

Iron Villages

VOSGES

BLACK FOREST

SWABIAN ALB

SHIP'S GRAVE
[RIES]

[Danube]

Fort Rusty

Ystroll

Hidden Springs

High
Vrazel

Proto-Rhine

Finiah

FELDBERG

Saône

Onion

BELFORT GAP

Upper Rhine

Constance

urask

de
Bresse

JURA

L. Geneva

HELVETIDES [ALPS]

Castle
ateway

Ronish

Rhone

Monte Rosa
4082 m

AL

Bardelask

FAMOREL
(Firvulag)

Sayzorask

MARITIME ALPS

Lac
vençal

Darask

GLISSADE

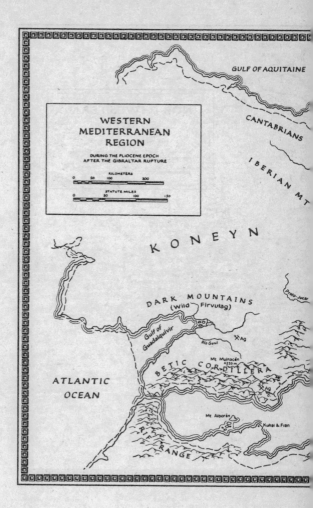

WESTERN
MEDITERRANEAN
REGION

DURING THE PLIOCENE EPOCH
AFTER THE GIBRALTAR RUPTURE

KILOMETERS
0   50   100   200

STATUTE MILES
0   50   100   150

GULF OF AQUITAINE

CANTABRIANS

IBERIAN MT.

KONEYN

DARK MOUNTAINS
(Wild   Firvulag)

Rio Jucar

Gulf of
Guadalquivir

Rio Genil

⚔ Ag

BETIC CORDILLERA

Mt Mulhacén
4235 m

✕ Ag

ATLANTIC
OCEAN

Mt Alborán

Kuhal & Fian

RIF

RANGE

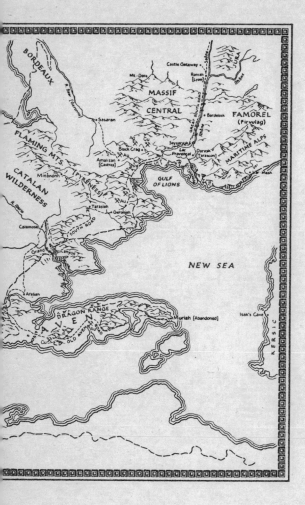

ABOUT THE AUTHOR

JULIAN MAY's short science fiction novel, *Dune Roller*, was published by John W. Campbell in 1951 and has now become a minor classic of the genre. It was produced on American television and on the BBC, became a movie, and has frequently been anthologized. Julian May lives in the state of Washington.